A COMPUTER VIRUS
IS A CURIOUS THING...

Like a virus that infects people or animals, it's invisible to the naked eye, requires a host to survive, and is capable of mutation. Once it's found a host, its internal coding instructs it to clone itself, and each copy is programmed to invade other hosts. Like non-computer viruses, such programs may or may not actually harm the host; again, their primary function is to reproduce and spread...

HARD DRIVE

One of the most exciting and terrifying thrillers of our time.

D1021198

HARD DRIVE

A NOVEL BY
DAVID POGUE

DIAMOND BOOKS, NEW YORK

This book is a Diamond original edition,
and has never been previously published.

HARD DRIVE

A Diamond Book / published by arrangement with
the author

PRINTING HISTORY
Diamond edition/April 1993

ISBN: 1-55773-884-X

Diamond Books are published by The Berkley Publishing Group,
200 Madison Avenue, New York, NY 10016.
The name ''DIAMOND'' and its logo
are trademarks belonging to Charter Communications, Inc.

PRINTED IN THE UNITED STATES OF AMERICA

10 9 8 7 6 5 4 3 2 1

For Poppa,
on his 103d birthday,
with thanks for the chromosomes

Acknowledgments

This book came about through the efforts of Steve Ettlinger, book producer, and Andy Zack. Special thanks to the editors of *Macworld*, air-traffic guru Michael Gibson, and beta-readers Marie-Claire Harris, Stephen Sondheim, Tracy, and, of course, Mom.

HARD DRIVE

prologue

THE WALL STREET JOURNAL, FRIDAY, APRIL 2, 1983

2 TOP EXECS TO LEAVE HUNTINGTON SYSTEMS

Huntington Systems, Inc., a major Silicon Valley software developer, yesterday announced the departure of two top executives. Robert T. Stroman, President of Operations, and Arnold McGivens, Director of Research and Development, will be leaving the company in June to form a new software development concern.

Industry analysts expressed surprise over the announcement. The departing Stroman was a founder of Huntington, along with current CEO M. Lars Huntington, in 1979. After developing a custom integrated circuit in a Stanford undergraduate science class, Stroman and Huntington founded Huntington Systems and built the company to its current size (1982 revenues: $120 million). Huntington stock fell $4.31 per share in the wake of the announcement.

October 12, 1992   By the third hour of the board meeting, the cigarette smoke was so thick the words No Smoking were barely discernible on the wall behind Lars Huntington's hairless head. The other executive committee members had long since filled their legal pads with doodles. One, a pale woman with her hair in a tight bun, had written *arc chip* over and over again, all the way down the margin. Her nerves were stretched taut as a wire; she dragged on her cigarette mechanically, ruthlessly.

Across the table, the chief financial officer was shading in his doodle with the side of his pencil; the sketch was of an insectlike ROM chip, but he'd added antennas to its end and little feet to each of its thirty-two legs. On a chair near the door was a burly man with a thick brown mustache and no notepad.

On a laser-printed handout, Lars had made his point exceptionally clear. It depicted a graph of the U.S. software market from the years 1985 to 1992. Superimposed on that healthy growth curve were two dotted lines. The upper dotted line, labeled HUNTINGTON, meandered slowly downward as it crossed the page. The lower line was steep and steady, appearing at zero just after the 1985 mark and shooting upward. By the time it approached the 1992 tick mark, it was high enough on the page that it was about to intersect the HUNTINGTON line. This lower line was labeled ARTELLIGENCE.

"We didn't build this company by being gentlemen," Lars repeated. The fluorescents reflected from his shiny bald skull as he blew dual streams of cigarette smoke from his nostrils.

"Or by being ladies, Sheila," he added with a smirk to the bun lady. "No, we built this company by playing *tough*. Tough means going after market share. Playing hardball. And doing *what has to be done*." With each word, his pudgy index finger stabbed the light green handout on the table.

The second handout was an outline—or, more precisely, a time line. Lars Huntington was the master of the time line; he drew time lines for everything. He'd drawn this one to illustrate his idea for reestablishing the balance of market power in the software business. He'd drawn it to convince the other executive committee members to endorse his special, rather unorthodox business plan.

And, above all, he'd drawn it to put Bob Stroman in his place for years to come.

The bun lady struggled to be diplomatic. "Lars, look . . . we all feel the pressure. We don't like what's happening, either—of course not. But this proposal," she said, peeling up one corner of the time line, "I mean, I'm sure it will be effective. But our concern is that it's motivated not so much by a drive to salvage market share as it is by . . . well, by personal vendetta?"

Her voice rose at the end, a subconscious attempt to take the accusatory sting out of the remark. "I—I'm just worried about the ethics thing." She stopped, her eyes flying to the faces around her for support.

Lars wasn't looking at her. He appeared to be staring ferociously at the light green handout on the table, but he was seeing nothing. Sheila became aware that the veins on his temples stood out, an indication of anger she hadn't seen since the day Robert Stroman left the company and took Huntington's best people with him.

"Let me tell you something about loyalty, Sheila," he said in an uncomfortably controlled voice. "Loyalty is worth more to me than all the market share in the world. I thought I've made clear to you how well I reward my people for loyalty—and I don't refer only to the pension plan. On the other hand, I think you're aware that life for a disloyal Huntington employee isn't always pleasant. Don't get yourself in trouble, Sheila."

The other committee members breathed shallowly and stole glances at Sheila. The mustache man leaned forward, suddenly paying close attention.

Lars's oily face relaxed into a thin smile.

"Now, then. Further questions?"

There were none. Sheila was suddenly keenly absorbed in her study of the table's Formica wood grain.

Lars Huntington mashed his cigarette butt into the ashtray. "Then I suggest we conclude our discussion and vote on this proposal."

chapter 1

Time Magazine • *September 7, 1993*

The Attack on Silicon Harbor?

The Japanese investment juggernaut turns to U.S. high-tech firms

By ANDREA LANDEFELD

First it was Rockefeller Center. Then MCA. Then Columbia Pictures. And now, if all goes according to plan, America's technologically fertile Silicon Valley will be the next national landmark to fall prey to Japanese investment dollars.

"You can't put all the blame on the Japanese," observes Software Developer's Association president Charlie Loomis. "Nobody's holding a gun to our heads; it's simple economic pressure. If you really wanted to resist, you just tell the Japanese 'no, thanks.' "

Targeted for takeover are several major

September 12, 1993   An intercom buzzed in Silicon Valley.

Robert Stroman, unconsciously tugging on his turquoise-and-silver bolo tie, acknowledged the second buzz. "Yes, Ellie," he said.

"Mr. Hirota is here to see you."

Stroman sat straighter in his chair. "Thanks, Ellie."

He took a glance around his office; it would be OK for this meeting. Not enormous, by any means; but appropriate for the hotshot CEO of an upstart, blossoming software company. *And besides*, Stroman thought, *the size of this office says something about humility. The Japanese seem to like that.*

As he leaned back in his chair, it occurred to him that the Japanese also liked *him*. They probably saw him as an American maverick; the essence of the young, driven entrepreneur.

Stroman was approaching forty, but he was solidly packed, tan, and obviously athletic; the California up-and-comer. Few would have guessed he was once the science nerd of his high school. Success had done good things for him.

Akira Hirota, dressed in a black three-piece suit, stood in the doorway. Two associates flanked him, dressed likewise. Hirota was short, graying, around sixty, but his aviator-style glasses gave him a shrewd modern-intellectual look. His adherence to etiquette belied a very American, very aggressive business sense.

"Mr. Stroman," he said.

"Please! Come in, sit down," said Stroman, rising. He strode forward to shake their hands. Hirota introduced his associates. Stroman ushered them into chairs, then sat and clasped his hands on the desktop.

"My friends," Stroman began. "I'm aware of the reason for your visit, and I want to assure you that this will be the last meeting of its kind.

"As you know, Master Voice is the most important, most dramatic new computer product in the history of personal computers. I mean, think of it: *true* speech recognition. I kid you not, gentlemen, it will be like nothing the world has seen before. People will speak into a microphone, and the computer will type out what they say, word for word, with better than 99 percent accuracy. Or people will control their computers: 'Print my thesis!' they'll say. 'Sort my Rolodex!' Trust me. One day you'll view your financial involvement with us as the best investment you ever made."

Hirota appeared not to have heard a word.

"Mr. Stroman, your original projections put this product on the market by June ten." He pronounced it *maahket*, with the soft *r*s of a man who had been sent to London to learn English, business, and ways of the Western world.

"Let me remind you that you failed to complete development by that date. At that time, you told us that you had been delayed. You told me that you were having trouble receiving quantity shipments of your circuit boards from Korea. So we intervened, and we assisted you."

Stroman nodded. "Yes, sir, you did. We're very grateful."

"At that point you promised that you would deliver the product by August fifteen. You will remember that just before that date, you phoned me to request additional funding, saying that the programming of the software was proving to be more expensive than your original budget allowed.

"Once again, Mr. Stroman, we were very patient with you. *We* have a software division, too, you know, in Tokyo. We realize that software is a complex thing to write, and that delays are inevitable. So we understood your difficulties, and we arranged a transfer of an additional hundred thousand dollars."

The room air seemed to be getting stuffy. "Yes, Mr. Hirota. You helped us out of a very tight place."

"At that point you assured us that the Master Voice product would be shipping in quantity by October five. A week ago, Mr. Stroman. The president of Mika/North America has sent me to find out why you still have not shipped the product."

He turned to regard the two mute accountant types beside him. "We have our own budgets to meet."

"Gentlemen," began Stroman, "as I'm sure you're aware, this company is called Artelligence. Our products combine *art* and *intelligence*. Now, the Master Voice technology is already very intelligent. On that chip is a vocabulary of two hundred thousand words, each programmed with a data path to other possible words. As you know, it's an amazing piece of work.

"But what can I tell you: the software isn't finished. We've achieved the intelligence, just not the *art* yet. It's working, it's running, but we won't put our name on anything that's not polished. We want to make people's jaws drop when they see this product. We want to sell *millions* of this item. We want you to think of your collaboration with us as a triumphant success.''

Hirota uncrossed his legs. ''Mr. Stroman, Mika Corp. views this joint effort as a business opportunity, nothing more. You showed us an impressive technology, and we agreed to capitalize you. But our involvement was based on some assurances you made to us. And now you are riding something that is out of control. You are like a cowboy—very showy. But Mika does not want to watch a rodeo, Mr. Stroman. Mika wants to make some money. *Soon.*''

He crossed his legs again.

''We want to know what steps you're taking to complete this product, and when you're going to ship it.''

Stroman squirmed slightly in his seat.

''Mr. Hirota, you're absolutely right. We've missed a couple of deadlines, and we're determined to do better. As you know, we're somewhat dependent on the speed of our star programmer, Gam Lampert. The kid's a genius—I mean it. Child prodigy. Twenty-one years old and the darling of the computer biz. Of *course* we needed more money—do you know what it takes to keep that kid happy? But listen, we're *so* close to finishing. Look, on December eighth we're introducing the product to the press in San Francisco. We're aiming to ship February first.''

Hirota started to interrupt. ''No, I mean it!'' Stroman went on. ''Look, we're taking steps. Gam doesn't like it, but I'm hiring new programmers to help us finish; I'm putting ads in the papers in both coasts. We've got wonderful marketing plans. We've got terrific beta-testers . . . ordinary people out in the field who can pound on the software to find any bugs. I've got a meeting with some military brass—they want to put Master Voice technology in their planes. Can you imagine? They'll have guys flying jets by talking to them. Listen, you gentlemen have nothing to worry about. You go back to Mika and tell them February first. February first, or I'm not fit to breathe the valley smog.''

Mr. Hirota was punching something in to his hand-held electronic organizer. Finally he snapped it shut and slipped it into his breast pocket.

''All right, Mr. Stroman. We will wait until February first. But we are going to hold you to your word this time.''

He leaned forward intently. ''If you do not ship that product by February first,'' he said quietly, ''you may consider our arrangement terminated. At that point, we will ask you to return the invested capital. Every penny. Do you understand me? You ship by February first, or Mika pulls out.''

Stroman swallowed hard, but concealed his terror. ''Whoa, now,'' he said. ''This is the software business! Nobody can live by deadlines in this business. What if something goes wrong? What if Apple introduces a new computer that our product isn't compatible with? What if Gam Lampert gets sick and can't complete the programming?''

He spread his tanned hands flat on his desk blotter in what he hoped was a subtle gesture of defiance. ''Listen, Hirota. You know as well as I do that we haven't got that kind of money on hand. We've *spent* it! We've worked for two years on this thing. If you pull out now, Master Voice dies. And this company dies with it.''

Hirota pushed his glasses higher on his nose and stood. His two associates rose simultaneously. ''Mr. Stroman, if your company dies, it will be your doing, not ours. All we ask is that you finish Master Voice by February first. If you do not have the cash on hand to repay, we will simply arrange a stock transfer. Artelligence will then belong to Mika Corp.''

He proffered his hand. ''Fair enough?''

Stroman shook it and nodded.

''You betcha,'' he said with all the conviction he could muster.

chapter 2

THE NEW YORK TIMES ● *SEPTEMBER 14, 1993*

September 20, 1993   At 11:07 P.M., Danny left his apartment
to make the last house call of his life.

The phone had rung at 10:49 P.M.—just in time to make him
miss the last ten minutes of the TV miniseries he'd been watching
all week. It was Mr. DaCosta, one in Danny's stable of computer
novices—''computer virgins,'' his friends called them. Danny
had patiently held Mr. DaCosta's hand through the intimidating
process of shopping for a Macintosh, hooking it up, learning how
it worked. For fifty dollars an hour.

But Mr. DaCosta called at 10:49 with an emergency. He said
his computer was talking.

Except for having to miss the climax of the miniseries, Danny
didn't much mind making a late-night house call; his clients knew
that he'd charge an extra fee for the service. And tonight, he'd
have a chance to say good-bye.

The cab stopped in front of Mr. DaCosta's Greenwich Village
town house. Danny grabbed his bag of disks, ran up the front
stoop, and pressed the buzzer. As he waited, he looked at his
own reflection in the brass plate that surrounded the peephole;
a lack of sleep made him look older than his twenty-five years,
and he had the pallor of a sun-deprived New Yorker. He plucked
at a wisp of his black curly hair. *Definitely Prell time*, he
thought.

His reflection swung away as the door opened. A thin, troubled-
looking white-haired man in his sixties appeared.

''Thank you for coming. I don't know what it's doing. I tried
everything.''

''No sweat, Mr. DaCosta. We'll get it fixed.''

Danny followed his client inside, up a spiral staircase, and into
a windowless, cluttered study. The Macintosh computer on the
desk looked fine.

''It says things,'' Mr. DaCosta said.

Danny slipped into the desk chair. He grabbed the computer's
mouse—the hand-held box that, when rolled across the desktop,
moved the pointer on the screen. He clicked the single button on
top of the mouse—and a recorded, digitized voice emerged from
the computer's speaker.

''*Gotcha!*''

Danny clicked again.

"Gotcha!"

Mr. DaCosta shifted uncomfortably. "It keeps saying this. I can't do any work."

"I know," Danny said, leaning back in the chair. He looked at his client sympathetically. "You've got yourself a computer virus."

Mr. DaCosta's bony fingers flew to his cheeks in a convulsion of alarm.

"What—what is that?"

Danny twisted in place to grab his Land's End bag off the floor. *Dr. Danny whirls into action....*

"Well, a computer virus is a piece of software. Just like your word processor," he said. "Except a virus doesn't do anything useful. Basically, it's programmed to gum up the works—and to make more copies of itself, so it can infect more disks. Anyway, I recognize the symptoms of this one. It's called the t-VIR virus. I think I read that some sicko teenager in Chicago wrote it. It doesn't hurt anything, except that it makes your Mac say that every time you click the mouse button."

Danny clicked.

"Gotcha!" said the computer.

Mr. DaCosta didn't seem relieved. "But how did this thing get into my machine? How did I get it?"

"Same way you get a flu virus: from somebody else." Danny extracted a box of disks from his bag, and began sorting through them.

"But who?" said his client, looking pale. "I sit here by myself. I write my stories. I send them to the publisher. How could I get this virus?"

"Let's see. You don't connect your computer to the phone lines. So you must've put an infected disk into your computer. Who do you exchange disks with?"

"Nobody! I write my stories, I send the disk Fed Ex to my editor. I don't use the computer for anything else."

"OK," Danny said. "And the editor never sends a disk back to you? For editing?"

Mr. DaCosta shrugged. "Sometimes. Of course." And then his expression changed. "You mean I . . . I got this virus from my editor?"

Danny smiled thinly. "Riding first class on a disk. No question about it."

He slipped a disk into the drive slot. In a moment, a tiny picture of a disk appeared on the screen, indicating that the computer was ready to access its contents.

The disk contained Danny's masterpiece: a little utility program he'd written himself that checked for computer viruses. He'd named it SURvIVor, hoping people would get the spelled-backward joke. It was a pretty good program, actually. If a virus made its way into your system, SURvIVor would beep like crazy, alerting you to the fact that you were being invaded. Once you knew you had a virus, SURvIVor's Cleanse command could even clean it out for you.

But the SURvIVor program—and Danny's career as a self-employed programmer—never got off the ground. By the time he had debugged and polished the program, there were six other anti-virus utilities already on the market, getting lots of press, good reviews, and heavy advertising by their big-bucks Silicon Valley developers. With lukewarm enthusiasm, Danny'd tried to market his own little baby, sending a disk, cover letter, and résumé to thirty software companies. Only four had even had the decency to send no-thank-you letters.

"This little program will clean up your disk in about ten seconds," Danny explained.

What kind of maladjusted creep would program a virus, anyway? he thought as the program went to work. He remembered that Robert Morris guy, the Cornell computer-science student who wrote a virus as a show-offish prank. Trouble was that it reproduced so rampantly that it eventually choked the national military and university network of computers. National headlines. As it turned out, the kid had never intended to do damage; a programming error allowed it to travel so far and so fast.

And then there was the Michelangelo virus scare: a little menace that was programmed to wipe out all your data on Michelangelo's birthday a couple of years ago. Had the world up in arms—since these things are invisible, you couldn't tell if you were infected or not—but hardly anybody actually had it, and little damage was done.

A message box appeared on Mr. DaCosta's screen.

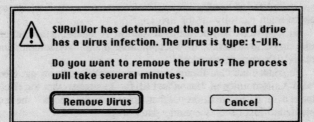

> ⚠ **SURvIVor** has determined that your hard drive has a virus infection. The virus is type: t-VIR.
>
> Do you want to remove the virus? The process will take several minutes.
>
> [**Remove Virus**]   [Cancel]

Danny clicked the Remove Virus button. The computer beeped to indicate SURvIVor's success.

Mr. DaCosta bent forward at the waist to peer at the screen. "Did it work?"

"Yup. You're clean. But you may as well let your editors know that they're infected, too. Along with any other writers they send disks to. And anybody *they* exchange disks with." Danny ejected the SURvIVor disk. "Here. Keep this disk on hand, in case it happens again."

"Thank you, Danny!" Mr. DaCosta withdrew a neatly folded check from the breast pocket of his jacket. It was already filled out—only the amount was blank. "Tell me what I owe you."

Danny looked at his watch.

"Let's see. . . I've been here fifteen minutes or so. Why don't you give me twenty bucks for cab fare and we'll call it even?"

Mr. DaCosta stooped to write on the check. "Thank you, Danny."

"Ah . . . the other thing is," began Danny. "I'm, uh . . . I'm leaving New York."

"You're leaving!? Danny! Where are you going?"

Danny didn't know how much of the story to tell him. After his entrepreneurial stint fell through, Danny had spent a year trying to build a decent life-style as a computer consultant. *Shoot*, he'd thought, *with my wits and my charm, they'll be beating a silicon path to my door.*

But being a consultant wasn't the lucrative, free-lance life he'd imagined it to be. His first corporate client used to phone him at home every time there was so much as a paper jam in the printer. Not to mention the time Danny rushed all the way to the Lower East Side to diagnose a computer problem; it turned out that the client had failed to plug it in. (*Power system dysfunction*, Danny had written tactfully on the invoice.)

But last week had been the last straw. A small-business client had called in a panic: "My screen went blank! My screen went blank! It's completely black!"

He'd used his Consultant Voice—his soothing, knowing, Obi-Wan-Kenobi voice of reason and calm—to suggest that the client look behind the monitor. "I bet a cable came loose," he explained. "Just check the cables back there."

But the Consultant Voice had no effect. "I *can't* look back there right now," the hysterical client said. "It's too dark—the power's gone out in my building!"

That night, Danny had decided to leave the consulting business.

"I've got a job as a programmer in California," was all he told Mr. DaCosta. "I'm pulling up stakes and heading west, y'know? I saw this great ad in the *Times*, I had an interview, and I'm outta here."

"But what shall I do when I have computer problems?"

Danny extracted his soon-to-be-obsolete business card from his wallet. "I'm glad you reminded me. Let me give you the number of a buddy of mine, who's much smarter than I am." He wrote the number on the back of his card.

Mr. DaCosta thanked him, accompanied him down the spiral staircase, and opened the door for him. Danny turned to wave good-bye as he trotted down the front steps; Mr. DaCosta looked genuinely sorry to see him go.

Danny's rent-a-car was a bright red Camaro. Like every car in California, it was new, sporty, and spotless. And like every car in the valley, it blinded him by reflecting the incessant, much-too-bright sunlight.

Silicon Valley was a different world: sixteen-lane highways, open-roof malls, and an endless succession of Sizzlers, pet hospitals, and 1-Hour Photos. And I-101—the highway Danny knew he'd become well acquainted with—was mile after mile of low-slung industrial parks and electronics companies; and always, in the background, those low, dusty mountains.

With a final squint at the directions he'd scrawled onto a yellow pad, he turned off at the Lawrenceville Expressway exit. A half mile later, he made a right onto a smoothly paved entrance drive. A white acrylic ARTELLIGENCE logo sign whipped past. *Yup,*

Danny thought. *Seeeerious money.* As software companies went, Artelligence was no Mom-and-Pop shop.

The building was low slung and very modern, all white granite and smoked glass. A Japanese garden was visible to the right of the building, complete with what looked like giant bonsai trees and a placid pond.

He swung into the parking lot, where his car fit right in among the showroom-shiny array of expensive cars. The entrance was around the building; he pushed his way through a set of chrome-and-glass doors. The second set was locked. A receptionist inside, seated at a sweeping semicircular console, spotted him; the inner doors buzzed. Danny opened them and walked into the reception area.

Admission by buzzer only, he thought. *What is this, Manhattan?*

"I'm Danny Cooper. I'm supposed to be at an orientation meeting at three?" He took a quick glance behind him at the reception atrium. Sunlight streamed in from the skylights; huge acrylic paintings of the company's package designs hung on the walls; carefully focused recessed lighting illuminated them.

"That's fine. May I see an ID?"

"ID!?" Danny pulled his wallet out of his jeans pocket and extracted his driver's license. "Course, it's a New York license." He grinned. "Probably no good here, right?"

The receptionist missed the joke. She studied the license and then dialed an extension on her phone. "Arnie, one of your new programmers is here. . . . OK, fine."

She hung up. "Mr. McGivens is on his way to meet you. He'll admit you into the main building." She flashed a quick apologetic smile. "We have to be a little bit strict about security."

With a glance at the array of security-camera monitors in front of her, Danny nodded.

Suddenly an Amish guy appeared—or so he seemed to Danny. He was tall and ruddy, with an orange fluffy square beard and sideburns. "Danny, good to see you," he said in a mellifluous voice. "Glad you could get out here on such short notice." He offered his hand. "I'm Arnie McGivens; I run the new products division."

Danny shook hands and made some polite noises. Arnie struck him as incredibly mild mannered, refreshingly free from the cut-to-the-chase impatience of most programmers he knew.

"Why don't you come with me; the meeting starts in about ten minutes," Arnie said. "Would you be up for a quick tour on our way to the conference room?"

"Sure," Danny said, grateful to be upright after the flight and the drive.

They walked down two nicely decorated hallways. "Here's what we call the Corporate Kitchen; you can whip up lunches in there, use the microwave, that kind of thing. Down those stairs is the gym—it's not bad for a company our size," he said.

They poked their heads into a large, centrally located room; around the perimeter were individual desks and computer systems. A heavy wooden table sat in the center of the room beneath the fluorescent lights. "Your home sweet home," explained Arnie. "The research and development lab. Customer Service is down that hall; the men's room is up ahead."

They approached a pair of dark oak doors laser-etched with the Artelligence logo. "Here's the conference room," Arnie said. He hesitated just outside the doors.

"Look, Danny. About the security thing. You're about to discover what's going on. It's a very, very hot new product we're working on—*you're* working on. A lot of people would love to have a look before it's quite ready.... We've had some prying inquiries from other companies, and some reporters. So I hope you'll forgive us if we play it on the careful side."

"No problem," said Danny. The guy was so . . . *nice*.

They pushed the doors open and went inside.

The overhead projector, the LCD projection screen, and the Macintosh IIfx were all ready. Bob Stroman, cowboy CEO, leaned back in his chair at the head of the conference room table. Today, he'd get to meet the Reinforcements, as he liked to call the new hirees. Their arrival marked the beginning of the homestretch in the development of the most important computer product ever created. Stroman relished the thought.

The heavy doors swung open. "Bob, meet Danny Cooper, our East Coast import," said Arnie with a smile.

Stroman stood and shook hands with the tall, curly-haired young man in front of him. "Welcome to Artelligence, Danny. We'll be starting as soon as our star programmer gets here."

Through the plate-glass window, Stroman could see the landscaping he'd commissioned for the approach to the new building. Beyond the Japanese garden, he could see most of the employee parking lot. The silver Maserati J10 still hadn't appeared.

Typically, the Maserati was fairly recklessly driven; if you stood on the lawn, you could hear its engines being gunned all the way from the exit ramp of I-101. To enter the Artelligence driveway, the car had to make a sharp right-angle turn; on more than one occasion, however, the turn wound up not being quite so sharp, to the continual disgruntlement of the groundskeepers whose thick green lawn was ripped up as a result.

But as far as Bob Stroman was concerned, the Maserati's owner was welcome to drive as recklessly as he wanted. It was all part of the deal.

When Stroman was particularly annoyed, he sometimes likened that deal to a pact with the devil. Stroman gets what he's always dreamed of: to become, at thirty-eight, head of an industry-leading software company with the best-selling product in the computer world. Artelligence, the impertinent upstart company, surges past the slumbering, corrupt giant: Huntington. Everyone makes box-cars of money. The stockholders love him, he lands a couple of military contracts, he pays back the Japanese investors. The future is bright.

In return, Bob Stroman had to give the agent of this alchemy enough money to afford the Maserati. And the pair of matching Mazda Miatas the employees hated hearing about so much. And even that goddamn Piper Turbo Arrow he flew around on weekends. And Stroman was required to bite his tongue as Mr. Maserati drove over his landscaping, violated employee policies, and ordered his superiors around as though he were a fifty-year-old executive instead of a skinny twenty-one-year-old brat.

But that was part of the deal, too. A deal Bob had spent months on; a preposterous gamble, in a way, that looked more and more as though it would pay off. A deal that wouldn't have been possible if Mr. Maserati *wasn't* such a materialistic jerk.

For Bob Stroman had *purchased* Gam Lampert, offering a profound amount of money to hire him away from his previous employer, a glittering list of perks, and an unprecedented amount of power in the development of the new product.

It was either that, Bob often reminded himself, or go on making mundane enhancements to existing programs. Touch up the spelling-checker in the word processing program. Add color to the graphics package. Come out with a spreadsheet charting module. Plod ahead, year by year, increment by increment. Keep the users in the stable.

But Bob Stroman's bronco streak made him a risk taker. Hadn't he risked it all when he dropped out of Stanford with Lars Huntington to start a new company? Hadn't he taken an even greater risk when he resigned from Huntington to start Artelligence? Hadn't he braved Lars's wrath as Artelligence slowly grew to become a rival software giant?

Bob smiled as he watched the parking lot. Well, not a giant yet, he reminded himself. A threat, sure, but not a giant. That, of course, wouldn't happen until February 1, when he unleashed Gam Lampert's neural-network brainchild upon the world, come hell or high water.

"Ah . . . Bob, perhaps we might consider getting under way," said Arnie tactfully. "I suppose Gam will get here when he gets here."

Stroman nodded, stood, tugged at his tie. He smiled at the four new faces around the conference-room table, winked at the other staff members.

"My name is Robert Stroman. I'm the founder of this company, and on behalf of the entire Master Voice development team, I'd like to welcome you all to Artelligence.

"I'm sure you've been wondering what this is all about. And, in a moment, I'll tell you. But first let's take a moment to sign the confidentiality agreements in your packets there. We've been working on this project for two years, full steam, and we just have to be very careful where our information goes. Yes, that's it—those five stapled sheets." He paused while the new programmers extracted the forms from their Welcome-to-Artelligence folders.

"You'll notice that these non-disclosures are a little more comprehensive than most. Especially read over page five, where we've outlined some in-house security procedures you may not be used to."

Danny sneaked a glance at the other new programmers. They were locals, he'd learned. The Asian guy moved like a bird, his eyes flicking from page to page, head nodding unconsciously, nose occasionally scrunching in a frenetic medley of tics. The fat, ponytailed guy next to him wore a pair of dark-tinted glasses that were completely wrong for his wide triangular face. And the third—could this guy be a programmer? He sure didn't look like one—broad shouldered and fit looking, he had chiseled GQ cheekbones, dark tan skin, and even a little lock of hair curling trendily across his forehead.

Great, Danny thought. *I get to spend the next three months sitting next to a fat hippie, a Chinese geek, and Clark Kent.*

All of them were reading page five.

Danny took a look at the confidentiality stipulations himself. *Man, oh, man . . . serious paranoia.* He raised his hand.

"Yes, what's your name again?"

"Danny Cooper. I'm looking at, like, number seven. 'No Artelligence employee may leave the Artelligence corporate premises with project code in any form without the advance and written permission of the product manager'?! Does that mean we can't take stuff home to work on?"

"I'm afraid that's exactly what it means, Danny," said Stroman. "On the other hand, you're welcome to work here as late as you want; we have security staff on duty here virtually around the clock. They'll just check you in and out."

Weird, Danny thought. *Can't take my hard drive home with me to touch up my code during Letterman.*

"We have to be strict on this, gentlemen. We even make Gam Lampert stick by this one," Stroman added with a quick smile to Arnie. "Gam is our . . . well, our team leader, I guess you'd say. This kid is a formidable code writer. He put himself on the map two years ago, when he wrote LightningWriter, which as you know is one of the hottest word processors in the IBM world." He chuckled. "No wonder he defected to work on our Macintosh computer project—can you imagine having to work on an IBM?" He grinned.

"You'll be working on the software under his direction; I think you'll learn a lot from him. He should be here any minute."

Danny read the rest of the non-disclosure agreements. *Well, can't exactly go back to New York at this point.* He signed. So did the others. They handed the sheets to the end of the table.

"Now, then," continued Stroman, "tell me what you know about voice-recognition systems."

The Chinese guy immediately raised his hand and identified himself as Skinner Hsiao. Stroman had barely nodded acknowledgment before Skinner began speaking.

"OK, speech recognition, right? So you wanna record your voice saying a command. You gotta microphone. You wanna control the computer by voice instead of by keyboard or by mouse, OK?"

Danny studied Skinner, from whose mouth syllables poured in a staccato rush; his entire body was animated—a double blink here, a backhanded wipe of the nose there. He was small and wiry; the fashionableness of the small gold earring he wore didn't come close to counteracting the nerdiness of his white-T-shirt-beneath-blue-cotton-button-down getup. At the very least, Danny noted, the guy didn't wear a pocket protector—but on the table in front of him there was, in fact, a scientific calculator.

"OK, so now you've recorded, well, OK, fifty words, right? You say every word a couple times so the computer learns the pattern, OK? So now you assign each little recording to a command. OK. So, like, you say 'print' and the computer recognizes the sound pattern, right?, and invokes the Print command you taught it."

Nobody's mouth could keep up with that *brain*, Danny thought.

Stroman was pleased. "You're absolutely right, Skinner. That's what they're calling voice recognition today. But is your computer really *understanding* what it's hearing?"

The fat guy next to Danny identified himself as Charles Bertaccini. "The only thing a computer *understands* is when the warranty is up," he said with a slow, dry drawl. "It doesn't do any speech recognition; it just sits there and does pattern matching. You could say 'Have a beer' and train *that* to invoke the Print command, too." Danny smiled despite himself.

"Fine," said Stroman. "OK, so what if someone came up with a *real* voice-recognition system? You could talk to it and it would parse your sentences automatically. You know what parsing is? You probably did it in high school, where you break a sentence down into noun, verb, and so on . . . to puzzle out its real meaning. Remember that stuff from English class, Rod?"

Stroman shot this question with a friendly wink at the male-model guy; Rod took on a furrowed, concentrated expression, trying to formulate a response.

Stroman let him off the hook. "Well, most of us have forgotten it, too." He smiled. "But the point is that training a computer to do real-time parsing is much harder. In fact, you'd need a special chip to do it, because no computer under fifty thousand bucks is going to have the power to handle it.

"To make a very long story short, we've developed this chip; you can read all about it in the folder Arnie gave you. But the important thing is that this chip, the arc chip, lets us write a program that can really *understand* what you say to it. We've got it working very well. . . . As long as your accent isn't extremely thick, it'll get you. I'm sure Gam will give you a better technical explanation." He glanced at the doors. "If he gets here."

Charles nudged Danny and peered over the smoky lenses of his glasses. "I like this Gam guy already," he whispered. "Pulls down six figures from these people and only comes to work when he likes the weather." Danny grinned.

Stroman was going on. "If you let your imaginations run wild a minute, I think you can understand the significance of a true speech-recognition system. We're not just talking about controlling your computer with spoken words like Print, Save, and so forth. We're talking about spoken *data input*. Entering numbers into a spreadsheet by saying them. Writing memos without having to type anything. Producing instantaneous transcriptions of phone conversations . . . you name it. We think we've got something that's really revolutionary."

Stroman took a sip of water and set the glass down. "At this time I'm going to turn the meeting over to Michelle Andersen, our product marketing manager for Master Voice. Michelle?"

He stepped back from the head of the table. Michelle stood up. Danny forgot all about arc chips and data input.

Well, hel-loooo, soulmate.

She was gorgeous. Her shiny blond hair was pulled back; she wore pearls and a businesary silk blouse that didn't suffice to conceal a cute figure . . . obviously a regular at the gym, if not a jogger. High cheekbones, blue Swedish eyes, not much makeup . . . *A true California blond*, Danny thought. If she were any taller than her perky five-five, she could have been a model.

"Thanks, Bobby. I just wanted to give you all a quick rundown on our plans for Master Voice, so you know what's at stake."

She smiled warmly at the new programmers; Danny instinctively smiled back. *OK, so maybe these other programmers aren't exactly Miss Manners School of Social Grace graduates,* he thought; *at least there's* one *glimmer of after-hours social-life hope.*

"As you know," Michelle went on, "you'll be working on the Macintosh version of Master Voice. There are twelve million Macs out there. We're expecting the product to be a must-have; not just a status thing, but a real productivity booster that every corporate manager in America is going to have to get. So we think sales will look pretty good there. We have plans for an IBM PC version, too, but that will come later.

"We've even had some meetings with some folks at the Pentagon. They have some very exciting plans for the Master Voice technology. Anyway, I'm sure you gentlemen will do a sensational job. Those government contracts would be a very big coup for us; I just wanted to mention the possibility." She closed the file folder in front of her, then stopped.

"Oh. One more thing. We've *got* to get the Mac version out the door by February first; that's why you've been brought in at the eleventh hour like this. Um . . . I guess you all know how software products never ship on time. In fact, I hate to admit it, but even *we* have never shipped a product on the projected ship date. But this one's a biggie, guys. Pull out all the stops for me, OK?" she said with the most adorable smile Danny had ever seen.

Nooo problem, he thought.

He was already composing his first words to her when the door flew open. Every head turned in time to see a tall, almost skeletally thin, very young man whirl into the room, Ferrari sunglasses still on his nose. He was wearing a nylon mesh Rams jersey, designer jeans, and a pair of new Nikes; he carried a dusty blue nylon gym bag. Without a word, he circled the table to a chair directly opposite Danny, laid the bag on the table, and flopped into the chair. He left his sunglasses on.

"Glad you could make it, Gam," said Bob Stroman, with complete sincerity. "Gentlemen: Gam Lampert, the mastermind behind the Master Voice software."

Gam jawed a couple times on a wad of bubblegum, then flashed a Garfield-the-cat smile at the rest of the room.

"Yo," he said.

Jeez, Danny thought. *How old is this guy? Twelve?* He scanned the other faces in the room. Rod's eyes were wide open in surprise. Skinner seemed awed by the dramatic entrance, and Charles was smirking. Michelle Andersen, for some reason, was engrossed with her watchband.

There was a momentary silence. Stroman and McGivens exchanged looks. "Well, then," said Stroman, "Michelle has put together a little welcome-to-Artelligence picnic for our Master Voice Reinforcements; you'll all get to meet each other properly, and Gam can show you something of what he's been doing. When we're finished here, just go downstairs to the lounge."

He switched on the overhead projector. "Now, then. Let me tell you a little bit more about what we're up to."

Danny settled back in his chair, wondering what this high-security, strangely peopled, sunny-weather world was going to be like. He let his eyes drift out of focus for a moment, and then suddenly his head jerked upright. There, directly on the table across from him, was Gam Lampert's blue nylon gym bag; protruding six inches from the partly unzipped opening was a stout gray SCSI cable used to attach a hard drive to a computer. Danny followed it with his eyes into the shadowed interior of the bag; sure enough, he could just make out the corporate gray plastic case of a portable hard drive.

So you sneak your hard drive in and out of work, eh, Gam? Danny thought sardonically. *Nice to know you're such a stickler for security.*

Danny was sure the jet lag was getting to him—his appetite was shot. Who decided avocado and tofu bits in a pita constituted a sandwich, anyway? He chugged away at his mango juice and tried to mingle at the Welcome Artelligence Reinforcements party.

But that was the other thing. This guy Gam, he'd decided, had the social skills of a walnut.

"Hi, Gam, my name's Danny Cooper," he'd said with a smile. "I just flew all the way from New York to be your hacker slave."

No response.

"And boy, are my arms tired," he'd added, trying for some reaction.

But Gam simply stopped chewing for a moment to stare. "OK," was all he said—which was nonetheless enough for a tiny bean-sprout fragment to escape the corner of his mouth and fall to the polished parquet floor.

Danny had taken solace in finding Skinner, Charles, and Rod

seated on folding chairs near the punch bowl. Skinner, gesticulating wildly, was in mid-anecdote.

"So think about it, OK? I mean, when you really stop and think about it, what is a RAM disk? It's virtual memory in reverse, OK? You wanna make the computer think it's got more memory than it does—OK, you use the hard disk and trick it. You wanna make the computer think it's got more hard disk— OK, you use memory, a RAM disk. They're *inverse.* They're inverse, right? Totally *righteous.*"

Rod looked studly—What is this guy *doing* here? Danny kept wondering—but thoroughly confused. His mouth hung open a fraction of an inch.

"Hello, there, Manhattanite," droned Charles, ponytail swinging. "Meet your cellmates."

Danny shook hands and exchanged introductions. "This one is going to be pretty tough to pull off, don't you think?" he said. "We've got a hell of a lot of code to write by the end of the year."

He lifted a leg over an empty folding chair and sat down. "But hey, we've got Gam Lampert on our side, right? The Rambo of the techno-nerds."

Charles regarded him dourly. "Hey, I'm just tickled to have Gam on our side. I just wish I didn't have to work in the same zip code."

"Yeah, OK?" Skinner burbled, nose twitching. "Like, OK, he's a good programmer, right? I'm sure he's a really super, super programmer. But I mean, hey! Maybe he could try being nice or something?"

Rod raised his eyebrows. "He hasn't done anything mean to *me,*" he offered.

"Don't worry," muttered Charles. "He just hasn't noticed you yet."

As they chatted, Danny liked the feeling he was getting. Sure, they were dweebs, but there was a pre-game huddle feeling to their conversation, a sense of us against the world. It made Danny feel like something good was going to happen.

As the party waned, he spotted Michelle getting ready to leave. He excused himself and walked over.

"Hi. I'm Danny."

She shook his hand. "I'm Michelle."

"So you're our public-relations guru?"

"You got it. Resident spin doctor."

There was that smile again. She seemed sure, solid, confident, and yet Danny bet she could be quirky and spontaneous outside of the workplace. He wanted to find out.

Danny glanced in the direction of the other new programmers. "How d'you like us new recruits?" He cocked a wry eyebrow. "Be pretty nice having all these models of manhood around, huh?"

"Oh, listen, the problem around here *isn't* a man shortage!" She glanced at some of the conversation clusters standing in various parts of the lounge. "Only a few women work here. Sometimes it's pretty hard to be taken seriously." She looked at him. "I mean, you're going to think this is silly, but I can't even wear my hair down at work. It's amazing—people immediately stop taking me seriously."

He nodded. "I gotcha. Well, count me among the enlightened ones. I'll appreciate you, with hair or without."

"Sounds good." She smiled.

He took a glance around the room. "So what's the story with this guy Gam? *He* must take work pretty seriously—he showed up at the crack of noon today."

Michelle's face darkened. "Gam is an amazing programmer," she said firmly.

Almost involuntarily, she shot a glance in Gam's direction; he was standing alone, near the doorway, staring at her. Or at Danny; it was hard to tell which.

It didn't matter. Her high spirits had vanished.

"Listen, I should get going," she said suddenly, apologetically. "See you Monday?"

"Right!"

She grabbed her purse and scurried away. As she passed Gam on her way out of the room, she stopped and said something to him, but they were too far away for Danny to hear anything.

But as Danny watched from across the room, Gam metamorphosed. His crossed arms unfolded and became animated. If he didn't actually smile, his expression at least melted as he spoke; something made Michelle laugh. Her eyes never left his face.

When the conversation finished, Michelle turned to leave; Danny saw Gam touch her briefly on the shoulder as he said one more thing.

Aha, Danny thought. *So it's the old Mr. Hyde and Dr. Charmer routine, eh?*

He took a last swallow of his mango juice just as Gam turned toward him, a hostile gaze back on his face. The hair rose on the back of Danny's neck.

Some picnic.

chapter 3

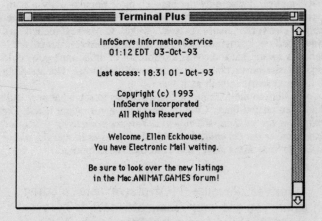

Terminal Plus

InfoServe Information Service
01:12 EDT 03-Oct-93

Last access: 18:31 01-Oct-93

Copyright (c) 1993
InfoServe Incorporated
All Rights Reserved

Welcome, Ellen Eckhouse.
You have Electronic Mail waiting.

Be sure to look over the new listings
in the Mac.ANIMAT.GAMES forum!

October 3, 1993   One of the best parts about college is these incredible computer deals, thought Ellen. *Everyone else in the world forks over a bundle for the same Macs I get for 50 percent off, just for being a student.*

As her modem dialed InfoServe, she stretched her arm straight forward to the screen to make sure she was seated at least arm's length away. *That ELF radiation gives you cancer, that's what Mike O'Massey says. I'm not getting any of that stuff.*

Her Mac beeped three times. *Aha—connected*, she said to herself. The InfoServe welcoming screen rolled up her monitor. *Yes, indeed. At fourteen bucks an hour, you'd better welcome me.*

Of course, it was only the biggest, most popular dial-up computer network/database in the universe. She could send and receive electronic mail (*E-mail*, Mike O'Massey called it), download cool programs, look up movie reviews... actually, Ellen was aware that there was a whole lot of other stuff you could do, but she never bothered to do much exploring. Her monthly bills were scary enough as it was.

She went to the Macintosh Games forum to see what new stuff had been posted there. Cool...three new games were listed. *The magic of the modem*, she thought. *You see something you want, you just use the Download command to transfer it over the phone wires to your hard drive.* She read their descriptions.

```
Dwarves_Revenge: Multiplayer role-playing
game. You and your teammates seek to recover
the lost gold of Anthrwar. Downloads: 228

Mindgame: You're the leader of an
international espionage ring. Your challenge:
blow away the enemy before he blows you
away! Downloads: 145

AirAttack.sit: Video arcade-type game. Shoot
rocket launchers and grenades to stop the evil
```

```
AirAttack squad from strafing your town!
Downloads: 1169

(D)ownload, (C)ontinue, (Q)uit
Press <Return> for more listings
```

Ellen's roommate Jo threw a poli-sci book onto the floor and flicked off her nightstand light. "I can't read anymore, El. I'm beat. G'night," she said, and flopped back onto her pillow.

"Dream sweetly," Ellen said absentmindedly. She read over the listing of the new games again. *Well, I'm certainly not going to download any multi-player games. If I get hooked on playing some game against other people on InfoServe, I'll never get off the line!*

Looks like that AirAttack thing is the one to get—if 1,169 people have already downloaded it, it must be pretty good. She pressed the D key. InfoServe told her:

```
Now downloading AirAttack.sit. Ellen Eckhouse
from Tampa, you have 30 seconds to begin the
transfer.
```

Ellen chose the Receive MacBinary command from her File Transfer menu, and picked up the copy of *Cosmo* that Jo had left on the desk.

When the transfer was finished, Ellen logged off the network. There, on her hard drive, was her new prize: AirAttack. She glanced at her clock radio—1:33 A.M. *What the heck*, she thought, *I can play with this for another half hour and then go to bed.*

She discovered that AirAttack was actually pretty good. "Hit the space bar to launch rockets at the incoming choppers; they appear from behind the mountains," read the on-screen instructions. "The more you play, the faster they come. You, hiding up in the oak tree at the right side of the screen, are the last line of defense for your city!"

As gently as Ellen pressed her space bar, she could tell it was still clacking loudly enough to keep Jo from sleeping. She decided to call it a night; even so, it was ten of two by the time she shut down her Mac and went to brush her teeth. She couldn't wait to show AirAttack to Mike O'Massey.

October 5, 1993   "I don't really give a crap!"

On Danny's first Monday morning in the R and D lab, those were the first words he heard from Gam's mouth. They floated in from around the corner and down the hall—Danny heard the storm long before he saw it.

Then a carefully modulated voice, also coming closer. Arnie's.

"Gam. Gam, please. Don't make this difficult. Look, it's nearly noon—the new hirees have been sitting waiting for almost two hours. *Please*, Gam. You just can't go making little flights when you *know* how tight the situation is here. OK?"

There was no response, but the quick footsteps approached. Charles, sitting next to Danny, swung his feet off the desk and sat up.

Gam burst into the room. Arnie was hot on his heels, fighting for self-control, his face almost the color of his carroty beard.

"I need to know that you're hearing me, Gam. This can't keep happening. I need you to stay out of the airplane business on company time."

Gam stopped short, took a glance at the other programmers, and turned to face Arnie, towering almost a foot above him. He spoke quietly, levelly.

"Arnie. Say one more word to me, and I walk out of here and that's the end of this project. It's that simple. *Not one more word*."

With that, Gam unslung his blue gym bag from his shoulder and moved over to his computer. Arnie stared, helpless, impotent, breathing hard.

At last he turned. "Good morning, gentlemen," he managed between clenched teeth. He moved toward the door. "Please excuse the disturbance." He left.

So this, Danny thought, *is my New Career*.

He'd expected a somewhat more formal introduction to the Master Voice project. Between bouts of apartment hunting and looking at crummy used cars, Danny had spent the weekend reading the Func Spec, the 400-page blueprint for the new program. In typical programmerese—a language something like English but without the distracting intrusion of syntax, spelling, and grammar—the Functional Specifications described how Master Voice would work when completed. For the programmers who would be writing the software, it was the Bible. Danny had hoped that perhaps Gam would spend Monday morning clarifying the program's structure.

But with Mr. Star Programmer in continual P.O.'ed mode, Danny didn't see how they'd all be able to operate as a team. As Gam began to explain, they weren't.

"So you each get one of these cubicles. You each work on the piece of the puzzle I give you, and I fit it into place. I give you the routine I want you to work on. You write it, you send it back to me on the network."

Skinner, eyes darting, voiced the question they all were thinking. "OK—Gam, OK? So you're the only one working on the big picture, right? I mean who's going to keep the Func Spec updated if you change how the thing's going to work, y'know?"

Gam stared. Skinner petered out, cowed.

"Looky here, little fella. If we're supposed to get this thing out the door by February, you boys are going to have to play ball with me. If you have a problem with that, you can go to Bob Stroman with it."

Gam, thy name is Attitude, Danny thought.

"OK, gents, let's hit the keys," continued Gam. "Look over the variable list. Learn it. I'll come around and tell you what I want you to work on."

Danny eyed Gam resentfully as he sat at the desk he'd assigned.

Each cubicle was equipped with a Mac IIvx—not top of the line, but powerful enough. Each was equipped with eight megabytes of memory—plenty of RAM—and a 265-megabyte external hard drive. *Well*, that *ought to hold a few files*, Danny thought. *Like the whole Library of Congress.*

Next to his Mac, Danny found a laser-printed, stapled set of pages that defined the variables in the Master Voice program. He read through a little bit of it, then switched on his Mac.

His portion of the software was to be written in the C language—practically his native tongue. He found the compiler in an electronic folder on the hard drive called MV Develop, opened it, and began to look through the program.

They're going to have to explain things to me a little better than this, Danny thought. Half of the routines that had already been written made reference to an external chip—that custom arc chip, he figured—and made no sense to him.

A thick breathing entered Danny's consciousness from the right side. It was Charles, leaning over from the next cubicle.

"Hey, Danny."

"What's up?"

"Did they do to your floppy drive what they did to mine?"

Danny scooted his chair back to look at Charles's workstation. The first thing he noticed was the six-pack of Swiss Miss plastic Individi-Serv pudding cups. Charles had nestled them neatly against the computer's side for later consumption. A spoon lay on top of the monitor.

But then he saw Charles's floppy-disk drive—or, rather, where it was supposed to be. Instead, there was an attractive plastic face-plate that matched the light gray color of the computer. It fit snugly in the slot, and four Phillips-head screws held it in place.

His own computer was similarly sealed.

He looked at Charles's expression—raised eyebrows and pursed lips—and he knew they'd come to the same conclusion. "Jeez," Danny breathed. "These guys are *paranoid*."

"Evidently morale around here ranks just above 'ceiling fixtures' on the priority list," Charles said acerbically under his breath. "Let me get this straight. We can't take our hard drives home from work. We can't discuss the project outside the office. And now inserting floppies is verboten? How are we supposed to get any work done?"

Danny shrugged sympathetically. "Guess we'll have to send code to each other over the network that connects the Macs."

"Lovely," Charles grunted. "If we all behave ourselves, they might even give us a stone tablet or two." With a disgusted look, he straightened up and disappeared around the cubicle wall.

"It so happens, friends," said a voice directly in Danny's ear, "that those drive slots were sealed for a very good reason." Danny's head whipped around as Gam, a condescending smile on his face, put one hand on his shoulder and one on Charles's. Danny flinched at the touch.

"If you haven't gotten the picture yet, *fellows*, Master Voice is a big deal around here. They've pumped mounds of money into it, have a boardroom full of nasty-looking Jap investors breathing down their necks, and they're not about to flush the whole project down the toilet because one of you boneheads gets careless with the software. One little virus you boys walk in here with, and our whole network is corrupted.'' He looked directly at Charles. ''And they're not about to risk having somebody 'accidentally' share our code with anyone outside of our little family, either.''

Danny and Charles exchanged looks. *What the hell is going on around here?* Danny fleetingly considered spilling the beans: *So what are you, Mister Clean? I happen to know that your hard drive rides home in that Ziplock bag of yours every night. . . .*

''Think of it as a urine test, boys,'' Gam continued. ''A urine test for the soul, OK? You do your job and play it by the books, and the floppy drive won't bother you. You pee straight, you'll have a good ol' time. You can do that, can'tcha, Danny boy?'' Gam patted him on the back, grinning in his face.

Danny bit his lip and turned to face the screen.

Gam moved on. ''OK, Chuck. Let me show you what to start on.''

Charles looked uncomfortable. ''It's Charles, if you don't mind,'' he said. ''*Chuck* sounds too much like a character on 'Cheers.' ''

Gam pulled up a folding chair and flicked Charles's ponytail with his index finger. ''Sure thing, Chuckles. No sweat.'' He launched Charles's copy of the program and began explaining what he wanted done.

The nerve of this creep, Danny thought, tuning out Gam's voice. Riled, he grabbed the mouse and began rooting through the folders displayed on the screen. Yes, everything they'd need was on the hard drive. He explored the E-mail system: the cubicles were all connected to the same network—even Gam's. He pushed back in his swiveling, castered chair, far enough to look into Gam's cubicle at the end of the room. He smiled: *Gam's* floppy drive, of course, hadn't been sealed.

''OK, Danny boy. Let's see what you're made of,'' said Gam, pulling the folding chair up next to him. ''You're gonna be our interface man. Mr. Pudding here is handling some of the standard Mac Toolbox routines. But you, you're out there in front, big guy. You're going to be the voice of Master Voice; when it requests more information from the user, it's going to pop up one of *your* dialog boxes. I want you to make everything clear and pretty to look at. Hope you like dialog boxes, 'cause you're gonna be making a million of 'em.

"But don't be a RAM hog," he said. "You use up more than forty K of memory for this code, and I give the job to someone else. Don't use three bytes if you can rewrite it in one. Write *tight, tight, tight,*" he said, knuckling Danny's bicep on each emphasis.

Gam began to explain how he saw the interface working. Half of Danny's mind tuned in. The other half raced, trying to process all the information pouring in, and resisting the urge to rub his arm where Gam had pounded him just a mite too hard for playfulness.

Actually, Ellen Eckhouse couldn't have cared less about bit-mapped graphics on the Macintosh. The only reason she was in Mike O'Massey's dorm room was Mike O'Massey.

"No, Ellen. See, the computer doesn't really know that the letter *A* is an A. When you type the A key on your keyboard, the Mac just draws whatever bitmap happens to lie in the A slot in the font. But it wouldn't have to look like an A, you know? I mean, it could be a bumblebee or an X or whatever the guy who made the font was thinking of."

He looked at her, not quite in time to see her gaze shift from his clean, bespectacled face to the example he'd drawn on the Mac screen.

"Cool," she said.

"That's just fonts, of course. That's when you're using a word processor. When you're doing other graphics, like a game or something, graphics are stored in the resource fork . . . here, where's that game you brought me?"

Ellen snapped to attention. She'd brought him AirAttack as a surprise midterm gift. "Oh, here," she said, picking up the floppy disk from the desk beside Mike's cool-looking rugby cleats.

Mike pushed the disk into the floppy drive.

"Have you played this much?" he asked as he moved the cursor to the AirAttack program icon and clicked the mouse button twice.

"Yeah, I downloaded it from InfoServe last week," she told him, hoping he'd be impressed by her modem prowess. "It's cool. You're defending this, like, guerrilla outpost against some helicopters that keep flying in. And every so often there's, you know, like a plane or something that you have to hit.''

Already the choppers were starting to flit across Mike's screen, making a little digitized beating sound.

''See, look, you press the space bar when you want to shoot him, and you use the mouse to aim.''

Mike tried for a few minutes. Two of the choppers went spinning crazily to the bottom of the screen with a funny slide-whistle sound. One of them crashed onto the oak tree at the right side of the screen.

''I love that little oak tree,'' Ellen said.

Mike didn't say anything. He quit the game, opened the Utility Programs folder on his hard drive, and launched the Resource Editor.

''What're you doing?'' Ellen asked.

''OK, this is ResEdit. The Resource Editor. This is a utility program that lets you look inside whatever program you want. It's neat, 'cause you can change things in the program. Like you can rewrite what the menus say, and stuff like that. In high school I used to freak out the other kids in my comp sci class, 'cause I'd change their menus to say stuff like— well, instead of File, Edit, View, and stuff, I'd make them say Puke, Belch, Snort, and stuff. They'd never know what hit 'em.''

Ellen laughed appreciatively, even though she didn't quite get it.

''So here,'' Mike went on. ''I've opened up your AirAttack game. Look, see this resource? See how it's labeled PICT? It stands for Pictures. That means this is the part of the program where all the little graphics are stored. Check this out. I'll bet we find all the planes and helicopters and stuff in there.'' He double-clicked the word PICT on the screen.

Sure enough, a scrolling window appeared, filled with small graphic images from AirAttack. ''Cool,'' said Mike. ''Here's the little bomb the plane drops, see? Here's the helicopter—there's four different pictures of it, with the rotors in different positions. When it's flying across the screen, the Mac is actually cycling really fast between these four pictures, so it looks like a little movie.''

''Cool,'' said Ellen. Mike clicked the scroll bar to see more pictures.

''Whoa!'' said Mike. He stared at the screen.

''What?'' Ellen leaned in to see what he was looking at. Next to the last helicopter image was the little oak tree. But next to the oak tree was something she'd never seen before in the program: a tiny Christmas tree, complete with all the trimmings, and miniature wrapped presents at its base.

"Where'd that come from?" she said.

"I don't know! That's neat," said Mike. "Sometimes the guys who write these things hide little surprises. I wonder what you have to do to make that Christmas tree show up when you're playing? Hey, let's see something." He quit ResEdit and launched the game again.

"You probably have to do something Christmasy," he said.

He tried typing Xmas, Christmas, Noel . . . nothing happened. He tried clicking the oak tree. Nothing.

Ellen had an idea. "Hey, maybe the Christmas tree appears if you play the game on Christmas?"

Mike shook his head. "No, that's impossible. How would the game know if it was Chr—. Hey, wait, I bet you're right! The game could check your Mac's clock! You know how the Mac has an internal clock? I bet the game just checks the date every time you run the program. Let's see."

Mike opened the Mac's Control Panel. Clicking the date icon, he changed the Mac clock to say 12/25/93. He closed the Control Panel.

"Oh, cool!" said Mike and Ellen simultaneously. Where the oak tree had stood on the screen a moment earlier, the little Christmas tree now grew.

"That's cool," said Mike, looking at Ellen appreciatively. She felt a surge of pride.

"Hey, we should send this in to the Mac magazines," he said to her. "They pay you money for stuff like this."

"We'll split it, how's that?" said Ellen. "And how about if I spend mine taking you out for dinner some night?" She put out her hand in mock businessman fashion.

When he took it, Ellen forgot all about bitmapped graphics.

Figures, Gam thought with a glance at the clock. *Danny Cooper, the New Yorker with Something to Prove, is the last of the brain-dead hirees to leave.*

If Gam were the type to show his emotions, he might have grinned: in less than two weeks, he had successfully established a reign of control over his new subordinates. They were slower, they were stupider, and they were already completely terrified. For the millionth time in his life, Gam marveled at how easy it was to establish control over another human being.

Power: the mutually accepted illusion of authority.

He snapped off his hard drive and began to unplug it from the back of his Macintosh SCSI port.

Before leaving the R and D lab, he took a glance at the calendar on the wall. October 5. That meant about three months before the Master Voice software was supposed to be completed, polished, and "frozen" into its final state. Then, after four weeks of user's manual binding, packaging, and shipping, tens of thousands of copies would be sent out. On February first.

Too bad they're not gonna make that date. Never yet happened in the software biz, never would; they'd missed their deadlines twice already. *Too many things crop up when you're working on a new program. Someone'll find a bug at the last minute. There will be a delay at the plant where the manuals are printed. And even if everything goes perfectly smoothly, then there's still...*

No, no, no. I'm supposed to keep my secret secret. Gam smiled.

He studied his hard drive as he listened to its fan's whine die away. It was the size, shape, and weight of a bible. The only break from its corporate grayness—"platinum," the brochures called it—was a now-dark LED disk-access indicator lamp. *Yep, thar she blows: eighty megabytes of my soul. My Rolodex, my business, my life.*

Then he grabbed the drive with one hand, his gym bag with the other, and stepped out of the R and D lab. The lights, heat-activated, shut themselves off a moment later.

Artelligence was eerie at night—eerie and yet somehow liberating. It reminded Gam of his high school, when he used to break in in the middle of the night to use the computer lab. In the darkened, locker-lined hallways, illuminated only by the light bridges in the trophy cases, he was simultaneously terrified that he'd be caught and giddy with the possibilities of being alone in the building. The Artelligence building was only slightly different at night. It had the same deserted, anything-is-possible calm, and it, too, was spookily dark—only the fluorescent accent lights along the tops of the hall walls were on. But this time, Gam wasn't breaking any rules by being there.

At least not that Artelligence knew of.

He made his way to the only unlocked exit, the receptionist's console at the front entrance. *Damn.* Hugo, the old, bald, black night security man, was uncharacteristically awake and at the front entrance. It was too late to shove the drive into the bag.

" 'lo, Hugo my man," said Gam as he approached the desk.

Hugo glanced at Gam's hard drive. "Hello, Gam. What that you takin' home tonight?" There was a Jamaican ring to his accent.

Gam reached into his back jeans pocket. *Well, won't be the first time for this old charade.*

"Too hard to explain, Hugo my man," he said. He pulled out his wallet.

This guy's got one reason for being here—to keep me from walking out with my hard drive—and a twenty-dollar bill shuts him up. Power is the illusion. . . .

He creased the bill and jammed it into Hugo's shirt pocket.

"Why, thank you, Mr. Lampert. I guess it really ain't my business, is it now?" He grinned his wide, gap-toothed grin.

"G'night, Hugo. Don't spend it all on one bottle." Gam pushed through the heavy glass doors and walked toward his Maserati.

Less than an hour later, he kicked open the kitchen door of his Woodside house. Periwinkle Lane wasn't anything like the winding, steeply inclined streets that were higher up the mountainside community known as Woodside; as such, it didn't seat any of the sprawling mansions of the super-wealthy that dotted the upper portions of the hill. Still, it was plenty large for the two people who lived there, and its elegance and landscaping fit right in with the rest of the affluent little suburb.

The lights in the house were out. He passed through the kitchen and took the stairway two steps at a time. As he walked down the hall toward his room, he passed her door. It was closed. The shag carpet was too thick for him to tell if the light was on in her room or not. He briefly considered calling her name to see if she was still up, but thought better of it.

She'll find me if she wants me, God knows.

His own door was open; a faint bluish light spilled out onto the hallway carpet. He laid the gym bag on his desk, took off his windbreaker, and closed the door. It was a cocoon, the way he wanted it. Dark, cluttered, and windowless—he had long since paneled over the room's solitary window—its only illumination, at this moment, was the Tensor lamp on his desk. It gave the desktop a stark, command-post look.

The high-tech aura was further enhanced by the perfectly symmetrical row of three color monitors, the plane of their screens at a right angle to Gam's desk. Each was attached to its own top-of-the-line Macintosh Quadra, their mice spaced equidistant on three identical mouse pads. Gam had named the three computers Hitler, Hussein, and Quayle.

He leaned back in his swiveling desk chair, the glow of Hussein's monitor lending an eerie cast to the contours of his face. It was going to be a busy night for Gam's modems; if it weren't for the fact that a bank in San Francisco unwittingly paid his phone bills, Pacific Bell would be collecting quite a bit from him.

He launched his telecom program and dialed the Artelligence mainframe; part of Gam's nightly ritual was to check for any electronic mail that had been sent during the day. *To me or anyone*, he thought to himself.

After making the connection to the mainframe, the computer prompted him.

Your name?

Gam typed Robert Stroman.

Your password?

It normally would have taken Gam some time to figure out his employer's password. Gam's favorite method was simply to watch over people's shoulders as they typed; he learned over time that, incredibly, nine out of ten people used their own first names as their passwords. A few even used PASSWORD as a password.

For the few that made up something more creative, Gam had to have patience and hope that the password was an easily remembered word, and not a hard-to-watch random combination of letters and numbers. He was rarely disappointed.

But Gam hadn't had much opportunity to hang out in Stroman's office, which was three hallways away from the R and D lab; when he first started working at Artelligence, days went by before Gam realized he'd never be able to watch Stroman enter his password. Fortunately, Stroman's password had been simple to determine. Like most people, Stroman didn't consider Artelligence's E-mail system a particular security risk; his password was MARGO, his wife's name. Gam had guessed it on his fourth try.

Tonight, Gam read through the various messages in Stroman's mailbox. Evidently Stroman had left the office early, because

there was a handful of mail he hadn't yet read. Something from
Arnie, something from marketing. Gam loved this; not only
could he intercept any messages that concerned himself, but he
got to see them before Stroman did. He was even working
on a way to edit them before the messages reached their recip-
ients.

Something from accounting. Something from tech support.
Something from Michelle.

LinkMail™
From: Michelle Andersen, PR
Time: October 5, 1993, 3:23 pm
RE: Ad draft

Bob, I've got to get these ads in to the glossies by the end of
the week. Please stop by to look over the copy. The photo
turned out great!

I'll be in early, around 7:30.

Michelle

Gam read the note twice. *Too early for me, Michelle baby*. He
signed off from the system. He'd never yet uncovered anything
worrisome perusing people's E-mail, but it was important to be
vigilant.

And, of course, it was part of the contract.

He remembered having spotted an envelope from National
Pacific Trust in the mail; he ran downstairs to the kitchen
table, picked it up, and returned to his desk. He tore open the envelope.

It was a confirmation of the account he'd just opened. *What a
deal. I deposit twenty bucks, you suckers send me an account
number. Hope that money's useful to you, 'cause the account
number is sure going to be useful to me!*

He quit the telecommunications program he'd been using. From
his top desk drawer, he pulled out the DirectLink disk. He slipped
it into Hussein's floppy disk drive and copied the DirectLink program to his hard disk. *Showtime, folks*. He double-clicked the
DirectLink icon to launch the program.

Welcome to

D I R E C T • L I N K™

Your home-banking connection to National
Pacific Trust

Press ⟨Return⟩ to continue

Gam pressed Return. The ''wait-a-minute'' wristwatch cursor
appeared on his screen as the program dialed the bank. From the
modem's one-inch speaker, he could hear the rapid dialing tones,
like a touch-tone phone gone mad.

Step one, of course, was going to be easy: Gam needed to find
another bank customer's legitimate account number. Preferably
someone with mucho money—although the pleasure, of course,
was in the pursuit.

He looked up at his screen when the whine-hiss sequence of
the modem connecting with another modem was complete.

Dialing National Pacific · · ·

Connecting · · ·

Confirming connection protocol · · ·

Connection complete!

Please enter your account number:

Aw, too easy! He entered the first eleven digits of his new account
number. Knowing perfectly well that these account numbers were
distributed in sequential order, he changed the final digit of the account number from a 9 to a 2. *Let's see who this poor sap is.*

Welcome, Paul Takishima

Gam's heart was pounding faster. Here he sat, master of somebody else's destiny . . . somebody helpless and unsuspecting.

**Please enter your Personal Identifi-
cation Number:**

OK, what's your PIN, you chump? Intense and charged, Gam snatched the literature he'd been sent by the bank and rapidly scanned it. How many digits were there in this PIN? He couldn't find any reference to it; all the brochure said was, "And, if you have a personal computer and a modem, you can access your own account twenty-four hours a day from your own home. Transfer funds, pay bills, check your account balance, with National Pacific's *DirectLink* Home Banking Service."

Fine. Gonna make this harder for me, aren't you? We'll see, you losers.

He typed 123456789, and pressed Return.

**Sorry, your Personal Identification
Number must be between 4 and 6 digits
long. Please try again:**

Why, thank you, Gam thought triumphantly. *Precisely what I needed to know.* He signed off from the service and quit the DirectLink program. Do not pass go, do not collect $200, go straight to Quick Pascal.

Within twenty minutes, Gam had written a program. He named it Guesser. Crude, dumb, and with almost no interface at all, it had only one main routine: to transmit 0000, check for acceptance from a remote modem; transmit 0001, check for acceptance; and so on up to 999999. *Not too tough.*

He launched it simultaneously with DirectLink, entered Paul whatshisname's account number, and switched to his Guesser program. *Let's roll.*

**Please enter your Personal Identifi-
cation Number: 0000**

**Sorry, that's incorrect. Please try
again: 0001**

```
Sorry, that's incorrect. Please try
again: 0002

Invalid password.

Thank you for using DirectLink™.

Disconnect

+++
```

Oh, so we think we're clever, do we? Gam's eyes were shining with the pleasure of the hunt. *So it's three guesses before you dump me off the system. Hey, that's OK; I've got three Macs, three modems, and all night.*

He thought a moment, then opened one of the three wall-to-ceiling closet doors that formed one end of his room. He pulled out a box of equipment and extracted two older modems.

He disconnected the laser printer from his computers, and hooked up the modems to the printer ports. *Let's get serious here. I'll run two copies of DirectLink under System 7; one will dial out on the printer port, and one on the modem port.* This way, he figured, he'd be able to try twenty-four combinations per minute instead of twelve. *Hell, it's just a hobby.*

By the time Gam went to sleep, all three computers were furiously redialing National Pacific Trust. Paul Takishima, a tax preparer in L.A., could not have known that he was the unlucky recipient of Gam Lampert's attention.

chapter 4

October 16, 1993   *Now,* this *is California,* thought Danny. Even after four weeks, he still hadn't quite adjusted to the breezy West Coast pop culture.

There was nothing in Mimi's Grill, for example, that wasn't made of driftwood or partially obscured by a fiberglass cactus. The specials, written in loopy girl's handwriting with fluorescent chalk that glowed under black light, universally included sun-dried tomatoes or avocado. The drinks were named for famous Western murderers, and there was no one at the bar older than thirty.

He walked in with Skinner, Rod, and Charles, thinking how much they deserved this night out after two weeks of intense concentration. *Of psychological manipulation*, Danny corrected himself; nobody on earth had a greater mania for controlling than Gam Lampert.

They sat down and ordered drinks.

Skinner: "One of these Jesse Jameses, OK?"

Rod: "I'd like a Charlie Manson, please."

Charles: "You winos are gonna dissolve your brains. Why don't you put something healthy into your bodies? Yes, miss, gimme a Pepsi and a basket of fries."

Danny scanned the potages list, found a cranberry/grapefruit concoction that sounded good. "A Yosemite Sam, please," he said. The waitress glided away, roller skates flashing.

Danny half focused on the TV above the bar, where a CNN correspondent was bringing the world into Mimi's.

"What *once* was called the *So*viet *Un*ion hasn't had a day of certainty since the *fall* of *Gor*bachev. For *years* the people here have known *conflict* as an ines*cap*able presence in their liiiives," went the singsong. "But for the *past* six months, Secretary of State Henry Masso has been working to *change* all that . . ."

"So check it out. Boys' night out," blurted Skinner, squirming happily on the booth bench after placing his calculator on the table. "Four crazy guys, right? Bachelors on the town?"

Charles regarded him dourly. "Our inability to get dates tonight is no cause for celebration, Hsiao. Take a Valium."

Rod perked up. "Oh, gee, were we supposed to get girls tonight?" He looked to Danny for an answer. "Because I could have gotten one."

Danny didn't doubt it. The guy looked like a Kennedy and was about as threatening as Snuggles the fabric-softener bear.

"Maybe you could have, Rod," deadpanned Charles. "But not all of us were born looking like Robert Redford's love child."

Rod looked sincerely shocked. "Robert Redford has a love child?" He blinked in disbelief.

Danny hoped the drinks would come soon.

Mercifully, Skinner changed the subject. "So OK, so how do we feel being the guys who get to write the coolest, coolest software ever?" He talked fast. He always talked fast.

"How does it feel?" Charles checked his pulse solemnly. "Blood pressure high. Dizziness, nausea, ringing in the ears. The only cure is a massive influx of starches and saturated fats." He smacked his lips.

Danny leaned back and sighed. "I don't know about you guys, but this schedule is wearing me out."

"You're gonna get wiped, y'know?" said Skinner. "I'm to'lly serious. You get into it, y'know? I mean a programmer, it's like, it's like a tax guy: don't do anything for months, right? You sit there. And then suddenly you're at full throttle for a few weeks. Do or die. All ya got. You know, while you get a new program out, OK, and then it's over—the deadline comes, you ship out the package, you take a couple weeks off, right?"

Danny nodded reluctantly.

"How lovely that we're just temps," sulked Charles. "Of that glamorous and fulfilling cycle you just described, the only part *we're* gonna see is the crunch. If I were you people, I'd be drinkin' it in, no matter how much it sucks. 'Cause in two months it's Unemployment Time again." He puffed on half a breadstick like a cigar.

"Except for Gam," Danny added. "He'll be basking in the royalties of our work for decades."

"That child pisses me off," said Charles. "If I hear one more stupid story about his stupid airplane or his stupid cars, I'll staple his nostrils shut. Where the hell does he get that kind of money, anyway?"

Danny rolled his eyes. "Probably the same place he gets the attitude."

"Know what he can do, though?" said Rod brightly. "He can dial into anything with his modem! He can bust into a company, or a bank, or anything he wants. He told me he called up the IRS mainframes and made it so he didn't have to pay any taxes!"

Charles grinned and tried to tousle Rod's hair. "I think Gam was having a little fun with the ol' Rod-man."

Danny wasn't smiling.

"Unless he wasn't."

There was an uncomfortable silence. Rod, annoyed, plucked at his hair to undo the damage.

"What about his programming?" Danny asked finally.

Another silence. Who'd be the first to admit he couldn't read Gam's code?

"Well, jeez, y'know?" Skinner finally said. "The guy writes in Assembly, OK? How should we know how good it is?"

The others exclaimed in agreement. While most programmers work in a pseudo-English structured language like Pascal or C language, Gam did his programming in Assembly language—almost the computer's own internal language. Most people didn't *write* Assembly, a nested morass of letters and numbers, like you'd jot down a grocery list; most programmers had to translate it, nugget by nugget, from a higher-level language. Danny knew they were all thinking the same thing.

"The guy's a genius."

The others chomped silently for a moment on their bread-sticks.

"Well, he has to be, OK?" said Skinner. "Assembly language is a hundred times faster and more compact than Pascal or whatever, right? OK, it's the only way they'd ever pull off a program this complex. What if he were one of us, OK? You couldn't write this program in C, you couldn't do it, y'know?"

Charles nodded. "Yeah, that'd be a *great* program. You'd tell your computer, 'Type my return address,' and you could do your laundry and come back by the time it was finished."

The waitress skidded to a stop and set the drinks on the table. "Who had the Manson?"

Rod raised his hand.

"Sorry, we don't have any more of the little plastic chainsaws. I gave you a sombrero instead." She skated off.

Rod held the sombrero up to the light, fascinated. "Cool."

"So that's why they let this creep walk all over them," Danny said. "They need him to pull this program off. Look, I'll be honest with you. On Wednesday afternoon I quit doing what I was s'posed to be doing. I took a couple hours to go over some of Gam's work. I mean, I sat there and walked through it line by line, translating it so I could figure out what he was doing. Took forever." He took a sip from his long, skinny glass.

Skinner leaned forward. "So? So like what?"

Danny swallowed and looked at him. "Freakin' amazing," he said. "This stuff is so tight, and so efficient, and so structured—it'll blow your mind. The guy *thinks* in Assembly."

Skinner slapped the table and blinked several times in succession. "So we've got this main programmer, OK, running the whole operation, writing code none of us can read, OK?" He was getting agitated. "Some team effort, right?"

"I know, I swear," said Charles. "If this jerk calls me the Swiss Mister one more time, I'm spray-painting his monitor."

Danny tasted cranberry, but his mind was racing. "Look, you guys, how are we supposed to come up with something integrated and clean if he's doing all the important stuff without letting us in on it? I mean, if we ask him to show us how he's building the main routines, he'll just laugh and tell us to learn Assembly better. This is only the third week, and Gam's already driving us crazy. What about in December, when the final code-freeze date is coming down and we're staying up all night? How're we gonna deal with that?"

Charles was stirring his drink with a swizzle stick shaped like a stirrup. He stared into the swirling liquid for a moment.

"Seems pretty simple, really," he told Danny. "You accept his control and he'll be nice to you. The one thing Gam doesn't like is not being in control."

"Yeah." Danny couldn't think of any alternatives. Yet.

He let the drone of the TV enter his consciousness.

"And *so* the United States has found itself in an *unlikely* position: an *al*ly to the rebellious Ukraine. If Masso and Ukrainian president Jure*nk*o have their way, the American plan just *might* help the fighting *Common*wealth states *tru*ly . . . become a *union* once again. *Jeannie* Spinks, *CNN, Mosc*ow."

They ordered nachos with melted goat cheese, laughed and drank, and talked about the economy, the Big One, and the Rams. But Danny couldn't get his mind off Gam.

By looking, it would be impossible to identify the sprawling, cubicle-filled office as the home of *PowerMac* magazine. Particularly not if you were a subscriber to this colorful monthly, whose 400-page, glossy look connoted something more of the chrome-and-glass high-tech corporate digs than three cozily cluttered floors of a San Francisco office building.

Tommy Daniel was in the delicate business of handling the monthly news column. Delicate, because in a business where a new product's image could make or break its success in the marketplace, Tommy had to make sure his reporting was objective and understated; he tended to use a lot of phrases like "the manufacturer claims" and "prototypes have been clocked at."

The news release in his hand, for example, was delicate.

ARTELLIGENCE TO UNVEIL TRUE
SPEECH-RECOGNITION SYSTEM

Tommy had been through the wave-of-the-future stuff before. First you get a press release; there's a lot of excitement; all the news editors run the item. By some not-so-surprising coincidence, this media coverage is usually concurrent with an ad blitz by the manufacturer's marketing department. Reader-service cards come pouring in. The manufacturer's mailing-list database builds up. And then comes the product demonstration, where you find out how little there really was to get excited about: some crude pattern-matching voice system that can only learn 200 words, and even then only interprets your spoken commands correctly 80 percent of the time. *Give us a break*, he thought.

He wondered, though, as he read this press release. This was evidently something new, and its development had required the design of a custom chip. Between the software, the hardware, and the money pumped into the project by Mika, the Japanese consumer-electronics firm, this thing might actually fly. And, after all, Artelligence was the developer. Tommy doubted they'd pour their R and D dollars into a dog.

He wondered if the item was important enough to run in the issue now being laid out—January. Of course, the release indicated that there'd be a product rollout for the press on December 8, over in Moscone. Tommy checked his calendar. Didn't matter what else was happening—he should be at that demo. Even then, there'd probably still be time to get the piece in for January. He dashed off an E-mail to the other editors, describing the event, and noting that a few *PowerMac* staffers should be on hand.

The contact on the press release was Michelle Andersen; he jotted down her number on a Post-It note and slapped it on the upper-right corner of his monitor.

Behind a space-divider panel from Tommy, Mila Moore grabbed her waist-length brown hair with both fists and threw it backward over her shoulders, as she always did unconsciously when getting serious. The task at hand was to check the camera-ready final proofs of her January-issue Tips'n'Tricks column.

She was about halfway through the proof copy when her associate editor, in the other crook of the S-shaped common desk, chucked a folded letter-size document over. Mila grabbed it: "What's this thing?"

Her assistant shrugged. "Got it today; maybe you can use it as a five-liner somewhere." Mila thanked her and dropped the letter in her In basket.

She didn't realize, however, how soon she'd be needing an item of precisely that length. The last item of the column, a hint for getting more speed out of local area networks, required a HyperRing card—but that very morning Mila had heard that HyperRing's release was being delayed. That meant it might not be available when the January *PowerMac* hit the stands, and that meant Mila'd better not run the LAN trick.

"Shoot," she said out loud, and crossed out the paragraph.

She called out to her associate. "Hey, Liz, do you have anything I could—" She stopped, remembering, and snatched the folded sheet from her In box. She unfolded it and read it quickly once, then again more slowly.

> *Dear PowerMac Tricks'n'Tips,*
>
> *Here's a neat little trick for you. We were playing the public-domain game AirAttack, which we got from InfoServe. We discovered that if you change your Mac clock to Christmas, the little oak tree turns into a Christmas tree. Pretty neat, huh?*
>
> *If you print this, please send the $25 to the address below. We like the magazine a lot.*
>
> *Sincerely,*
> *Ellen Eckhouse & Mike O'Massey*
> *Farrow House 125a, Rollins College*
> *Tampa, FL 82882*

Mila picked up the phone and called the features editor who spent the most time with games. Within moments, he had a copy of AirAttack running on his computer. She directed him to set his clock to December 25, and, from his exclamation, she knew immediately that the trick had worked.

"Hey, great. Is it cute?" she asked him. "All right, that's what I needed to know. I'm gonna run it for January. Thanks for checking it out. I'll be down later to get a screen shot of it, OK? Thanks, Ted. Bye."

She hung up. "Never mind, Liz. I was going to ask you if you had a little quickie I could use, but I've got it fixed."

She turned to her Mac and started writing it up. She wouldn't give the item another thought until months later—but by then it would be too late.

October 29, 1993   Danny's left hand held the half-finished plum with thumb and forefinger, and the other three fingers steadied the vinyl-wrapped steering wheel of his '79 Rabbit. As usual, it didn't start immediately. With his right hand, Danny tried the ignition again after each patient pump and release of the accelerator.

At last it sputtered to life. Danny licked the plum juice that had run all the way down to his wrist, buckled up, and headed for I-101.

He felt good. As the Rabbit's speedometer moseyed up toward sixty, he wondered why his spirits were so high. Could be that he had something significant to do every day—something meaningful. *Man, if Dad could see me now*, he thought. *What a cue for his Squandered Gifts speech.*

"Use the Brains God Gave You, Daniel," Danny's head recited as he drove the eternally pothole-free highway. "You've been blessed with the gifts to do something meaningful; look at your brothers. Don't squander your gifts, Daniel. I'd like to see you make something of yourself." The pause, the official throat clearing, then: "I'll mention one more time that Chuck Deegan is the dean at Chicago Business. He was my roommate in law school. The day you decide you've finished playing around with your computers, you let me know."

Gotta give Dad a call one of these days.

Danny found something fun and dancey on the AM radio—the Rabbit's sole amenity—that he was still humming as he walked from the parking lot, through the Japanese garden, and into the Artelligence building. He had a feeling nothing would be able to crush his mood. . . . If Gam got unpleasant, Danny vowed to just smile and work harder at the piece of the program he'd been assigned.

As he rounded the corner toward the R and D lab, he decided to poke his head into Michelle's office, as he'd been making it a point to do more and more often. He'd been getting the feeling she looked forward to it.

"Hail there, Media Goddess!" he greeted her. "How are things in PR-Land?"

"Just dandy, Danny," she said. She looked sunny and neat, her hair, as usual, carefully tied back. "All systems go on my end; you guys gonna be ready for me?"

"Of course we will," said Danny, grinning. "The Japanese may be baying at the door, the public may be screaming for their voice control . . . but we're gonna finish this program on schedule for you and you alone. Never was a roomful of computer nerds so adoring."

"That's my boys!"

"Hey, cool terrarium."

On a castered TV stand behind her desk was a small aquarium, a microcosmic forest. The hard plastic plate from a microwave frozen dinner served as a miniature lake.

"That's Myrtle," she said, lifting the mesh lid. "I thought she needed a change of scene, so I brought her in to work."

Danny peered inside. "Myrtle?"

Her fingers burrowed through the leaves and wood chips. She grabbed something and carefully extracted it from the aquarium.

"Behold: Myrtle, mother of all dimestore turtles."

She set the tiny turtle on her desk and watched it. No bigger than a half dollar, the turtle blinked sleepily in the fluorescent light and took a single tentative step forward.

"Morning, Myrt," said Danny grandly. To Michelle, he stage-whispered: "How do you know it's a *she*?"

Michelle arched an eyebrow at him. "I don't. But I give her the benefit of the doubt."

Myrtle, evidently bored by the proceedings, half receded into her shell. Michelle lifted her gently by the edges and put her back inside the terrarium.

"Technically, poor Myrtle is contraband," she told Danny. "Pet stores in this country aren't allowed to sell turtles anymore, did you know that? But I got Myrtle from the lady who used to have my apartment, and that was two years ago. Myrtle has already outlived her life expectancy in captivity by a year; I think she and I were meant to be together."

"Of course you were," he said. "Look at all you have in common. Myrtle is a leathery, toothless, egg-laying reptile; you're a bright, with-it, *very* attractive media relations director at a major software firm."

She folded her arms and gave him a flattery-will-get-you-nowhere look.

"Well, OK," he conceded, caught in the act. "I guess you don't have that much in common."

He turned toward the door. "Well, I'd better get to work. Gam here yet?"

"No," said Michelle. "He's not coming in today. Oh, yeah—he says for you guys to leave his Mac alone. He's got some kind of virus."

The mood was shattered: he froze. A gush of adrenaline made his stomach muscles clench involuntarily. A computer virus? Now? After all their weeks of work? Desperately, he mentally traced the connections in the R and D network; what if it spread to the other connected computers? Oh, God, he thought. Depending on when Gam's hard drive had become infected, there might not be a single healthy copy of the program! Even the backup copies would be corrupted . . . they were all made from the copy on Gam's hard drive!

He looked hard at Michelle, a wave of panic washing over him. "*What?*" was all he could get out.

"He's got a nasty virus," she repeated. "He's not coming in today."

"Oh God, oh God . . . *How* could this happen?!"

Michelle was staring. "Danny, what's your problem? Who cares? He touched some doorknob and didn't wash his hands. Someone sneezed on him. How does anyone get a virus? It's no big deal; he'll be back in tomorrow."

Danny exhaled audibly, drowning in relief. "Oh . . . oh, jeez. I get it. He's got the flu or something?"

She nodded with a quizzical look.

His pulse was returning to normal. "Michelle, do you know what a computer virus is?"

She gave him a sharp look. "No, Danny. I'm a female. With no grasp of anything technical. I've only been in the software business for six years, and I also don't read the newspaper."

"Sorry," Danny said, ashamed, but still relieved that Gam's virus was a biological entity instead of an electronic one. "Look, I was just afraid you meant a *computer* virus. See, I may as well let you in on this: Gam takes his hard drive home every night. He hooks up to a lot of those dial-up modem services—that's where most people pick up viruses, so I thought you meant. . ."

She nodded.

"You can imagine how hairy it'd be if some virus held us up

for a few days," he continued. "We'd probably miss our ship date, for one thing."

For the first time, a tiny furrow of concern appeared on Michelle's brow. He'd almost forgotten how important that shipping date was to her.

"Well, it's bad enough that we're losing a day of Gam-programming time to a *human* virus," Michelle said, sitting on the front edge of her desk. "But I'm a little concerned about this modem thing. Does Arnie know that he's exposing the project to that risk?"

Danny shook his head.

"Maybe we ought to tell him."

Danny scratched his neck thoughtfully. "I don't know. From what I've seen, Arnie's not much of a match for anything Gam feels like doing."

She rested her hand lightly on his wrist. "I think you ought to talk to him. There's got to be some way to protect ourselves."

She even smelled good.

Inspiration struck; Danny snapped his fingers. "Michelle, you're brilliant!"

"What'd I say?"

His mind raced—it would be so simple. "You're absolutely right. Of course we can protect ourselves. How could I be so silly?"

"What?" she asked.

And then another idea . . . now or never. He smiled mysteriously. "I can't tell you now. But I'll tell you what: have dinner with me tomorrow. I'll let you in on my sordid past." He started backing deliberately toward the door.

"I don't know, Danny. I try to keep my professional and personal lives a little separate."

He had one hand on the doorframe. "OK, I promise not to say anything personal. Seven o'clock?"

She hesitated only a moment longer. "Well, I guess it's OK." She hopped off the desk. "For the sake of the program."

"Naturally," he said. "For the sake of the program." He threw her a half smirk and sprinted into the hallway.

October 30, 1993   Taxes. Taxes. Taxes. Taxes.

With each footfall, Stroman chanted the word in his head like a mantra. Yes, here was the taxpayers' money—in every carpeted office, in the glow of the computer screen on every desk, in every pair of swinging conference-room doors. Bob Stroman strode down the hallway, struggling not to let his dovey, Democratic past get the better of him.

And Hamilton Air Force Base wasn't even the most frivolous expenditure of his country's citizens' money, either, Stroman knew as he checked door numbers for the office he sought. He wasn't sure what the citizens' action leagues would say if they knew what *he* was doing here today.

Nonetheless, Stroman had decided to treat the U.S. government like any other Artelligence customer. Stroman would sell them the product; it wouldn't be his responsibility to monitor what they did with it. If he started worrying about the ultimate reason for his presence in these hallways, he'd probably back right out of the deal out of sheer guilt; finding better and faster ways of killing people wasn't quite his cup of tea.

There: room 1831-A. Past the open door was a cluttered reception area. The receptionist, a young lieutenant, looked up.

"Good afternoon, Mr. Stroman," he said. "Colonel Oskins is expecting you; go right on in." He gestured to a second doorway.

Stroman walked in to Oskins's office. Oskins, a corpulent, puffing man in his fifties, threw out his hand. "So! The man himself!" he boomed.

Stroman shook hands and sat down; Oskins struggled back into his desk chair. "Ah'm glad we could finally git together on this," Oskins said. Stroman was always amazed at the man's vestigial Alabaman accent—the guy was a walking movie-general stereotype.

"As Ah've been tellin' you on the phone, Ah had to go through the usual red tape on gittin' the funds for this project from the GAO. But now they're saying they'll sign whatever needs signin' as soon as they can see a demo."

Stroman smiled. "Right," he said. "You told everyone about our little show on the eighth, didn't you?" From all indications, the official public unveiling of Master Voice would be an incredible event.

"Course. That's why Ah think you and Ah should assume it's on, and maybe we can talk more about specifics."

"Sure." Stroman opened his briefcase. "As you know, the arc chip is sort of like a genius who can't talk; it's a brilliant piece of engineering, but it doesn't do much without a software front end. It needs something to interpret our instructions into a language it understands—and vice versa.''

Oskins nodded.

"So, in essence, we have a couple of choices. We can give you what we've got right now—the chip and the software for the Macintosh, which we're finishing up now. You might use that kind of system internally, administratively, you know—the same way anyone in any office anywhere would use it.''

"That's this Master's Voice thang?''

"That's right, Master Voice,'' said Stroman, correcting him gently. "Now, of course, the real military possibilities of the arc chip don't involve sitting around in an office calculating the cost of paper clips; I think you might be more interested in having us adapt the software specifically for you, so you could incorporate the voice-recognition technology into anything you wanted. Navigational controls, weapons systems. . . whatever.''

Stroman could tell from the gleam in Oskins's eye that he'd found the colonel's weak spot.

"Actually, Bob, Ah've been talkin' to the boys in the Infidel offices here, and they been talkin' to the brass at the Pentagon. They're all convinced we should pursue it, full steam ahead.''

"The *what* office?''

"Infidel,'' Oskins answered. He pronounced it Infa-dale. "It's a new cruise missile class. For the last decade, this department been developing so-called smart bombs. You know . . . once they're shot off, they got enough sensors on board to home in on the heat of a jet exhaust, the metal bulk of a tank, and so on. In other words, you don't actually have to aim the suckers when you launch 'em.''

"OK,'' Stroman said.

"Well, the smart bombs got one big ol' problem: they can't tell the heat of an enemy plane from one of ours. Ah guess you could say that smart bombs aren't quite smart enough.'' He looked at Stroman, leaning back in his chair. Stroman took the cue and faked a smile.

"Infidel, though, is a little more ambitious. These little fellers have a much longer cruisin' range, and much more sophisticated computer imaging on board. They got maps of the terrain stored right on board—or else they talk to our mainframes on the ground for that information—so they literally look for some'm to hit. They go flyin' around, takin' their sweet time, comparin' the images from their cameras with the information in their topographical databases. When they spot somethin'—say, an enemy installation we know about—off they go. Kamikaze bombs, you know.

"The great thing about Infidel is the psychological edge we git. All of a sudden, enemy troops got no warnin'. They don't pick up any scramblin' of our jets or movements of our tanks to tip 'em off that we're attackin'. The smart missile can be out there lurkin' all day, huntin' them down."

Stroman didn't quite follow. "Well . . . how does speech recognition enter all this?"

"All right, here's what happens. The Infidel Eights are workin' right now. They've been shootin' off dummy Eights in Nevada for six months. Trouble is, the Eights are expensive as all git-out. Every Eight costs us about two million bucks in circuitry and imaging gear. And what happens if the things work? Two million bucks go up in a puffa smoke when they hit the target. Kinda crazy . . . you waste taxpayer money when the damn things *do* work!"

Stroman pretended to be amused.

"And they *still* can't tell a good plane from a bad one," he added.

"So, OK, now we got Infidel Tens on the drawin' boards," Oskins continued. "The Pentagon boys got a great idea: keep the databases and the processing gear on the ground. Keep the Tens in radio contact with the mainframes on the ground at thirty-six thousand bits per second, sendin' instructions all the time, instead of kickin' the missile out of the nest and wishin' it good night. If we can get the Tens workin', they'll cost a fraction of the Eights, because the missile itself only carries weaponry. The expensive stuff—the computers—stay on the ground. The Tens'll work better, too, 'cause we can afford a helluva lot more number-crunchin' power if the computers are in a truck somewhere. And, 'course, the computers don't get blown off the goddamn map every time an Infidel hits its target."

Stroman nodded, encouraging Oskins to elaborate.

"OK. So the boys have been thinkin'. First of all, they're in love with the idea of making the Infidel command post mobile. They want to send a coupla semis out there into the desert, or the tundra, or wherever the battle happens to be, so communications with the actual missile remain good and strong. So that means transportable computer gear. And that means powerful but cheap. In the testing they been usin' a pair of modified Mac Quadras to simulate the ground Infidel computers.''

Stroman snorted involuntarily. "You mean they're running this trillion-dollar defense program off a coupla Macs!?" he asked, astonished.

"Easy with the figures there, son. The Infidel program's budget is well under a billion," Oskins said earnestly. "Anyway, with the custom software we got, these Macs really cook. And the GAO loves 'em, 'cause Macs are something they c'n understand.'' Stroman mumbled apologetically and sat back to listen.

"So we were thinkin' about this voice-recognition stuff. The idea is this: we want the man on the ground system to feel like he's right on that sucker. We want him to actually *see* whether that missile is chasin' an enemy plane or a friendly one, double-check its decisions about where it is, maybe help it scan for enemy installations, and so forth. The point is for a human eye to work together with the Infidel's video.

"So we got this crazy idea: outfit him with this voice thing. We want him tellin' that bomb what to do. You know, 'Right thirty degrees,' 'Circle that valley again,' that kind of thing. He'll be sittin' back in that truck with a martini, starin' at the video from the onboard cameras, while the bomb is three hundred miles away, tellin' it where to go and how it's doin'.''

Stroman considered for a moment. "Well, it's completely doable,'' he said. "I mean, it doesn't sound that tricky for Master Voice, even unmodified. If you wrote the right interpretive code for the kinds of instructions your men will be speaking, you could use the product as is.''

"That's exactly what we were hopin' you'd say, Bob.'' The colonel extracted a pair of minuscule half-moon glasses from the desk drawer and perched them almost daintily on his nose. "Now, our worries here are about the time line. We need to see somethin' on this fairly ASAP.''

"Of course," Stroman said. "We've been meaning to draw up a proposal. We've just been so busy getting our first consumer-level product out the door, this Master Voice package, that I just haven't had any time. But listen, the minute that product ships—''

Oskins interrupted. "Bob, look, Ah'll be straight with you. Ah don't know that Ah can wait until the spring, or whenever you're done with your home-market device. You probably know that you're not the only speech-recognition developer in the world; we're also lookin' into a couple of other promisin' packages. Now, Ah like what Ah've seen of your system, so Ah'm happy to keep in touch with you on this. But time is of the essence." He clucked his tongue a couple of times.

Stroman jerked involuntarily. Other systems!? *What* other systems? *What* other developers? Oskins couldn't possibly be talking about one of the old pattern-matching voice systems. Did he know about some other true speech-recognition system Stroman didn't?

"Colonel, I'm sorry, I didn't realize that . . . I didn't know there were other candidates for this contract."

"We have to consider all the options, Bob. Course, these projects will represent a healthy chunka change for some company, and we just want to make sure we're doin' the right thang."

"If I may ask . . . how many other candidates are there?" Stroman's mind raced. There weren't any other true speech-recognition systems anywhere near completion! There were some experiments at M.I.T., but they wouldn't be courting the Pentagon. . . .

"Aw, look, Bob, you know Ah can't go inta that. Let's just say that there's at least one major player sayin' they're ready to talk to us. You git me the write-up soon as you can, and you got nothin' to worry about. All right, sir?"

For another twenty minutes, they discussed the specifics of the arrangement that might be struck. Oskins talked money, manpower, and fiscal budget years; Stroman did what he could to help with information about development time. But all he could think of was the other bidder. Suddenly Stroman's place in technological history wasn't so secure as he'd imagined.

At precisely nine A.M., Oskins rose.

"All right, Bob, Ah think we done some good work here. Ah think the next step is for me to bring the boys in to see your big demonstration on the eighth." He walked from behind the desk.

Stroman bent forward to close his briefcase—and froze. There, in square center of the blotter, was Oskins's file folder, still open on the desk. What he saw there shocked him.

He looked away, stunned.

"We talk next week then, Bob?" came the big friendly voice from behind him.

Stroman straightened, turned. "Yeah . . . yeah, thanks," he said in a breathy voice, and coughed twice to cover for his paralysis.

He squeezed past the burly colonel in the doorway, giving him a quick, firm nod by way of farewell.

He plowed out of the building, clenching his sunglasses nearly to the breaking point, his nerve shattered. He should have expected this; somehow he should have seen it coming. He scanned the parking lot for his car, his confusion turning to rage.

In that one second, Stroman had seen a sheet of letterhead paper clipped to each leaf of the open folder. Even upside down, he recognized his own Artelligence logo at the top of one page. It was his original proposal.

The logo on the other page said NOⱢ⅁NⁱⱢNⵑH.

So this was Huntington's game. This was his ten-year-old punishment for Stroman's defection—to beat Artelligence to market, steal their thunder, shoot down Stroman's brilliant dream.

He wouldn't let it happen. His jaw tightened: he'd get Master Voice finished on time or die trying.

"Danny! What a nice surprise," said Arnie kindly. The R and D director always reminded Danny of some benevolent grandfather. A thirty-five-year-old grandfather. With a big bushy squared-off beard.

"Sorry to bug you," Danny said, sitting down.

"Not at all! I'm sorry we haven't had a chance to talk lately. Is everything all right? Did you wind up finding a good place to live?"

"Well, *good* might be stretching it. Let's put it this way: there are fewer roaches than there were in New York."

Arnie nodded. "So you're saving some money, then. Good idea."

"Yeah."

Danny couldn't believe he was doing this, but his conscience drove him to make the attempt.

"Listen, Arnie. I had quite a scare yesterday." He described his conversation with Michelle.

". . . and for the sake of allegiance to our star programmer, I probably shouldn't be telling you this . . . but I think you should know that Gam takes his hard drive home with him pretty often. That's why I assumed he'd caught something."

Arnie smiled. "Well, Danny, I know we must seem awfully strict to you. You must think we're crazy; I don't blame you. But if Gam needs some time at home to work on the Master Voice code, I think I can overlook that one security breach. Frankly, I'm more concerned that the project be finished on time.''

"No, that's not what worries me," Danny said, shaking his head. "He doesn't just take it home to *work*; he takes it home and uses his modem. He exposes himself to every little virus and bug out there, and then he brings his drive back into the lab and connects it to our network.''

"You know this for a fact? I'd normally give Gam credit for being more careful than that.''

"It's a fact. He brags about it, for God's sake!''

Arnie leaned back in his high-backed chair, pondering. Danny, a quick thinker and snap decision maker, would have sighed if he weren't trying to show some courtesy—he sometimes had trouble tolerating people whose mental wheels turned so methodically.

At last Arnie returned to the conversation. "What do you suggest we do, Danny?''

At last.

"OK; actually, I have what I think is a pretty good plan. When I was back in New York, I wrote a program, a really smart anti-virus utility, called SURvIVor. I never could get it sold, but it's done. It's debugged and stable. And it's good.''

Arnie smiled. "I always suspected you were a fine programmer.''

"So my idea is simple," Danny went on. "Just let me install SURvIVor on Gam's hard drive. That's all I ask. Simple, quick, he'll never know. In the meantime, we can all breathe easier knowing that we're protected in case he gets himself infected.''

Bingo. Score. Bull's-eye.

But Arnie scowled. "I don't know, Danny. . . .''

That drawn-out thoughtful look again. Danny nearly rolled his eyes.

"I don't think that would represent very good faith on our part, Danny; it certainly does seem like an invasion of privacy.''

Invasion of privacy? Give me a break, Danny thought. *What about our sanity?*

"But I'll tell you what," Arnie continued. "Let's take this a bit more democratically. Let's install your program, by all means. But let's ask Gam for permission first." He smiled, pleased with his Solomonic wisdom. "That way we don't step on anybody's toes.''

Man, you should be in the Guinness Book: World's Biggest Conflict-Avoider.

"Please, Arnie. You know that he'll just say no, and then for the rest of the year he'll despise me for suspecting him. Look, nobody loses with my plan: you call him out of the lab one day, I slip the protection onto his drive."

"Danny, Gam is a very, very bright young man. He's also a very promising programmer with a lot riding on the Master Voice project; we're paying him a considerable sum to write it for us. I don't think he'd be so careless as to allow his work to be at risk; I think I can give him the benefit of that doubt."

"But—"

Arnie held up one finger with a Socratic expression. "Danny, I appreciate your concern. You're showing excellent care for your work, and you're certainly an asset to the team."

Danny sensed that that was supposed to be his exit cue. He ignored it.

"Arnie, come on. The guy's got some psychological screws loose, and we both know it. Just give me five minutes alone—"

"Danny. I think I've made my position plain. You're not to put anything on Gam's drive, is that clear?"

What's clear is that you let Gam wipe his feet on you.

"Yes, Arnie. It's clear." He stood slowly and rose to leave the room.

"And, Danny?"

He stopped in the doorway to see what Arnie wanted.

Arnie waved cheerfully. "Have a happy Halloween tomorrow."

Danny left Arnie's office and went back to the lab. *Who needs Halloween?* he thought. *This place already gives me the creeps.*

Secretary of State Henry Masso felt like a shepherd in some kind of twisted modern-day Nativity scene, standing there, motionless, for five minutes at a time. He knew he should have been used to photo ops by now, but it was still a trial. Standing on the dais, his hand firmly in that of Ukrainian president Jurenko, he kept his head turned ninety degrees to face the press. Flashbulbs blinded him over and over again, creating a starry field of blurred blue dots everywhere he looked, but he kept the tight diplomatic smile of confidence plastered on his face. Every five seconds he and Jurenko convulsively jerked their clasped hands up and down again, in the slim hopes of making the handshake photos look more spontaneous.

The diorama was for a good cause, though, he reminded himself; appearing on the front page of every daily in the country never hurt a politician. And that much coverage was assured, not just because an accord among the Commonwealth factions was nearing, nor that this third round of delicate summit talks was beginning; no, what made this set of meetings unusual was that they were taking place on American soil. If they could iron out the fine points of the agreement here at home . . . Jesus, Masso kept thinking, what a PR coup.

He pumped Jurenko's pudgy hand once more just to keep sane. Under the heat of the photo lamps, it was warm; Jurenko was perspiring and beginning to look miserable.

At last, the Secret Service men drifted in front of the cameras. "Thank you, ladies and gentlemen of the press," shouted a deputy from the press office. "We'll see you again on Thursday at two o'clock. These gentlemen have some work to do." The crowd thinned; Masso was grateful that Jurenko's was the last hand he'd have to clutch. He glanced to his left, where the honchos from Russia, Belarus, Georgia, Armenia, and Azerbaijan stood, no doubt nursing their own aching necks and wrists. But today the spotlight was clearly on Jurenko: Jurenko had the nukes.

The Service staff cleared the salon and ushered the delegates into the adjoining conference room. A long, dark oak table had been carefully prepared; at each place was a stack of transcripts from the previous summit meetings, stacks of legal pads, pens, and crisply sharpened pencils, and a pitcher of water. Next to each seat was a chair with a shorter back, pulled back two feet from the table's edge; these would seat the translators.

Masso, smiling, turned and genteelly ushered President Jurenko through the double doorway. God, but these affairs were delicate; Masso remembered the first of these summits, where there was enough hostility among the participants to poison a platoon.

Masso took his seat, which had been carefully placed a third of the way along the table's edge, neither too prominent nor too artificially out of the way. The others, with their translators and secretaries, were also seated; only Jurenko remained on his feet. He was rubbing his left arm, up and down, hard, shuffling toward his seat with a furrowed brow.

Hoping to alleviate the tense silence, Masso rose slightly and leaned forward. He pointed to Jurenko's arm and grinned. "Didn't squeeze too hard, did I, Vladimir?"

Jurenko was a good English speaker, but responded only by looking up from the floor for a moment. Then, suddenly, his eyes squeezed shut, tight with pain. With a glottal grunt, he clutched at the back of the chair occupied by the Armenian ambassador, who half rose at the incivility; for a fleeting moment, Masso was sure there was going to be a confrontation.

But Jurenko was now clawing at his collar, pinched tight around his thick, fleshy neck, and wheezing something in his own language. The translator leaped to his feet and tried to support the president by the elbow. "It's his arm," he shouted to Masso. "Something's wrong with his arm and his side!"

"Jesus, Bernie," Masso shot to his aide. "Get a medic in here." Bernie raced from the room.

Jurenko looked at him, with a glazed expression, for a long moment, still clutching the back of the chair, his speech finally slurring to a stop. The other diplomats stood, but remained where they were; the protocol for this one didn't appear in their foreign-policy manuals. "Heart attack," observed the Russian delegate loudly.

Jurenko never made it further; his wheezing stopped, his knees buckled under him, and he fell, clutching his torso in pain and cracking his head on the table edge as he went. Too late, two Secret Servicemen and a bodyguard rushed forward to catch him. The room was filled with sudden commotion and expletives in five languages. The president's arm flopped across the polished shoes of the Belorussian prime minister, who now stood looking downward at it with an almost indignant expression.

"Oh, Jesus," Masso said, looking around frantically for the arrival of the medics. He wondered if Jurenko was dead.

chapter 5

November 10, 1993   *PowerMac* magazine has a monthly cir-
culation of 600,000. Of those, 475,000 are subscriptions.

The January 1994 issue hit the stands—and the postal system—
on November 3; for maximum newsstand shelf life, each issue
was shipped over a month ahead of its printed cover month, to
the eternal bewilderment of some readers.

The magazine published a larger-than-usual number of copies

of the January issue, however, because nearly 50,000 copies were given away at the Macintosh Superfair show in San Francisco.

By November 10, roughly 480,000 copies had been received in the mail (or purchased at newsstands) and read. Just under 60,000 people read the Tips'n'Tricks column in its entirety. Only eight thousand of those readers owned the shoot-'em-up computer game called AirAttack, described in that column.

The blurb mentioned that AirAttack would display a fully dressed Christmas tree when the Macintosh clock was set to December 25.

In the days following the magazine's publication, 1,911 readers actually took the trouble to change the date, using the Macintosh Control Panel, to see the effect. Most of them were delighted by the little graphic surprise.

One of them was Tobias McLuhan, a Loews theater manager in Solon, Ohio. He even called his nine-year-old daughter over to his computer screen to see the little Christmas tree.

The two of them played a round of AirAttack just for fun. Just as they finished the game, the phone rang; the caller was one of Toby's drinking buddies, proposing a get-together. His daughter climbed down from his knee and skipped back to her own room. Toby smiled as he continued the conversation. Absently, he quit the AirAttack game and shut down his computer.

Like 109 other *PowerMac* readers across the country, Toby had unwittingly made a tiny mistake.

He had failed to reset his Macintosh clock to the current date.

"Danny, Jesus. What's your problem?"

For the second time, Charles's meaty arm shot out beneath the table and clutched Danny's bouncing knee. Danny stopped jiggling and whispered, "Sorry."

Charles flicked his leg with a forefinger. "What's the deal? You never had a second date before?" he whispered back.

Danny smiled in acknowledgment and tried to tune in to what Arnie was saying. Something about the product introduction on December 8. Something about press passes and hors d'oeuvres. But he was far too tense to concentrate... and his date with Michelle was hardly the reason.

He looked at the clock again. The meeting would be ending in fifteen minutes. He unconsciously fingered the hard square edge of the floppy disk in his shirt pocket. The other programmers, as well as the sales staff, were all listening to Arnie. Except Gam, who sat across from Danny, slouched in the chair, looking arrogant and bored. Every few minutes he'd stare directly at Danny.

As though he knew what Danny was about to do.

The minute hand on the wall clock jumped. It was time.

As slowly as he could, Danny wedged his fingers into his right jeans pocket to find the Kleenex, wadded up, just under the opening. He withdrew it carefully; the only one who might have been able to see it was Charles, and Danny wasn't worried about him.

He glanced down at the tissue; the red Magic Marker stains were all over it. *Am I nuts? Is anyone gonna buy this?* His palms were sweating, but it was now or never. *Well, it worked in twelfth grade.*

He brought the Kleenex up to his nose and blew.

"At that point, the trucks will meet us at the loading dock," Arnie was saying. "If you could all just help us carry the equipment back to the trucks before you disappear into the night—"

"Oh, jeez!" said Danny.

Arnie stopped. Gam frowned and stared.

"I'm sorry, Arnie. I just. . .It looks like I've got a nosebleed." He stood, shifting the Kleenex in his hand just enough for them to see a flash of the bright red stain. Just a flash, then it was wadded against his nose again. "I'll be back in a couple minutes. Sorry." Tilting his head back as best he could, mouth hanging open, Danny walked from the room.

"Take your time, Danny," Arnie shouted after him. "Get some ice from Tina."

Danny was already halfway down the hall. "OK!" he shouted back.

He went into high gear, sprinting toward the R and D lab. *No Academy Awards for that performance, bucko.* He fumbled for the disk in his pocket as he ran into the lab and dropped into Gam's chair.

His heart was pounding; he felt the paranoiac desperation of sitting, much too obviously, in off-limits territory.

He slammed the floppy into the disk drive. *Nice thinking, Gam. Thanks for leaving your own disk drive slot uncovered.*

A window appeared on the screen, displaying Danny's disk's contents. It had only two files on it: two little items he had carefully prepared just for Gam's hard drive. The first file was SURvIVor—what Arnie didn't know wouldn't hurt him, Danny figured.

The second file was a surprise.

Using the mouse, he moved the cursor to the files and slid them carefully onto the on-screen image of the hard drive, which Danny saw had been named Hussein.

Gam names his hard disk after a Persian Gulf dictator. Why doesn't that surprise me?

"Files remaining to copy: 2," said the message on the screen.

Hurry up, dammit. He looked at his watch—unnecessarily. Having rehearsed this routine at his own Mac, he knew perfectly well that the copying would take thirty-five seconds. He glanced at the open doorway of the lab: all quiet.

Quickly, he ejected the floppy disk. There were the two files on Gam's hard drive, represented by two small, neat rectangular icons on the screen. This was the hard part—to make them invisible. It wouldn't do to have Gam discovering his hard drive had been...visited.

Jerking the mouse across the desk, Danny whipped the cursor up to the Apple logo, pressed the mouse button to produce the drop-down menu, and guided the pointer down the alphabetical list of mini-programs. Alarm Clock ... Calculator ... Control Panel...

DiskFixer! He let go of the button, and the DiskFixer window popped up. Danny's mouth was dry, and his heart beat like a rabbit's—but there was only one more step. DiskFixer showed him a list of every file on the outer level of Gam's hard disk directory, including the two he'd just copied. He clicked carefully on the SURvIVor file, moused up to the Fixer menu, and selected the Invisible option.

He repeated the process with the second file. The surprise. At last the deed was done.

Thank you, God.

He closed the DiskFixer window and took a look: sure enough, the icons for the two files he'd donated to Gam no longer appeared. Unless he knew what to look for, Gam would never find them. Danny shoved his floppy back into his shirt pocket—and, out of the corner of his eye, spotted something small and pink stuck to his cuff.

He plucked it off: a two-by-three-inch slip of warm pink paper, a Post-It note that must have been lying on Gam's desk. Danny looked at it.

In blue ballpoint, it said "NICE code. Love the V-mem routines."

Nice code? Well, of course, but who—

There was a sound in the doorway.

"Danny! What are you doing?"

He leaped from his chair—caught. His breath stopped.

It was Michelle. She came toward him, angrily. "What are you doing to Gam's Mac?"

"Oh, Michelle...," he managed.

"What do you think you're doing? You tell us you have a nosebleed. I come in here to see how you're doing, I think I'm being nice, and you're screwing around with someone else's *stuff*?"

"No, no, Michelle, listen—"

"I don't think that's a great way to operate, Danny. I don't enjoy being around manipulative people." She started for the door. "And I think Gam should know what you've been doing."

"*Michelle!* Listen to me! I'm protecting us! It's what we talked about, remember? About viruses?"

She stopped in the doorway.

"Look, I've only got a minute before they come back in here. Last year I wrote an anti-virus program. It's a watchdog against viruses, OK? If you get one, it'll pop up a little message on the screen and offer to kill it for you. See? That's all. I just copied it onto Gam's drive, so now we don't have to worry. He can hook it up to modems all he wants, and our software is protected." He stopped, gulped a breath. "It's for our own good."

She looked at him, and her features softened. "That's all you did?"

"That's all."

She looked down for a moment.

"Well..." She smiled. "Then I guess we should get the hell out of here."

He didn't need further prodding.

"C'mon," he said as he shoved the chair back into place. He sprinted with her into the hallway.

"Let's really go get you some ice," she said. "To make it look good."

Danny thanked her as they ran to the corporate kitchen. There would be plenty of time to tell Michelle about the second file he planted on Gam's drive. Maybe at dinner.

He didn't give the Post-It note another thought.

Clive Witmark was getting fed up with S.C.A.N., the virus checker he'd had watching over his hard drive for a month or two.

The program's modus operandi was at fault, really. Whenever something tried to modify any of his programs, S.C.A.N. would beep and display a message:

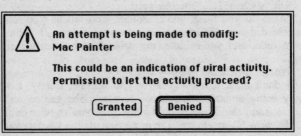

> ⚠ **An attempt is being made to modify:**
> **Mac Painter**
>
> **This could be an indication of viral activity.**
> **Permission to let the activity proceed?**
>
> [Granted]   [[**Denied**]]

In the beginning, Clive always clicked the Denied button. For a week or two, he was convinced that he was in the midst of the biggest virus blizzard of all time, because the beep/message would appear several times a day.

But Clive, a computer consultant in Houston, was no newcomer to the Macintosh. He began to realize that all of this beeping wasn't caused by viruses at all. Instead, it dawned on him that S.C.A.N. was reacting whenever *anything* tried to modify a program's code—even when the program was trying to modify *itself*.

For instance, every time Clive ran a program for the first time, it would ask him to "personalize" his installed copy by typing in his name. Once branded in this way, the program stored his name in its own internal code—to discourage him from making illegal copies, he supposed. Trouble was, every time a program attempted such a procedure, S.C.A.N. would erupt, beeping and flashing . . . because, after all, the program was being modified. Eventually, Clive got in the habit of clicking Granted every time S.C.A.N. asked for permission to modify something on his hard drive.

Same thing with floppy disks. S.C.A.N.'s other heavily hyped feature was that it would scan every floppy disk he inserted, checking for viruses. But it took about ten seconds to scan each floppy. And 99 percent of the disks Clive put into the drive were his *own* disks that he used every day. After a few weeks, he got tired of the way S.C.A.N. wasted his time scanning the same few disks every time he put one into the floppy drive.

And so when S.C.A.N. would ask him, upon the insertion of a floppy, "Scan floppy disk for viruses?" Clive got into the habit of clicking the Bypass button instead of the Scan button. *Damn thing is too oversensitive*, he thought. *Cries wolf all the time.*

And so it was that on a Tuesday afternoon, Clive tried a new program, for which he was a beta tester. S.C.A.N. beeped once, as usual with new programs. Clive automatically clicked the Granted button—*yeah, do what you gotta do*.

Over the course of the day, he would use several other programs. For some reason, S.C.A.N. beeped at random intervals, flashing "An attempt is being made to modify...." messages, one after another.

Damn thing's freaking out, Clive thought. He clicked the Granted button a few times, then finally opened the Control Panel and turned S.C.A.N. off to save himself the bother. He made a mental note to check the manual to find how to change the thing's sensitivity.

It never occurred to him that the sudden infection might be connected to the Christmas-tree trick he'd read about in *PowerMac* magazine that morning.

SYSTEM:	**WELCOME TO USA ONLINE! YOU ARE IN A CHAT AREA.**
SYSTEM:	**TREKKIE IS LOGGED ON**
TREKKIE:	hello, is anyone here? I'm new here, how does this work?
BOBSTER:	Welcome to USA Online, Trekkie. What kind of modem do you have?
TREKKIE:	Cortech 2400-baud, just got it today, this is my first time trying out one of these dial-up services.
BOBSTER:	Well, if you've found your way to the Conference Room here, you probably pretty much know what you're doing.

SYSTEM:	**MISS BROOKS IS LOGGED ON**
TREKKIE:	what else can you do here
BOBSTER:	Oh, you name it. There's a lot of neat software you can download to your computer, there's stock quotes and weather reports, all kinds of stuff. At midnight there's a trivia contest here in the Conference Rm.
TREKKIE:	This is neat. so everything I type appears on evryone elses screens?
BOBSTER:	That's right. And vice-versa. Like a CB radio for computers.
TREKKIE:	except it costs 5 $$ an hour right?
BOBSTER:	Right. But you'll have a lot of fun here. It's just like being at a party, except you don't have to dress up.
MISS BROOKS:	LOL
BOBSTER:	Hey, a lady online! I didn't even see you lurking there, Miss Brooks.
TREKKIE:	what's that?
BOBSTER:	What's what?
TREKKIE:	what is LOL?
BOBSTER:	Stands for "laughing out loud," Trekkie. Saves typing. People here also use BRB (be right back), IMHO (in my humble opinion), and ROTFL (rolling on the floor laughing).
TREKKIE:	Oh, I'm new using these things, sorry
BOBSTER:	Don't worry. We'll teach you everything you need to know.
MISS BROOKS:	And also you can meet people from all over the world without even leaving your desk.
TREKKIE:	hey its "our miss Brooks," get it
MISS BROOKS:	Yes indeed, Trekkie. I've had to endure that particular joke all my life.
BOBSTER:	My God you type fast!!!!
MISS BROOKS:	I used to be a secretary. For a long time.
TREKKIE:	so is you're name really miss Brooks?

MISS BROOKS:	That's really and truly my name, Trekkie. I take it "Trekkie" isn't yours?
TREKKIE:	haha! I mean, LOL!
BOBSTER:	Why sure it is, Miss B! Yes, his name is Sebastian T. Trekkie from Enterprise, Calif. (kidding)
SYSTEM:	**DANNY THE C IS LOGGED ON**
DANNY THE C:	Hey, gang. Wha'ts shakin'?
BOBSTER:	Hi Danny. How've you been? Haven't seen you up here in awhile.
DANNY THE C:	Guess where I'm calling from?
BOBSTER:	Last I heard, you were a New Yorker.
DANNY THE C:	Aha, you see? I've swapped coasts. I'm calling from Santa Clara! I moved!
MISS BROOKS:	Welcome to the West Coast!
DANNY THE C:	Thanks, Miss Brooks.
BOBSTER:	Us Midwesterners just sit happily where we are, while all you coast people fly back & forth over our heads trying to decide where you want to settle.
DANNY THE C:	LOL, Bobster. So what's going on tonight?
BOBSTER:	Nothing much. This is Trekkie's first time online.
DANNY THE C:	Get psyched, Trekkie. You're going to get addicted to this system.
TREKKIE:	I already am
MISS BROOKS:	<--heavily addicted
BOBSTER:	<--me 2
DANNY THE C:	How old are you, Trek?
TREKKIE:	25
DANNY THE C:	Me too. Believe it or not, this is a great place to meet women. I've seen some very hot relationships start right here.
TREKKIE:	no way
BOBSTER:	For sure, Trek.

MISS BROOKS:	It is true that surface characteristics such as appearance, ethnicity, and social stratum don't enter into the way social contacts are made here.
DANNY THE C:	Man oh man, Brooks, you type fast!!!!!!
BOBSTER:	She used to be a secretary.
TREKKIE:	she used to be a sec'y
DANNY THE C:	Oh. Where's everyone calling from?
BOBSTER:	Okiboji, Iowa. You, Trek?
TREKKIE:	Bishop, Vermont, way north
MISS BROOKS:	Livermore, CA
DANNY THE C:	Hey, we're neighbors practically. I'm in Santa Clara.
MISS BROOKS:	So you said. Nice to meet you. May I call you Danny?
DANNY THE C:	You got any other options? :)
MISS BROOKS:	I have to go. Boss caught me. Bye.
SYSTEM:	**MISS BROOKS HAS LEFT THE CHAT AREA**
BOBSTER:	Man, that's what I call beating a hasty retreat.
DANNY THE C:	I gotta go too. I have a hot date tonight!
BOBSTER:	Danny, you devil!
DANNY THE C:	Everybody, say hi to Michelle.
TREKKIE:	hi michelle!
BOBSTER:	Treat him right, Michelle—he's our buddy!

"That's neat," Michelle said, reading the screen over his shoulder. "I've been on InfoServe, but I've never tried this USA Online thing before."

She leaned back in the desk chair Danny had pulled up for her and took the last swallow from her Heineken. "But here I was, having a great time at dinner, complimenting you for not being a computer geek after all . . . and what do you do? You open doors for me. You invite me up to your apartment—I'm thinkin', hey, this guy is way smooth—and then you show me stuff on the *computer*?!"

Danny grinned. "Pretty romantic, huh?" He logged off the

system and shut the Macintosh off. "It's all part of the grand plan; don't be deceived."

She looked at him with sleepy eyes. Tonight was the first time he'd seen her hair down. Long and silken, it curled easily at her shoulders, strikingly gold against her black linen jacket.

"And what grand plan would that be, you beast?"

"To get you off your guard, so you'll believe me when I tell you you're the most interesting person I've met on the West Coast."

"Compliment accepted."

Danny laughed. There was something strong and independent about her, and yet she thrived on chivalrous treatment.

"Woops," Danny said. "I think I just violated the terms of our date, didn't I?"

She looked puzzled.

"I promised to talk nothing but business. To say nothing personal."

She considered this. "Oh, that's right! Better say something about work, then, to compensate."

"OK, how about this: why on *earth* is Arnie so terrified of Gam Lampert?"

Michelle's playful mood evaporated. "What do you mean?"

Danny's eyes widened. "Oh, come *on*! The guy's a complete, arrogant jerk! Arnie absolutely cringes every time Gam opens his mouth! Or the way Gam shows up at work when half the workday is over already, you know?"

She was looking away, suddenly tense. *Uh-oh*, he thought.

"Danny, I think there's a lot you don't know about Gam." She crossed her legs. "And I don't think you should pass judgment before you know the whole story."

Danny hadn't expected her to rush to *Gam's* defense. Too late, he remembered Gam's ladies' man mode, and the couple of times he'd seen Gam and Michelle laughing together at the office.

"Look," she said. "Do you know where Gam worked before this?"

Danny shook his head.

"Huntington Systems. They discovered him, really. He'd been working there for two years before Bob Stroman came up and bought him out. I saw some of the figures—you can't believe how much they're paying Gam. Enough to make him jump ship.

"It's all much stickier, of course, because Stroman *founded*

Huntington Systems.'' She noted his look of surprise. ''You didn't know that?! Oh, yeah. Stroman started it with his old Stanford buddy, the guy who runs it now—the 'Huntington' in Huntington Systems. And then one day Stroman left to start Artelligence. So he and Lars Huntington haven't exactly been best buddies since then.

''Anyway, the point is, hiring Gam away probably made Lars really ticked off. So at this point, Stroman's hands are sort of tied: Gam's the only one who could pull off Master Voice, and Stroman basically told him he could run the show if he came over to our side. And so that's the deal. They're doing what they can to keep him happy and working, that's all. And Gam happens to be a very, very brilliant person.''

''I don't know, Michelle. I don't doubt that he's brilliant—I just don't trust him.'' Suddenly he felt as though he were on thin ice. ''I mean, like, when you ask him about specifics of the program—what he's calling some variable, or the name of a subroutine—he answers you incredibly clearly. But if you ask about the program's overall structure—the flow, the big picture—he just gets cranky and says that the helm is in good hands.''

''And it *is*, Danny. Believe me, the guy's got his name on this project in ninety-point type. He'll do everything in his power to make it great. Don't forget he's staking *his* reputation, too.''

Danny considered this. ''Well, all I know is that he's a very screwed-up, controlling, unpleasant person.''

Michelle looked away, self-conscious for just an instant. ''Could we change the subject?''

''Sure. Sure we can. I mean—Michelle, is it . . . did you . . . have feelings for Gam?''

''Let's not talk about it, OK?''

She looked at her watch abruptly. ''Actually, you know what? I've got to be up kind of early.'' She picked up her purse.

''Michelle, listen: I'm really sorry if I said something. I'm just trying to understand things better, you know?''

She looked at him and nodded. Finally, a forgiving smile broke on her face, and she stepped up close to him. She smelled amazing.

''I know, Danny. I like that in you.'' She stood on tiptoe and kissed him, gently, briefly. ''Thanks for a great evening.''

He hugged her warmly, then showed her to the door. ''And thank *you*. Please give my apologies to Myrtle for not choosing a restaurant with a more liberal reptile policy.''

She laughed and stepped out the door. He savored her farewell smile, but knew that he'd unearthed some emotions he hadn't expected. And he knew he had much more to learn about Gam.

chapter 6

Say "Hello" to the future of computing.

Actually, say anything you want.

You know how to work your computer, right? You press the keys
on the keyboard.
You roll the mouse around. You've always communicated
with the computer on its terms.
Until now.

Introducing Master Voice™ from Artelligence Software:
the world's first true speech-recognition system.
Imagine. You *speak* to your computer. . .
and it *understands you*.
It does what you ask it to. Immediately. Efficiently. Simply.

But we can't describe the power of Master Voice.
You have to see it for yourself. So call
800-384-5838 to find out where you can catch a demonstration.
After which, we're convinced, you'll be speechless.

ARTELLIGENCE®

December 8, 1993 The programmers, minus Gam, sat on the loading dock at the back of the Artelligence building, drinking Jolt cola ("Twice the caffeine—and all the sugar!"). Charles slowly scooped the occasional spoonful of Swiss Miss from his pudding cup. Danny tried to clear his head. After nearly forty-eight continuous hours of bug fixing, configuring, and rehearsing for the big demonstration, he was suffering from sleep deprivation. If pressed, no one could honestly say he'd ingested members of all four basic food groups in the last two days, either.

Charles actually looked as though he might have lost some weight.

The sunrise was still a few minutes away. But the cool of the evening had left a foggy dew in the air, and the first morning rays formed misty beams through it like a Kodak commercial Danny had seen. He almost called Charles's attention to the phenomenon, but decided it was too much effort. He closed his stinging eyes and swigged some vile cola.

"What time's the truck again?" asked Charles froggily. Half opening his left eyelid, Danny looked at his watch: 6:40 A.M. In New York, he realized, the day was already well under way. And here . . . well, here he hadn't even seen the end of yesterday. Or the day before that.

"Leaves at nine," he said. "We set up at the convention center until three, they open the doors at three-thirty, showtime at four." Charles knew most of the drill; he managed to acknowledge the information with a " 'kay" before closing his eyes, trying to summon the energy for one more stressful day.

"Where's your earring, Skinner?" asked Rod, perking up. Danny glanced over. Sure enough, Skinner's little gold ring was missing. Normally an endless fount of verbal energy, even Skinner seemed subdued this morning.

"I don't know, you guys. I was so tired last night, OK? So remember when I went out to the Quik Mart, right, remember I went out to get us sodas. So I go inside, right? I get the sodas. And so I'm buying them, and there are these three girls, OK? They're buying ice creams. And I hear this one pointing to me and saying what a fashion dropout." He stared downward.

Danny studied Skinner's outfit: the same tan long-sleeved

button-down shirt he'd had on for two days, and a pair of black polyester slacks that didn't quite reach the tops of his black lace-up dress shoes.

"Fashion dropout, OK?" repeated Skinner disconsolately. "I don't even know what that is, really."

Danny reached over and swatted Skinner's shoulder sympathetically. "You're not a fashion dropout, Skinner. You have . . . an independent style, that's all."

Charles peered through his tinted glasses. "Exactly, Skinner. I think it's a safe statement to make: that you are no slave to the whims and caprices of today's ever-changing fashion establishment."

Skinner seemed to appreciate it. "Really?"

"For sure." Charles belched loudly. He took another glance at Skinner. "Then again, I think those pants went out of style with the Nixon administration."

"Skinner, I could take you shopping," offered Rod earnestly.

Skinner blinked nervously twice. "Shopping?" He pronounced it as though it were Sanskrit.

"What a great idea," said Charles. "After all, Rod is certainly the resident expert on looking good."

Skinner looked at Rod with new respect. "So this weekend, OK?" Rod thrust out his hand to shake hands. "Righteous!"

"And hey, Rod," said Danny, lolling his head back far enough to see him at the edge of the loading dock. "Thanks for cleaning up the demo code."

In the crush of the preceding programming marathon, Danny had discovered why Rod, who never ceased to amaze them with his apparent dim-wittedness, made such an ideal teammate: he didn't *think*. The guy could sit there tirelessly, trudging through the world's most boring and repetitive code, happy as a clam. Lunchtime, dinnertime would come and go, but Rod would slog cheerfully through the dullest tasks without a peep. He didn't even seem to need sleep.

Rod smiled wide enough for a rare glance at the gap between his two front teeth—as Charles had once remarked, the sole reason Rod did not get regular death threats for having been dealt a perfect hand by Nature.

"Sure, Danny, it was fun!" Rod said. "In fact, I think maybe I'm gonna go back in and get back at it." He hopped up.

Exchanging miserable glances, shamed into action, Danny,

Charles, and Skinner struggled to their feet and followed him into the building.

Just inside the half-open slatted steel door of the loading dock was a roomful of equipment being readied for the afternoon's festivities: computers in their original shipping cartons; rented lighting equipment and their heavy black cables; audio equipment for the PA system and the demonstration itself. As Danny walked by the last stack, a pair of temp employees struggled in with a fifty-pound box of glossy Master Voice brochures, still reeking from the offset printing ink.

"Hey, guys!"

Danny angled his attention, if not his throbbing head, toward the voice. *Much, much too perky for this hour*, he thought grumpily. It was Michelle, clutching a stack of eleven- by fourteen-inch computer printout pages. She was dressed smartly in a designer suit, her hair back in a French braid tied with a blue velvet ribbon. She was a vision of energy.

"Check this out!" She fairly skipped over to them and slapped the printouts into Danny's arms.

"My God, Michelle, do you have any idea what time it is?" he said.

"It's almost seven," she said. "C'mon, guys, you're acting like zombies." She stabbed her finger onto the printouts. "Look at this. You know what those are? Those are the RSCs from the January *PowerMac* ad. Can you believe it? It's only been out a week!"

Danny tried to focus on the list of tiny, monospace, dot-matrix names and addresses. There were eighty names on a page, and about 250 pages in the fanfold printout.

"Michelle, although I appear to be fully ambulatory, I want you to know that my cerebral cortex is still in the middle of a very nice dream about a nudist beach in Carmel," said Charles. "Perhaps you can rephrase that in layman's terms."

"RSCs," she chirped. "Reader-service cards. You know, you circle our number on the customer-response postcard in the back of the magazine, and send it in. Or you call us direct—Customer Service has been swamped all week," she said proudly. "Don't you get what this means? That's an unbelievable response rate for the first week. That's only been the first ad, too. I tell you guys, this is going to be one very, very hot program. Get psyched!"

She grabbed the stack from Danny and turned on her heel in mock pirouette. She started briskly down the hall toward her office, turning to walk backward just long enough to shout, "And wake up, you sleepies! Today's the big day!"

Danny and Charles exchanged sardonic glances. "Easy for *her* to say," Danny said. "She must have gotten a good three hours last night." They made their way back to the R and D lab.

There was only one person in the Customer Service room, which they passed en route: Tina, an unflaggingly conscientious CS part-timer who'd showed up for the big day to show her support.

"Yo, Danny!" she shouted as she saw him pass the doorway. She grabbed a yellow pad and chased him. "Danny, here's one more for ya." She ripped off a page and thrust it at him.

"Morning, Tina," Danny said, taking it. "How lovely to be greeted by another irritating, hard-to-find bug from some beta tester. You're a sweetheart," he said.

Over the past three weeks, Danny had relished his role as bug-list compiler less and less. Of course, he acknowledged the importance of a beta-test program; by sending early copies of new software to a bunch of average Joes out in the field, a software company discovered plenty of bugs and problems that in-house testing might miss.

A software company's relationship with beta testers is a curious one, each thinking it's doing the other a favor. Beta testers, already busy computer users with their own lives to lead, assume they are helping the software company perfect its software-to-be. They are paid nothing, have to endure frequent system crashes, and are rewarded only by a free copy of the program when it is finished.

But the software company can argue that it's doing the favor, Danny often thought, especially in this case. Artelligence sends the tester a copy of exciting new stuff that nobody else will see for months. And answers their questions, trains them to use it, adds features they request. *And sometimes*, Danny thought, *we waste time with—what was that polite term they used in CS?—* "*user errors.*"

Like this one. Tina's loopy handwriting spelled out some guy's problem.

Beta Report #:	3884	Date/Time:	12/7 5:03p
Tester ID#:	14	Name:	Clive Witmark
CPU:	Mac IIsi	System/RAM:	7.0/5 megs
INITs/cDEVs:	see back of sheet	Reported to:	Tina

Summary:
*Is thrilled with MasterV. beta 2, but says it makes his anti-
virus program beep. Can we send him a fresh disk?*

It's called, Why Don't You Have a Backup? Danny thought. *When
do people learn?*

He and the others swung around the doorway into the R and
D lab. He glanced at Gam's cubicle, as he did several times a
day in hopes of being alone with Gam's computer. *One of these
days, I've got to retrieve my little surprise.* No such luck this
time; the room was buzzing with people.

Danny tossed the bug report into his BETAS folder.

There are four ways a virus can infect a computer. First, it can
be accidentally sent along with legitimate data over the phone
wires, if the computer is equipped with a modem (telephone
hookup). Second, the virus may enter through the SCSI port on
the back of the computer. This small computer serial interface
port is usually used for connecting an external hard drive; if such
a drive is infected, then any other disks in the computer also
become infected.

Third, a computer may be infected by other computers, if they
are linked together into a network. And finally, a virus may arrive
at a computer aboard a floppy disk. As soon as the disk is slipped
into the disk drive, any hard drives (or other computers) attached
to the computer are at risk.

A computer virus is a curious thing. Like a virus that infects
people or animals, it's invisible to the naked eye, requires a host
to survive, and is capable of mutation. Once it's found a host, its
internal coding instructs it to clone itself, and each copy is programmed to invade other hosts. Like non-computer viruses, such
programs may or may not actually harm the host; again, their
primary function is to reproduce and spread.

You can protect yourself against both kinds of virus, of course,
but only to an extent. Just as the only surefire way to avoid getting
a flu virus is to spend your life sealed in a sterile bubble, the only
way to be absolutely sure your computer never gets infected is to
avoid any connection with other computers. That means the computer may not be attached to a modem, a hard drive, or another
computer, and no floppy disk may ever be inserted. Of course, if

you never insert a floppy disk, you can never use software. Without software, a computer is no more than a paperweight, and can't perform any function at all.

However, the analogy between human and computer viruses isn't perfect. Computer viruses are created by people. They are computer programs; creating one takes time, patience, and discipline. Viruses must be debugged, polished, and tested. They're written for any number of reasons, usually having to do with the programmer's desire to show off or to exert anonymous control over a community he feels has done him damage. And viruses are coded with explicit instructions; some do nothing, some simply reproduce. A very few are also programmed to damage the data in the computer.

Although Clive Witmark had no way of knowing it, the virus that had infected his computer arrived on a floppy disk. It was a particularly dangerous virus for three reasons. First, it infected any program it was exposed to, even on a different disk, whereupon that program became an infector itself.

Second, it was programmed to deliberately destroy data by erasing it.

Third, and worst of all, the programmer had written a routine to make the virus's effects especially potent. Before doing anything, it checked the modification date of every file. Every Macintosh computer file gets automatically stamped with a modification date; it indicates the day and time each file was last changed or updated by its user. Once the virus learned this information, it proceeded to methodically erase files according to their modification dates—oldest first.

Because Witmark's oldest files would begin to disappear first, it would take him some time to notice that anything was wrong; that is, the first files to disappear were ones he hadn't used or thought about for some time, filed away into a forgotten electronic folder. By the time he did become aware that things were missing, of course, the virus would have had ample time to clone itself, invade every program on his hard drive, and infect every program even on his backup drive.

Most unfortunate of all, however, was Clive's status as an active and enthusiastic member of the computing community. He helped run a local Macintosh User Group and ran a thriving consulting business in Houston. He was usually busy nine hours a day visiting clients, driving from building to building with his portable hard drive in the passenger seat, ready to hook up and diagnose a client's computer problems.

In the week before Clive noticed that his system had been invaded by a virus, he exchanged infected floppy disks with four user-group members, and connected his infected hard drive to six corporate computer networks.

"My name is Robert Stroman, and I'd like to welcome you to the new world of computing."

In four-track Dolby, a throbbing, insistent electronic beat filled the auditorium as a thirty-foot projection screen smoothly unrolled from above. Even as it approached the bottom of its path, a rear-projected, full-color, animated Artelligence logo spun and tumbled into place.

Having attended dozens of these rollouts, Tommy Daniel didn't think much of the glitz. He knew he'd be sitting here for ninety minutes just to see four minutes of demonstration. Nonetheless, it'd make a good blurb for the *PowerMac* news column.

And the hors d'oeuvres were primo.

"Today, we can't imagine life without computers," the man onstage was saying. "They wake us in the morning, guide our train rides to work, track our expenditures and our earnings. They help us get our work done, get us where we're going"— on the screen, a pair of homely video-dating customers appeared—"and even help us meet new people." The audience chuckled.

"After we unveil Master Voice, you won't be able to imagine life without voice control. You'll not only tell the computer what you want it to do, but you'll be able to speak to it. You'll not only tell it to take a letter, you'll also dictate the letter and let the computer do the typing.

"Social scientists have feared the arrival of true speech-recognition systems; they say our society will lose the ability to type. But Artelligence says: Terrific! Let's spend our energies exploring new frontiers, and not be held back by old technologies." A series of still images appeared: a monk illuminating a page; a horse and buggy; a printer placing movable type.

Tommy glanced at his watch, then at his blank clipboard. He scanned the back of the brochure he'd been given.

At last, the demonstration seemed imminent. "Without young minds like the one you're about to meet, our technology—and our society—could never move forward. So, without further ado, I'd like to introduce the mastermind behind Master Voice, a young prodigy in the art of programming: Mr. Gam Lampert.''

There was an uncomfortable do-we-know-this-guy? smattering of applause as Gam strolled onstage. He was wearing a shiny gray jacket several sizes too large, a pencil-thin red tie, and jeans. Before approaching the podium, he stopped by the computer on the center table and did something with the mouse. On the large screen, the audience saw the familiar menus and blank white screen of a word processor, evidently running on the computer at center stage. Gam finally stepped to the microphone.

"Master Voice is the best thing you have ever seen."

The hall was instantly buzzing. Most people uttered involuntary "whoas" and "oh my God's"; a few applauded; those in groups were instantly chattering. As Gam pronounced each word, it appeared nearly instantaneously, correctly typed on the word-processing screen, larger than life. It was astounding. It was so impressive that it looked rigged, but of course it was not. Standing in a clump with the other programmers at the side of the auditorium, Skinner helplessly danced with excitement; Danny smiled, enjoying the moment.

"What you are about to see is no longer science fiction (period)," Gam continued. Once more, his words were transcribed as fast as he spoke them. "The sound of my voice is conducted from this microphone into the Artelligence voice-recognition chip installed in this little box on the table (comma), which analyzes each incoming word (comma), finds a match in its dictionary (comma), considers whether or not that word makes sense in context (comma), and finally displays it on the screen (period)." Gam had to pause again as another murmur filled the room. The system was performing flawlessly; a few cameras clicked.

"As you see (comma), Master Voice doesn't care if you have an accent (period). Master Voice is speaker independent (period). It's not matching sound patterns you've previously recorded (dash)—it's looking for auditory clues in your words, like the pop of a T, or the hiss of an S or F, to point it to the right words in its dictionary (period).

"Now you may wonder what happens when Master Voice encounters a word that may be in doubt (period). I'll show you in the following sentence (colon): 'I'm filled with a nameless feeling.' ''

There was a beep from the Macintosh, and a neat, small dialog box appeared on the screen.

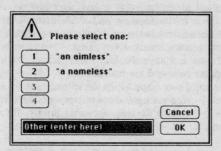

Danny caught a warm look of pride by association from Charles. "Now I, for one, am *deeply* moved by that dialog box," he whispered.

"You see, I didn't enunciate properly," Gam was saying. "Master Voice has pointed out that these two phrases are pronounced almost identically. So instead of making a guess that I may have to correct, Master Voice just asks me which alternative I want. To make a selection, I type the appropriate number. Of course, it's much easier simply to *say* the appropriate number. The arc chip is going to ignore anything I say until I pronounce a number."

He glanced at the screen for reference, then said "Two" into the microphone. The program typed *a nameless feeling*.

"You have no idea how smooth all this becomes after a few minutes of practice," Gam went on. His words were once again transcribed.

"You start to interact with the system. You start to save incredible typing time. You don't make typos anymore. You don't even have to say (open quote) 'period' (close quote) at the end of each sentence (comma), once you get the hang of it. That's because the software lets you set a voice-level threshold and a time-interval threshold. If your voice drops and you wait whatever lag you specified (comma), Master Voice knows you've reached the end of a sentence."

Gam reached for the keyboard with his left hand, pulling away from the microphone. "Now, entering text is only one thing you can do with Master Voice. The other thing is controlling your computer itself, as I'm about to do.''

He struck a key on the keyboard. "Save this file."

The standard file-saving dialog box appeared on the screen, prompting for a folder location and a file name. Gam struck a key, said, "Master demonstration" (which the program typed into the file name blank), struck a key, said, "Put it into the Demonstration folder and save the file," and stepped back to watch as the computer followed his instructions.

"Quit the word processor. Open the spreadsheet I was working on last week." Sure enough, the word-processing screen disappeared. The Macintosh desktop appeared briefly, then a dialog box appeared.

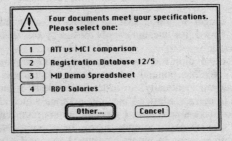

Four documents meet your specifications. Please select one:

1 ATT vs MCI comparison
2 Registration Database 12/5
3 MU Demo Spreadsheet
4 R&D Salaries

[Other...]   [Cancel]

Gam gestured at the screen. "You see, the program found four spreadsheets that were modified within a week of today's date. It offers me a selection." He stepped back to the microphone and said, "Three." The spreadsheet he'd requested appeared on the screen.

"Or let's try this: Open my Rolodex." A database window appeared. "Look for Hilton." Three records appeared, each listing the contact information for a Hilton hotel. "Now the cool part," Gam announced. "Copy the fax number of the San Francisco Hilton and paste it into the letter I was typing yesterday." Flying through the steps, the computer executed the command flawlessly.

"You may wonder how the computer knows when I'm dictating text and when I'm giving it computer instructions," Gam said. "Very simple: you can specify any key on the keyboard to be the toggle switch between Dictation mode and Command mode. In this case, I have the Escape key set up to be the switch.

"So imagine the possibilities. Complete, word-for-word transcripts. Total computer control for the handicapped. Instant written records of anything you can speak: phone numbers, brainstorms, E-mail messages."

He picked up a floppy disk and waggled it between his fingers. "And the dictionaries are on the external chip, folks. We don't clog up your hard disk with a bunch of data files. In fact, the Master Voice software is a little baby thing: seven hundred seventy kilobytes. Fits on a floppy. It's the tightest code you've ever seen; over seventy percent of it was written directly in Assembly language." A murmur went through the programming-savvy spectators.

Danny exchanged glances with the rest of the team. Gam, in his Smooth Charmer Mode, had the audience captivated; people were stirring and buzzing. Reluctantly, Danny admitted to himself that Gam had a certain charm when he was trying to impress.

Rod, looking resplendent in a blue sport coat and a red-and-white pinstripe shirt, nudged Danny and, with his eyes, directed Danny's attention to a row of men in khaki military uniforms, eyes bulging; everywhere, journalists were scribbling furiously or aiming cassette recorders in the general direction of the stage. Even Tommy Daniel made a few notes on his clipboard.

Danny was so thrilled with the proceedings, in fact, that he was only dimly aware of the massive presence next to him: an obese, shinily bald man whose reaction to the demonstration was a small, tight smile. There was a fluttery middle-aged woman with her hair in a bun next to him; flanking the bald man on the other side was a muscular man with a thick brown mustache who had stood expressionless, arms folded, for the entire presentation.

As Stroman began the Q and A session, the bald man turned and pushed his way out of the room. "Nick. Sheila. Let's go," he grunted.

"Yes, Lars," Sheila responded automatically, scurrying out after him.

Procedurally, the surgery went very well. Dr. Ankner had performed dozens of bypasses far more complex than this. In fact, were it not for the fact that the sternum he was wiring back into place belonged to the leader of a powerful nuclear-armed nation, he probably would have forgotten all about the operation by the time he was having his first sip of dinner wine.

"Staple gun."

Of course, such a casual attitude would also have required his failing to notice the eleven three-piece suits lining the glass operating-theater windows above him, intently watching his every gesture. *Well, to each his followers,* he thought to himself. *Mine just don't carry briefcases that fail airport security checks, that's all.*

"Thank you, gentlemen. Let's wrap it up."

He completed the operation eighty minutes after it had begun. Nobody at Walter Reed Army Hospital could miss the fact that something major, and of delicate international import, was taking place in the operating theater. The presence of a tinted-glass van full of State Department officials assured that. So did the presence of two muscle-bound operating-room technicians, looking uncomfortable in the scrubs they'd been forced to wear as they watched Ankner's every move.

Nonetheless, this wasn't the first time foreign heads of state had been rushed to this hospital for specialized surgery. Few medical centers were as well equipped with high-tech lifesaving gear, or as well staffed. And when the heart surgery went well, the hospital looked good, Washington looked good, and the state of American medical science looked good.

And Secretary of State Henry Masso, hooked by hot line to the operating room, dearly wanted it all to look good. Russia and Moldova had announced they would proceed no further in the negotiations without Jurenko's participation; that meant that the summit was on hold until he recovered. Masso found the timing excruciating; for the first time since the dissolution of the USSR, a lasting power arrangement was at hand. If the treaty was successful, Masso knew he could essentially write his own results for the next election.

But with Jurenko anesthetized on a table somewhere, Masso could do nothing but hold his breath along with the rest of the administration.

Ankner nodded to the attending surgeon in charge and went to wash up. A resident took care of the operation's remaining details.

Ten minutes later, Ankner walked over to the cardiothoracic unit—intensive care for post-op thoracic patients. Walter Reed's CTU was state-of-the-art, with a computer terminal for every two beds. Each tracked every patient's chemistries, blood count, even their insurance records. A nurse could consult a monitor and learn the results of the latest lab report when they were only a minute old. And each terminal was linked to the CTU's powerful central computer—a Macintosh Quadra.

An hour after the last giddy journalist had left Moscone Center, Danny watched the rented trucks trundle out of the parking garage, headed for Artelligence. He and Charles propped each other up in their weak, slap-happy exhaustion; Skinner passed out bubble-gum cigars he'd bought at the Quik Mart the night before. Michelle wore a confident smile, hugging her briefcase as she leaned on a Mercedes hood. Danny gave her a thumbs-up, and she closed her eyes in contentment.

At last Bob Stroman, Arnie McGivens, and Gam emerged from the stairwell, joining the others in the garage. Gam was clearly pleased, although his joy manifested itself as an even more intense smugness than usual. Stroman bore two bottles of champagne and a plastic-wrapped stack of paper cups, which he rested on a Volvo.

"Lady and gentlemen, we are on our way!" he said, handing the bottles to Arnie to open. "That was a simply sensational demo. The press went ape, did you see that!? The army guys are in love...I'm told there's to be stories in the *L.A. Times* and the *New York Times* on Monday. Mr. Lampert: you, sir, manipulate crowds as well as you manipulate code. Our hats are off." They gave him a smattering of applause and thumbs-up signs.

"Tank you, tank you," said Gam. "I couldn't've done it without me."

"And my thanks to the Reinforcements. What a team, what grace under pressure! And what an up-and-coming interface whiz: how about that Danny Cooper?"

Charles tousled Danny's hair and the others clapped briefly. During those few seconds, however, Danny was keenly aware of Gam's very, very cold gaze; among the other members of the moving, celebrating Artelligence family, Gam was icily still.

Lighten up, Gam, I'm not after your job.

"So now we've got seven weeks to get this puppy on the shelves," Stroman continued. "Get some sleep tonight, don't worry about getting to work early tomorrow, but start gearing up for the final push." He considered adding that Artelligence would cease to exist if they didn't meet the deadline, but decided to let them enjoy the moment.

"OK, who's going back to the base with me?" he asked. Michelle, Rod, and Danny raised their hands. "I'll get the van. See you in a second." He walked briskly away to find the car.

Gam shot a superior look at the others. "See you suckers back at the ranch. If you need me tomorrow, I'll be at thirty-five thousand feet, en route to San *Frrr*ancisco." He exaggerated the Spanish pronunciation.

"I'm sure you'll be in good hands, though. 'How about that *Danny Cooper*?' " he mocked. Without another word, he strode away toward his car, his rail-thin frame swaggering deliberately.

"Gam—" started Danny.

"Let it alone," cautioned Charles. "He's just a brilliant, messed-up dude."

"Yes, sir," acknowledged Danny. "The brain of Einstein. The personality of battery acid."

Rod pursed his lips. "Well, *I* like him."

Michelle gave Rod's strong, sculpted shoulder a friendly rub. "*That's* the spirit, Rod," she said. "Give the guy a break."

Danny tried to give her a dirty look for flirting, but she wasn't going to give him the opportunity.

Stroman pulled up in the van. Danny gave Charles his best oh-what-mysteries-these-women-be look, swatted him on the shoulder, then got into the van. He scooted over to the far side, making room for Michelle to follow him in. But Rod got in next, and Michelle climbed in last.

Once on the highway, there was little talk in the dark of the van. Stroman drove, Rod dozed. Arnie was lost in thought.

"Michelle," Danny said softly, craning his neck to see her on the other side of Rod's nodding head. She sat with her head back on the seat, blond hair pinned up, looking angelic and Michelle Pfeifferish in the oncoming headlights.

Her head rolled a quarter turn so she could see him. "Mmm?" she said.

"Michelle, what did I say?"

She regarded him for a moment. "What do you *always* say, Danny? You condemn people without knowing the first thing about them."

"Oh," he said. "You mean Gam?"

She turned away and watched the telephone poles flashing by.

He sighed. "OK, you're right. I promise to make more of an effort not to trash the guy, OK?"

He was dying to know what her connection was with Gam. Tomorrow he'd have to do some research.

"In the meantime," he continued, "I want you to know that I thought the rollout was fantastic. The slides and stuff looked amazing. . . . I know how much work you put in, and I think it turned out just awesome."

At last, she warmed up. "Thanks."

With difficulty, he stretched his arm behind Rod's curly head to rest his hand on her shoulder. She rubbed her cheek against his hand.

"So when this is all over," he went on softly, "and the product ships, maybe you and I—"

Michelle sat bolt upright. "Oh God, that's right! I completely forgot! Hey, Bob!" She reached forward to grab the back of the front seat, pulling herself forward.

"What's up, Michelle?" Stroman said.

"In all the running around today, I completely forgot to tell you guys the good news!" She glanced at Danny. "Danny, this is confidential, OK?"

"No sweat," he said, wishing he hadn't changed the subject.

"All right, listen. I've been talking to all these different printers, trying to find someone who can do our manuals in less than the three weeks we've allowed. Well, don't breathe a word, but I talked a printer in L.A. into doing the work in *five days*. He's going to run double shifts and have the paper pre-cut when we deliver the galleys. Know what that means?"

Stroman was beaming. He hadn't told anyone that Huntington was breathing down his neck with a rival product; the team's morale would plummet. But knowing made this news all the sweeter. "Sounds to me like we're going to ship on schedule," he said.

"Or . . . God forbid . . . dare I say it? . . ." began Arnie. "*Ahead* of schedule?"

He and Stroman whooped loudly enough at the improbability of it that Rod stirred next to Danny, photogenic mouth smacking once or twice in his sleep, heavily moussed hair clinging slightly to the seat.

Michelle sat back against the seat and closed her eyes.

"Hey, Michelle," Danny whispered.

Her eyes fluttered open for a moment; she looked at him.

"Nice going, gorgeous," he said softly.

She smiled in response and closed her eyes.

Even through his exhaustion, Danny felt a sense of calm and security. He stretched his arm along the back of the seat, behind Rod's head, toward Michelle's sweater-draped shoulder to give her a friendly neck rub as they returned to the base.

His fingertips were only a few inches from her soft cascading hair when Rod shifted in his sleep, head lolling, and nestled right into Danny's armpit.

Danny froze, pained. He couldn't move without waking Rod, and he was too self-conscious to wake Rod and alert Michelle to the presence of his hand, pinned en route to her.

For the last twenty minutes of the ride, Danny sat stiffly in that position. Michelle either didn't notice or was too tactful to smile.

December 18, 1993

```
Welcome to the InfoServe Bulletin Board.
Messages since your last call: 51
================================
Message:  #49531, S/9 Macintosh Hardware
Date:     Sat, Dec 18, 1993 9:39:24 PM
Subject:  Weird new virus?
From:     Clive Witmark 73260, 1455
To:       ALL
Reply:    #49545 (2 replies)


Can anyone help me? Either I'm mis-filing my
data like crazy in my old age, or something's
eating my files. In the last day I've lost 3 files
I'm sure I had. No big deal, I thought... I'll just
use my backup copies. But would you believe:
as soon as I copied the backup copies to the
hard drive, they disappeared again within 10
minutes. Can't figure it out.
```

Is there some weird new file-eating virus I
don't know about?

--Clive
```
==================================
```
Message: #49533, S/9 Macintosh Hardware
Date: Sat, Dec 18, 1993 11:30:12 PM
Subject: Weird new virus?
From: Terry Tulley 73954,023
To: Clive Witmark 73260, 1455
Reply: #49546 (1 replies)

Sounds like you just mis-filed them, Clive.
Happens to me all the time. What you need is a
good file-finding util like SpeeDemon.

What kind of files were they?
```
==================================
```
Message: #49543, S/9 Macintosh Hardware
Date: Sun, Dec 19, 1993 13:02:22 PM
Subject: Weird new virus?
From: Raybo 73260,1455
To: Clive Witmark 73260, 1455
Reply: #49547

I haven't heard of anything. You should get a
good virus-checker going on your hard drive
though. Doesn't really sound like a virus
anyway. Never heard of a virus that would eat
the same files over and over.
```
==================================
```
Message: #49545, S/9 Macintosh Hardware

Date: Sun, Dec 19, 1993 13:02:22 PM
Subject: Weird new virus?
From: Clive Witmark 73260,1455
To: Terry Tulley 73954,023
Reply: #49549

Thanks, Terry, for your idea. I'm really sure I didn't just misplace them, because (1) I keep using the backups, and they vanish as soon as they hit my hard drive, I mean a few minutes later, and (2) now a bunch of other files are gone. I can't even tell WHAT files are missing, but this morning DiskUtility said there were 4059 files on my hard drive, and now it says there are only 4044. Weirdest thing I ever saw.

I DO have a virus-checker program. That's what makes me so mad. you know S.C.A.N.? It runs in the background, and every time anything tries to modify a program, it beeps and says "Something is trying to modify MacWriter" (or whatever). "Permission granted?" But it does this so often that I've just gotten into the habit of clicking OK.

So I have a feeling this is a real virus, and S.C.A.N. just cried wolf once too often, you know? It's my own damn fault. I'm a beta tester for a bunch of programs, and kind of a power-user nut, so I'm sure I put myself at the mercy of every little virus that comes along. But that doesn't make me any happier.

So I ask again: Anyone heard of anything like this?

--Clive

chapter 7

THE NEW YORK TIMES, DECEMBER 10, 1993

As the New Year Begins, A Space-Age Speech-Recognition System Debuts

By PETER LOOMIS

SAN FRANCISCO, December 8—Fans of Star Trek and science-fiction stories will have to dream up some other futuristic vision to wait for: a true speech-recognition system for computers has just become a reality, according to Robert Stroman, CEO of Artelligence Systems in Santa Clara, CA.

"Computers have never really been hard to use; they've just been hard to communicate with," Stroman said at a press conference this week in San Francisco's Moscone Convention Center. "They've always forced you to work the way *they* do. But once you install Master Voice [the new speech-recognition package], you'll talk to your computer in plain English. You'll forget how to type."

At the demonstration, presenters spoke to an Apple Macintosh computer through a microphone, commanding it to open files, print, and even transcribe correspondence into word-processor format as it was dictated. Industry analysts are heralding a new wave of human-computer interaction, sparked by a new

(Continued on page A4)

December 21, 1993 "Nectar of the Gods," proclaimed Charles as he crammed another entire folded slice of pepperoni pizza into his mouth. His cheeks bulged, utter ecstasy on his face.

Skinner looked aghast, his eyes blinking rapidly. "That's like really gross, OK? Charles, you're gonna get the keys all greasy, OK? Just don't come near *my* keyboard." He picked up the pizza box and perched it on top of Charles's monitor.

Danny took a long, cool sip from the straw in his milkshake. Gam, feet on his desk, keyboard in his lap, pecked away at the keys, characteristically ignoring the other programmers.

For a few minutes, there was no sound except Rod's voice, quietly running Master Voice through test after test. "Open MacPaint," he'd tell it. "Select the paintbrush. Select the pencil. Save the document." With the program approaching completion, all efforts were focused on debugging and testing; Rod, with his stomach for endless repetition, was the perfect man for the job.

"Danny, you see this?" asked Charles when his mouth was empty. He tossed a section from the *L.A. Times* into Danny's lap.

"Pretty great," Danny confirmed. "We're famous now. Get used to it: the adulation, the free pizzas, the women throwing themselves at us . . ."

Charles cracked up. "In your dreams, hacker."

They turned their attention back to the program. Danny smiled to himself; he'd come to love the rhythm of alternating bursts of work and banter the group had established over the months. He decided he'd miss them. He knew the importance of getting Master Voice out the door by February, but it would also signal the end of an exciting era for him. And then he'd have to find some other place to use the Brains God Gave Him.

Danny took the next sheet of yellow-pad paper off the pile to the left of his Mac. "Okie-doke: what's the *next* problem?" he muttered to himself. He glanced at the sheet. As official Bug Collator for the team, he'd spent days going over his list of bug reports, hunting down one after another. It wasn't always easy, of course; some of the beta testers' reports were as vague as "doesn't work right," which didn't give Danny much opportunity to nail the problem.

He recognized the name on this one, written in Tina's careful handwriting: Clive Witmark. Some guy in Texas. "Says sorry, lost MV disk to a virus. Can we send another one?'' Danny hefted it helplessly, wondered what he was supposed to do. *Oh, all right. Do your job and call this guy.*

He went over to the phone, installed on an empty desk next to Gam's cubicle. '' 'Scuse me, Gam,'' he said as politely as possible, and reached for the phone.

Gam stopped typing and sighed loudly. He also grabbed his swivel monitor and twisted it so Danny couldn't see what was on the screen.

''Listen, Danny boy. If you're going to start making phone calls, I'd appreciate it if you'd use one of the phones in Customer Service. It's a little hard for me to work with your voice blasting in my ear.''

Danny looked at Gam, who didn't once look up from the screen. Was it his imagination, or had Gam's hostility become even more pointed since Danny had started seeing Michelle?

Danny put the receiver of the phone back down. ''No problem, Gam,'' he said carefully, and he went out into the hall.

Well, count your blessings, Danny thought as he walked down the carpeted corridor. At least Gam hadn't discovered the invisible software Danny had planted on his disk. Better still, Danny hadn't heard the familiar beep of SURvIVor finding a virus. So far, it looked like Gam was clean.

''Hey! Danny!''

It was Michelle, rounding the corner from her office.

He was glad to see her. Despite the increasing pressure to finish the project, they'd managed to get away for a few evenings over the last weeks—a dinner here, a Sunday afternoon at Great Adventure there—and Danny was learning more about her with every passing day. She was a rare bird, he'd decided: plucky and strong, but with a soft streak that betrayed an obviously romantic core.

She was struggling to carry a heavy cardboard box; Ragù Extra Hearty was stenciled on its side. Danny grinned.

''Would you allow me to assist you with your spaghetti sauce?'' He gestured grandly toward the box.

''Allow!?'' She shoved it into his arms. ''If you hadn't asked, I would've smacked you.''

She walked close beside him toward Bob Stroman's office.

''What's *in* this box, anyway?'' he asked her. ''Cinder blocks?''

"Nnnnnope," she said. "It's a surprise."

"Man," he said, shifting its weight. "We really should have gotten Rod to do this."

Michelle scowled. "What's that supposed to mean?"

Uh-oh. "Well, you know . . . he's just right for hauling spaghetti boxes: big, good looking, and not very sm——not very particular." He smiled, but she was looking irritated.

"Danny. You should be more tolerant. Rod is an incredibly sweet guy. What have you got against him?"

"Nothing, Michelle, I'm just kidding."

She softened slightly. "Danny. Just as an exercise: why don't you try to find something to like in every person you work with?"

"A lesson in tolerance, eh?"

She nodded. "Find something in everybody. Even Gam."

He feigned shock. "Now, let's not get carried *away* here."

She took his arm supportively. "Everyone here is talented, Danny. Everyone here was hired for a reason."

"I know."

But let's face it . . . Gam's got about as much to like as a tarantula—and less personality.

They swung into Stroman's reception room. Danny's arms were already starting to ache, so he swept past Stroman's secretary with a quick "Hi, Ellie!" and strode into the office beyond. Michelle fairly skipped in anticipation. They burst into Stroman's office to find him on the phone, head bowed, elbows on the desk.

"Mr. Hirota, I understand your point of view. I recognize the pressures Mika is under. But at this point, I think the die is cast. I don't see how an additional set of meetings would——"

Danny set the box down quietly on the credenza along the side wall of the office. He stood quietly. Stroman looked up, gave them both a weary smile, and gestured to a pair of chairs.

"Yes indeed, my friend. You have made it very, *very* clear. Clear as a bell. If it were any clearer it would be Saran Wrap. As I've said several times, I think we are going to ship on time. Having the lawyers start drawing up stock transfer papers at this early date is both premature and . . . and—would you let me finish?"

Evidently the man on the other end wouldn't, because Stroman closed his eyes wearily and listened. An occasional "Uh-huh" or "I understand" punctuated the silence. At last he said, "I'll do that. He'll give you a call this afternoon."

He slipped the phone into its cradle. "The Japanese," he indicated apologetically. "Why do they want to pick on *us*? Why don't they go buy the Statue of Liberty?"

"Don't worry about it, Bob," said Michelle. "I've got enough good news to compensate for anything they just said to you."

Stroman sat up in his chair. "I could use it. Whatcha got?"

She stepped over to the box and tugged open the corrugated flaps. Grabbing it from underneath, she dumped its contents onto Stroman's desk. Forty rubber-banded bundles of credit-card slips jostled and bounced slightly as it landed.

"Ohhh, myyyy, Gooooddd," was what Stroman said.

"Five days' worth," Michelle said. "A thousand orders in each bundle: forty thousand orders. Even with the six temps working all day, we're still getting complaints that the order lines are busy all the time. And you know that big mail-order place, Mac Storeroom?" Stroman nodded, priming himself for more good news. "They want to place another order of twenty-five thousand. Bob, we're not going to make it. There's no way we can fill all these orders in time."

Danny watched Stroman sit back, eyes on the ceiling.

"You know what?" Stroman said. "We underpriced this thing. If this many people want us, we should have listed it for fifteen hundred bucks instead of seven ninety-nine."

"You wanted this thing on every desk in America," Michelle reminded him. "And don't forget that you're setting the groundwork for years of add-ons and upgrades from us; the more doors you get your foot in now, the more your repeat business will be in the next few years. Think of the eight hundred bucks as just the entrance fee."

Stroman's dream was coming true right in front of him, and he found himself unable to handle it. How would they meet the demand? They could install more phone lines, hire more temps; they had already added a second paper supplier, printer, and bindery for the boxes and manuals. The Moscone rollout had been a stunning success, generating massive and overwhelmingly positive press for Master Voice, and now Stroman's main concern was handling the demand. Not an unpleasant position to be in, Stroman told himself.

"Well, I guess there's only two things left to do," he said cheerfully. "First, hire some more temps. And second, schedule the code-freeze party. We ready for that, Danny?"

He referred to the imminent day when the programming was complete, the last beta tester's report was in, and the last bug worth fixing had been chased down—the day the master disk was pressed and sent to the duplication company. To make 250,000 copies, Stroman smiled to himself. . . for starters. He had a feeling that this particular code-freeze party would be one helluva celebration.

"At this rate, I don't know why we couldn't finish the code completely by next week," Danny replied. He thought of Gam's skulking behavior. "As long as nothing unexpected happens," he added.

Michelle, checking her daily planner, perked up. "Hey! New Year's Eve! Let's make it a dual-purpose party. . . . Oh, it'll be great."

Stroman agreed, scratching it on a yellow sticky note.

"Great idea," Stroman said. "The manual's done; we got the last round of edits back from the copy editor this morning, so it's essentially ready to roll. We've had the chips coming back from Seoul for several weeks. So as soon as the software is done— bam, we're in good shape!"

"There's only one thing, Bob," said Danny. He'd been meaning to mention this, but the time never seemed right. "There's only one thing that's not really in good shape."

"What is it?"

"Well, there's no technical documentation. We've all been working full force on the software, but nobody's been documenting the code itself." He looked at Michelle, hoping she wasn't interpreting this as another sign of intolerance.

"See, whenever Gam makes a change, alters the way something works, adjusts a variable or something, nobody keeps track. Nobody's been updating the Func Spec. At this point, the program really exists only in one place: inside Gam's head. It's no problem, really, as long Gam's working on the project. But eventually somebody else should learn the program, so there'll be somebody who can write an update next year, or fix bugs, or help the Customer Service people."

"I agree that's not a good position to be in," said Stroman thoughtfully. He studied Danny's face for a moment.

"What would you say if I asked *you* to make that your responsibility, Danny? What if you became our Func Spec man? You just meet with Gam at the end of every day and keep tabs on any changes he's made. Learn the code. Learn the structure.''

Danny didn't relish having to approach Gam every afternoon, but he nodded. ''That's fine. I think having something written down will be a big relief to all of us.''

Stroman thanked him. ''I'm pleased that you'll be in charge, Danny; you've got a good head on your shoulders. If Gam gives you any trouble, just let me know. Deal?''

Danny nodded.

''Now, then,'' Stroman continued. ''Who's going to order the champagne?''

Clive Witmark sat alone in his study, near tears.

Christmas in Houston wasn't exactly a snowman-and-sleigh-bells affair even under the best of circumstances. But he'd never known a holiday season with less magic than this one.

''Isn't there anything I can do, hon?'' asked his wife Eileen. She stood leaning against the doorframe, a cup of coffee in her hands.

Clive turned away from the screen and looked at her. Eileen wasn't ravishing, but she was eternally impeccably well groomed; she projected an aura of being together, confident, supportive. In the year they'd been married, he valued that characteristic above all others.

''No. I'm sorry, babe. I'm just sorry to botch our Christmas like this.'' He rubbed his reddened, burning eyes.

Eileen came over to the desk and sat down. ''How bad is it?''

For the three hundredth time, Clive switched on his Macintosh IIcx. It played its familiar perfect-fifth chimes; the usual smiling-computer logo appeared; the ''Welcome to Macintosh'' banner appeared. That was as far as the computer got before displaying the message that was, by now, etched in Clive's brain:

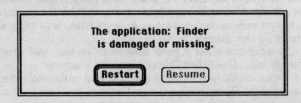

"I don't get it," said Eileen. "What does that mean?"

Clive sighed. "This virus, or whatever it is, has been systematically eating every file on my hard drive, one after another. Remember on Tuesday when you asked for Dr. Abrams's phone number and I couldn't get it for you? Remember how I had to look it up in the white pages?" He flopped back in his chair. "I didn't know it at the time, but the reason my computerized Rolodex didn't work is that the data file, where it stores all the names and addresses, wasn't on my hard disk anymore. It was just gone, without a trace.

"So no matter what I do, or how careful I try to be, one file after another just disappears from the disk. It's so infuriating."

His mind raced to track his interactions with other computer users. What disks had he exchanged? What program had he downloaded from InfoServe? Where could the damn thing have come from?

In his efforts to remember, he failed to link his disappearing files with the S.C.A.N. anti-virus program's alarms, which had gone off en masse exactly ten days earlier. And had he even noticed that his Macintosh clock was set forty-five days ahead, he probably would have forgotten why: because on November 10, he had changed the date to December 25 while trying out a little game he'd read about in a Mac magazine.

Eileen rubbed her husband's clasped hands sympathetically. "Don't you have backup disks or something?" she said.

"That's just it. The last time I backed up was Sunday—and this virus, or whatever it is, got backed up along with everything else. As soon as I hooked up my backup hard drive to the Mac, the whole thing started all over again with *that* disk. Yesterday afternoon, I lost twenty files in half an hour—from the backup disk. I finally realized what was happening and shut the thing off." He gestured to a disconnected hard drive sitting on the couch. "That's the backup disk; I couldn't risk leaving it on any longer, or I'd have nothing left."

He pointed to the error message on the screen. "And now this. Now the thing has eaten the Finder—part of the main system software. Without the Finder, I can't run the Mac at all. I just get this error message. I've got other copies of the system files, but as soon as I put them into the drive, they'll be infected, too."

Eileen bent forward to kiss him. "Poor darlin'," she murmured. "I just don't get it. I thought you bought some kind of anti-virus program."

"That's what gets me!" Clive exploded. "God, I'm going nuts! I keep the virus checker on all the time. The thing is—" He sighed. "I leave it on when I get new software from electronic bulletin boards—you know, BBSs and stuff, because that's where I thought I'd be most likely to get a virus. But at some point I hit the Ignore button when a *real* virus was trying to get at my System file. The only thing I can figure out is that maybe this virus came from one of the beta versions of software I'm supposed to be testing."

Eileen nodded. She knew how much pride her husband took in being on the cutting edge—in being a handpicked beta tester for several different computer companies.

"And you know what the sick part is?" he said. "You know what really gets me?"

He looked intently into Eileen's eyes.

"Today my anti-virus program disappeared, too. It got eaten by the virus."

SYSTEM:	**WELCOME TO USA ONLINE! YOU ARE IN A CHAT AREA.**
SYSTEM:	**MISS BROOKS IS LOGGED ON**
MISS BROOKS:	I just got here. What are we talking about?
COWLADY:	Welcome to USA Online, Miss Brooks. Tonight's topic is The Future Mac. We're talking about where the Mac is going, in light of the new models and so on.
BAGHEAD:	I want the color PowerBook II. I want that and I want Master Voice.
TAIWAN:	Oh, me too. I rilly want m.voice
DACAPO:	Me three.
COWLADY:	Well, you three sure came to the right Chat Area then. You won't believe who happens to be in this room at this very moment.
DACAPO:	Who.
COWLADY:	Danny, shall we tell 'em?

DANNY THE C:	Sure, I don't care.
MISS BROOKS:	Tell what?
DANNY THE C:	Hi Miss B! From Livermore, as I recall?
MISS BROOKS:	Right you are!
COWLADY:	Danny is one of the programmers of the Master Voice software.
TAIWAN:	No, no way!!!!!!!!
BAGHEAD:	Really?! That is so neat.
DANNY THE C:	*blushing* Yea, 'tis true.
DACAPO:	You work for Artelligence?
DANNY THE C:	Well, at the moment.
TAIWAN:	Yer so lucky. m. voice is the COOLEST, I saw them demonstrate it at our user group
DANNY THE C:	Where's that?
TAIWAN:	Berkeley
DANNY THE C:	Oh, yeah . . . our R & D guy went up last week. Did he do a good job?
TAIWAN:	Blew everybody away.
DR. DOOM:	What did?
TAIWAN:	Master Voice!
DR. DOOM:	What isi it?
MR.DEAL:	Good god, man, where have you been hiding!?
TAIWAN:	LOL
COWLADY:	Master Voice is speech-recognition hardware/software for the Mac, Doom.
DR. DOOM:	Meaning?
BAGHEAD:	You talk into the mike and it writes down what you say.
MR. DEAL:	Danny the C why don't you tell him what it is.
DANNY THE C:	Well, Master Voice uses a custom chip we developed using neural-net technology. Instead of the data just being passive, acted on by the program, the data itself is active, directing itself through thousands of individual decision-making nodes,

	and eventually teaching itself to make fewer errors. It's really something. Up till now, it's sort of been a technology in search of an application.
COWLADY:	Uh. . . what HE said. :)
DR. DOOM:	Wow! Sounds supercool.
MISS BROOKS:	How do you like Artelligence?
DANNY THE C:	Lots. They're great people.
BAGHEAD:	When will mastervocie be available?
DANNY THE C:	Shipping February first. We're pretty heavily backordered tho.
BAGHEAD:	Can we order M. Voice online? right here?
DANNY THE C:	No, I don't think so. But you can call their 800 number to order.
TAIWAN:	You guys have to see this thing. Really amazing.
MISS BROOKS:	I've heard Master Voice is sensational. How fortuitous to have run into you here.
DANNY THE C:	Yeah. It's pretty neat.
BAGHEAD:	Do you have to talk really slow like?
DANNY THE C:	No, actually. You can speak at a pretty normal speed, and Master Voice will understand you. There's nothing like it anywhere.
MISS BROOKS:	Have a happy New Year, everybody. May the economy pick up, the international scene quiet down, and our computers never crash.
BAGHEAD:	Man she types fast.

"Yo, Luis."

"Hey, Gam."

The two young programmers didn't shake hands, but acknowledged each other with a little head toss. Luis led Gam out of the Huntington Systems foyer into a vacant conference room; he closed the door after them.

Luis ran his fingertips through his short-cropped back hair and slid into a chair. "So you have the new version?"

Gam managed an "uh-huh" and unzipped his gym bag. He pulled out a manila envelope folded several times and rubber-banded around its contents—a set of disks. He tossed it across the table to Luis.

"You fix the virtual-memory bug?" asked Luis.

Gam nodded. "This is as far as I go. It's our final beta version. That was the deal."

Luis nodded. "OK. I hope you gave us a little more annotation to go by this time. We've had some trouble making our way through the Assembly code."

Gam snorted. "Yeah, well, get used to it. Even more of this version is in Assembly language. If it weren't, it wouldn't run fast enough. *You* know that."

He was right; next to Gam himself, nobody knew more about the Master Voice software than Luis, a recent Cal Tech graduate and a key player on Huntington's programming staff. He opened the rubber-banded package, peered at the disks inside, and then closed it up again.

"OK, man. Well, thanks a lot. I guess I'll give you a call if we run into any problems." He stood up. "Oh, yeah. This is for you."

He tossed a business envelope onto the table.

Gam snatched it up, flipped up the flap, and glanced inside.

"What the hell is this?" His voice was a notch higher than usual.

"What?"

Now Gam stood up. "There's a problem with this check, Luis. It's not even a tenth of what it should be."

"I don't really know, Gam. You'll have to work that out with Lars. I'm just a programmer."

Gam held out his hand. "Then give me the damn disks, Luis. The deal was one check at the beginning, the rest at the end. What is this crap? Either give me the whole amount, or let me have the disks back."

Luis threw up a hand. "Hey, don't go crazy. I'll get Lars, all right? You two can battle it out." He started for the door, but Gam's long wiry legs were fast enough to meet him there.

"I'll come with you," Gam said. "Let's go."

Luis glanced uneasily at the tense young man who followed him down the hallways. *Lars is gonna go ballistic*, he thought.

He led Gam into Lars's secretary's office. "OK, Gam. This is where I'm out of it. You want to argue with Lars, you do it yourself.'' He turned and left, package in hand.

Without a glance at the young woman at the desk, Gam rammed through the door to the inner office. It swung open, and he stood, slightly out of breath, in front of his former employer, who was in the middle of dialing a phone number.

Lars turned his head only about fifteen degrees—just enough to see who the bristling intruder was. He paused a moment, then hung up the phone.

''Where's my money, Lars? What is this crap? You know this isn't what you owe me.''

Lars turned in his high-back swivel chair. ''Why, hello, Gam. Yes, I'm fine. And you? How lovely to hear it. Why, we're doing very well indeed; good of you to ask.'' He made a tiny sniff sound, a hint of the amusement he seemed to bring himself.

Gam approached the desk, breathing hard. ''I want the money.''

''I'm awfully sorry to disturb you, Mr. Huntington,'' Lars continued, extending his private joke, ''but then I'm just a skinny kid with an inflated sense of self-worth. I'm having a little financial question I'd like to discuss with you. Perhaps you could find the time to—''

Gam smashed his palm onto Lars's desk. ''*Shut up!* Shut *up*. Look, this whole thing was your idea. I would've been happy to take the job at Artelligence and get out of here. So I listened to you, I went along with your plan, and now you *owe* me.'' He threw the opened envelope at Lars. ''You still owe me two hundred fifty. What is this twenty thousand crap? I put myself on the *line* for you, man.''

The envelope lay near the edge of Lars's heavy desk. He regarded it thoughtfully. ''Young man, I paid you a quarter million dollars when our little arrangement began two years ago. Most young men your age would be delighted to be honored with such sums.''

''That wasn't the *deal*!'' shouted Gam, losing himself.

''What can I tell you, my friend? Read the papers. Our industry is in a slump. Now, if you'll excuse me...''

Gam was seething. ''You pay me, you bastard, or I'll spill the whole thing! I'll *do* it!''

''I don't think you're in much of a position to threaten *me*, young man.'' Lars leaned back, and as Gam watched, actually smiled. "It's an adorable performance, but simply not convincing. For example, you'd be expected to provide some proof of our arrangement. Ah, but alas, you have nothing to show, do you now?"

Gam didn't respond, but his eyes were narrowed with anger.

"How would you explain that first check I gave you, hmm? The most you would accomplish by speaking up," Lars continued, "is to ruin your own reputation. Even your *claiming* that you've been doing some work for me would render you virtually unhirable in this business. No, you've got nothing to threaten *me* about. Quite the contrary."

"What's that supposed to mean?"

"Simply that I wield considerable clout in this industry. Son, you have an uphill climb as it is. But if you get in my way, you'll feel like you're trying to climb a glass wall." Lars rubbed his chin absently. "I suggest you take the generous amount I've given you and get on with your life."

Gam glared. "You pathetic *asshole*. I don't care *what* you think you can do to me, Lars. I swear to God, you pay me what you promised, or I'll *find* a way to expose you." He knew Lars was right; exposing his own participation in Lars's plan could ruin his own career. But at this moment, Gam didn't care.

Lars tapped the COM button on his phone. "Rhonda, would you send Nick in to see me right away?" He glanced, mock-apologetically, at Gam. "You remember Nick, don't you? He's our head of security. Formerly of the Chicago Police Department, but he ran into a little legal trouble. Wonderful fellow; I'm thrilled to have found him. He'll enjoy seeing you out."

"Don't jerk me around, Lars," Gam hissed. "I'm not going to answer one more question about the code; if Luis calls me, I'm just going to hang up, until you pay me the rest." He stopped as the muscular man with the thick mustache entered the room.

"Nick, this is my friend Gam. He's having trouble finding the exit."

Gam shot Lars a look of venomous hatred as he was dragged from the room and escorted out of the building.

chapter 8

From the President

On a closing note, we at Apple took great pride in welcoming the five-hundredth Macintosh User Group to the global network of Macintosh users. It's a group of twenty people in Delta Point, Wyoming.

We feel that this is an important milestone. Naturally, we're proud that 12 million people own Macintosh computers. But we're even happier that all of them are connected. . . some by a cabled network, some by modem, but more often by the *human* network: friends, neighbors, and user groups.

Connections mean a better flow of information. Connections mean exchanges of ideas. Connections mean nobody is alone: we're all part of one personal-computing family.

Even in Delta Point, Wyoming.

We think that the connections in the Macintosh world are what makes this computer remarkable. We think it gives our community the power to grow. The power to communicate.

And the power to be your best.

December 31, 1993   This wasn't in my job description, Danny thought.

"OK—OK, Mrs. Javed. I understand. . . . No, no, listen to me. Please stop panicking, Mrs.—''

He sighed and pulled the phone away from his face. He shot a look at Tina, whose phone he was using. She grinned at him, jerked her head at the clock on the wall of the Customer Service room, and pointedly swilled beer from an imaginary bottle. He nodded with a silent pained look on his face and gestured helplessly with the receiver. Tina slipped on her jean jacket and left for the party.

"No, that's impossible, Mrs. Javed. Now, look, I need you to calm down. I need you to sit down, take a deep breath, and tell me carefully what you see on the screen.''

For thirty minutes he'd been on the phone with a Master Voice beta tester's wife. Hysterical and barely computer literate, she'd been ranting that as soon as she tried the Master Voice program, file icons began to disappear from the hard drive window of her husband's Macintosh Plus.

Never mind that it's New Year's Eve, lady. Never mind that the last thing I want to think about, on the night we're freezing the code, is some beta tester with some piece of buggy software or something. Never mind that twenty-four other testers have reported no problems at all . . . and that's why we're having the party tonight.

"All right. Now. How many files are there in the window? Are you sure? OK, I want you to take your—wait, Mrs. Javed, just let me finish. I want you to take your hand off the mouse. Yes, that's right. Hands off the compu——''

Once again, the voice on the other end was squawking. "*Quiet!*'' Danny shouted, nearly losing his cool.

Naturally, Michelle chose that moment to pop her head into the doorway. She smiled to Danny, looked at her watch, compared it with the wall clock in mock horror, waggled her finger at Danny mother-in-law style, blew him a kiss, and dashed away. Danny threw his head back in frustration, eyes closed.

"Mrs. Javed, look. It's New Year's Eve. I have to go. But I'm going to ask you one more time to try an experiment. Do you understand?''

Mrs. Javed did.

"All right. Take your hands off the keyboard. Put them in your lap. I mean it. All right. Now. Count the number of icons in the window on the screen. Do not touch the computer. OK? Now. How many are there?"

She told him. There were five file icons.

"All right. Now think very carefully. Have you ever actually seen files disappear? In front of your eyes?"

She told him she'd never seen one vanish in front of her eyes. *Ah, sweet Mac virgins,* Danny thought. *This poor soul is probably opening up different folders, thinking it's the same folder every time. No wonder she keeps getting a different file count.*

He looked up in time to see Skinner and Charles passing the doorway en route to the parking lot: Charles, with his characteristic heavyset stride, and Skinner, fairly skipping along beside him with preparty excitement. It was 7:05, and Danny was losing patience.

"All right. Now. You're looking at these five icons, right? Now—don't touch the mouse yet, all right?"

There was no answer.

"All right? Mrs. Javed, what is it?"

Mrs. Javed was sniffling on the other end of the line.

"Tell me, Mrs. Javed. It's OK, you can tell me what's happening. I didn't mean to snap at you."

She told him that, even as she sat there, not touching the computer, she saw first one, then another icon blink off the screen. There were now three left in the folder window.

Danny's mood darkened. So evidently this *was* something. Something he hadn't heard of before.

"All right, listen very carefully. There's not much I can do from here, without actually seeing what's happening. Now, where are you again?"

She told him she was in Boulder, Colorado.

"That's too bad; I was hoping we could send someone to help. But I guess all I can suggest is that you make a copy of your Master Voice disks and Fed Ex them to us; there's a freak chance a disk miscopied, and we could—"

Mrs. Javed was yammering about something else now.

"Oh," said Danny. "A videotape?"

A videotape? Why not?

"Why not?" he said. "That's actually a pretty good idea. Yes, that's right. Get that camcorder. And I want you to sit there and point it at the screen. Just sit there until you've filmed one of these disappearing files, all right?''

It was.

"And then I want you to send the tape to me personally, OK? Send it Federal Express; here, let me give you our Fed Ex number."

He did.

He knew, of course, that the video image—if she could operate the camcorder at all—would roll, since the screens of computers and TVs are painted at different rates by their electron guns. Still, it was better than flying to Boulder only to find out that some lady was accidentally dragging files to the on-screen Trash Can, or something.

"You, too, Mrs. Javed. Again, I don't think it's really something in Master Voice. I think probably you've just—I mean, I don't know precisely what the problem is, but I'll know a lot better when I get your tape. OK?''

It was.

"Thanks, Mrs. Javed. If it's possible in the middle of your computer troubles, have a happy new year, OK?''

She said she'd try. Sighing, Danny hung up and walked briskly back to the lab to get his jacket.

Clive Witmark had written a database-formatting program for Traxis, a subcontractor for the city of Houston responsible for managing the city's municipal parking garages. The first thing Clive did upon arriving for his consultation on this day was to copy it to the Traxis network file server, a dedicated central hard drive that stored the company's files for easy retrieval by any of the connected computers. The next thing was to demonstrate his handiwork to the MIS director who had commissioned the programming. Clive double-clicked his program's icon, looking forward with great pleasure to showing off his work.

A computer program is something like a recipe: it's simply a list of instructions. The computer reads them from the beginning and executes each instruction, line by line—at dizzying speed, of course. These instructions not only tell the computer what ingredients to use, but also where to look for them: one line might direct the computer to look in a particular "cupboard" (memory location) for a certain "ingredient" (piece of data).

Most computer programs are far more complex than recipes,

however, because they are rarely completely linear—that is, executed from start to finish. Along the way, one line of code might tell the computer to repeat the last ten instructions—in other words, to loop. Or an instruction might tell the computer to skip over part of the program if certain conditions aren't met—just as a tax form might say "If self-employed, skip to line 49."

As he sat in a desk chair on the tenth floor of a Houston office building, Clive Witmark couldn't know that on this occasion, the Macintosh didn't begin by reading his code; at line 0, there was a "JSR" (jump to subroutine) instruction that had been inserted by a computer virus. It directed the computer to jump to line 14,566 of the program code. Line 14,565 was the last line of code that Clive had written; 14,566 was the beginning of the virus's tacked-on code.

The Macintosh, unable to tell genuine code from foreign code, proceeded to perform the viral code's instructions. Among other things, these instructions directed the Macintosh Toolbox file-management routines to copy the virus to the active System file—the computer's software brain—and then to all other programs on the hard drive.

It then made an interesting modification to the System. Under normal circumstances, the entire Macintosh screen image—that portion of the monitor that gets illuminated—is not a perfect, sharp-cornered rectangle. Rather, the Macintosh ROM chips—its hardware brain—round off the corners of the screen image ever so gently. This rounded-corner look is purely cosmetic, but is one of many details that gives the Macintosh its reputation for graphic elegance.

The virus now installing itself into the Traxis network, however, added a special feature to the screen-redrawing routines. In the upper-left corner of the screen, it turned one pixel on—a single phosphor dot of the thousands that make up a computer monitor. This pixel lay at position (0,0). That is, it was the very first dot on the screen, the one that would have formed the sharp upper-left point of the display area if the Macintosh did not round the display's corners. Because this pixel lay at the outer tip of the rounded—and thus darkened—area, it was clearly visible: a white dot, the size of a period, within an eighth-inch triangle of rounded darkness. Clearly visible, that is, to anyone who knew to look for it.

Clive Witmark, anticipating the pleasure of demonstrating his program to his client, certainly did not notice that the first screen pixel was glowing. As a matter of fact, he probably should have noticed that his program was taking longer to load than usual; he certainly should have noticed that the hard-drive access light was blinking frantically, an indication that files were being modified on the drive.

But if anything, he subconsciously welcomed the delay, because he had prepared a gorgeous opening screen—a splash screen—to appear when the program was launched. This screen, a full-color, 3-D word TRAXIS and logo, remained on the screen long enough for Clive to sneak a look at the MIS director's face, reading it for first impressions.

After four seconds, the Macintosh processed the second-to-last line of code in the listing, and proceeded to the final line. This last line was an RTS instruction, meaning "return to subroutine"; it directed the computer to continue reading the program listing at the beginning—that is, to proceed with Clive's code as though nothing had ever happened. The viral code had simply inserted a detour, then referred the computer back to the point at which it left the main road.

The virus immediately began to destroy files, oldest first. For several days after Clive's visit, nobody at Traxis detected anything unusual.

On the third day, an administrative assistant named Janet Cavalier copied a program called DictionDoctor—an electronic dictionary of sorts—from the Traxis network server onto a blank floppy disk. Her boyfriend Ned, a systems analyst for AT and T in Houston, was a Macintosh nut who collected software, even pirated (stolen) software, from anyplace he could get it. After days of his "whining," as Janet called it, she finally agreed to see what cool stuff Traxis had on their disk. And DictionDoctor is what Ned wanted.

When she gave it to him, Ned kissed Janet with the joy of a teenager obtaining a terrific comic book. But within moments, Janet found herself alone in his bedroom, a Charlie Brown zigzag smile on her face, as Ned pounded down the hall to his computer to try out the new software. *I should've known*, she told herself. *Give the guy a computer and I spend the night alone.*

And thus it was that Clive Witmark's virus made its way to a second Macintosh network in a different part of town: it was carried by Ned's sweaty hand on a 3.5-inch, 800k floppy disk.

Janet Cavalier's boyfriend worked in AT and T's regional administrative offices, an environment rich with interconnected Macintosh and IBM machines. He had no intention of copying the DictionDoctor program he'd stolen onto the central server disk. Instead, he hustled over to his own desk and copied the program from the floppy disk onto his own hard drive so that he could try it out. ·

But every computer in the office was connected by network cable. By the end of the day, the upper-left pixel of every Macintosh screen at the office was glowing white.

"The Bee-Gees? Ohhh, mannn!" Danny laughed when he finally arrived at the Artelligence New Year's Eve/Code Freeze Bash in the cordoned-off second floor of the Santa Clara Hilton's restaurant. Classic disco trash boomed from the PA system; a few normally staid, pale-skinned computer types were dancing with abandon; a diskette painted in gold paint dangled from a nylon monofilament tied to the chandelier, a gold metallic ribbon streaming from each corner. A banner draped across the length of the granite mantelpiece said, The Master Voice Master Disk: Masterful Job!

Danny scoped the room to see who was there: everyone. There was an amazing, electric feeling in the room. As though the completion of the two-year project wasn't enough, pre-orders of the product were through the roof, and everyone had received an unanticipated bonus check at the end of the workday.

And, of course, it was New Year's Eve.

At one end of the room was a white-covered banquet table, holding a Macintosh II rigged and ready to go for some kind of presentation. He didn't see Michelle. McGivens and Stroman were at the bar, shoulder blades to the wall, surveying the party like lords surveying their lands. Danny went over.

"Mr. Danny Cooper," said Bob Stroman as he approached. Danny gave a military salute, and joined Bob and Arnie in their leaning-against-the-bar postures.

"Well, Danny, you can be proud. You've done a great job," Arnie said. "I don't know how you got the dialog-box messages to come up so quick, but the thing works." Arnie slapped Danny on the back.

"Thanks, boys," Danny said with exaggerated modesty.

"Have you been able to keep the Func Spec up to date? Have

you been documenting all the changes?'' asked Stroman.

Danny shifted and glanced down. ''Ah. No, not really. I've had some trouble there.''

Stroman looked concerned. ''Oh?''

''Well, for one thing, there hasn't been much time. We've been working so hard on the code and everything.''

A few measures of ''YMCA'' wafted by.

''And there's another problem: Gam hasn't been completely forthcoming on explaining the program to me.''

That was the understatement of the century.

''I'm sorry to hear that,'' Stroman said. ''I was hoping he'd cooperate; it's important that somebody else understand the code, and I think you're the man.'' He shook his head in frustration. ''I know he's hard to deal with, Danny. Yeah, he's a screwed-up S.O.B. . . . but my God, he can churn out some amazing code.''

''That he can,'' agreed Danny, sipping from a tall thin plastic champagne glass.

He turned to watch Gam from across the room. He was sitting, legs sprawling, on a restaurant chair against the wall. He was looking directly at Danny, with a look that could have been burning resentment. It occurred to Danny that Gam might not be happy to see him hanging out with the company's directors.

''Hey, Danny, guess what?'' offered Stroman. ''We delivered a prototype to the air force guys yesterday afternoon. They're gonna tell their missiles who to blow up now, just by talking to 'em.''

Danny whistled. ''Oughta be a few bucks in *that* contract, eh?'' he said. Stroman and McGivens half looked at each other and nodded, smiling.

''Well, if they mention they're in the market for an anti-virus program, tell 'em I can deliver one for the low, low price of ten million bucks. Military Special.'' Danny grinned.

Stroman looked to Arnie for an explanation.

''In a past life, Danny wrote an anti-virus utility,'' Arnie said, scratching his big orange beard. ''Never did get it marketed, right?''

Danny shook his head.

''Well, that's a shame, Danny. You're a fine programmer.''

Danny glanced across the room. Gam was standing now, staring at the three of them. Danny quickly looked back at Arnie.

''Thanks,'' he said. ''My inspiration comes from the environment I'm working in. You know, morale comes from the top, and all that stuff."

"Speaking of morale, Danny," said Stroman, looking beyond his shoulder, "I'm told you have a romantic interest?"

Danny cocked an eyebrow. "You *do* have your hand on the pulse of this company, don't you?"

"Naturally. And I do believe your date has arrived."

Danny turned. Michelle had just come into the restaurant, looking stunning in a deep blue satin dress, hair pinned back, high heels.

"Will you guys excuse me?"

He jogged over to her. "Who are you, O radiant vision of Gorgeousness, and what have you done with Michelle?"

She kissed him quickly. "Do you mean to imply that I'm not *always* a radiant vision?"

"May I have this dance?"

She grabbed his arm. "You may have all of them."

The hired d.j., dreadlocks dangling, had put on a soft, rocking ballad. Michelle slipped into Danny's arms, warm and relaxed.

"You dance pretty well for a computer jock," she conceded after a moment.

"Thank you, Miss Andersen. And you do computers pretty well for a dancer."

Danny basked in the uncomplicated pleasure of that early evening. With Michelle, warm and graceful, beside him, he drank champagne and gorged himself on the reddest, ripest strawberries he'd ever plucked from a platter. He was with friends, among his new family; they were all in the highest spirits; and a promising new year was dawning. The specter of business school had begun to recede; he could almost forget that in three weeks he would be looking for a job again, and his time at Artelligence would be reduced to a line of twelve-point Helvetica type on his résumé.

And then it was twenty minutes before midnight. Danny stood with Michelle near the entrance, champagne in hand.

"Oh, God, poor Gam," Michelle said suddenly.

Poor Gam!? He turned to see what she was looking at. Gam was slumped sourly in a chair near the d.j., staring listlessly—coldly, Danny thought—out at the dance floor.

"Michelle. . .come on. He's antisocial by choice. If he wanted to have a good time, he could just get up and mingle."

She looked at him. "Do you really believe that?"

"Sure!" he said. "Look, he goes around alienating everybody he talks to, he doesn't show up at work on time, he spends the party sitting by himself. . .I think a person controls his own social destiny."

"Danny, you are *never* going to understand, are you." It was a statement, not a question. She took a step back from him.

"Don't you get that Gam has a lot of stuff to work through? Hasn't it occurred to you that there must be more to him than computers and being a little isolated? Isn't it possible that there's something to like in him? Even something to—" She caught herself.

Danny was startled. "Michelle, what *is* it? Why can't you just tell me? Was there something between you two?"

He glanced over at Gam. He wasn't staring listlessly now; he was staring at Danny.

"You don't *know* him, Danny. He used to treat me like a princess. He treated me better than any guy I've gone out with. I know that must be hard for you to see." She looked away. "Look, I don't really want to get into it. It didn't last very long, anyway. But it was enough to teach me that there's a great, tortured mind in that kid. He's just so young. He's so vulnerable. You have to see what's under the surface in people, Danny."

He almost scoffed. *Vulnerable?* Gam, staring with what Danny thought was murderous jealousy, was the last person in the world he would have called vulnerable.

"He hates my guts, Michelle."

"No, Danny. He doesn't hate, he . . . he just gets controlling sometimes. He *has* to, you know? He has to create a feeling of being in control wherever he can, because. . ."

She sighed, and looked at Gam again. Suddenly she grabbed Danny's forearm.

"Danny. Will you do something for me?"

"Anything, good-lookin'."

She looked at him earnestly. "Talk to Gam."

"*What!?*"

"I mean it. Talk to him. Let him tell you the story. Do it for me, Danny. And for yourself; try to understand him."

"Michelle, come *on*. The guy thinks I'm out to steal his spotlight. He'd probably knife me."

"Danny, answer me truthfully. In the three months you've been here, have you even *once* tried to strike up a conversation with Gam? Computer-nerd talk not included.''

He shrugged. "No, I guess not."

"Do it, Danny. You're not going to become his best friend or anything. Just go right over and talk to him. What have you got to lose?"

He regarded her for a long, hard moment, then glanced toward Gam, who was once again gazing at the floor.

He sighed heavily. "All right."

She placed her hands lightly on his shoulders and kissed him.

"You'll probably learn something, you know?" She stepped away. "I'm going to get a drink."

How the hell was he going to *do* this?!

He walked along the edges of the rectangular room, trying not to make this incredibly contrived act seem so contrived. As he rounded the last corner of the restaurant and began to approach Gam, he caught a glimpse of Charles, watching him with a curious look from where he stood at the buffet table.

Gam sat at the end of a row of five restaurant chairs. Danny sat three chairs away and tried to develop a misty-eyed look surveying the dance floor. He tried to predict whether Gam would stare him down or ignore him.

Gam ignored him.

Danny waited for what he hoped was an adequate period for Gam to get over the shock of being approached.

"D'we get that Command-period shortcut put into the code in time?" he began.

Gam didn't stir.

"Gam?"

After a moment, Gam leaned back in the chair, still seeing nothing in front of him.

"What the hell do you want, Cooper?"

Hmm. Nice rejoinder, Gam. Guess it's a little tough to be caustically witty with no audience, eh?

"Nothing at all, Gam. I just asked if—"

"I heard what you said."

Ah. Well. Been nice chatting, Gam.

"But you didn't slink over here to talk about the program. Michelle made you come over here. So you could stand in the other guy's shoes, that it?"

Danny was really getting irked now. To make matters worse,

he was missing a slow dance. He scanned the room, but couldn't spot Michelle.

"Gam." As long as he was going to crash and burn, Danny decided to get some mileage out of it. "You act like you can't stand me. You always have. How come?"

"What do *you* think?"

Danny thought for a moment. "Hmm. Well, let's see. I don't think it's my work habits; I've done a good job on my chunk of code, and I've never missed a deadline."

Gam said nothing.

"And I don't think it's me personally; I doubt if you'd resent me for my money, 'cause I don't have any, or for my brains—I guess you take the brains cake around here."

Say something, Gam buddy.

Danny cleared his throat self-consciously. "Could it have something to do with Michelle?"

Sharply and frighteningly, Gam turned in his chair and strained forward. "*Could it have something to do with Michelle? Could it have something to do with me personally?* Maybe it has something to do with things you don't even dream of, *pal.* Maybe you come from a nice East Coast family with a dog and two-point-three kids. I doubt if people like you even have the imagination to know what it's like—"

He stopped, already having gone too far. He exploded a gush of air and saliva, weirdly, abruptly; it could have been a scoff or a sneeze.

Danny looked at him closely.

"What *what's* like, Gam?" he said slowly.

"You don't give a goddamn. Get out of my face."

"Gam, give me some credit. I—"

"*Leave it.*" Danny could see Gam's knuckles, white, clenched on the molded-wood front of the chair seat.

A full three minutes passed. Danny sat very still, knowing that if he walked away now, things would be worse than when he began. Finally, his voice low, he spoke again.

"Gam."

Gam turned his head slightly.

"Let me hear it, OK?"

Gam looked at him. Something on his face told Danny that a struggle was taking place inside, a clash between the mask of aloofness and the compulsion to confide.

"Aw, you don't give a crap." There was less violence in his voice now.

The d.j. had turned off the music, and the sound of the Times Square New Year's Eve show blasted from a color TV mounted high on the wall. Most of the Artelligence employees drifted toward it to watch the countdown to the new year.

"Better get the hell over there, Danny," Gam said bitterly. "You'll miss the big moment."

Danny leaned forward.

"Tell me, Gam."

Gam looked out at the emptying dance floor.

"What do you want to hear, all right?" he blurted, his voice hard and defensive. "You want to hear about my father? You want me to sit here and tell you what a sick bastard he was to my mother and me before he blew his brains out?" He was staring so hard that Danny almost had to look away.

"Or you want to hear about my mother? She's a basket case. She lives with me. Want to hear about that? Wanna hear what she yells in her sleep sometimes? Wanna come over and help wash her sheets some night? Come on over, Danny, you'd love 'er. Yeah, come on over, meet Becca; you'll learn the whole goddamn story you're so interested in."

Danny could hear Gam breathing. He could hear himself breathing. He couldn't say anything. Mercifully, Gam finally looked away.

Some band was playing driving rock, tinnily, from the TV speaker.

He spoke feebly. "Gam—"

"Oh, skip it." Gam stood suddenly and snatched his leather flight jacket from the back of the chair. "*You* don't give a goddamn."

And then he was gone, jogging a beeline across the empty dance floor and disappearing down the grand staircase beyond. A hoarse, drunken chant began from the group and the TV: "Ten! Nine! Eight! . . ."

Danny sat still where he was, incapacitated by some new and untrustworthy emotion.

"Five . . . four . . . three . . . two . . . one. . . . *Happy New Year!*"

There was screaming and hugging; cocktail napkins flew into the air; and then Michelle emerged from the middle of the crowd, looking for him. She spotted him, held his gaze. The hooting and celebrating thrashed around her.

There was no other face Danny wanted to see more at that moment. She smiled sympathetically and beckoned; he stood slowly and crossed the room.

They had a lot to talk about.

Gam was shaking. Even under normal circumstances, his metabolism ran too fast for its own good. But today was worse; he hadn't had anything to eat since breakfast, and the champagne wasn't helping him to think straight. And New Year's Eve wasn't the world's greatest night to be running red lights in the streets of Santa Clara. On the other hand, he figured, at five past midnight, the drunks were still at their parties guzzling themselves silly.

The deep burgundy Sentra that followed him out of the Hilton parking lot and onto the highway, however, was driven straight as an arrow.

Gam's Miata looked like a TV commercial for itself, glinting in the light of the streetlights and the occasional neon sign. Gam had always liked the way it cornered; as he swung off the highway at the airport exit, his flight bag didn't even tip on the seat next to him. *Freakin' great suspension on this thing*, he thought.

He parked at the hangar, in the space marked Reserved for Airport Personnel. He snatched the flight bag, opened the door, got out . . . remembered something, went back into the car, pulled out his hard drive, and tucked it into the flight bag. He stood by the car and folded his arms on its low-slung roof, then rested his head on his arms. He looked out at the airfield, lit by only half a bank of halogen-arc lights that gave it a misty "Field of Dreams" look. There was a voice from his memory:

I believe in being aggressive in this business, son. So I've decided to let you in on a little business plan of mine: Don't turn down the Artelligence job. Go ahead and take it. Negotiate the hell out of them. Scare them silly. Get rich. Then you call me and tell me what you settled for. I'll pay you ten times what they give you. In return, I only ask a simple favor.

By lifting his head a little, Gam could see the staggered rows of private planes parked in the tie-down area to the right of the little Palo Alto terminal—if the one stained-wood building could, indeed, be considered a terminal. The faded General Aviation sign was barely visible on the chain-link fence behind them. He thought they looked like a bunch of sleepy cattle, all standing close together for company.

Look, you're not going to be damaging anything, son. Nobody gets hurt. You're not going to be a criminal. I only want you to buy me some time. That's all.

The wind was chilly, even through his leather jacket. Leaning on the cold metal of the car probably wasn't helping keep him warm, either.

So, at last, Gam stood upright and grabbed his flight bag and walked toward the private planes. If he had turned, he might have seen the dark Sentra, lights off, nosing into view just beyond the Quonset-hut hangar.

And there was his baby—his darling Piper Turbo Arrow twin-engine, still looking as shiny and new as the day he bought it. He untied the yellow nylon rope from the grommets at each wing tip and the tail. He opened his flight bag; the keys were in the side pocket, where they always were.

Luis tells me you're doing impressive work. You're a clever one, son. They say they've never seen code like yours. Keep it coming.

There were a few muffled pops as New Year's Eve firecrackers went off somewhere. *Little late, creeps.* It was twenty minutes into the new year.

He unlocked the Turbo Arrow's door and climbed in. He started the engine; the Piper sprang to life at the first twitch of the key, the way he loved so much. A little getaway ten miles up, Gam knew, was just what he needed to get calm whenever he started feeling...cornered. Technically, the Palo Alto airport closed at eight P.M., but Gam doubted anyone would be around to object to a solo flight.

Feet on the pedals, Gam began to taxi. He looked forward through the little windshield, the purring motor's sound all around him. He turned the plane due north onto the runway. Far away, there was a tiny, wimpy shower of sparks from some backyard firework.

Finally, Gam lowered the Piper's flaps and pushed the throttle forward. The Piper responded beautifully; save for the loud drone, the lift-off could have been an angel sweeping into the sky.

Below, on the ground, the burly, mustachioed driver of the

Nissan Sentra peered through his windshield at the graceful little plane. Just to make sure everything worked.

Forty seconds after the plane left the ground, Gam retracted the landing gear. The two wheels folded smoothly into their die-cast sockets in the plane body with a hydraulic hiss, slowing as they approached their locked positions. As the right landing gear nestled into its housing, a copper strip on the inside hub made contact with a plate that had been fastened to the inside wheel assembly with duct tape. A charge from the lantern battery wedged in the fuselage sent a six-volt surge through ten feet of electrician's wire, which had been carefully taped along the black sport stripe on the right side of the plane.

In an instant, the fluid in the fuel tank completed the circuit and ignited. The force of the explosion ripped the plane in half, sending a shower of shredded steel outward. The jet fuel mixed with the oxygen-rich air—the plane had only reached an altitude of 500 feet—and became a hundred times more volatile. The result of the combustion was a gigantic fireball that spewed particles of steel and aluminum alloy over the airfield a quarter mile in each direction.

From where the Sentra was parked, the muted boom and the bright eruption could almost have been a particularly expensive firework.

chapter 9

ARTELLIGENCE SOFTWARE CORP • NEW PRODUCTS DIVISION

Dear Clive,

Enclosed you'll find your release-version copy of the Master Voice software, as well as a photocopy of the manual galleys. We thought you might appreciate receiving the final working version now, instead of having to wait until the packaging is finished being assembled later this month.

Thank you again for all your valuable feedback over the last six months. Helpful people like you and the other beta testers have made Master Voice the success that it already is. We will be shipping nearly 250,000 copies of the product—as soon as we can produce and package them all!

Again, thank you for your patience and assistance during this process.

Sincerely,

Arnold McGivens
Director of New Product Development

January 3, 1994 "I can't take much more of this," Charles sighed. "You people don't seem to understand. I'm still on day three of my New Year's Eve hangover."

Skinner laughed. He looked almost normal in the pre-washed jeans and the blue-and-white polo shirt he and Rod had bought that morning.

"Come on, Charles," reprimanded Danny. "We need your brain cells, no matter how sloshed."

"Oh, nice," said Charles. "He calls *me* to the front line, but it's OK for Gam to not even show up for work."

"He's got an excuse, y'know?" perked up Skinner. "He has a quarter-million-dollar airplane, OK? He prob'ly flew off to Vegas for a week. To'lly righteous."

They were hunched around the seven-inch portable black-and-white TV they'd swiped from Arnie's office. After renting a VCR, they had gathered to watch Mrs. Javed's videotape.

Over and over and over.

"Seriously, though, I just don't get this," declared Danny. "Look at this one here. Just look. Now pause it. Pause!"

Rod, manning the VCR, slapped the freeze-frame button. It was as clear as a videotape could be, showing, very obviously, a Macintosh Plus nine-inch monitor. In the open window were three file icons, labeled Receipts/June through Receipts/August.

"All right. Now check it out," continued Danny, as though to convince himself. "Watch these two on the left—the May and June ones. Roll it, Roddy."

Rod let the tape continue. As they watched, they saw first one file, then the other blink out of sight. The cursor wasn't anywhere near them. There was nothing else unusual about the screen. A menu-bar clock blinked quietly in the upper-right corner of the screen. In the background of the videotape's audio track, they could hear Mrs. Javed and her beta-tester husband exclaiming excitedly when, after staring at the computer for twenty-five minutes, they finally captured the mysterious file-vanishing act on camera.

"Well, whatever it is," announced Charles, standing and stretching, "keep it the hell away from *my* computer." He started to walk back to his cubicle.

" 'Kay, so, Danny," began Skinner. "So you talked to this

guy, right? You talked to him?''

Danny nodded. ''Yeah. To his wife.''

''When was this?''

''About a week ago. No, wait, I'll tell you exactly: it was New Year's Eve day. She'd been calling poor Tina every day for two weeks, so Tina finally had me try to talk the lady down. I'll tell ya, though, I didn't believe her for a second. I mean, who's ever heard of anything like this before?''

Skinner was staring intently at the video image, not hearing a word Danny said. He chewed his lip rapidly.

''Danny...hold it, OK? New Year's Eve?''

''That's what I said, ol' buddy,'' Danny said.

Skinner acted as though he were onto something. ''So check it out, right? So what's going on here? You told her to make the video? So Rod, rewind to the beginning again.'' He rubbed his nose rapidly.

Rod did so. As the tape began again, they heard the Javeds' funny Midwest voices at the beginning of the tape—the voices that had made the programmers laugh uproariously the first time they played it.

Hello, we are testing. We are testing. Honey bear, is it on? I can't see anything through this thing.

You have to take off the lens cap, dear. Look, let me—

I can do it! I'm not a cripple.

Shh, honey, the tape is running. . . .

By this time, however, nobody was amused. Skinner stared, riveted, at part of the image.

''What's the deal, Skinner?'' asked Danny.

Skinner just kept saying, ''New Year's Eve, right? New Year's. God.''

''So?''

Skinner sat upright. ''OK. So you talked to her December thirty-first, right? Right. OK. So you tell her to make a videotape. So. She makes a videotape, maybe New Year's Day. She Fed Exes the thing yesterday, we get it today, here we are.''

''OK, Skinner,'' said Charles. ''Your formidable powers of chronology leave us all breathless.''

''No. No, you don't get it, OK? Look at this lady's menu clock.''

They all leaned in to see the tiny menu clock at the top right corner of the Macintosh screen.

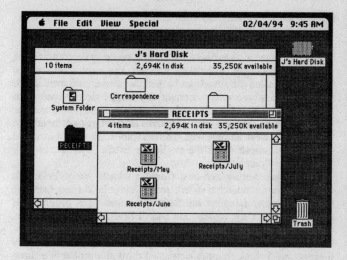

The colon in 9:45 blinked once per second.

"So?" said Charles. "She's got her clock set wrong. So sue her."

Danny didn't even hear him. Now his mind was racing, too. Here was an isolated pair of beta testers out in Colorado. They didn't own a modem. They didn't exchange floppy disks with anyone. The only programs they owned were Mac Write, a spreadsheet, and a painting program. In fact, Jack Javed wouldn't even have qualified as a beta tester for Artelligence if he weren't a linguistics specialist at the University of Colorado. Arnie McGivens had thought his expertise in spoken language would provide a valuable point of view.

Charles wasn't getting it at all, and the silence in the room made him nervous. "Yup, that sure is nutty," he was saying. "Why on earth would someone set her clock wrong? We should definitely call her and complain."

Danny kept returning, over and over again, to the same cycle of thoughts. What could make files disappear like that? A macro program, possibly. Some bizarre conflict of INITs—self-loading background programs. But the Javeds had no macro program, and the only INIT they used was the menu clock that was now showing 02/04/94 9:47 AM. So what could be causing the disappearance of the files?

It almost had to be some kind of virus.

And yet there was no way the Javeds *could* have contracted a virus. This morning, after they watched the tape a few times, Danny had called the Javeds and asked them, over and over again: "Are you *sure* you never brought any floppy disks home from the university? You *swear* you don't own a modem? You *promise* you haven't bought any new programs in the last two months?" The answers were all negative. The only software they'd installed on their Macintosh since the beginning of the summer, in fact, was Master Voice.

Danny was getting nervous. Could a Master Voice beta disk have become infected? It didn't seem likely; he'd been listening for the warning beep of his SURvIVor anti-virus program on Gam's hard disk for weeks, and hadn't heard a peep. Of course, Gam's clock was set correctly. . . .

"All right, look, you guys. Those people have what's probably a virus, and I think Skinner's right—I think it's probably a time-bomb virus. I think it's set to go off on a certain day or a certain time. Something had to trigger it. And what makes me really worried is the isolation of these people. They haven't had a *single contact* with the outside world of computers except for the floppy disk *we* sent them."

Charles scowled. He was starting to get the scenario Danny was painting.

"So I believe the only way these people could have contracted a virus is if it came from us."

Skinner swore loudly. Charles was frowning. Rod paused the VCR.

"I don't know, Danny," Skinner said finally. "How could it come from here, OK? I mean, our Macs are to'lly sealed off. There's no way a virus could have infected one of these hard disks, you know? I mean, the only one of our hard drives that's been exposed to the outside world is—"

He stopped short. As if on cue, every programmer turned his head to look at Gam's desk, where only empty space marked where Gam usually placed the hard drive he transported to and from his home. Everyone was thinking about the same thing: Gam's late-night modeming exploits. In the back of their minds, they had always been aware that anyone using a modem exposes himself to the outside world . . . that every time a modem user downloads a file, a virus may be along for the ride. Could Gam have been so careless?

Danny dismissed the thought for the moment. "So help me figure this out. Who's been the liaison with the beta testers?"

"Arnie," said Skinner. "Arnie sends the disks out to the beta testers, OK? But it couldn't have come from him, the virus couldn't have come from him. Arnie virus-checks everything before he sends it out, y'know? I'm to'lly serious. He runs everything through Antidote—I've seen him do it."

"I know it doesn't make much sense," said Danny, "but bear with me for a second. What copy of the software does he send out? Who gives him the version he's supposed to duplicate and send them?"

"Gam," said Skinner with a double face-blink.

"Fine," said Danny. "So we need to look at Gam's hard drive. Where the hell is he today, anyway?"

Charles looked at Danny through the smoky lenses of his glasses. "Evidently two days off weren't enough for him. *You* know how Gam spreads himself so thin—squeezing in his programming here in between stints at the soup kitchen. . . . "

Rod started to react. "Really!? I didn't know he works at a—"

Charles clamped his hand over Rod's mouth. "I'll explain it to you later, Rod-man. Right after I sell you some shares in my Brooklyn Bridge Mutual Fund."

"All right, no big deal," Danny said. "When he gets here, we should check out his hard drive, because there's only a few places Mrs. Javed's virus, or whatever it is, could have come from. And almost all of them start with us." *Although that theory doesn't make sense either, because SURvIVor never sounded any alarm. . . .*

They were watching him with "So now what, Mr. Expert?" looks. Danny suddenly realized that he had been silently designated the ringleader.

All right, let's get this over with.

"OK, so does Arnie send each beta disk to a disk-duplicating company? Maybe Mrs. Javed's disk got infected there."

"Nuh-uh," said Rod. "Arnie always makes the guys in Customer Service dupe the disks when they're on the phone. Maybe it came from Customer Service?"

Danny nodded. "Definitely a possibility. But I'll tell you what

I want to do. Just so I can sleep easier, OK? I want to isolate one of these Macs. Cut it apart from the network. And I want to set its clock ahead to February fourth, just like Mrs. Javed's clock. Then let's try the latest beta disk we sent out to her, just in case. Just so I get good and positive whatever they've got didn't come from us. OK?''

Skinner shrugged. ''What else we gonna do? We can't get started on updating the Func Spec until Gam shows up, right, and the program's done, so we may as well try to earn our dollar a day, y'know?''

It was a shame that Steve Trevir wanted to be an artist.

He always told himself that repairing computers at ComputerCentre/Dallas was only an interim job; of course, he'd been telling himself that for six years already. Pretty soon, he knew, he'd have to make some career moves.

As part of his plan, he'd decided to combine his skills: he'd get himself a copy of the $795 Bezier-based graphics program Freeform Pro, teach himself to use it, start doing commercial line art, print his files on ComputerCentre's laser printers . . . next thing he knew, he'd pull himself out of this job by his creative bootstraps.

Naturally, he had no intention of *paying* eight hundred bucks for a program. Every hard drive in Dallas passed over his workbench; he planned to swipe himself a copy of Freeform Pro as soon as he came across a computer that had it installed. That was one of the perks of being an authorized service center: an endless parade of free software. *I get a free program, the computer's owner never knows the difference. . . . The perfect crime*, he thought. Nobody gets hurt. Nobody even notices. Everybody wins.

He pried the outer casing off a sick SE/30. A student at a community college had brought the SE/30 to him saying that the hard disk was dead.

Man, oh man, the things I've seen pass over this bench! For instance, he'd nabbed a pretty cool Rolodex or two with some satisfaction. He remembered the NRA lobbyist whose hard drive contained a mailing list that was probably worth millions: names, home phones, and personal information for every politician in the region, not to mention a bunch of congressmen and presidential aides. He'd laughed, too, because there was also a file of ''Tentative Spokespersons 1995'' that included some of the biggest names in Hollywood and professional sports. (He hadn't minded making a copy of that particular list for himself. Not that he knew quite what to do with it, exactly. What was he gonna do, call up Michael J. Fox at home one morning? "Hey, Mike. You don't know me, but..." Oh, sure.)

Steve set the casing aside and began to disconnect the wires that ran to the SE/30's mother board: the speaker cable, the hard drive's broad gray ribbed ribbon, and the multicolored cluster of wires from the CRT display.

It didn't take him long to find the problem with the hard drive; like many of the SpinKing series of hard-drive mechanisms, this one's motor oil had gummed up after a year or so of heat and dust inside the computer. He doused a nylon swab with alcohol and set to work, bending over sideways to get at the top of the platter spindle on which the gunk had accumulated. *Brain-dead design*, he thought. *You're supposed to completely seal these babies—yes, even the mechanical parts—inside a steel case in a clean room somewhere. You put the drive mechanism on the outside like this ... well, sure, they're cheaper to crank out, but cheezus; they're gonna fail.*

Steve got lucky. When he reassembled the SE/30, the newly lubricated drive mechanism worked fine. Better yet, he found a gold mine of graphics software on the disk as he undertook his typical perusal of its contents. Not only did he find the most recent version of Freeform Pro, but its rival PostScript environment-drawing program, too, and a pair of CAD/CAM programs. He knew he was no architect or engineer, but he thought the CAD/CAM stuff might be fun for trade value with other guys. He hooked up his own external hard drive to the SE/30 and began happily helping himself to the graphics software, copying program after program to his own disk.

What Steve didn't know, however, was that his role as a clearinghouse for computers from all over the city also made him an unwitting viral Grand Central Station. His software-copying escapades had, in the past, helped to spread viruses to otherwise widely separated sectors of the computing community. On occasion, he had even formatted the hard drives of new computers sold by the store by running the Apple System Installer program off his own infected hard drive. If he had stopped to think about it, he would have realized what an unpleasant first week of com-

puting he'd accidentally prescribed for the customers who purchased those machines: a week learning about computer viruses,
data corruption, and hopelessly lost work.

Tonight was worse. In copying Freeform Pro to his own hard
disk, he also infected his disk with the virus that had originated
in Houston. It would be two weeks before he even discovered
that fact; in the meantime, the virus on his hard drive installed
itself in every new or repaired computer that passed through
ComputerCentre/Dallas.

"All right, now, let's be really careful about this thing. That's
it, slowly...slowly..."

Michelle smiled to herself. Danny was acting like James Bond
defusing a missile. The male of the species, showing its plumage.

They had completely dismantled the wiring of the R and D lab,
and had put one Mac on a card table by itself. The only cords
coming out of it went to the power outlet, the hard drive, and the
keyboard. The computer looked small and helpless on the card
table, the boys in a semicircle around it; Michelle thought the
scene smacked of an underworld interrogation.

"All right. That's fine. Now let's power up the hard disk,"
Danny was saying. With all eyes upon him, he felt a little self-
conscious, as though he were watching somebody else play himself in a movie.

"Pencil ready, Rod?"

Rod was into it. "Check!" he shouted.

"Now: computer on, please."

"You didn't say Simon Says," sang Charles.

"Come on, man..."

Charles flipped it on. After a moment, the Macintosh desktop
screen appeared.

"All right, Charles, quick: how full is the hard disk?" Charles
put on his tinted glasses and looked.

"Eleven thousand, five hundred three kilobytes free."

"Fine," Danny said. "Rod, it's now four-oh-nine, and there
are eleven thousand, five hundred three kilobytes. Get that
down."

"Check!"

There was no sound in the room save the hum of the hard drive
fan. The tension, Danny thought, was palpable. Here he was,
thrust into the fore, based on his knowledge of computer viruses,

summoned forth to save the galaxy . . . he felt like Luke Skywalker. Or Einstein.

He wished Michelle didn't have that small bemused smile.

"Now: Charles, let's change the date of the Mac clock. Control Panel: open. Good. I want you to set it to February fourth, 1994." Charles did so. "Close Control Panel, please."

Charles closed the window. "Very logical, Captain Kirk."

They all watched the screen. "All right, quick," Danny said. "Open the Programs folder, and let's see what we see."

Charles opened a directory window. It was filled with program icons. They seemed fine. None of them disappeared. Danny was perversely disappointed.

"Well, all right . . . we'll just be patient for a minute."

They were patient for twenty minutes, in fact, before there was a buzz on the speaker phone. "Arnie, it's Bob. I need to see you in my office. Immediately." Arnie and Michelle exchanged worried glances, and Arnie sprinted from the room.

Nothing happened on the screen.

"Well, I give up," said Skinner. "I mean, we've essentially duplicated the lady's setup, right? This is the exact copy of the Master Voice beta that she had, right? Same version of the System file, OK. Same everything. I give up, Danny."

Danny didn't understand, either. "Rod, how much disk space left on the disk now?"

Rod looked. "Eleven thousand, five hundred three K. It's the same amount." He looked at the list of files, each displaying its modification date. "No files have been modified in the last half hour, either."

Danny began to pace. Rod clutched his legal pad expectantly. Charles peeled the foil top off a butterscotch Swiss Miss.

"So what are we missing?" said Danny to no one in particular. "We've got the same computer setup, with the same software these beta-tester people have. So how come *our* files aren't disappearing?"

He tried to remember everything he knew about computer-virus behavior. *What's a virus?* A piece of code. *What's it live on?* It attaches itself to a host program. *How does it spread?* It runs when the host program is run—

"I might have it," he said suddenly. "Suppose this Mac here *is* infected. But a virus doesn't actively run around like a little man in there, right? It has to be attached to a legitimate program.

And we haven't tried running a program yet! Charles, man that mouse!"

Charles was licking the back of his pudding spoon lovingly. "I delegate my duties to Skinner," he said. "I'm experiencing oral afterglow."

Danny rolled his eyes. "Skinner, would you—"

That was as far as he got. Suddenly there was running and shouting in the hall. Something was happening.

They dropped what they were doing and followed the sounds to the atrium, near the reception desk, where a throng of Artelligence employees were standing. Something urgent was unfolding as Danny arrived, slithering between a pair of rapt, white-faced secretaries. The assembled employees were focused intently, straining to catch the words of a cop. He was accompanied by three other uniformed men. Stroman and McGivens were up front, answering questions. It was a weird scene.

"He phoned in a VFR flight plan at sixteen hundred hours that day," the cop with the mustache was saying. "That's plane talk—visual flight rules. From a little uncontrolled-airspace airfield like Palo Alto, that's the system most of the pilots use. Means they're not watched or governed by a control tower, like they are under instrument flight rules, like the big airlines. Means they fly at even-numbered altitudes flying east, and odd-numbered flying west."

Stroman was nodding nervously. Danny didn't quite know what was happening. But he only knew one person at Artelligence with an airplane.

"Now, under VFR, the destination airport has the aircraft's ETA and course in the computer. If the pilot confirmed the flight plan as he took off, then they give him an hour past the ETA before they start sounding the alarm. Vegas Center phoned the FAA here at oh-one-thirty hours to tell them that the plane did not arrive as planned. Unfortunately, Vegas Center didn't have a pilot ID on file for the aircraft."

The painfulness of the jargon was clearly getting the better of Stroman. He kept nodding with tense little jerks of his head.

"The body was found in the early morning, but we had no leads on the ID. Then this morning a white '93 Mazda Miata was towed to the pound by the Palo Alto Traffic Violations Bureau. It was parked at the airport illegally."

Arnie McGivens couldn't stand it anymore. "So what's the upshot, all right?"

The cop shot him a condescending glance, all protocol.

"We obtained a home address by tracing the automobile's registration; on the cars in the garage at that address in Woodside, we discovered parking stickers. Yours. We assumed you might be able to tell us more about the deceased."

Danny wildly searched the eyes of those around him. Were they getting this? Tina was crying. A pair of women from sales were hugging each other. Stroman looked ill. Danny looked for Michelle. He spotted her, but he wouldn't have been able to name what she felt if you paid him. Her jaw was set, and she was listening intently to the cop; her eyes showed nothing.

Deceased? His mind raced, trying to fend off the feelings that crowded him like bats in a cave. How could it happen? Had Gam been drunk?

Summoning his wits, he walked through the crowd to stand beside Michelle, still staring stonily ahead. If she saw him, it was peripherally, because her eyes never flickered. Danny stood there, troubled, then placed a hand on her shoulder. Instantly, the dam broke; Michelle buried her face into his shoulder and let out a silent torrent of tears. Danny wrapped his arms around her.

He closed his eyes as his sense of reality failed him. Guilt and frustration skirmished just beneath the surface of his consciousness. Maybe he'd been wrong about Gam. . .maybe Michelle was right. . .maybe the pain Danny had glimpsed at the code-freeze party was a deep river indeed.

But no matter what Danny thought now, no matter what resolutions he made, he knew it was too late. Gam was dead.

chapter 10

MAC WEEKLY, JANUARY 5, 1994

Don't just sit there . . . say something!

Well, of *course* you're all excited. We fully understand. Who wouldn't be? Who wouldn't go wild hearing about a true speech-recognition system: you talk to your computer and it obeys. It types. It files. It chops, slices, and dices. You have every reason to want to be the first on your block.

Except that you'll pay a cool $800. And for that you get a box you have to plug in. And a rat's nest of cables. Still interested?

Well, now Huntington Systems has something to say: You can do much better.

It's called SpeakEasy.℠ And it works precisely as well as the one everyone's buzzing about—but costs half as much. And there's no ugly box to hook up; the SpeakEasy neural-net chip is built right into its microphone.

So do yourself a favor: keep quiet until you've seen what *we* can do.

Available second quarter 1994.

H·U·N·T·I·N·G·T·O·N S·Y·S·T·E·M·S

January 5, 1994 "So that's it, then. A memorial service Monday, a quiet press release from Michelle. Arnie, any luck reaching Gam's mother?"

Arnie shook his head. "Nobody's answering the phone. I'll drive by and see if she's okay."

"All right, then," Stroman said through a sigh.

Danny thought Stroman looked less like a cowboy today than a beleaguered executive. It was too much stress—suddenly, Stroman's most valuable asset, and the brains behind the software, was gone. Only the fact that the software was officially completed protected the company from dying along with Gam.

Stroman looked around at his staff. The programmers were looking disturbed. At the very least, Stroman knew, he still had momentum—amazing press and public enthusiasm. *Now, God*, he thought, rubbing his eyes, *please just let us ship the product and be done with it for a while.* Only that morning a Mika lawyer had called him up to inquire about his Artelligence stock certificates.

"All right, let's move on. Danny, you said you had some new business?"

Danny caught the other programmers watching him carefully.

"Um . . . yeah." He got out of his chair and pulled Skinner's laptop computer, a Macintosh PowerBook, out of its case. He gently laid it on the table in front of his employer and opened it so that he could clearly see the screen.

"What's this?" said Stroman. Arnie McGivens scooted his chair closer to Stroman's so that he, too, could see the display.

"Well, we may have a little problem," Danny said. "I don't know how it happened, or when it happened, but I think you should have a look at this."

Stroman shrugged wearily. "Sure. Go ahead."

"OK," Danny said. He pointed to the PowerBook screen. "I'm going to open the Alarm Clock." For portable use, the Power-Book had a built-in track ball that controlled the cursor position instead of a mouse; Danny rolled the arrow cursor to the Apple menu at the left side of the screen, and selected Alarm Clock from the list of mini-programs. The Alarm Clock program displayed its tiny window, containing the date and time, in the middle of the screen.

"Now, I'm running a copy of the final Master Voice beta in the background. Check this out. First, I set the date of the Macintosh clock to February fourth." He typed the new date into the Alarm Clock. Skinner, incapable of remaining still, had now joined the standing cluster of spectators at Stroman's end of the table.

"All right, I'm with you," said Stroman.

"And now, the scary part: we launch a program. Any program." He guided the cursor on the screen to MacODex, an address-book program, and clicked the track ball button twice to launch the program.

In five seconds, the address-book window opened, containing the names and phone numbers of Skinner's contacts. But that wasn't what Danny was interested in.

"Now. Look here." He pointed not to the active window, but instead to a remote corner of the screen—the upper-left screen dot.

It was white, not black.

"You set the date forward, you run any program, you get this: the first screen pixel turns white. It's got to be either a freak bug that makes no sense, or—" he remembered the panic in Mrs. Javed's voice as she watched her files disappear from the screen—"or we've got a virus in the Master Voice software."

Stroman pursed his lips thoughtfully. "Is that it?"

"Is what it?"

"Is that the extent of the damage that this...this bug does?"

Arnie, stroking his bushy square beard, stood upright after having stooped to view the screen. "I agree, Danny. I don't think this is anything to get excited about. We'll just patch the code to turn that pixel off again. Take five minutes."

"Ah...may I, gentlemen?" Charles said, raising one finger in the air. He cleared his throat. "I think what Danny is concerned about here is not that there's a white pixel on the screen, but instead that this may just be a symptom of a more destructive virus."

Stroman's patience was wearing thin. "As far as I can see, gentlemen, you've just shown me evidence of an extremely minor cosmetic bug. Bugs are to be expected, gentlemen. We've had 'em before, we'll have 'em again. This is the way of the software world."

"Well, we don't have conclusive proof," Danny responded, "but we have a very isolated beta tester who's been losing files off her hard disk. We've seen it happen; she videotaped files disappearing off her screen. And," he concluded with intensity, "*she* had the white dot in the corner of the screen."

Stroman snapped his fingers. "Well, OK, then. That's the question: have *you* seen any files disappearing in your tests? If not, then there's *no* reason to think this first-pixel bug is related to disappearing files in any way, is there?"

Danny stared in disbelief. These guys were giving him Corporate Denial Syndrome, and they had just *seen* this infection take place.

Arnie chimed in, too. "Besides, Danny, why don't you just run a virus-checking program on it, to see if we've caught something? There's your answer."

Danny took a deep breath, trying to stay cool. "All right. Look. No, we haven't been able to make it eat our files. And I *did* run a virus checker." *In fact*, he thought, *it's been running for weeks now.* "The virus checker drew a blank: it reports no infection. But I still think there's something going on. I'm just saying, maybe we should chart a map of this program. Figure out what Gam's doing in there. Let's just take some time out to figure out what's happening."

Stroman shook his head. "I don't know, Danny. We're actually in pretty good shape for meeting our February first ship date, but I don't want to take any chances. If one element of the puzzle doesn't fall into place right—if the manual is late, if the binding takes more time, if the chips don't arrive in quantity from Seoul—then the whole project gets delayed." He glanced at Arnie, then back at Danny. "I don't think we can afford the time."

Danny's sense of deference to authority left him. "So you'd rather torpedo the whole project by shipping out a buggy program?" His voice rose slightly. "Or a program with a *virus*?"

Stroman responded coolly. "There's no reason we can't discuss this in a civilized way, Danny."

Arnie, ever the mediator, intervened. "OK. All right, look. Have we established that this anomaly is in the *final* version of the program? Or just the last beta version?"

Danny looked down for a minute, flustered. Charles took over. "We . . . we actually haven't tested the final version yet, but . . ." He let his voice trail off.

"Rod," said Stroman bluntly, "run to Customer Service and grab one of their Mac SEs. Bring a power cord. Let's settle this once and for all."

Minutes later, the Mac was set up, and the shipping version of Master Voice was installed.

"Let's get this over with," said Stroman.

Arnie leaned forward to observe the proceedings on the nine-inch built-in monitor of the SE. Charles shot a look at Skinner hoping Danny wasn't about to look foolish.

Danny opened the Alarm Clock, feeling resentful that his expertise on viruses was being challenged. He set the date forward to February fourth, exactly as he had a moment before, and swallowed hard. Then he launched a program, the final step that seemed to trigger the virus. . . *if there is one*, he thought.

Nothing happened.

The rounded corners of the Mac's screen image remained rounded and dark.

Dammit! Danny thought.

Stroman cleared his throat. "Well."

"Looks like Gam fixed whatever it was in the final version, Danny," said Arnie gently.

Danny felt stupid and ashamed; he should have made that test on his own. He was about to speak when Michelle flew into the room.

"Michelle!" said Stroman. "I thought you must have forgotten about this little mee———"

"Look at this, Stroman," she said sharply. She was clutching a copy of the tabloid-size glossy *Mac Weekly*. She slammed it down on the table.

"What. . ." was all he managed. He followed her pointing finger to the half-page ad. *Don't just sit there . . . say something*, it began.

He read it, the color draining from his face.

Danny exchanged glances with Arnie. "Bob. . .what is it?" he said quietly.

Stroman sat motionless for a moment, his grip on the magazine tightening. "It's Huntington," he managed. He swallowed hard.

Michelle filled them in. "It's an ad for a new speech recognition package from Huntington Systems. It says they'll be shipping second quarter." Anger flashed in her eyes. "I think it's a scam."

Arnie was stunned. "How could they? That's impossible! It took *us* two years just to get to the *testing* stage. . . . How could they just whip something together? There's no . . . possible . . . way!" He grabbed the magazine from Stroman's hands and read the advertisement furiously.

Stroman stared, still in blind shock.

"Maybe you're right, Michelle," he said softly. "Maybe it's a sham. Maybe he wants to make buyers hold off. He doesn't want them to buy Master Voice. He wants to buy time until he *can* ship a competing package."

Rod raised his hand unnecessarily. "Who's 'he'?"

Stroman half focused on Rod. "Lars Huntington," he murmured. "My ex-partner. Good old 'Bloodsucker' Huntington."

"But what's the big deal?" Rod went on. "Why is he out to get—"

Arnie lay a cautioning hand on Rod's forearm. "Tell you later," he whispered.

"I don't understand. What am I supposed to learn from all of this?" asked Stroman miserably to nobody in particular. "Our whole vision was coming true. The press, the market, Wall Street . . . everybody was hailing us! And now Gam's gone. And now this . . . this *psycho* is trying to steal our thunder. . . ." He shook his head, nearly defeated.

When he really thought about it, of course, Lars's behavior didn't surprise him; Lars had always been unscrupulous, aggressive, and moral free. This ad for a new speech-recognition package smacked of the same tactics that drove Stroman crazy when they were working together a decade earlier.

He remembered the year Lars was determined to win one of those dime-a-dozen computer-magazine awards. It was called The People Speak trophy; the readers of the magazine were supposed to send in ballots for their favorite software. Lars, naturally, set four employees to the task of buying crate after crate of the magazine, filling out the ballots with phony customer names, and mailing them in. Naturally, Huntington's program won its category—but Stroman had struggled daily with his conscience to show up for work.

There were always smaller irritations along the way, too—Lars was always in it for the market share instead of the thrill of breaking technological barriers. Lars insisted on sending expensive desk sets as gifts to reviewers of his products, a tactic that only occasionally backfired. And he'd sue anyone in sight for software piracy, for the publicity value alone—even the Chicago School for the Deaf, who made the mistake of buying five copies of a program for use on fifteen machines.

But in 1981, Huntington Systems was completing its development of a program called #Cruncher, destined to become one of the early greats of accounting software. Trouble was, Huntington planned a little feature nobody knew about. In the name of promoting the paperless office, Lars wanted to include a special floppy disk with #Cruncher. It was to be labeled Registration Disk. The instructions were for the purchaser to insert it in the floppy drive of the PC, then run the Register.EXE program. Once launched, this program would simply prompt the customer to type in his name and address; he was then asked to mail the disk back to Huntington, in a prepaid envelope, to complete his product registration.

In fact, Register.EXE did most of its work behind the scenes; while the name and address were being entered, the program sought out, and recorded, all kinds of statistics about the computer that was running it: how much memory was installed, what version of the operating system was running, what model computer it was, and so on. It would also copy the catalog of files; the user would then unwittingly send all of this information to Huntington.

Once he was equipped with a list of a customer's files, Lars would be able to see if a particular customer owned other Huntington programs (and, if so, whether or not they were legitimate owners), what competing programs the customer owned, and so on. Stroman had always suspected that Lars planned for the little program to delve even deeper into the customer's data . . . but the possibilities of what Lars could learn, and how he would use the information, were too terrifying to contemplate.

It didn't much matter. Stroman and Arnie McGivens had both opposed the registration-disk scheme violently. For days they fought viciously with Lars and the other board members behind closed doors. For Stroman, the Register.EXE program was a gross invasion of privacy—not to mention a twisted kind of breaking and entering—and a humiliating breach of integrity. For Lars, the fight was simply a power struggle. He figured that Stroman, his college pal, his comrade in arms, had become dissatisfied with his goody-two-shoes life and had decided to challenge Lars's leadership. Lars began to circumvent Stroman and McGivens in policy questions, making categorical decisions without them. His manner soured, and communications became first strained and finally nonexistent.

And so, at a time when Lars needed them most, Bob and Arnie left the company. Stroman remembered hoping that his departure would be as painful as possible to Huntington, a sentiment he was no longer proud of. Even so, Stroman sometimes wondered if Huntington had gone ahead with its registration-disk scheme once he was left alone with his delusions of grandeur.

"Well," Stroman said finally, clearing his throat, "this little stunt of Huntington's settles it. We *will* ship Master Voice by February first. Or *earlier*." He was on a roll. "Arnie, Michelle, and I are going to pull out every stop. We'll hire temps. We'll bribe the truckers. We'll make a phone call *every hour* to the supplier in Korea. Whatever we have to do, we'll do it."

Danny struggled with himself, still chagrined at having cried wolf. "Bob, look. I'm sorry about flying off the handle, but seriously: at this point we don't really know our way around the program. Gam's the only one who knows the code! There's no documentation on it, hardly any notes. The. . .the general concept and structure of the software was generally kept . . . I mean we weren't able to—"

"Yes, Danny. You're going to be flying blind for a while. You're going to have to grab whatever time you can to hash through the program, to learn it; I never said this was going to be easy. But I have faith in my team. My Reinforcements."

"What I mean is . . . I really would like to take a couple days to find out about this pixel virus. Or bug, or whatever it is. Even if it's fixed, we should—"

"No *possible* way." Stroman cut him off, holding up the issue of *Mac Weekly*. "There is no way in hell we're going to let *this* bastard beat us to market. Sorry, Danny. We simply don't have any time to worry about some bygone cosmetic glitch." He turned to Charles and Rod. "You guys keep Danny in line, now, you hear me? I don't want you guys spending one minute more on it. I want all your time spent on documenting this code. Figuring out what Gam did and why. Clear?"

"Clear," Rod murmured.

Stroman stood. "All right, then. I'll see you tomorrow morning."

The staff filed out. Stroman remained in the conference room, wondering if Lars was bluffing about having a competing product. With a pain in the pit of his stomach, he remembered that he'd seen Huntington's name listed as a candidate for the Infidel military contract. It was there, even months ago, in the folder on Colonel Oskins's desk.

But *how*?

Stroman closed his briefcase and made a mental note to call his Korean arc-chip supplier when the business day began in the East. He needed to assure himself that they weren't supplying anyone *else* with the chips . . . just in the crazy off-chance that Lars Huntington really was close to delivering a better speech-recognition system of his own.

By January 4, the big day, Lt. Terry Gibbs had stopped reflexively grasping for a joystick that wasn't there. It was too weird, talking to her equipment. At last, however, she was able to keep her eyes on the screen without worrying about her hands.

She had to admit, it was a beautiful system. It wasn't the Taj Mahal inside the truck, but she had a comfortable enough seat in front of the monitor console, and she'd been lucky to land this assignment. Her palms were only slightly sweaty.

There were maps spread on three sides of her, and she was nearly buried by powerful computers in water-cooled metal housings. It was just Gibbs, a microphone, and an expensive remote-controlled death robot.

And that's what it was, too, she'd decided. The thing did what she told it to. It could fly for eight hours without a whimper, cameras trained, constantly responding to the navigational signals transmitted at unimaginably high speeds by the computers at the mobile base. *Pity the enemy if we get a bunch of these babies flying at once*, Gibbs thought. *There won't be anywhere to hide.* The Infidel missiles were much worse than accurate—they were *patient*.

On the leftmost monitor, Gibbs had a computer-generated schematic of the five hundred-square-mile patch of desert. She hadn't even been told where the target was. She did know what she was looking for, however: an enemy airfield that may or may not be camouflaged. Finding and destroying it was up to her. And the Infidel.

At last things seemed ready. The three guys who'd been working on the backup systems had finished, and Colonel Duke OK'd the Infidel for launch. Gibbs sat in front of her main monitor—a modified Sony Trinitron, no less—and fingered the microphone.

"OK, Colonel. I'm ready to roll when the missle is."

"That's affirmative, Lieutenant. We're ready for launch; once she's off the ground, it's your ball game."

"All right," she heard Duke say. "Launch it."

The Trinitron showed a neutral dark green, as it would continue to do until the missile's bow cameras were on. She couldn't switch them on until the missile was in the air, since it was feared that the violence of the launch might disturb the electronics. Therefore, the only clue Gibbs had that the missile had, in fact, been launched was the small five-digit altitude readout at the bottom of the right-hand monitor. She watched the numbers climb: 00000, 00300, 00900, 011450. . . .

Colonel Duke's raspy voice popped into her headset. "OK, Gibbs. Start talking."

She cleared her throat self-consciously. "Bow cameras on," she enunciated carefully.

The Trinitron flickered on, and Gibbs caught her breath: the missile had already begun to level off, and a dusty brown vista appeared before her. The top half of the picture was a deep azure blue. There were no clouds on the display.

"Uh. Down thirty," she said tentatively. The picture on the Trinitron responded smoothly seven-tenths of a second later, shifting the image slightly in favor of the valley floor. *This is wild*, she thought.

"East five. East five." With each command into the microphone, the Macintosh Quadra CPUs sent a translated command to the Infidel missile, and the missile's course changed. Lieutenant Gibbs's hands remained free to grab at the terrain maps she had arrayed in front of her, to manage her microphones, and to work with the computers, if necessary. A few minutes passed as she scanned the monitors, followed her maps, and guided the tons of expensive machinery with the sound of her voice.

There it is! In the lower-right quadrant of the Trinitron, she spotted a familiar formation. *Some camouflage*, she thought . . . the airstrip was about as hidden as a skyscraper in a cornfield.

Off to the sides, she could see about a dozen gray X-shaped objects, which she knew were planes. She could make out a hangar and a couple of other buildings, all surrounded by a faint grayish fence.

"Down ten. Up five. West eight-point-five. Show me the cross hairs." A fine grid appeared on the screen image; she was discovering that controlling the missile's flight with precise numeric information was much more accurate than trying to do it by hand. Her cross hairs were homing in at a right angle to the paved airstrip that was now in screen center. She completely forgot that she was speaking to a machine.

"Focus and lock." That was almost all . . . her job as a human directional coach was complete for this run of the missile. "Kill it."

The airfield formation loomed larger and larger; the altitude numbers flew downward toward ground zero; the gray airstrip rushed up at Gibbs. She flinched involuntarily at the moment of impact. As the missile struck its target, Gibbs heard no explosion, saw no cloud of smoke, dust, or sheet-metal shards flying through the air; the Trinitron merely blinked back to its neutral green.

The right-hand monitor, however, did say MISSILE DOWN.

"Sheeeeeee-*itt*!!!" roared Oskins's voice in her headset. He was cackling like a schoolboy. "Did you *see* that mother! Shee*it*!"

Colonel Duke was pleased. "Target killed, Lieutenant. Nice work."

She leaned back in her seat and allowed herself to breathe again. "Uh, can I come out of here, sir? I'm feeling a little cooped up."

"Come on out, Lieutenant." It was Oskins again.

She pulled her headset off and stood up, stretching, as somebody on the outside cracked a door panel open. Bright fluorescent light burst into the darkened truck, and Gibbs let a technician help her down the three small stairs.

Colonel Duke emerged from behind his own console at the side of the testing lab. "Hey, I think it's safe to say this project is more than on schedule. Nice work, Gibbs."

"Nice simulation, you mean. Is the real missile going to work that well?"

Duke grabbed her hand and shook it. "I don't know why not.

You were using the real electronics and computer gear—we're only simulating the missile itself. Anyway, let's give you another few runs in that overgrown video game, and then we head out to Nevada to try the real baby, OK?''

"Fine, sir." Lieutenant Gibbs smiled at him. "I can't wait."

January 8, 1994   Danny sat slouched in his desk chair. One window of his small apartment was open, and the chilly night air raised goose bumps across his skin. He stared miserably at the computer screen. If the first two days were any indication, 1994 was going to be a rotten year.

His eyes kept returning to the upper-left corner of his screen, and he couldn't get the memory of Mrs. Javed's videotaped virus out of his head. *What the hell are you, little bug? I've got the last beta version of Master Voice on my Mac here, the same version Mrs. Javed had. . . . Why aren't you on my screen?*

Of course, he already knew the answer to that. The bug hadn't affected Danny's computer because its clock wasn't set incorrectly. Despite Stroman's order not to waste any more time on the topic, he'd experimented with three computers at the office. First he copied any useful files off them, protecting the data if there *was* a virus. Then he'd set each computer's clock to February 4, and then he'd run a program; the infuriating white dot appeared instantly every time. And that was all; no further damage. All three computers contained the Master Voice beta software. Uncomfortable, he'd reformatted each computer's hard drive to clean it off completely, then restored the backed-up information. Once he'd cleaned off the hard drive and re-loaded software, the computers were fine once again.

His wrist flopped to the desk, almost reluctantly, and he grabbed the mouse. He was about to change the date on the computer's Alarm Clock. He would watch more closely this time. He'd learn *something*.

He was about to set the clock to February 4 again—the date that Mrs. Javed's video showed—when he stopped. When had she *reported* the problem? Not February fourth. No, she'd reported the problem on New Year's Eve.

Danny moved the mouse to the Alarm Clock and set it back to the night of the big party at the Hilton. . . the night everything, for a while, had seemed to be going right.

Then he launched a program and watched the corner of the screen.

Nothing.

He sighed, slunk lower in his chair, and grabbed the half-finished bottle of Orangina on his desk. *What is going on? What am I missing?*

He finished the bottle in one long slug and absently clicked the up-arrow button on the Alarm Clock displayed on his screen. The date clicked forward to January 1. He clicked again: January 2. And again: January 3. *It's so easy to trick a computer...the poor thing has to trust us to tell it what time it really is.*

And then he nearly jumped out of his chair.

Why did we keep testing February 4 on the company's computers?

Because that's what Mrs. Javed's clock had said—when the programmers watched the video, *on January 3*. So her clock was running—Danny did the math—thirty-two days fast.

But Mrs. Javed first reported her problem to Danny on New Year's Eve! If her clock was a month fast even then... Danny flipped open a calendar and counted squares. So on the *real* December 31, Mrs. Javed's clock thought it was January 30. *The trigger date isn't February fourth*, Danny realized. *It's some date between now and January 30.*

With a faster heart rate, Danny set his Alarm Clock set to January 5, and launched WordWriter. No white dot appeared. He quit the program, set the clock to January 6, and launched WordWriter again. Nothing. And again: January 7, January 8, January 9 ... *Come on, you damn dot, I know this is how you like to come out. Why don't you do it?* January 18. January 19. January 20—

And then it happened. The white dot appeared on Danny's screen when the computer's clock said January 20.

Danny's thoughts whirled. *So we've got ourselves a time-bomb virus. It's set to go off on January 20, and it makes a little white dot on the screen. Or, if you're not very lucky, maybe it starts eating your files.*

He turned his calendar over, grabbed a pen, and began writing questions on the cardboard back.

Is the white-dot business the same as the file-eating thing?
What makes it start eating files?
Why isn't the virus in the finished program?

Why was Mrs. Javed's clock set ahead?

Then he wrote one more question and underlined it three times.

WHY DIDN'T SURvIVor SET OFF THE ALARM?

The week of January 7 was one of those weeks that made CNN look good. Events were unfolding at an amazing pace. There was so much hard news every night that the twenty-six-minutes-past-the-hour human-interest tales of second-graders building papier-mâché rain forests never made it into each newscast.

Ukrainian president Jurenko's heart surgery at Walter Reed Hospital had gone off without a hitch, to the immense relief of the diplomatic community, although his recuperation hadn't been as brisk as some would have liked. The third and final set of summit talks were frozen in mid-session, since several of the factious states refused to take part unless Jurenko was at the table. Now recovering at the hospital, Jurenko was expected to resume his duties in a matter of days. They were days of agonizing suspended animation for the White House, where the Administration dearly needed this foreign-relations coup.

At an air force test facility in Nine Lakes, California, a new technology was replacing the joystick for military pilots: voice control. In a specially modified flight simulator, air force pilots were being trained to operate their bombers through spoken command. Without the requirement of handling flight controls, a pilot would have both hands free for manipulating weaponry, thus allowing one flier to man each sortie instead of the usual two.

There were also, of course, a number of stories CNN did not cover. The news organization was largely unaware, in fact, that 110 computers and computer networks in the Southwest were already infected with a dangerous computer program; those in the computing community were calling it the Houston virus, named for the city where the first infections were discovered. There was no report on the congressional aide who was fired for tampering with a senator's mailing lists—and certainly no revelation that she was completely blameless; the senator's files were corrupted by the Houston virus that had managed to cross the country embedded in a file sent by telephone. No story covered the bewilderment of a technical-help agent at Apple Computer, who received a phone call reporting a monitor defect in which the upper-left screen dot was continuously lit.

And there was certainly no coverage of a strained and awkward memorial service held in a Roman Catholic church outside of Santa Clara, where thirty-five people honored the life of a brilliant young programmer who, as the pastor put it, had burned too brightly for this world.

chapter 11

January 13, 1994   "You, sir, are a man of your word," Michelle said. It took every ounce of her self-control not to puke at having to play the cute blond PR chick.

It was working, though. The guy was utterly hormone driven, with about as much brains as a grapefruit. His name was Ringo, of course.

"Hey, hey, I say I'm gonna get the job done, I get it done, you know what I'm saying? Doll like you comes in here, I says to myself, I says, Whoa! Now, there's someone with class, you know what I'm saying? There's a fine classy lady who deserves to be treated right. I told you I was going to put on extra shifts for you, did I not? And I did. I put on extra shifts for you, honey. Oh, we had to burn some midnight oil, sure we did. But for you, I'm happy to do whatever I can, you know what I'm saying?"

Michelle smiled and turned to inspect the boxes.

Fine little butt, Ringo thought.

The first run of 100,000, boxed and shrink-wrapped, was sealed into huge cardboard cartons now sitting on the printer's loading dock, but Ringo had left a few out for the blonde babe to look over. Most of the time, guys who came in here were corporate-suit types, guys who pushed him around like he was a gardener or something. That's why he liked this little filly. Perky, blonde, treated him nice. Cute little bod, too.

Michelle peeled the shrink wrap off one of the finished Master Voice packages. *So this is it*, she thought. *This is what we've been building all these months*. The heavy cardboard box inside looked great—the colorful Master Voice design was printed on shiny coated stock that gave the whole affair a slick sheen. She pulled the primary box out of its sleeve to take a look.

There, nestled in a Styrofoam shipping block, was the three-inch-square metal box that housed the arc chip; its cable to the Macintosh serial port was neatly folded and tied with a twist-tie. The microphone, complete with a Velcro patch to fasten it to the edge of the computer, lay in its own hollow of Styrofoam. Inside a plasticized-paper envelope was the manual—still with its just-printed, inky smell—and the two Master Voice software disks. It all looked sensational; Michelle had to give the Neanderthal bindery man a little credit for having done such polished work.

"They look terrific, Ringo. Really great. You've done a wonderful job," she said, aiming her most heart-melting smile directly at him.

Ringo stood up. "And lemme tell you this, too, awright? There's no other binder in the valley gonna do this for you. The thing is, is that they just don't work that fast. They don't have the facility, know what I'm saying? You would have had to build the box at one place, build the manuals at another, do the shrink wrap somewhere's else. . .but us, we see a fine customer like you, we say: Hey. Let's do the job right, you know what I'm saying? Let's do the job right, and then the next time they need a run— well, hey, they'll call us, won't they?" He was standing closer than Michelle liked, and his breath reeked of cigarettes.

She nodded. "You bet, Ringo. Get me the rest of the boxes by the end of next week, like we said, and I'll make sure you get lots of repeat business from us. OK?" She stepped tactfully away from his hulking presence and grabbed her purse from the couch against the wall. "The shipper is picking them up here?"

That Ringo had finished boxing the first run of Master Voice packages in four days was too good to be true. Michelle figured that the shippers would probably be late for the pickup; the law of averages dictated that she couldn't be so lucky twice in a row.

"Three o'clock, sweetie."

Fabulous, she thought. *In forty-five minutes, a couple of trucks are going to roll in here, pick up those boxes, and take them to the DHL terminal at the airport. A hundred thousand boxes en route to their new homes; a hundred thousand computers will never be the same. A star is born.*

She offered her hand. "Thanks again, Ringo. You've really saved the day for us." He took her hand with both of his and tried to look warmly into her eyes.

Michelle, however, just wasn't up for following through with the bimbo routine. She made a halfhearted hand-shaking motion, withdrew her hand briskly, and strode out.

"See you next week, Ringo," she called out.

Now, there's a spirited one, Ringo thought to himself as he watched her leave. Ringo knew that the good ones were the hardest to get.

As Michelle piloted her Civic out of the industrial park, she had to utter three shuddering primal grunts before she recovered from the clammy sleaziness of the bindery guy. He left such a bad taste in her mouth, in fact, that she almost forgot to gloat about the extra two weeks she'd helped Artelligence win. The packages would be on air freight by dinnertime, she knew...two full weeks before the scheduled ship date. Stroman would be ecstatic.

She merged with the other northbound traffic.

It wasn't simply a matter of riding the crest of the program's pre-release popularity, either, she reminded herself. That wasn't the only cause for celebrating the fact that, for the first time in software-publisher history as she knew it, a program had gone out the door *ahead of schedule*. Not counting their first two missed deadlines, of course.

No, Bob Stroman had made it more than clear to her that there were some critical business reasons for the timeliness. Dampening Lars Huntington's hopes was one. Most of the other reasons were Japanese, powerful, and eager to see whether or not Stroman-san could pull off what he had promised to do. The sooner those gents—whom Michelle had seen only twice at the office—started making some return, any return, on their investment, the happier they would be. And the more likely it would be that Artelligence would thrive and continue to grow. Of course, if they *hadn't* shipped on time...if no income started rolling in...if something went wrong...

She stopped herself. No need to dwell on precisely how much of the company's future depended on the success of the Master Voice project.

And why worry? In the last week, to Stroman's considerable joy, she had helped to pave the way for several co-marketing agreements with other companies. An audio-equipment maker in Edison, New Jersey, wanted to develop a wireless mike for the program, so that corporate brass could dictate memoranda even as they strolled the office. Sharp, by no small coincidence another company in which Mika had substantial holdings, was close to releasing a telephone module. Placed between the handset cord and the phone itself, it actually allowed Master Voice owners to telephone their own computers. That was Michelle's favorite; if she'd had that and a car phone, she could be getting work done on the computer even now, as she drove back to Santa Clara. She certainly hoped the boys in R and D would be able to decipher Gam's handiwork enough to let the program continue to grow and improve.

The boys in R and D. The boys in Sales. The boys in Finance.

She unconsciously shook her head as she drove. Sometimes she felt like a mother/sister figure, one of the company's sole footholds in reason and grace. No, a *lot* of the time she felt that way. And she knew that the Artelligence boys thought of her more frequently as a computer outsider—as a quietly efficient supersecretary—than as one of the boys, so to speak. Nothing new, she guessed. Especially not in this biz. Still, it baffled her that even as she pulled off coup after coup lately, the boys still seemed to value her cheerleading capacity more than her PR prowess.

Like the *PowerMac* review. She'd been sent an advance copy by an old friend at the magazine: a total triumph. The review was as glowing as the magazine's terse Consumer Reportsy, painfully objective tone allowed. The only thing they didn't like was that there were few foreign terms in the chip's dictionaries.

She adjusted her rearview mirror. *Well, fellows, I suppose you're only victims of your hormones. And centuries of stereotyping. I love you dearly, boys, but how about doling out a little credit?*

Danny's first act as acting head programmer was to remove the faceplates from the floppy-disk drives of the computers in the lab. He thought they weren't good for the programmers' morale—in any case, they weren't good for his.

His second act was to virus-proof each computer in the R and D lab. He installed his SURvIVor program on each, and then set its clock *back*, so that January 20, as far as the machines were concerned, wouldn't arrive for months.

For a surreal week, the programmers were in a peculiar limbo; the official Master Voice software had been rushed to the disk duplication firm several days ahead of schedule, so there was no actual programming work to do. Instead, Danny and the other programmers devoted their working hours to poring through the Master Voice code, in an effort to chart its structure. This documentation task had to be done sooner or later. But without Gam on hand to explain some of the program's twists and turns, it was slowgoing; for most of them, reading his brilliantly compact Assembly-language code was like trying to pluck out a melody on a strange new instrument.

As far as Danny was concerned, however, they weren't just charting; they were hunting. Hunting for a string of stray commands that didn't belong in the program. Hunting for something that watched every second of the clock, waiting for it to be twelve A.M. on January 20.

"What I don't understand," Charles kept muttering to Danny next to him, "is what happened to this white-dot business between the last beta version and the final shipping version of this program."

Danny glanced over. In characteristic busy-programmer style, Charles's shaving habits had fallen by the wayside, and his ponytail was now joined by a stubby incipient beard.

"Hey, you guys." Danny cleared his throat.

Skinner, frenetic, continued working at his Mac. The others paused to listen.

"I have a little confession to make."

"Jesus, Danny," moaned Charles. "I think we may have some slightly more important things to do than listen to you bare your soul. What'd you do, go through Michelle's lingerie drawer?"

"Shut up, Charles. I'm serious. A few weeks ago I snuck in when Gam wasn't in here. I planted SURvIVor on his hard disk. He never found out."

"Righteous, Danny," murmured Skinner.

"Don't you get it?!" exclaimed Danny. "It's been on his hard disk all this time! But it never went off! It never beeped, it never flashed a dialog box—*it never detected a virus.*"

"Danny, rilly," said Charles. "Let's assume that the virus thing got fixed, OK? Yes, it's possible that there was some little mother in a beta version. But I'm afraid you're gonna lose too many brain cells stewing about that virus thing."

Danny seemed not to hear him. "Look, I just want to know: if it was a virus, how come SURvIVor never beeped?"

"Maybe it wasn't turned on," offered Rod.

"Rod. It was turned on, OK? I'm telling you, my program sat there next to every version of Master Voice on Gam's disk, and it never once sniffed a virus."

"Personally," intoned Charles, "I think Danny needs to cultivate some extracurricular activities. Anyone up for a foreign film?"

There was a rap on the doorframe; it was Bob Stroman. "Gents? May I direct your attention to the intercom?"

Danny looked up carefully; he hadn't felt completely at ease around his boss since he made a fool of himself about the virus.

Stroman approached the phone next to Gam's empty cubicle

and hit the intercom button. "Go ahead, Michelle. . .I wanted the boys in the lab to hear your news."

Michelle's voice emerged from the speaker, with all the sound quality of a truck-stop pay phone. "Guess what, you guys?!" she said, a good-mood sparkle in her voice. "Master Voice is born! We got a break on every single element of the time line—the *shippers* even came an hour early! The one hundred thousand copies of Master Voice will be in the hands of its adoring public in two days!"

Stroman shook a triumphant fist in the air, and the programmers whooped. "Come and get us now, ye Japanese invaders!"

"That's right!" said Michelle. "We just crossed the finish line! Hey, how come I don't hear the champagne being uncorked?"

"We're saving it for your return to the office, Michelle," Stroman said to the phone set. "Drive safely." He hung up. "Didn't want to disturb you, gents. I just wanted my Reinforcement gang to hear the good news. A hundred thousand—*yess*!" He disappeared jubilantly into the hallway.

There was excited chatter and back slapping in the room around him. But Danny was less than exuberant; a doubt still nagged at him.

Lars was so large and imposing a man that the guys could always hear him puffing toward the door of Development, even if he hadn't alerted them over the intercom first. Luis, the lead programmer on the SpeakEasy project, once snickered when he pictured Lars wearing corduroys. "Can you imagine? Spontaneous combustion of the thighs," he told the others on the programming staff.

It hadn't taken long for somebody to set him straight on the propriety of such jokes. A week later, Lars summarily fired a programmer who took off an afternoon; it turned out that the young man had gone to attend his grandfather's funeral without asking Lars first.

Lars Huntington, Luis learned quickly enough, ran a tight ship.

"Lars alert," said someone. Nobody stopped what he was doing—it was no longer a secret that Lars sometimes quietly listened in on their activities over the intercom, so they never exactly spent their days telling dirty jokes—but there was an increased aura of concentration as they heard their employer stride into the room.

"How goes it, boys?" he asked. Nobody responded. "Luis? How about a report? Our time is running out, you know."

Luis stopped what he was doing. He ran his fingertips through his short-cropped black hair.

"We're going as fast as we can, Lars. But don't forget most of this stuff is written in Assembly language. It'll run like a jackrabbit—that's the nice part. But in the meantime, we really need some docu on it. We're making progress, but it's like translating the Rosetta stone."

Lars's bushy eyebrows knit together. This, of course, was the wrinkle he hadn't anticipated. The project should have been farther along by now. That meant Lars wouldn't be able to ship SpeakEasy, his own voice-recognition system, in time to destroy Artelligence as soon as he'd hoped.

He almost wished he could use Gam's code just as it was. *The stuff works already*, he thought. *What a pathetic waste of time that we're sitting and rewriting routines to make them* worse, *just so we won't get nailed in some copyright-infringement suit six months from now.* He almost wished he hadn't listened to Sheila's voice of reason on that point.

That wasn't all Lars wished, however. He also wished he had some kind of documentation of the work Gam had done on the program. And he wished he could pick up the phone and call Gam at home, just as he had done for months.

But now, of course, that wasn't an option.

But can you trust him, Lars? I mean he's just a kid, for God's sake.

He's nineteen years old, Sheila. I believe I can make it worth his while to stick to the plan.

What if he talks? What if he tells some girlfriend? Or his crazy mother? All they'd have to do is mention it at some party, somebody overhears...

He won't talk, Sheila.

How do you know, Lars? This is going to be over in two years. That's not the problem. The problem is persuading him to keep the secret for the next sixty *years.*

It won't be a problem, Sheila.

What power will you have over him once you've paid him? How will you keep him quiet?

Not a problem, Sheila.

Luis was still standing in front of him, saying something about rewriting key routines in C language.

Lars hadn't heard a word. He compensated for having let his mind wander by berating the young man.

"I don't pay you idiots to sit around picking your noses," he snapped. Luis shut up, eyes wide. "Don't you people realize what's at stake here? Didn't your mothers ever breed some competitive spirit into you?"

He clutched Luis by the shoulder, whirled him around, and shoved him back toward his desk.

"I want that program, *gentlemen*, I want it very soon. I don't give a goddamn what troubles you're having; if you're any good at all, you'll translate that code and have it ready for me by second quarter. I'll see to it that you're plenty motivated," he added with a stiff smile.

He turned his expansive back on them and strode out.

January 18, 1994   It had been a mildly depressing day for Danny. With a jolt of realization, he had glanced at his calendar: his time at Artelligence was rapidly drawing to a close, at least as far as his contract was concerned. In fact, he only had three more weeks of wrapping up loose Master Voice ends, and then he'd be answering help-wanted ads around the valley. It was definitely time to update the ol' résumé.

After dinner with Michelle, he returned to his apartment, threw the windows open, and poured a glass of OJ. He flipped on his Mac SE/30. The familiar sights and sounds greeted him: the little ding sound, the smiling computer face, the tiny white dot in the upper-left corner of the screen, which he'd never been able to get rid of. While the computer started up, Danny whipped some miscellaneous articles of clothing off his chair and into the Hefty trash bag he used as a laundry hamper.

He sat down and launched ParaGraph, his integrated word processor–painting program. He located his résumé file and brought it up on the screen.

Using the mouse, he placed the insertion point after "Freelance consultant," and hit the Return key. Looking down at his hands, he typed: "1993–94—Programmer, Artelligence Software Corp."

He looked up: the letters were still appearing on the screen, lagging behind his typing by at least a full second.

Danny frowned. *What the. . . ?*

He moved the mouse up to a pull-down menu of commands at the top of the screen, and clicked the mouse to make the menu appear. It did—after a second and a half. The computer was responding as though it were on sleeping pills.

It could be any number of things, Danny realized. A virus, of course. Or a bloated directory file. Or some multitasking software working in the background that he'd forgotten about.

Danny decided he could live with the slow motion for a moment; he only had to change one more thing on the résumé.

He decided to change the typeface of the words *Employment History* to Palatino bold. In normal Macintosh fashion, he selected the phrase using the mouse, and chose the font name from the menu at the top of the screen.

But now the mouse cursor froze, immovable, on the screen. There was a flickering of the screen pixels around the perimeter of the screen for two seconds, followed by an error message that only half appeared. He could barely make out the wildly flickering words "Sorry, a system error has occurred."

Goddammit. Danny hated system errors in commercial software; once they occurred there wasn't much he could do to figure out *why* they had occurred. He sighed heavily and wondered what sequence of events had caused the crash—when a hideous, loud, electrostatic buzz came out of the Macintosh speaker. Combined with the rapidly deteriorating screen image, the effect was terrifying. Danny quickly reached out and punched the Restart switch on the side of the computer. The screen went dark, and the start-up process began again—*dinggg*, said his computer.

He took a swig of OJ.

The computer started up normally. Same smiling Mac, same white pixel, same desktop.

Although Danny didn't notice immediately, everything was not, in fact, back to normal. First, had he looked in his System folder, he would have found five files he'd never seen before, called PG Temp-1 through PG Temp-5. These temporary files were left behind by the ParaGraph program he'd been using; when the program was in use, it transferred data in and out of these temporary files constantly. Under normal circumstances, the program deleted its temp files when the user quit the program. Because Danny hadn't had the chance to exit ParaGraph properly, the temp files were left behind in his System folder.

What Danny did notice, however, was that he couldn't find his ParaGraph program; it wasn't out on the gray "desktop" area of the screen where he usually left it. *That's odd.*

So Danny tried the next-best thing: using the mouse cursor, he double-clicked the file icon of his résumé, which would automatically launch ParaGraph, wherever it might be. Instead, a message appeared:

The file "9/93 Résumé" could not be opened or printed. The application is busy or missing.

OK

It was as unhelpful a message as Danny had ever read.

He was soon to discover, however, that the application—ParaGraph—*was* missing. It had begun to disappear even while he was using it five minutes earlier, vanishing virtually out from under him.

When Danny had used the font command, the Macintosh attempted to read a line of code in ParaGraph that no longer existed. It was as though someone tried to drive across a bridge that appeared on the road map, but in fact had collapsed in an earthquake. The result in the computer's case: a violent system crash.

Danny cursed and crossed the room to the bookcase where he kept his blue plastic Flintstones lunchbox. He popped open the lid and flipped through his collection of master disks. There it was: ParaGraph 2.0.

He went back to his Macintosh to recopy the program when he noticed something else: now his résumé was gone, too.

A cold lick of fear shot up from his stomach: he knew exactly what was happening. He'd seen it before. *Goddamn you, virus!*

He opened up a the directory window of his electronic Stuff folder as large as it could go, and read the number at the top: "17 items." *OK, great. Now*:

He closed the window and waited for sixty seconds, then reopened it: "15 items."

Jesus!

He left it open this time. The numbers at the top of the screen didn't change, since the Macintosh only counted a window's contents each time the window was opened—but Danny didn't need the counter to see the marching destruction. Individual file icons popped off the screen, leaving blank white space where they'd been, every sixteen seconds. Panicked, Danny slammed the power switch to off.

The Macintosh went dark and silent.

Danny was breathing hard. He clutched the front edge of the desk in an effort to stabilize his whirling thoughts.

There's something inside this computer . . . and it's the same thing that's in Mrs. Javed's computer. But what woke it up?

And why didn't my SURvIVor program alert me to the attack?

Danny struggled to make the connection. What did he have in common with Mrs. Javed? The white-dot screen infection. Master Voice software. What else?

The date. What's the date?

With some trepidation, Danny turned his Mac on again and checked the on-screen Alarm Clock: 1/30/94, it said. Of course! Danny had set it ahead during his experiments, and forgotten to reset it. To preserve what files hadn't yet been eaten, he switched the machine off again.

He desperately wished he knew what was happening. The feeling that something was inside his Mac, out of his control, made him frustrated and hot. And the thought that he knew almost nothing about it made him feel worse.

Why doesn't the final version of the program have this problem?

And then his jaw clenched involuntarily. *What if it does?*

He looked at his watch—10:45. He grabbed the phone and dialed.

"Charles? Listen, it's Danny. What're you doing now?" He listened to the response.

"Well, can't she watch TV by herself for an hour? I need you to meet me at the office. Big time. It's important."

Charles was already waiting at the front entrance when Danny arrived at Artelligence. The place looked different at night: the sleek and sculptured architecture looked alien and forbidding in the darkness.

"This better be good," said Charles.

"It is," said Danny. "C'mon."

They burst through the first set of doors. Hugo, the night man, looked up from his portable TV, recognized them, and buzzed them in.

"Evenin', gennelmen," he said broadly.

"Hi, Hugo," Danny blurted as he ran past the security console and down the hall toward the R and D lab.

Charles jogged beside him. "Danny, what's the deal?"

"We may be in some major hot water," Danny managed.

They burst into the R and D lab.

"OK. Isolate that Mac IIsi over there. Unhook it from the network," Danny panted. "I think I've got the key to the virus thing. The white dot, the disappearing files, the whole thing."

Charles, ponytail flopping, pushed his glasses up his nose and began to dismantle the connections between the IIsi and the other computers. "Perhaps Mr. Holmes would care to share his insight with his bumbling yet lovable assistant?"

"I'll do better than that. I'll show you."

Danny flipped on the IIsi. When it was finished starting up, he moved the mouse to the Master Voice control panel inside the System folder. "OK, look. *Voilà*. The last beta version of Master Voice, yes?"

Charles nodded. "To this point, my feeble mind is with you, O Sleuth."

"OK. Now we use the Alarm Clock, and we set the date ahead two days from today...to January twentieth. Like so. OK?"

Charles was intrigued.

"The next time we run any program—like I'm doing now—presto, the little white dot appears in the corner of the screen."

It did.

"So it's not February fourth, eh? So it's January twentieth. OK. But at least only the prototype was infected, and not the shipping copy, right?"

"Just hold your horses," Danny responded. He bent over and maneuvered the mouse again. "Now...if I'm right, this is the really scary part." He clicked the date-advancing button ten times, so that the clock now said January 30. And he restarted the computer.

"This is the really awful part."

When the computer was running again, Danny opened a few windows and watched their contents carefully.

"There! Charles!" He pointed to a folder called Archive Stuff.

Once every sixteen seconds, a file disappeared from the screen.

Charles wrinkled his nose. "Jeeeeesus H. Christ," he marveled. He stepped back to lean on the table in the middle of the room, trying to grasp the ramifications of what he'd just seen.

"So we're talking about a *two-stage* time-bomb virus?"

"You got it," said Danny. "It wakes up on January twentieth, yawns, looks around, and starts infecting everything in sight. And every time it spreads to a new computer, it marks its path with that little white dot in the corner of the screen."

"And then, ten days later, it gets hungry, and starts gobbling up everything on the hard drive," Charles concluded for him. "This thing was written by one malicious mother."

"But that's not the worst part," Danny told him soberly. "What I'm worried about is the *shipping* version."

Charles frowned. "But I thought we'd established that this virus wasn't on the final disk."

"Nope. We established that the *white pixel* syndrome—the virus's stage one—wasn't on the finished disk. We never determined that the finished disk didn't contain the virus at all."

"Whoa," protested Charles. "Last time I used my brain cells for anything constructive was today at five o'clock. Can we go slower?"

Danny smiled thinly. "This is why I needed you here, man. We've got to run a little test on the finished program."

He looked around for another computer to use; the IIsi, which he'd just infected, was now out of the running. After a moment, he tracked down a Macintosh SE on a desk in Shipping. He set it up in the R and D lab, turned it on, and examined its contents. Since it was used primarily for generating shipping labels, there was very little data on it. Charles found some floppy disks, and they made a backup copy of everything on the SE's hard drive. "Just in case I'm right about what's gonna happen," Danny explained.

When they were done, Danny changed the computer's clock to January 20 and ran a program.

"No white pixel," Charles acknowledged. "Either we're in good shape, and there's no virus, or we're in it deep."

Danny adjusted the date, click by click, until it said January 30. He restarted the Mac and held his breath.

After sixteen seconds, he saw a file disappear from the screen. His blood ran cold.

"Um. How many copies of this did Michelle send out last week?" ventured Charles.

Danny fell weakly into a chair.

"Like a hundred thousand," he responded.

chapter 12

NBC NEWS ● NEW YORK, NY ● TELE-PROMT-R ™

Good evening. I'm Bill Barton, sitting in for
Christopher Nyles, and this . . . is ActionEye News.

Our top story: a Long Island songwriter wins the
New Jersey lottery, to the happy tune of twenty
million dollars. Congress votes the so-called "guns
for butter" law into effect. And Kristi Loames will
have our special report, High Stakes in the Lower
Republics. You'll find out why Secretary of State
Henry Masso is biting his nails about the touchy
situation in the Commonwealth of Independent
States this weekend.

We'll have these stories, plus Grave Carmichael
on sports and Hank Johns on weather, after this.

January 19, 1994   It was nearly midnight by the time Michelle, Arnie McGivens, Stroman, and the other programmer
were all assembled in the lab. Danny and Charles hadn't performed any more experiments; they were running out of uninfected computers.

They did try running Danny's SURvIVor program, in an effor
to kill the virus. The program successfully detected the infection

and—at least according to its on-screen report—successfully killed it. Yet each time they started the computer up again, it became riddled with the destructive invisible program once again. SURvIVor clearly wasn't able to ferret out the virus's original hiding place.

"So what you're telling me is that this virus, or whatever it is, is on our master disk?" said Stroman angrily after Danny demonstrated his January 30 experiment for the new arrivals.

Danny nodded, still feeling ill.

"What about it, Michelle?" Stroman said, not feeling good about having been dragged out of bed for news like this. "Any chance we can stop the shipment?"

She shook her head helplessly. "We shipped Wednesday, mostly to the big mail-order houses. They probably turned the packages around the same day, sending them out to their customers. Those boxes are long gone."

Arnie was looking agitated, and kept glancing at Stroman to gauge his reaction.

"Well, why the hell didn't somebody run a virus checker on this thing?"

Danny swallowed. "Um . . . that's the thing we can't understand. Whatever this virus is, it's undetectable by virus checkers—until *after* it's infected a computer. So we thought the program was clean."

There was a moment of tense silence.

"Now I'm sorry I pulled so many strings to ship the product early," murmured Michelle. "If we hadn't shipped early, this thing would have just attacked our own computers in-house. We never would have exposed the rest of the world to it."

"Well, what are we going to do?" said Stroman irritably. "We don't know a goddamn thing about this virus. We don't even know *if* it's a virus. How are we supposed to recall a hundred thousand—oh, Jesus." The realization of the potential damage was spreading through the room.

Danny was staring at Michelle as though seeing her for the first time.

"You're right, Michelle," he said quietly.

Michelle exchanged mystified glances with Stroman. "About what?"

Danny stood up. "If we hadn't shipped Master Voice early, the virus would have been confined to this building. It would have woken up *right here*, in-house, on January thirtieth—two days before we were supposed to ship.''

He met Stroman's gaze.

''*And that is exactly the way Gam designed it to work.*''

Arnie: ''Oh God—''

Charles: ''What the hell is that supposed...''

Michelle: ''Wait a minute, he would never—''

Rod: ''*Oh*, man. *Oh*, brother. I don't like this.''

''*Hold it*,'' Stroman barked. They looked at him.

''Go on, Danny.''

Danny spoke slowly, trying to fit all the pieces into place. ''Listen. *Why* would the virus be set to start going crazy on January thirtieth?'' he demanded. ''Whoever wrote it didn't just pick the date off the wall.''

The silence in the room was taut and tangible.

''Look, you guys. We were supposed to ship on February first, *get it*? This is no accident! This thing winds up in *our* program, two days before *our* ship date? There's no way this is just *some* virus. It wasn't written by *some*body out there.''

Rod was saucer eyed. ''We've been sabotaged?''

''You got it,'' Danny said. Stroman sighed painfully.

''I bet the idea was,'' Danny went on, ''to have it blow up in our faces, just before we shipped, so we'd have to pull Master Voice off the market. It'd be back to the drawing board for weeks while we fiddled around on a wild goose chase, trying to find what went wrong, going through another beta-test cycle, the whole thing.''

''Well, Gam didn't do it,'' declared Michelle firmly.

''OK, then explain this: who took the little white-pixel indicator out of the final version of the program?''

He searched their faces for a flicker of understanding.

''There's only one person who could have fixed the code. That dot was a telltale; a signal. It was a debugging tool! While he was writing the code, he could tell at a glance whether his virus had worked or not, or whether the first stage had been activated or not, just by checking for that little white dot. Of course, none of *us* would ever *see* the white dot, because he planned to take it out long before the virus was supposed to wake up on January twentieth. And he did.''

Skinner was beside himself. ''So, like, the only reason we

found out at all, is 'cause of that lady and her video, right? God!''

"What about the two-stage business, Danny?" asked Arnie, stroking his beard unconsciously.

"I don't know."

"Probably to make sure the office was good and infected," offered Charles. "Ten days would give the virus plenty of time to spread, behind our backs, to every network in the company. That way everybody would start screaming at the same moment."

There was a moment of tense silence. Stroman looked pale. Danny closed his eyes for a moment, trying to find some way out of the mess. When he opened them, he was staring at the waste-basket under Gam's desk. *What's that?*

Michelle felt a violent, overpowering surge of helplessness and betrayal. "But *why*? Why would Gam sabotage his own work? Why would he deliberately destroy everything he'd built over two years? He *cared* about his work!"

Danny squinted at the wastebasket.

Arnie agreed with Michelle. "And why would he throw away the money? He was lined up for some major royalties on this thing, not to mention the salary we were paying him."

Stroman ran a hand through his short gray-flecked hair. "Jesus. What the hell did he have against *us*?" He looked at Danny, who was walking, stooped over, slowly toward Gam's desk, as though drawn by an invisible force.

"Danny, what are you doing?"

Danny stopped at the desk and crouched down. With one hand, he grabbed the wastebasket. With the other, he reached just inside the rim and peeled off a small pink slip of paper.

"I can tell you why," he said quietly.

Michelle exchanged mystified glances with Stroman. "Why what?"

Danny stood upright, still staring at the scrap of pink paper that clung to his extended fingertip. "Why he bothered."

Stroman held out his hand for the tiny square of paper. Danny gave it to him.

"Nice code. Love the V-mem routines," Stroman read aloud.

It was a pink Post-It note. . .it was *the* pink Post-It note; weeks of janitorial services had failed to dislodge it from the inside lip of the wastebasket.

"I don't get it," Stroman said weakly.

"It's the answer to all of this," Danny said, becoming angry. "I found this thing over a month ago, and didn't think anything of it. Look—whose handwriting is that?"

He showed everybody. Nobody knew.

Danny could have predicted that, of course.

"It comes from somebody outside this company. It comes from whoever hired Gam to plant a time bomb in our program."

Stroman slumped weakly into his chair. "Huntington," he said miserably.

"What?!" blurted Skinner.

Arnie looked surprised. "Oh, come on, Bob. Would he go that far?"

And suddenly Michelle stood up, livid. "He's gone a lot farther than that!" They looked at her.

"Remember the ad we saw? For a speech-recognition product from Huntington? And we couldn't figure out how he pulled it off, remember? *That's* how they were able to come up with a program in such a short time. *It's our program!*"

"What?" asked Rod, not following.

She was staring into space. "They've got our program," she murmured.

It was finally making sense to Danny. "So Gam would write the code here, and then turn it over to Huntington, and they gave him feedback . . ."

Arnie finished the thought. ". . . and then, when Master Voice got delayed, because of a virus infection we would discover two days before shipping, Huntington would beat us to market."

Stroman swore viciously. Danny had never heard him so distressed. Looking haggard and small, he slouched even deeper in a chair. His fists were pressed close to his head in a reflexive posture of self-preservation; tufts of flecked brown hair protruded from between his clenched knuckles.

Stroman saw it all coming unhinged. If this were all true, he was buried alive. How could he ever have trusted that kid? How could he make himself so vulnerable? Why didn't he see it coming?

The virus was out of control now, beyond their reach. What would have been a dirty enough trick had backfired on everybody—even its authors. The booby trap designed to gum up the works in-house was now about to explode all over the country, taking thousands of gigabytes of data with it: research, contracts, documents, brainstorms, archives, proposals, records, artwork, compositions, treaties, schedules, formulas... all wiped away. It could go anywhere from there; the greatest miracle of the Information Age—the awesome interconnectedness of the computers on every desk, in every office, at the end of every phone line— was about to become its greatest menace.

His mind struggled to keep control of his body; as it was, he was bathed in a cold sweat. Images flashed through Stroman's mind: faces of 10 million computer users losing years of work, headlines castigating Artelligence, armies of lawyers wielding class-action suits... Lars Huntington riding triumphantly into the breach with a rival, uninfected program... a nightmarish phone call from Mika Corporation...

Panic washed over him: a sensation of loss and helplessness he hadn't felt since childhood. His mouth fell open. A single, agonized vowel sound escaped his lips.

There was silence.

Arnie tried valiantly to fill the void. "Listen, Bob, we're not dead yet," he said gently. "All we have to do is make sure the media doesn't get ahold of this. We can't let them track the virus back to Artelligence."

His words penetrated Stroman's delirium.

"No!" he glowered suddenly, lifting his head. What little fight was left in him rose to the surface.

"No. We won't conceal anything. There's more at stake here than this company. At this moment, losing Artelligence would be a small price to pay, if we can derail the chaos we're headed for. We're going to start by telling the press everything we know. They're going to hear about it from *us*." He was standing straighter now, looking like a man possessed. "The only way we can stop this thing is by warning everybody in sight. As soon as possible."

Arnie and Michelle were watching him closely. They'd never heard him speak like this. Until today, he had always put the company before everything else. Danny glanced around the room. Rod, who hadn't uttered a syllable, looked deeply frightened. Skinner was a bundle of nerves. Charles peered through his dark lenses, deep in thought.

"You're right," Michelle added. "From a PR standpoint, if Artelligence *can* be saved, that's the only way it'll happen—if we're up front about it. But if we keep quiet, and the virus gets traced back to us . . . we're finished.''

"Along with everyone else in the country," Charles murmured.

"All right. All right, listen to me," Stroman said suddenly. "This is what we're going to do."

He wiped his face with both hands, slowly, top to bottom, psychologically regrouping. Then he snapped into action.

"Michelle, you're going to orchestrate the biggest PR blitz in history. Hire temps. Do what you have to do. I mean, I want you to call *every* name in your contact list—I don't care if it's *Boys' Life*—and tell them what's going on. Tell them we'll have the problem fixed by the time the virus is triggered on the twentieth— Jesus, that's tomorrow—but that they should set their clocks back as a precaution. Tell them to tell everyone they know. We've got to get the word out, or Artelligence won't be the only thing wiped off the face of the earth."

She nodded.

"Arnie, call all the beta testers; they may have been spreading the thing for weeks without knowing it," continued Stroman. His face was taut with the strain. "Call them first thing in the morning. Tell them everything you know, and find out everything *they* know. Find out who they've been in contact with, who they've shown Master Voice to, whether or not they have modems. Get back to me as soon as you've got a picture."

He looked at the programmers around him, summoning his strength. "Look, gentlemen. The chips are down. I think you can understand what's at stake here. We are talking about a virus that spreads very quickly, and destroys data. And we just sent *a hundred thousand copies* of this virus into the world.

"But that doesn't mean that only a hundred thousand people are at risk. Every computer is connected to every other. Maybe not by cables. Maybe not even by the phone wires. But by accidents, by user groups, by buddies. It doesn't matter where you live, or how isolated you think you are . . . this virus is going to be able to get to you. It has a hundred thousand *starting points*.

"But we have time to act; the bomb is still ticking. We can find it. I believe in you. We didn't come this far to be thwarted at the eleventh hour."

He turned, all business. "That means you have one mission. *Find the virus*. I mean study *every single line* of code, no matter how long it takes. Somewhere in that mound of spaghetti, there's a couple of pages of code that has no business being in the pro-

gram. We won't sleep until we find it. Danny—I want you in
charge of the hunt. Report back to me every time you learn
anything."

He looked down for a moment, then stood up straight, his voice
level.

"You're looking for something that was designed to *kill us*,
gentlemen. To survive, we've got to kill it first."

The programmers, with time pressing like a gun to their heads,
hastened to their computers. Danny had a feeling they wouldn't
be getting any sleep tonight.

"Bob?" he asked. Stroman paused at the door. Danny could
sense that Stroman was fighting to remain optimistic, but there
was one thing that had to be asked.

"What'll we do when we find it?"

Stroman said nothing for a moment. "We'll cross that bridge
when we come to it, Danny," he finally said. "All I know is, if
Lars wants a fight, he's got one."

He slammed the door behind him.

As with a human virus, the spread of a computer virus accel-
erates geometrically among tightly packed populations. In its first
regeneration, as it spread from program to program within the
confines of a single hard drive, a single copy of the Houston virus
had become 32; as the virus spread by cable and disk to other
hard drives, the second generation split into 829 copies, and so
on.

By January 21, the Houston virus had spread to over two thousand computers and networks in the Southwest states and beyond,
its presence marked each time by a glowing pixel in the upper-
left corner of the computer screen. Few of its victims in the computing community even noticed it. After all, there are over
300,000 pixels on a typical Macintosh monitor. Even those few
who did notice something amiss with their monitors couldn't possibly understand what had caused the problem.

Until Artelligence made its first shipment of Master Voice
packages, the virus's spread had been somewhat localized. That
is, its spread was primarily limited to beta tester Clive Witmark's
immediate contacts, their contacts, and *their* contacts—associates,
networked co-workers, and computing friends. Large otherwise
isolated communities, such as universities and scientific establish-
ments, were thus far unaffected by the virus.

The one hundred thousand Master Voice packages that were opened and installed during the first days of the new week, however, gave the virus a healthy foothold in thousands of new computing communities; it was as though a flu virus had been sprayed on towns and cities by a squadron of airplanes. Most people installed Master Voice as soon as they received it, and thousands upon thousands of infection cycles began again.

Worse, the virus in the finished Master Voice software was a much more devastating strain than the one descended from Clive Witmark's computer—this one left no tracks, no white dot. The new epidemic was undetectable—and several thousand times more widespread.

On nearly 10 percent of the affected computers, virus-guard programs had been installed. And, to an extent, these programs proved useful. As the Master Voice software was run for the first time, releasing the virus's first stage, the virus-watchdog programs beeped wildly—one beep for every program infection attempt— and refused to allow the infestation to proceed. Yet, as with any virus attack, this alarm only signaled the user that something had been infected. But it provided few clues to the virus's source, the path it had traveled to the hard drive being invaded, or the nature of the virus. Worse, because these virus-protection programs detected nothing wrong with the Master Voice software itself, they never succeeded in completely cleaning out a computer; as soon as the program eradicated the infections from other software, Master Voice immediately attempted to begin the infection cycle again. For owners of anti-virus programs, the result was an unending and unendurable torrent of warning beeps and dialog boxes.

Hardest hit, of course, were the networks in companies where Master Voice itself was installed. Thomson, Cheney, and Walter, an accounting firm in Chicago, was completely overrun with the virus inside of an hour. In Durham, North Carolina, another easy target was the new pan-campus Macintosh terminal system, recently installed by Duke University at a cost of $1 million. The oceanographic institute at Wood's Hole, Massachusetts, was another lattice of interconnected computers that the virus easily navigated. In Little Rock, Arkansas, a multimillion-dollar astronomical institute and deep-space telescope facility fell victim.

At the very stroke of January 20, in the middle of the night, the replication instructions in the viral program code executed itself. It did its spreading invisibly, silently, and efficiently, and then lay dormant.

Then, once every sixteen seconds, each copy of the virus consulted the Macintosh clock to find out if it was January 30 yet.

The virus that had infected the Macintosh Quadra at the blood lab of the Walter Reed Hospital's Cardiothoracic Unit on January 15 did not come directly from an installed Master Voice program. In fact, it was a thirty-eighth-generation descendent of Clive Witmark's originally awakened viral invader. En route, it had crossed nine hard drives, been transmitted twice by modem, was inadvertently copied from a floppy disk three times, had spread on seven networks, and had infected one program from another on the same disk too many times to count. The virus had finally been downloaded to an administrative computer elsewhere in the hospital complex from MedNet, a national physician's modem service, riding in a demonstration version of a medical-office management program.

Its most recent host was the hospital's sophisticated custom relational database called CTU-Base. The hospital had commissioned it for tracking the statistics, medications, and even the insurance and payment status of post-operative patients. One of them, only days away from being released from the hospital, was President Vladimir Jurenko of the Ukraine.

January 21, 1994   In three days, Danny had only slept a total of five hours. His senses were both dulled and sharpened: every stimulus seemed to be grating or painful, and yet he could tell that his brain wasn't processing as well.

A caterer had arrived just after midnight with a roomful of cold cuts and salad; half-filled plates cluttered the computer lab as the programmers tried to eat, became engrossed in charting the pro-

gram, and then left the physical world—and the sandwiches—
behind.

Danny's eyes stung from staring at his thirteen-inch monitor,
poring over the code, looking for anything out of place. It was
infuriating: he had almost reached the end of the listing, and there
were never more than a few lines whose purpose the team hadn't
been able to puzzle out.

Like this passage, for example:

```
clr.l      -(sp)
move.w     dCtlRefNum(a1),d0
not.w      d0
lsl.w      #5,d0
ori.w      #$C000,d0
move.w     d0,-(sp)
clr.l      -(sp)
move.l     #-1,-(sp)
tbx        GetNewWindow
move.l     (sp)+,a0
move.l     a0,getDateTime(a4)
move.w     dCtlRefNum(a4),wKind(a0)
jmp        lin(28333)
```

It was all perfectly legitimate, part of the routines that drew
one of Danny's custom dialog boxes. The only instructions he
didn't recognize were the last four lines, which were probably
pointers to an extension somewhere else in the code. Rod, ever
the Saint Bernard, kept careful, studious notes, and they had
nearly completely charted the program; nowhere could they find
a several-page stretch of Assembly code that didn't have to do
with the program's speech-recognition capabilities.

Michelle, in the meantime, was only slightly better rested. She
had equipped a telemarketing firm with the mailing lists that had
been faxed to her from the mail-order companies. The lists included the names of everyone who had received the first batch of
product. The telemarketing firm was instructed to call every single
name on the list and explain the possibility that a virus might be
present, and to take the immediate precaution of setting the computer's clock back one year.

As she wearily hung up after leaving another message for her college roommate—now a correspondent for CNN's Future Watch technology segment—she knew in her heart that the tele-marketing idea was doomed to failure. First of all, the phone numbers were a problem. Many of the customers had failed to provide phone numbers when they ordered the product. Michelle reasoned they were probably trying to avoid landing on a million Mac-product mailing lists; for one contradictory moment, she cursed the telemarketing industry.

Worse, she knew that, for most of the customers, it was too late; the infection cycle had already begun.

To this point, Michelle hadn't contacted the broadcast networks. If Danny and the others were wrong in their assumptions about the virus's behavior, such national negative coverage would destroy Artelligence. This was not a time to cry wolf, she figured. Nonetheless, she had called each network a number of times, climbing as far up the assistant-to-the-assistant ladder as she dared, making sure she'd know whom to call if the moment arrived—the moment when the programmers had come up with some way to stop it.

Down the hall, draped in his desk chair, Bob Stroman's mind ran in the same well-worn circles. Of *course* this was some plot of Huntington's; it was completely in character for Lars. A file-eating virus? An ex–Huntington programmer at the helm, writing in the cryptic Assembly language few people could read? A time-bomb virus set to awaken just before the ship date?

It made perfect sense.

He'd phoned everyone he could think of to phone. The lawyers were already scrambling . . . but how would they prove the connection to Huntington? And then there was the copyright issue; Stroman vowed to rip Huntington's code to shreds in search of similarities to Master Voice. That is, *if* Huntington ever shipped a voice-recognition package. And if it was in fact the same code, Stroman knew, he'd prosecute to within an inch of his life.

Not for the first time, Stroman thought about Gam. The kid had never been terribly well adjusted, of course . . . always angrily defensive, condescending and manipulative to co-workers, tight-lipped about his past, his family. . . . Once again, Stroman had to wonder about Gam's bizarre plane accident.

Could it have been suicide?

And then, for a fleeting moment, an even darker thought crossed his mind. He'd known for years that Lars Huntington would do anything to protect his business. But *anything . . .* ?

His speaker phone chirped.

He hit the speaker button. "Stroman," he said.

"Bob, it's Danny. I think we've found something."

God, the boy sounded exhausted. "I'm listening."

"Well, we found a funny side road in the program. We found a jump-to-subroutine instruction, really, that had no business being where it was in the code."

"OK?"

"So we looked at the routine it directed us to. It was miles away. In a different part of the program. So we opened that up. It could easily be part of the viral code. It's a GetSpecs routine that goes out to the disk and returns a list of applications on the mounted volume. Now, that's something the real code *might* need to do. I mean, when you say to the computer, 'Open a spreadsheet,' it's got to know where your spreadsheet program is. You with me so far?"

Stroman was sitting up straight now. "Sort of."

"OK. So we wanted to find out how it used this information. So we followed it to *another* pointer instruction. One that sent us way back to the beginning of the listing. I mean, it's jumping all over the place. So then we—"

Stroman cut him off. "Danny, just give me the punch line, will you? What's the upshot?"

There was only a moment of silence. "Well, I guess the upshot is that there is no virus planted in the program."

Stroman's head jerked in confusion.

"The program *is* the virus."

Sheila wasn't looking forward to this meeting. Her floppy leather briefcase in hand, she walked nervously down the stairwell to the conference room.

Lars Huntington was already seated. The meeting wasn't his idea. He had the look of a king who'd been summoned for a consultation with his interior decorator—an expression that said "I've got better things to do." The two other committee members arrived as Sheila sat down.

"All right, what is it?" said Lars.

Dick Rankert, Huntington's head of R and D, had never been much for Lars's autocratic style. Normally, he wasn't cowed at all, but on this occasion, he took a deep breath before he spoke.

"Lars, we have a little problem," he began. As he spoke, Lars scowled at the other two committee members. Both were staring at the tabletop. Both knew about whatever it was already.

Lars didn't appreciate communication that went on behind his back.

Rankert went on. "Artelligence shipped their Master Voice program ahead of schedule, Lars. They shipped last week."

At first, all Lars could think about was the sales advantage an early ship date gave them. "Those scum," he snapped. "All right. We'll just work a little bit faster, that's all. We'll keep the programmers a little bit later every day."

He prepared to push himself away from the table. "Is there anything more?"

Rankert was looking at him, scratching his graying crew-cut hair. "No, Lars, I don't think you understand the problem." Rankert was starting to get nervous; Huntington had been known to shoot the messenger. "It's the virus."

Sheila bailed him out. "According to your time line, the virus was supposed to activate Saturday. Two days before they were going to ship. But they shipped early, Lars. They sent the boxes out already. The virus is out there." She swallowed. "I think we'd better come clean with this."

"And what exactly does that mean, Sheila?"

Uh-oh, she thought. *There go the veins in his temples.*

"You know very well, Lars. We're responsible for this. We're responsible for infecting another company's master disk. We can't just sit back while a virus eats up hard disks all over the country. This was not the purpose of our plan." She glanced at the other two committee members. "Look, when we voted on this, the idea just was to hold up their development a little. The idea was to trip them up in-house. Give 'em something to chew on for a while so we could finish SpeakEasy. Make 'em a little nervous, right?"

Lars's face was expressionless.

"It's out of control, Lars. If he programmed the thing right, it's going to start eating data in a couple of days. *Lots* of data." She glanced at Rankert for confirmation.

"We need to alert people, Lars," concluded Rankert. "We need to tell Artelligence so they can tell their people. You were trying to wound Artelligence—not the whole damn world, right?"

Lars still wasn't responding.

"You're not going to sit here and let it destroy the lives of people all over the country, are you, Lars? Innocent people. They weren't supposed to be part of this."

Sheila watched Lars slowly swivel his head to look at the committee member who hadn't yet spoken. It was Chad Huntington, Lars's nephew—the most spineless, pathetic, talent-free CFO Sheila ever hoped to meet. The guy cooked the company's books like a short-order chef—to suit Lars's palate. Chad voted only one way at meetings: Lars's way. Chad was thirty-five and still lived with his parents; his mother, Lars's sister, had persuaded Lars to hire him despite his utter lack of training or experience. *Here we go again*, Sheila thought, spotting Lars's famous "Back me up, boy" look.

But Chad said nothing. Eyes wide as saucers, he just looked at Lars like a deer caught in the headlights.

"Chad, may I have your thoughts?" asked Lars with cruel faux-politesse.

Chad cleared his throat. Sheila and Rankert exchanged glances.

"I. . .I guess it's not right to make innocent people, you know, suffer," he began. "I mean, couldn't we just—I don't know—"

But he had said enough. Lars smashed the tabletop with his fist. Hard. Sheila flinched.

"I don't think you people under*stand*," he snarled. "This is *business*. In business, we do not *hold hands*. We do not aid the *enemy*. And we most certainly do *not* shoot our own feet off in the public eye!"

He glared at each of them.

"Business is war. We compete. We struggle. We sacrifice the weak so that the strong may survive. If innocent bystanders fall in the way, I'm sorry. We are all sorry. But the matador does not leave the ring when a few spectators get spattered with blood."

Lars was breathing hard, his pudgy nostrils flaring.

"We have a choice here. We can go to our rivals: the people who have made it their ambition to *crush us*, need I remind you . . .the people who have been working for ten years to teach *us* a lesson. We can go to them and admit defeat. We can say, 'Oh, we're sorry, we planted a virus in your program, but we were wrong. Please, help yourself to a slice of market share.'

"Let's think for a moment. What will happen then? They will alert their users. They'll fix the virus, their product will flatten us like a steamroller. And then our little business plan will hit the front pages. What happens to Huntington? We go to jail. *You* people go to jail. The company dies. Everything we've worked for dies. Is that what you want? *Is it*?'' he shrieked.

Nobody moved. Not an eyelash twitched.

''Or''—his face changed—''we could do nothing. They can't trace that virus. They have no evidence whatsoever. There's not a chance in hell that they could track it back to us. All right, they have an infected master disk. It's happened before, at other companies. Could've happened anywhere. Could've crept in at the disk duplicators, I don't know.

''So what happens? Yes, some data gets wiped out. So a few housewives lose their favorite meat loaf recipes. Big deal—if they're smart, they've made backups. Word gets out: Artelligence products are infected. Don't buy them. The company looks bad: poor quality control. They didn't check before shipping? People think: 'Holy Jesus, I'd better wait for that *other* voice-recognition package.' We'll send out a couple press releases: *We*, at least, screen our master disks for viruses. *We*, at least, care for the customer.

''We win. Artelligence loses.'' He snapped his fingers. ''Is it really such a difficult decision?''

Chad was looking greenish with the intensity of his discomfort. Sheila shot Dick Rankert a grave glance.

''Lars, be reasonable,'' she began. ''Look, I don't think it's as dire as all of that. Why don't we—''

Lars cut her off, booming. ''Why don't we *what*, Sheila? Why don't we *slit our own throats*?'' He was shaking slightly. ''No, Sheila. I'll tell you what we're going to do. I'm good at predictions. Let me try a little prediction now, shall I?'' He looked maniacally at each of their faces.

''We're going to take an executive committee vote. That's how we do things around here, right? The good old democratic way. We're going to settle this issue right now.'' A wall of mistrust grew in Sheila.

''But before we vote, I want to tell you something. I started this company. I built it from the ground up. In the early years, I wrote the manuals. I took out the ads. I designed the goddamn *boxes*.'' He stabbed the tabletop with a stout index finger.

''So I *think* I may know a little something about this business. I just *might* know what I'm doing. Maybe that never occurred to you people.'' He paused, almost as though expecting a response.

''Now. On this particular issue, I know the correct course of

action. I believe I've made it more than plain: we will do nothing.
We will let Artelligence wallow in their own incompetence.

"But I said we're going to vote, and I mean we're going to
vote. But there's something I want to make clear to you. I want
to talk about consequences."

Uh-oh, thought Sheila.

"Chad, I certainly expect you'll support me in this. You're a
young man, with a bright future—why, this entire corporation
could be yours one day." He leaned over until he was almost in
Chad's face to whisper, "But you vote against me on this and
you'll be back in your mother's house all day long, wetting your
bed because nobody will hire you. I'll make certain of that."

He turned to Rankert. "And you, Dick—I feel certain reason
will prevail with you. You must remember that it would be a
special shame if I had to fire you this afternoon—let's not forget
the pension plan you'd be throwing away. Not an inconsiderable
token of my appreciation for loyalty."

Rankert winced, struggling with his conscience. It was true: in
another year, he stood to receive a colossal lump payment from
Huntington. The pension fund was indeed Lars's way of keeping
his employees "loyal"—of keeping their mouths shut when Lars
practiced his less savory business tactics. And for fifteen years,
Rankert had stood by quietly, suffering from conscience twinges
at first, but gradually accepting the way things were. Was it worth
throwing away a gigantic retirement sum, a payment his family
had been counting on for years?

He turned to Sheila and smiled. "And, Sheila. Sweet Sheila,
our voice of conscience and reason. Vote however you choose,
my dear. But you know how I feel about disloyalty."

He paused for a moment, choosing his words carefully. "I simply want you to remember—I want all *three* of you to remember—that God rewards the loyal, and punishes the betrayer. Think
of Gam Lampert. A young man with so much to offer." Lars
flicked his hand airily. "Of course, who knows how cause and
effect works in this world. But perhaps he became covetous, and
that's why he was struck down. I simply want you to remember
what becomes of traitors."

Sheila's throat constricted, and her adrenaline rushed. "You
murderer! You *did* kill him!" she screamed, tears welling in her
eyes. "You disgusting, pathetic *asshole*!"

Lars reached out to grab her wrist. The pain was enough to

make her stop breathing. "No, no, Sheila," he cooed. "We don't use that language in our little family." Using her wrist like a pole, he guided her back into her chair; she choked back a sob. "I'm only saying I want you to consider carefully before you cast your vote."

He released her wrist, which she immediately cradled in her lap.

"Frankly, I'm surprised at you, my dear." He swiveled to face her, shifting his corpulent frame in the chair at the head of the table. "You have been with this company as long as I have. Eighteen years at my side, Sheila. Don't you remember the day Bob Stroman and I hired you to type up our incorporation papers? Just the three of us. Remember how we used to rush around to computer fairs, showing off our little circuit board? And there you would be, vacuuming the sawdust off the floor of our booth before every show. So that we would look like a good, reputable company."

Her shoulders were tense. Rankert and Chad wore bleak expressions.

"Nothing has changed, Sheila. We still have a reputation to keep. We still have to protect impressions."

She shifted miserably in her chair.

"Now, Sheila. All I ask is that you, shall we say, vacuum the floor of our little booth one more time. If you tell me you're going to vote against me, that's certainly your choice. But I cannot tolerate disloyalty, Sheila."

"Lars, I—" She struggled to get out the words, tears still visible on her cheeks. "Please. You *must* know this isn't right. Those people out there have done nothing to deserve what they're about to get! Infected with a virus *you* created, Lars. People who will lose months or years of their work. Records. *Whole lives*, Lars . . ." Her voice was rising, trying to preempt the explosion she saw building in him. "What have they done to deserve this, Lars? *What have they done?*"

"I'll *tell* you what they've done!" Lars shrieked. He half stood, planting his palms on the table and leaning over her.

And now his voice was a whisper.

"They bought *his* products: they supported *his* efforts to defeat me. And *that* is why they deserve it, Sheila. When the day of judgment comes, *I* will be at the head of the table, laughing at the rest of you as you struggle with your consciences. Because I do justice, Sheila. I punish those who deserve punishment. And I reward those who remain loyal.''

He was breathing through his flared nostrils. A tiny fleck of spittle bubbled in the corner of his mouth.

''And I would have rewarded you, too, Sheila. I saw promise in you. You've seen the company grow, and stood by me. I would have rewarded you.'' A moment passed, and the storm seemed to wane. Lars guided his bulk back into the chair, and the furrow in his brow grew shallower.

''But I've taken enough of your time, my good people. You've made your positions clear now, and so have I. Let us vote. Do we condemn our own company to death? Or shall we let market forces do what they will, and ride them to success?''

He thought, but did not say: . . . *and bury Robert Stroman at last?*

Stroman rounded the corner into the lab, where the team was clearly at the edge—unshaven, grumpy, and exhausted. Michelle, on a break, was doing her best to give Charles a shoulder rub.

''How're my boys?''

Only Michelle looked up. ''Hi, Bob.''

''Gentlemen, may I interrupt?''

They gradually stopped what they were doing and looked Stroman's way.

''Listen, ah . . . I wanted to bounce something off you.'' He noticed how bloodshot their eyes were.

''It's about this virus, and—first of all, I wanted to apologize for not taking it more seriously when you guys first presented it to me. I guess I just wanted this project to work so much I . . . well, anyway. I'm sorry.''

Their expressions didn't change.

''Anyway. Now, don't get alarmed or anything, but I need to know something about this virus of ours. I guess I'm just a natural worrier, but there's something I need you to give me a straight answer about.'' He sat down.

''Could this virus migrate to UNIX?''

A terrible light dawned for Charles. ''Jesus,'' he sighed.

Michelle glanced at their faces in hopes of getting a translation. ''I don't get it,'' she said. ''I thought eunuchs were little castrated guys.''

Danny had little patience. "No, Michelle. UNIX machines are the big mainframes. The computers that run the military, the government, the universities. The banks. The satellites. The phone system. Basically, the country."

Stroman's eyes were closed as though he couldn't bear to listen anymore.

"If this thing crawls into the UNIX and mainframe world," Skinner volunteered, "it could get onto the InterNet!"

Danny shot an explanatory glance at Michelle. "InterNet is the phone network that connects every mainframe in the United States. Like the national highway system, except it's made of phone lines. Every corporation, branch of government, and satellite hooks into the InterNet." At this moment, he didn't want to think about it.

Stroman was focused, intent; he was trying to stave off the nightmare that was taking form too fast for him to cope. "Danny. You know more about these viruses than I do. Could a virus written for the Mac survive in the UNIX environment?"

Danny thought a moment, trying to piece together what he knew of the virus code.

"I need to know," Stroman prompted. "If this thing gets onto the InterNet, it won't be about people losing a few files," he said. "It'll be about hospitals and communications and air traffic... people losing their lives."

He was holding the back of a chair tightly.

"We're safe," Danny said. Charles was nodding, having arrived at the same conclusion.

"Yeah. Assembly language is machine specific," Charles added. "In fact, it's processor chip specific. That's why you never hear of an IBM PC virus showing up on the Mac, or vice versa. Thank God Gam made up his mind to make the code as difficult to read as possible; since it's all in Assembly for the Mac, so is the virus code. It wouldn't make any sense to a UNIX machine."

Stroman looked at him hard. "You're sure?"

Danny raised his eyebrows at Charles. Both nodded simultaneously.

"Yeah," said Danny.

"Until the day they come out with a Mac interpreter for machines that run UNIX," added Charles, "no UNIX environment knows the first thing about running Mac code. At least we've got that tiny blessing."

Charles's comment reminded Danny of something; but he was too drained to focus on it, and time was running out.

SYSTEM:	**WELCOME TO USA ONLINE! YOU ARE IN A CHAT AREA.**
SYSTEM:	**DANNY THE C IS LOGGED ON**
DANNY THE C:	Hello? Hello, is the SysOp here?
AQUA VELVA:	Yes, Danny the C. I am the acting Sysop tonite. Do you have a question about USA Online?
DANNY THE C:	Yes. I have a very important message concerning a computer virus. Where should I post the info where everyone will see it?
AQUA VELVA:	Let me see. You should post it in the New Members section, and in the Hot News forum, I would think.
DANNY THE C:	So there's no way to post it on the welcoming screen, so everyone will see it?
MR. BIGGS:	WHAT IS THE VIRUS?
DANNY THE C:	It's a very, very dangerous virus that eats files, and it got shipped out on a commercial program disk.
AQUA VELVA:	Then I will ask my manager if you can post the message on the welcome screen. It sounds pretty important.
SYSTEM:	**MISS BROOKS IS LOGGED ON**
DANNY THE C:	It IS, it is. I've typed it up as a little text file. Do I send it to somebody in particular? I'm in kind of a hurry.
AQUA VELVA:	Just a moment, I will contact my manager by voice phone. Can you wait a minute?
DANNY THE C:	Yes, go ahead.
MISS BROOKS:	Danny?
DANNY THE C:	Oh, hi, MIss Brooks. Sorry, I really can't chat tonight. We're having something of a crisis where I work.
MISS BROOKS:	At work? It's 10 pm, you know.

DANNY THE C: I know, I know. We're in pretty rough shape. I actually have to get back to work, but I was supposed to post this message on all the electronic bulletin-board services.

MISS BROOKS: What message?

DANNY THE C: Well, it's 3 paragraphs long. But basically we have discovered a virus in the master disk of the software we've been working on.

MR. BIGGS: WHAT SOFTWARE

DANNY THE C: It's called MasterVoice.

MISS BROOKS: Danny is one of the programmers, Mr. B.

DANNY THE C: Wow, you remembered that!

MISS BROOKS: Yes. I remember everything you've ever told me about yourself.

MR. BIGGS: SHOULD WE BE WORRIED

DANNY THE C: Not too much. Just set your computer's clock back a year, and read the message I'm going to post. If the SysOp ever gets back.

MISS BROOKS: Danny, I have to talk to you. In a Private Room.

DANNY THE C: Sorry, I really have to go.

AQUA VELVA: OK, Danny the C, I am sorry. I am back now. I talked to the manager. SHe says to E-mail the information to her right now, and she will post it on the welcoming screen so that everybody sees it.

DANNY THE C: What's her E-mail address?

AQUA VELVA: Curly Shirley.

DANNY THE C: OK, great. I'll send it right now.

MISS BROOKS: Danny, I mean it. Can I talk to you in a Private Room just for a minute?

DANNY THE C: Look, why don't you tell me your real name and your phone number and I'll call you at some point.

MISS BROOKS: I can't do that.

DANNY THE C: Why not?

MISS BROOKS:	I don't feel comfortable with that. I'm sorry.
DANNY THE C:	<-- not a serial killer. Not going to come after you.
AQUA VELVA:	Danny the C is a good guy.
MISS BROOKS:	LOL! I know that.
DANNY THE C:	Well, sorry, then, Miss B. But we're up against the wall, time- wise, here at work. Gotta go.
MISS BROOKS:	Meet me again here tomorrow?
DANNY THE C:	Doubt it. Bye all!
MISS BROOKS:	DANNY STOP!
DANNY THE C:	what!?
MISS BROOKS:	Look, there's something I have to tell you. It's very important. I'll send you an E-mail here. Just log on later and read it, all right? It's urgent.
DANNY THE C:	OK. I'll log on and read it.
MISS BROOKS:	You promise? It's VERY imp
DANNY THE C:	YES YES OK
MISS BROOKS	ortant.
AQUA VELVA:	OK, let the poor guy go.
MISS BROOKS:	You're a good person, Danny.
DANNY THE C:	U-2. OK bye.
SYSTEM:	**DANNY THE C HAS LEFT THE CHAT AREA**
MR. BIGGS:	NOW THERE GOES A MAN ON THE RUN
MISS BROOKS:	He's in trouble, I'm afraid.

Etienne had always liked bucking the techno-weenie stereotype. He chewed tobacco, for one thing, which he assumed gave him an air of nonchalance and manhood; he was rarely seen without a paper cup into which he'd spit the juice from between his teeth, to the eternal dismay of his co-workers at Wright/Knowlton, the national credit-reporting agency. He also carried a hunting knife in an embossed cowhide sheath on his belt.

Joe Schorr, the graduate student who came in to work three evenings a week, always made fun of the knife. "What's that for, Etienne? In case a grizzly comes rampaging through the lab?"

But this week, for the sake of additional coolness, Etienne had topped himself. He'd bought a Master Voice voice-recognition system for the company's UNIX mainframe, for which he was one of the technical administrators.

Joe Schorr had scoffed at him for making what appeared to be a gross lapse of intelligence; no Mac program could run under the UNIX operating system.

"Correction, chump," Etienne had said. "*Any* Mac program can run under UNIX . . . with this."

He had reached for the shelf over the terminal and pulled down a striking four-color cardboard box. It looked like a software package; the logo said CrossOver.

"Cool," Joe Schorr had said on his way out. He promptly forgot the whole thing.

Etienne, however, thought CrossOver was freakin' great. He had already spent one delirious morning with it, learning how far he could push it, how fast he could make it run, how many kinds of Mac programs it could run.

CrossOver was a Mac emulator—technically speaking, it was a Motorola 68000-series interpreter. Etienne had no doubt that it had been designed with more mundane tasks in mind: running a Mac spreadsheet under UNIX, for example. Things like word processors and spreadsheets. Etienne had no doubt that CrossOver's marketing people had been thinking "business."

But Etienne never liked doing things the conventional way. His first experiment with CrossOver involved the Talking Seal, a fun little Mac doodad that made a sarcastic cartoon seal pop up on the screen every couple of minutes and utter some snide remark, like "Yo! How 'bout gettin' some work done?"

Etienne's favorite idea, though, was to freak out the lab assistants by voice-controlling the UNIX mainframe.

Installing CrossOver under UNIX wasn't difficult; it had taken him about twenty minutes. Installing Master Voice, however, took him longer; his UNIX terminal had no appropriate jack into which he could plug in the Master Voice microphone cable. It took him most of the afternoon to jury-rig an RS-232 cable that would serve as an adapter.

By dinnertime, Etienne had Master Voice running on a $100,000 mainframe computer almost as comfortably as if it were a Mac Classic. Not without bugs, and not terribly fast, but it was running. He'd have to wait until the next day to show it off to the others, but he knew it would be worth the wait. He fired stream of brown juice at the Styrofoam cup by the leg of the chair, missing slightly. "Quit this program," he told the computer. "Log me out." Master Voice responded as though by magic.

Etienne carefully put the CrossOver box and manuals back on the shelf, and tucked the microphone behind his terminal. This was gonna be good.

CrossOver was so good, in fact, that it successfully interpreted 100 percent of the Macintosh Assembly code in the programs it was handed; the product went on to win *InfoByte* magazine's Best New Product of 1994 award.

Of course, the viral code laced through the Master Voice software was equally persuaded—it never even knew it was on an alien platform. It sought out a central memory address in the mainframe, just as it would on a Macintosh, and lurked there, consulting the computer—via CrossOver—as to whether or not it was January 30, and time to start destroying data.

During the night, it exploded into thousands of copies, infecting every application on the mainframe. When, at four A.M. PST, the automated batch system kicked in to upload the previous day's data files to the L.A. office, the Houston virus went along for the ride.

And by nine A.M. the following day, the virus made it onto the InterNet.

chapter 14

THE SCREEN OF A MACINTOSH PLUS ● *TAMPA, FL*

InfoServe Information Service
1:12 EDT   Wed 22-Jan-94

Last access: 18:31   11-Jan-94

Welcome, Ellen Eckhouse. You have
Electronic Mail waiting.
****
MACINTOSH VIRUS ALERT
Several members have reported the spread of a new
Macintosh comptuer virus called the Houston virus.
Symptom: The top left pixel of the Macintosh monitor
becomes permanently illuminated. The virus apparently
does no harm, but we recommend eradicating it with an
anti-virus program such as Antidote as soon as possible.

To the best of our knowledge, no software in the InfoServe
software libraries has been contaminated with this virus.
For further information on the virus, download the text
file HVIR.TXT from the Macintosh Business User's Forum.
****

January 22, 1994   As the programmers went into their third
day of combing the complex program code for a clue to the virus,
sleep was in short supply. Danny discovered that he could get by
for seven or eight hours at a time, as long as he slept one solid
hour between stints. He felt like hell, but at least his brain could
still function.

He used a mat in the company's mini-gym as his bed, and was
usually stone unconscious thirty seconds later. He saddled Ellie,
Stroman's secretary, with responsibility for waking him at the end
of an hour.

As he lay down at 6 A.M., his brain seemed to sting. Suddenly
he knew the meaning of the word *overtired*. He closed his eyes
and lay flat, but little memory-pictures kept flashing past his eyes.
*Gam at the New Year's Eve party, carrying around his hard drive
even then . . . a call for a duplicate Master Voice master disk from
a beta tester . . . "Don't use this phone, Cooper; it distracts
me . . ." "Danny, let's get some ice for your nosebleed . . ."*

He sighed/moaned and changed position on the mat.

*What was that nosebleed business, anyway. Later. Something I
was gonna do later. Before all this came up . . .*

His eyes were closed, but he squeezed them tighter. He forced
himself to remember . . . *left a meeting, went to Gam's computer,
put something on it. Oh yeah, SURvIVor. I put that on there. And
that other thing. It was . . .*

And now his eyes were open, and he was frowning with the
effort; he had a strong feeling of having forgotten something, like
a man who's halfway to the airport and remembers he forgot to
lock the house. *Wait. I can't retrieve it now. It was on Gam's
portable hard drive. It's gone forever. . . .*

Danny fought his grogginess and struggled into a sitting position. *No, wait; I put it on the internal hard drive, the one inside
the Macintosh.* As the memory came back, he pulled to his feet
and loped back toward the R and D lab. *It's been sitting there all
this time. . . .*

"Some nap. You were only gone five minutes," ventured
Charles. "Danny Cooper *is*: Rip Van Winkle. Rated G."

Danny cleared the gunk from his throat. "Remembered something," he mumbled. He sat down at Gam's Mac. The room was
filled with the soft plastic clacking of computer keys.

Danny turned on the machine. The internal hard drive whirred to life, its LED light flickering on the outside of the Macintosh case.

"Give it up, Danny. He didn't leave any clues on *that* hard drive, you can be sure of that," said Charles.

Weakly, Danny used the Find command. In the blank labeled "Find what," Danny typed the name of the *second* file he'd planted on Gam's hard drive that day. The one he had made invisible in hopes that Gam would never find it.

He typed LIFESAVER.

Under normal circumstances, a computer displays what you type on the screen, but it's a purely electronic memory. If the power plug is pulled—or if the computer suffers a system crash—everything on the monitor disappears forever. Only when you choose the Save command is that text permanently stored on a disk.

Most people use the Save command, therefore, every ten or fifteen minutes, so that only a few minutes' worth of typing is ever at risk. But losing even a few minutes' worth of typing can be a terrible inconvenience, and if you're engrossed in your work and forget to Save, you may lose hours of work if something goes wrong.

Danny first heard about LifeSaver back in New York. It was a tiny utility program, a one-piece safety net for just such circumstances. Once installed, LifeSaver created a text file, letter by letter, of everything typed on the keyboard . . . day in, day out, completely independent of the Save command. With LifeSaver installed, Danny ceased to endure the sickening, infuriating feeling of helpless loss every time the computer crashed—because he knew that he could open the text file and recover everything he'd typed that day. Or the day before. Or any day since LifeSaver was installed.

But Danny had used LifeSaver as something it was never intended to be—he had used it as a wiretap. In the days of excitement, possibilities, and suspicion, he had planted it on Gam's hard drive. He'd thought it was a brilliant idea; the little text logger would record everything Gam typed: passwords, E-mails, program code . . . all kinds of things that might prove useful. Danny thought that by retrieving the LifeSaver file weeks later, he'd be able to check up on Gam, to find out what he was up to, to discover how much of a security risk he posed to the project.

Of course, that was while Gam was still alive to ask about it.

He slid the mouse across his desk, moving the on-screen cursor to the text-file icon. He clicked the mouse button twice to open the file. It felt odd; he was peering, like some sick voyeur, into the life of the dead. He felt a guilty little shiver as he opened the recorder file.

When its contents appeared on his screen, Danny sat up higher in his chair and squinted. He should have expected this, of course: LifeSaver recorded only text. No formatting was preserved, so paragraphs weren't indented, there were no breaks between paragraphs, and sentences were out of order. They appeared on Danny's screen in the order they'd been typed, not in the order they were eventually word-processed into.

Worse, LifeSaver recorded every keystroke, even backspaces; every time Gam had made a typo and backspaced over it, Danny could see the original word, a bunch of rectangular backspace symbols, and then the retyped word. The result: an incredibly messy and difficult-to-read mass of text.

Nonetheless, he tried to puzzle it out.

```
MOVE.L          A0,D0
SBI.□□T         #$000A,D0$$$
LSRS.W          #2□□□, D0
ADD.W           D0,A0
JSR             Fix□□□Address
□□□□□□MOVE.L Time,A0 CMPA.L
```

A bunch of programming code. Danny figured that was what Gam had spent most of his time typing on this computer. He scrolled down farther into the file.

MOTHER— I am going to be home very late tomorrow night. Do not waty□□□□ stay up for me. I have□□□have left □□□□ brought some Isanya home and If□□left it on the counter for you, you cn□□can heat it in the mcr□□□ microwave for dinner. —$$$y

29238 (213) 838-3849Paul Takeshita ∎

Dear Tim Lach□hann□ssc□□ce,

Thank you for your letter about my old□□□
first program, Lightning □Writer. I have
alws□ays bed□n□en very proud of it. And so
your letter ws□as vr□ery much apr□
preciated □□□□ □□□□□□ □□□ □□□□ □□□□
□□□□□□□□□ I appreciatd□d□ed your letter.

I am sorry that I cn□annot helpy□□p you with
your difficulties though, becas□use□□□se I
quit□□am no longer working for the original
pub□□□□□□□□□□□□□□□ Huntint□□□tington
Systems, the original publisher. You will have
to call them to find out why □□□□ □□□ □□□
for technical help of this kind.

"Danny, what're you doing over there?"

Danny turned to look at Skinner. True enough, since Gam's
death, his Mac had been universally left alone, as though in tacit
tribute—or else as a result of habit and fear.

"I'm looking for clues. I'll let you know if I find anything."

Danny rubbed his eyes, feeling like a crook, but somehow hor-
rifically fascinated by the life being revealed on the screen. He
scrolled down some more, wading through the garbled programming code in search of real English. Here was more:

```
MOVE.L   A0,D0 CMPA.L  #□□□□□□BLE
Early   JSR FIX□□□  FIX□□ixAddress
#$000A,□,D)□□;  ADD.With D0□□,A)/EXIT
```

Yo Luis,

OK here is the latest. It mainly contains
bug□g-fixes□es and some □□□□□□□. I hope
all goes well there, I am really getting sick

an□tired of□□□□□□burned out over here. You
c□c□ can call me at home but please stop
calli□□□□ □□□□□do not call aftre□□er 10
p.m. as my mother isn't wle□□el a□□□l and
needs the sleep. She gets very u□cra□z□□
upset of □□ifi□□if she is awakend□ed.□

Gam

"You guys know anybody named Luis? Friend of Gam's?"
The other programmers barely glanced up. "Don't know,
Danny," murmured Charles.

Via MCInet

Yo Luis,

There was a problem in the screen update
routines of□□in the last rev i□l sent you□□to
you. PLe□□lease use the ew versino□□on I am
seinding□□□□nding attache □□d to this E-
mail.

Gam.

"Whoooaaa," Danny breathed. Here it was in writing: Gam
had been feeding code to Huntington. *This could be useful*, he
thought. He read on into the stream of ASCI-code secrets.

9328□-4993 ▪ Glampert▪ 60890   Read
New Ma□ail
▪ flour▪ budget gourmey□ts▪ salda□□□ad
stuff▪ envelopes▪ hamburgers▪
Send All Wiati□□□□□aiting Mail▪

New Mesa□sage
M□Yia MCInet 60890

Yo Luis,

Could you tell Lars to tell Nick to lay off a
little. He is beomceing a□□□□□i□ing a real
hardass□□□□□□□ very irritating.
Thank you, Gam.

To: Palo Alto Flight Center
From: IDLicense @□#NC100389
Date: CvDecembr□er 18□□28

Gentlemen,

I am enclso□□osing my ehcch□□□□ check for
the comm□ing year. Ples□ase renew my
hangar space and parkign□□ng stickers. Feel
freet□ to call me if you have g□to reach me.

Sincerely
Gam Lampert

OK Luis,

I'm going to deliver the final copy of the
sftw□□□□ program to you next week. pls note
I took out the pixel (0,0) indicator, so even if
the inf□□□ virus p□□ part is working, your
not going to see it in the final version.

Please tell Lars that he is supposed to give me
my mo□□ check upon delivery of the final
code. I havent heard him mention it for a long

time, I just wanted to remind you to remind
him.

Thank you, Gam.

Danny frowned. *OK Luis?*
Danny sighed and scrolled quickly through some more of the
200-page text file, looking for anything that seemed important,
but there were just too many garbage symbols for him to get much
out of it. He reached for the mouse to quit the program when one
block of text caught his eye.

OK Luis,

Lars said for me to sort of □□□□□□□ write
up a kind of □□□□ □□ a cod□□□ map of the
code so he can tell what he needs to keep and
what to kill,□□□□□cut out, so here it is.

To kee it od□□□□□□□□□ protect it from
pry□i□ying eyes I have encrypted it though.
The password is the same one as always.

Thank you, Gam.

Code map!
Grimly, he called the other programmers over to see.
"Jesus. So we've been busting our butts for nothing?" said
Charles. "You mean there's already a chart so we can find our
way through this mess of code? Where the hell did you get this
text file? I can't believe Gam would leave it on his hard drive for
all to see."
Danny briefly explained how LifeSaver worked. He scrolled
through the endless document, showing them the little clues and
the big ones, the bread crumbs left behind and the cryptic, frightening glimpses into Gam's personal life. The other programmers
were astounded.

"Jeez, y'know?" said Skinner. "Like, these files could sort of expose his whole deal with Huntington, you know?"

Danny knew.

Michelle sat at her desk, arms folded, head collapsed on them. One hand still clutched the phone receiver she had just hung up after what seemed like the thousandth phone call. Her strength was wearing out.

Her eyes, barely open, watched Myrtle the dime-store turtle blunder contentedly across her blotter. The tentative, one-at-a-time way Myrtle lifted, then placed each leg gave Michelle's flagging spirits a tiny boost.

"Now, there's *one* hardy soul who's not getting depressed by all this."

Michelle looked up. Danny stood in the doorframe: a tall, curly-haired presence with a pen mark on his cheek.

"I take it you're referring to Myrtle?"

He nodded and came around behind her. He kissed the top of her head and began to massage her shoulders. "C'mon. It's time for the meeting," he said.

"Jeez, Danny. What have *you* got to be so up-and-at-'em about?"

"You wouldn't believe what we just found out—" He stopped. Maybe it still was too soon to talk about Gam with Michelle. "Anyway. We're making great headway," he lamely finished.

"I miss you," she said.

He stopped for a fraction of a second. "What?"

"I miss having you around. I guess once you become the company hotshot, things like romance sort of drop by the wayside."

"Michelle," he protested. "We've been under just a *little* bit of pressure."

"I know. But think about it. Your contract here expires what— next week? And then where will you go? Back to New York? You're just going to go away and that's that. Leaving Myrtle and me behind, to wallow in our respective terrariums."

"No! Of course not. I'll still be *around*, even if I'm not in this building," Danny countered. "I mean, depending on what kind of job I can get after this."

Or if I cave in and go to business school.

"You better be, Cooper. I don't give my heart to just any computer nerd."

"Thanks ... I think," Danny said. He glanced at her desk clock. "Come on, Juliet. Bob's waiting."

She got up, plucked Myrtle up from the edge of her desk, and put her back in the terrarium. They left her office and walked around the corner to the conference room.

With only eight days remaining before the virus awoke, Stroman sat wearily at the head of the table. The programmers lined one side of it, dark circles under their eyes, but attentive. Danny found a seat and unfolded the laser-printed report he'd typed up.

"OK, Danny," said Stroman. "Let's hear what you boys have discovered."

"OK. Well, first of all, we've found some pretty incriminating stuff on Gam's Mac. Memos he's been writing to Huntington. There are references to money Huntington's paying him ... the whole deal."

"Oh, Jesus," Stroman muttered.

"I can print that out or print out the good parts, and send them around later. In the mean time, we've been bulldozing our way through the Master Voice code, and we think we've figured out some of what's going on. Ellie's making copies of this report, and she'll hand them out when she gets back. In the meantime, I guess I'll just read it to you. First of all, there's a summary of everything we know about the virus.

" 'One. The virus is embedded in convoluted threads through the code of the Master Voice software.'

"In other words, Gam constructed our program, from day one, with the viral code embedded in it. Obviously, the idea was to keep us busy hunting around for it for quite a while. I mean, it's *buried*. The point is, there's no way for us to rip the virus wholesale out of the legitimate code, all in one chunk; it loops and doubles back and makes detours.

"That's an important point, because it answers one of the great mysteries for us—why my SURvIVor program never detected any viral activity. SURvIVor looks for something amiss. It looks for something that's tampered with a program, like a separate entity that's invaded. It just looked at Master Voice, noticed nothing there that Gam hadn't *put* there, and assumed everything was OK.

" 'Two. The virus has two stages, or forks. The first fork keeps checking the Macintosh clock until it's twelve A.M. on January twentieth, 1994. At that point, the virus seeks out the System file and embeds itself. Once in the System file, it continues to infect other programs, even if the Master Voice is removed. And once a System file is infected, it doesn't matter what the computer clock says; so you can't turn your clock backward after you're infected and hope you've turned it off. The virus then attacks any other application it can find, by installing a JSR instruction early in the code. This "Jump to Subroutine" command directs the program's execution to the end of the application, where the primary viral code has been appended. The figure below shows a simplified flow chart that indicates how the computer executes a program, both before and after it's been infected by the virus.'

"I'll hand this around as soon as Ellie gets here," Danny added, "so you can all see this diagram."

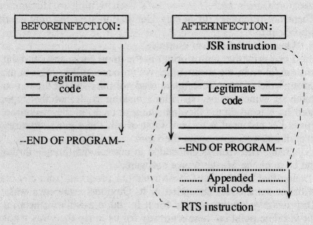

"As you can see, the virus works by changing the infected program's table of contents—the jump table at the very beginning—by inserting a jump-to-subroutine instruction that shoots it off to the viral code.

" 'The second fork of the virus does the damage. When the call to the Macintosh clock returns a value of twelve A.M. on January thirtieth, 1994, the second fork is activated. These final instructions direct the virus to consult the modification dates of every file on any mounted volumes. Beginning with the earliest-modified, it proceeds to delete one file every sixteen seconds.'

"Once again, you can't put it back to sleep once it's begun eating. You can't change the Mac clock back to 1991 or something, hoping to lure the virus back into its dormant state.

" 'Three. The virus in the Master Voice code is considerably different from the virus that embeds itself in other programs and continues to clone itself. That is, the Master Voice code is not so much a virus as it is a virus-construction *kit*. It is much larger and more elaborate than the virus-child it creates described in Item Two.

" 'Four. Once activated, the System file-based virus continues to delete files up to, and including, the Master Voice program—thus erasing its own tracks. Ultimately, it deletes the System files of the computer itself, which the Macintosh requires to run. In other words, eventually the virus even eats its own host file out from under it, causing a system error and rendering the computer incapable of running.' "

Danny set his paper down. "By the way, I guess the only good thing about this is that it wipes your hard drive as clean as it can get. When the virus is done eating, you have no choice but to erase the hard drive and reinstall the System files—which, as it turns out, is precisely what you have to do to get rid of the virus. In other words, once you deliberately reformat the hard drive, you effectively wipe out any remaining viral code. Remember," he added for the benefit of the nontechnical attendees, "a computer virus is just software. It's not alive. It doesn't live in the circuitry of the machine. Once that hard drive is erased, the virus is gone."

Stroman interrupted. "So that's a sure way to eliminate the virus? To completely erase your hard disk?"

Danny nodded.

Charles leaned back and rested his feet on the conference table. "Oh, *that*'d go over big. We can just tell people: Protect your data in one easy step—just erase it."

Stroman's secretary had reentered the room, and began to distribute a photocopy of Danny's memo.

"So that's it," Danny concluded. "That's everything we know about the virus. At this point, I'm not exactly sure what we can do about it. Even telling people to set their Mac clocks back a year isn't going to help the ones who have already installed Master Voice; the first fork of the virus woke up two days ago."

Stroman was looking disturbed, although he actually was gratified that his team was making some headway. "Arnie, what'd you find out from the beta testers?"

"Well, about what you'd expect. We have twenty-three testers. I've been able to reach twenty, and when I asked them about it, every single one has the white pixel. We figure that that white pixel was something Gam put into the beta-test versions for his own benefit, so only the beta testers have been seeing it."

"So nobody's lost data yet?" asked Stroman.

"Well, I wouldn't say *nobody*," McGivens replied. "As you know, the Javeds have lost everything. One of our testers in Houston, Clive Witmark, lost everything weeks ago. Evidently he had set his Macintosh clock way ahead, so his virus got an early start; he started losing data just before Christmas. The funny thing is, he never reported it to us; he's a beta for so many different products that he never suspected Master Voice. He thought he'd just contracted a rogue virus from someplace. His Mac eventually shut down completely. But he had enough presence of mind to reformat the hard disk and reinstall what he could. He's back in business now. Beyond those two, looks like no viruses have gone off yet. For one reason or another, both of those two testers had set their clocks forward, so they received Gam's little gift a couple weeks early."

Danny didn't follow. "Why would you would set your clock ahead by two months or whatever?"

Danny hadn't read the November issue of *PowerMac* magazine; he knew nothing of the hidden Christmas tree in the Air-Attack game.

"I don't know, either, OK, but I mean thank God, y'know?" interjected Skinner, blinking in tic frenzy.

Arnie looked at him quizzically.

"If they hadn't, we wouldn't have found out about the virus until it was too late!"

"OK," said Stroman. "I feel like we're starting to get ahold of this."

Charles was raising his hand, pudding spoon dangling from his fingers even in this time of crisis.

"Charles? Got a report?"

"I just thought I'd let everyone know that I signed onto Info-Serve last night," he said. "I don't know how this could happen, but everybody's buzzing about a new virus that sounds an awful lot like ours. They're calling it the Houston virus, and the description fits our little guy—right down to the white dot in the corner of the screen." He looked around the room. "Sounds to me like our Texan beta-tester friend let the thing loose into the world."

"Damn," muttered Stroman.

"So nobody's tracing it back to us?" said Arnie.

"Well, not from what they're saying on InfoServe, anyway," said Charles.

"So what're we going to *do* about it, OK?" burst Skinner.

"Steady there, Skinner," said Arnie. "We're working on it."

Stroman turned. "All right, Danny. What *are* we going to do? Can this thing be cleaned up? We've got—what—eight days before the thing starts eating out computer guts. Is there anything we can do?" His voice cracked slightly from the stress. "C'mon, team, I'm trusting you to be brilliant under pressure now."

Danny fidgeted as the focus, for the hundredth time since the crisis began, seemed to shift to him. His brain wasn't functioning at full throttle.

"Well," he began. "See, originally I thought it might be possible for us to write a patch program. A little program that goes out and looks for the viral code. If it finds the virus, it could delete it."

"Well, that sounds like exactly what we need," said Stroman. "A virus eater. So why don't we get started?"

Danny shook his head. "There's a problem. The virus code is threaded through the legitimate code. In, out, and around, like a tapestry. It's not all in one contiguous chunk we could rip out. If we wrote this . . . this virus eater, we'd have to give it directions. We'd have to give it a map to follow as it ate away the virus code, leaving the good code behind. Kind of a Func Spec for the virus."

Skinner and Rod were nodding in agreement.

"So . . . what's our next step?" Stroman dearly hoped Danny had an answer.

"What we need is a map . . . you know, a structure hierarchy, identifying all the pointers to code pieces. We need a guide through this maze of spaghetti." He shot a sly look at the other programmers. "And it *just so* happens that such a map exists!" He turned to Stroman. "Gam wrote one. He delivered it to Huntington."

"Yeah, I'll *bet* he did," muttered Stroman. "He had to provide a way for Lars to scrape the virus out of the real code; wouldn't do Lars much good to market his *own* virus-ridden program."

"So do we have a copy of this code map?" asked Arnie.

Oops, thought Danny. *Hadn't thought that far ahead yet.*

"Prob'ly on that hard drive he carried around," offered Rod.

"Of course!" exclaimed Danny. "Remember how he used to

cart that thing around? No wonder he was so protective of that disk!''

Charles peered through his tinted lenses. "Of course, that particular disk probably got blown to smithereens in the plane crash with Gam, *n'est-ce pas*?"

Michelle shot him a glance for his tactlessness.

"Oh yeah," Danny said.

"If there's another copy, Lars Huntington probably has it," said Stroman. "And I can promise you Lars isn't feeling generous right about now...now that his little plan is working perfectly."

No one spoke.

Danny sighed. He took a long, slow look at the faces around the table. They were all watching him, eyes full of despair, tremulous hope, or simple glassy exhaustion. What could he tell them?

"I forgot about that hard drive. I'm sorry," was all he could come up with.

Stroman turned his eyes away to hide his desperation.

"There would have been only one way to find our way through the program. And that's if we had the code map."

Stroman spoke in nearly a monotone, still looking away.

"So there's no way to stop the virus without this code map. And there's no way we're going to get our hands on a copy."

He was nearly inaudible.

"So we stop here."

Danny, embarrassed to see his employer nearly breaking down, turned his head away. His eyes fell on the legal pad Michelle had on her lap next to him. She hadn't written a word while he read. Instead, she had neatly sketched a rather good cartoon turtle, one leg poised in midstep.

Too bad we can't go back in time, he thought. *Too bad we can't just back up and...back up and...*

Suddenly he slapped the table. "He's got a backup," he said quickly. "He's *got* to have a backup."

The eyes of the room were on him.

Stroman didn't know whether to dare hope. "Well, Jesus! Of course he did! He'd have to have a backup copy of everything he did. Where would he have kept it?"

"At his house," said Michelle simply.

Danny turned. "What?"

"He's got a big computer setup there. In his bedroom. I'll bet anything he kept his backup copies right there."

"You know where this place is?" asked Stroman, a glimmer of hope reawakening.

"Sure," she said. "Up in Woodside. I'll drive over right now, if you want."

"Meeting adjourned, goddammit! Get the hell over there!" Stroman shouted.

She stood up, snatching her pencil from the table. "I'm outta here."

"We should go with her," Danny said, standing. "Charles, wanna come?"

Stroman grinned for the first time all day. "All right. It's you three musketeers off to Woodside. I want a report the minute you find out."

"What are you *doing*?"

The others froze in their tracks; it was Skinner. "You're kinda forgetting something, OK? I mean like that's great and everything, right? But so what if you find the code map. We'll be no better off." He sounded much less turbocharged than usual.

Michelle sat down again, looking concerned.

"What do you mean, Skinner?"

His eyes snapped forcefully shut a couple of times—his Stress Tic.

"OK, so like what if we find the map of the virus, OK? OK, good. So what do we do with it? We write some kind of a patch program, right, like Danny said. We write a little program that eats Gam's virus. Goes out hunting and eats it, right? So, OK . . ." He took a breath. "How are we going to get it distributed?"

Danny's spirits clouded. "Oh, God. He's right. I mean, by the time all this happens, there's only going to be a day left, or less, before Gam's little masterpiece wakes up. And that thing must be *everyplace* by now." He slunk back into his chair. "So let's say we do write an anti-virus program: we can't possibly ship out five hundred thousand disks by January thirtieth. Even with a surefire, super-duper Gam-virus killer, there's no possible way we're going to get it installed all over the country in time."

Stroman's expression darkened, but Arnie perked up. "We could send it electronically. InfoServe, USA Online, all of those BBS services. And we could make sure all the dealers had it. And all the user groups."

"There *is* one thing in our favor," Michelle added. "I have a hunch that the national networks will be interested in this story. At least I think we can count on media coverage, so most people will find out about it."

Charles interrupted. "But Danny is right: Realistically, you're not gonna cut it that way. If *everyone* knows about it, and *everyone* acts, you might defuse—what—a quarter of the infected sites in time. But the majority of these guys don't have modems, so they can't get to those dial-up services. And even if someone does download the patcher, what if there are fifty Macs on a network? Is someone going to run around, patching one hard drive after another?"

Danny looked down, the weight of reality on his shoulders, the drag of extreme fatigue in his soul. "So. . .what's the consensus? That we just aren't going to make it?"

After an afternoon of dashed hopes, Stroman was getting tired of the roller-coaster ride. "Oh, God," he sighed.

Michelle wasn't giving up. "Come on, you guys. There's got to be some way. Think, Danny. Isn't there any faster way? We can do mail. We can do dial-up services. What else?"

"There just isn't anything!" Danny said, getting irritated. "OK, sure: load half a million disks on an airplane and fly across the country, spraying them like insecticide. Drive trucks around ringing a little bell. Or, hey, I know! Let's shrink to the size of atoms and invade every computer through its power cord!"

"Don't get nasty, man," said Charles.

"Sorry," Danny said miserably. "But there's no way we could follow the virus's footsteps everywhere it went. It's probably spread to a couple million machines by now."

But Michelle was staring at him. "Follow the virus . . ." Her mouth hung open while her brain spun out an idea. "You know what? That's right, Danny. That's exactly it! *That's* how we could distribute the anti-virus program in time," she said intensely.

"*What?*" said Danny, not registering. Then, a query: "What?"

She was gaining confidence. "Yes, I'm *sure* of it. I know how we could saturate every computer, every network, every computing community. Just as thoroughly, and just as fast, as the virus did."

Nobody breathed.

Stroman said quietly, "Tell us, Michelle. What could blanket the country in a matter of days?"

She sat back, a smile of supreme confidence on her face.

"*Another* virus."

● ● ●

Miss Brooks closed the door to her office quietly. She slipped into her chair and dialed USA Online; from the modem speaker, she heard the rush of static that indicated the connection was made.

She grabbed the mouse and edged up to the Mail menu on her screen. She rolled down the list of commands until she found the one she was looking for: Read Mail You Have Sent.

A small window appeared, listing the last ten E-mail messages she'd sent. There, at the top of the list, was the one she had sent most recently. Next to its name were three columns, labeled TO, DATE SENT, and DATE READ.

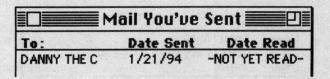

To:	Date Sent	Date Read
DANNY THE C	1/21/94	-NOT YET READ-

"Damn," she said aloud. She should have known he wouldn't have time to waste on the modem. Not at this point, anyway.

She logged off the system and stood slowly, thinking.

She opened the door to her office and stepped down the spiral staircase to the second floor. She could hear the booming echo Lars's voice produced when he was excited from all the way down the hall. She followed the sound to the development room.

Lars was standing behind Luis, one of the programmers, staring at the screen. "Lovely," he was saying over and over. "Lovely, lovely, lovely, lovely." And then he would laugh.

Miss Brooks slipped through the doorway and stood a few feet behind them.

Lars saw her out of the corner of his eye. He turned to face her for a moment.

"Why, Sheila! What a lovely surprise."

She glanced nervously at the floor. "Lars. I'm sorry if I was out of line in the meeting."

He regarded her carefully. "Does that mean I can count on you?"

After a hesitation, she looked down and nodded almost imperceptibly.

Lars didn't trust her for a moment—but at this point, he thought he'd show her just how much the deck was stacked in his favor.

"Then come look, Sheila. Look at what we've discovered."

Tentatively, she shuffled close enough to see the computer screen.

"You see?" said Lars. "There's no way we can lose on this one. This is the Artelligence E-mail system. Our good friend Mr. Lampert was kind enough to share the passwords with us. And as you can see, our ability to monitor the competition's progress has turned out to be very valuable."

On the screen was an E-mail message.

LinkMail™
From: Robert Stroman
Time: January 22, 1994, 11:34 am
RE: Oskins

Ellie, here are the phone numbers I told you about. I need you to dial these guys until you get through. They're doing some weapons testing with MV, so it's rather critical that we reach them.

If you reach Col. Oskins, explain the situation. Tell him that Danny will be back from Woodside with the code map by dinnertime, and meanwhile we'll get started writing the anti-virus virus. Anyway, have him call me immediately, regardless.

Lars waited until Sheila had straightened up after reading it. She looked at him for an explanation.

"You see, they're a little smarter than we gave them credit for, Sheila," Lars beamed. "Woodside is where Gam's home is, you see. They are going there in hopes of finding some sort of map. Apparently they hope to undo Gam's good work by piecing its structure together from what they find at Gam's house. *So* clever.''

Luis fingered his T-shirt collar. ''Actually, it won't do them any good, Lars.''

''No?''

''Nope.'' Luis shook his head. ''There *is* a code map, but Gam kept it locked up. It's password-protected. Even if they get the file off his hard disk, won't be able to read it. It'd take them a trillion attempts before they came up with the right password.''

Lars beamed. ''Luis, I thank you for your skill and expertise. I trust your judgment completely—and yet, just to make sure all systems are go, I believe I'll need to send Nick on an errand anyway. I think he misses the action of his days on the old Chicago police force; now I can make it up to him.'' He strode out of the room.

Luis turned around; his eyes met Sheila's. Nothing was spoken, but Sheila knew from his expression that she shouldn't step over the line. *I know how you feel, lady*, his face said, *but you're not dragging me into it. I know who signs my paycheck.*

Had there been some way to track the Houston virus's progress through the national InterNet system, its spread would have astonished even UNIX specialists. Because of its speed and the efficiency of its design, the virus—modified by the CrossOver software into a UNIX-friendly mutation—leaped freely over the phone wires from one major corporate hub to another. Twenty-four hours after the virus infected the InterNet, it was deeply entrenched in the mainframes of IBM in Armonk, New York; Continental Airlines in Houston; Stanford, M.I.T., Yale, UCLA, Michigan, and thirty other universities; Citicorp in Manhattan; Federal Express in Memphis; Bank of America in San Francisco; Lockheed Aircraft in L.A.; Pepsico in Purchase, New York; British Petroleum in Cleveland; Ford Motor Company in Lansing; and hundreds upon hundreds of smaller corporations and organizations.

In each location, the virus's active first stage oversaw an immediate and rabid explosion into thousands of additional copies. Because this strain originated from the shipping version of Master Voice, there wasn't even a telltale white pixel at screen position (0,0) to indicate that anything was amiss. Every sixteen seconds, the virus made a call to the UNIX system's date routine to find out if it was time to awaken; as soon as the answer was yes, the virus's second stage was programmed to begin devouring the seams of the nation's electronic infrastructure.

The interpreters in the offices of Dr. Jay Ankner, chief thoracic resident at the Walter Reed Army Hospital, were as good as any in the world; Ankner noted that they didn't even stumble on the trade names of the medications.

"And tell them," Ankner added, "that as long as there's no instability with President Jurenko's heart rate, I don't see any further problems. We've been gradually reducing his medications, and we should be able to take him out of the CTU tonight. We'll have the computer keep monitoring his lab results and blood counts. He should be able to return to the talks Wednesday or Thursday."

The translator told Jurenko's advisers. They were greatly relieved; pressure on the hospital had been increasing from the White House, as the world waited for the summit peace talks to resume. If all went well, Ankner said, the president would be bidding the hospital farewell in only a few days.

When Secretary of State Masso received the good news from his aide at the hospital, he heaved a sigh of relief. He sure as hell hoped Ankner knew what he was talking about.

Danny pulled his noisy maroon Rabbit just behind Michelle's Civic at the sandy edge of Periwinkle Lane; because of the street's incline, he turned the front wheels and set the parking brake. He took a look at the house—an impressive, even stately Tudor mini-mansion, set back fifty yards from the steep, winding street. Suitable, Danny guessed, for a kid of Gam's astronomical double salary.

The only other car on the street was a dark red, tinted-glass Sentra that was parked a hundred yards higher up the hillside.

Michelle climbed out of her car and walked over.

"OK, boys, let's go." Danny and Charles climbed out of the Rabbit.

"Did we really need two cars for this?" asked Charles. "Don' you thoughtless children ever consider our fragile ecosystem?" They had only walked halfway up the steep driveway, and already Charles was starting to breathe hard.

Michelle smiled at him, noting that he was out of shape bu

trying nobly to keep up. "I have to drop a mailing list off at a PR firm in Cupertino when we're finished here. My contact said she'd be there all day, so I'm going to deliver the names for her to call."

Danny glanced at the house. "So you've been here before?" *How could you ever date that scary guy?*

"Yeah. A few times. I know where his room is, anyway. And her room."

"Her?"

She glanced at him. "Becca. Gam's mom."

A shiver of gooseflesh ran down Danny's arms. He suddenly heard an echo of Gam's voice.

Come on over, Danny, you'll love her. Come on over and meet Becca. Come on over...

The bushes were manicured, the house neatly painted—the work of a maintenance crew. They walked along a slate stone path across the lawn to the front door. "I don't know if she'll be home or not," she said. "Arnie says nobody's answered the phone or the door since the funeral. I tried her again before we left. No answer."

Michelle stepped onto the porch and rang the doorbell. "Becca's a little bit unstable," she explained to Charles. "Gam's father wound up committing suicide about ten years ago; Becca's never been the same since. I only saw her once, when Gam first brought me here. She was sitting naked in the living room watching TV." Michelle shrugged. "I was never really introduced."

She rang again. The house was dark and silent.

"Wonder where she is?" said Danny. He looked at his watch; they really needed to get this code map and get back to the lab.

Before leaving for Gam's house, he'd spent a tense half hour with the rest of the team designing the anti-virus. He whipped together a structured flow chart for them to follow, and told them to write as much of it as they could without the map itself. The idea, he explained—actually, Michelle's idea—was to fight fire with fire; to release this counter-virus into the world, programmed explicitly to hunt down and kill Gam's virus...and to reproduce.

Danny had never dreamed he'd wind up using his knowledge of viruses to write one of his own, but at this point, he had little choice.

"Come *on*, lady," he muttered, grabbing the heavy brass lion's-mouth knocker and slamming it three times.

And still the house was quiet.

"She must have moved out or something," said Michelle. She watched as Danny tried the door; it was locked tight.

"Come on," she said. She started striding back to the driveway.

"Where are we going?"

"He kept a key around back. Follow me."

In back of the house, they found another gorgeously manicured lawn and a two-car garage. Both garage doors were shut. The whole house had a deserted, ghostly feeling to it.

Michelle was scrabbling around in the wood chips that formed the bedding for some shrubbery along the back wall of the house. "It used to be right here."

Suddenly she perked up. "Got it!" She extracted a key from the wood chips and shook the dust off her hand. She slipped it into the lock, turned it with a click, and swung the back door open.

Danny and Charles stepped in after her.

They were in the kitchen. It was a stylish, shiny black-and-white tiled room, with flush-mounted appliances and a peninsula table surrounded by stools. The table and the counters, however, were piled with encrusted plates and silverware. Stacks of mail, opened and unopened, added to the clutter on the table.

"Hello?" shouted Michelle into the silent house. Danny winced at the sudden sound.

"Stephen King's *Bachelor Pad*. Coming soon to a theater near you," muttered Charles, looking around at the filth.

"Hello? Becca?" Michelle moved through the kitchen and into the hallway beyond, then made a right onto the front staircase. Danny followed, hand on the banister, taking in the surroundings as fast as he could.

He felt like an intruder, a voyeur. He recognized the feeling back in New York, the lady across the hall used to ask him to take care of her cats when she was away. He was always willing. But every time he let himself in to her apartment, he felt an almost nauseating urge to do his business and get out of there. It was psychologically distressing to learn things about this stranger by passing among her furniture and knickknacks.

They reached the top of the stairs. The boys padded behind Michelle across the thick shag carpeting. Danny almost smiled despite her apparent fearlessness and familiarity with the house, he noted that she, too, was almost tiptoeing.

They reached Gam's bedroom. The door was open. Michelle flicked on the lights.

"Jeeeezus," Charles murmured.

It was a womb, a cocoon—windowless, dark, insulated. The room was dominated by three gigantic computer monitors, each attached to a Macintosh CPU. There were no posters, no photographs; the bed, unmade, had a dark brown coverlet that now spilled onto the floor.

Danny walked beside the bookshelves, marveling. *Inside Macintosh. Motorola 68000 Series: A Technical Guide.* And then a tiny photo, in a silver frame, on a shelf, stopped him.

It was a picture of tall, thin Gam, bent at the waist wearing a rare smile, and proffering a single rose—to Michelle, who was looking at Gam with a teasing grin.

Danny frowned, not understanding, some unwholesome emotion welling inside. *What is there that somebody's not telling me about the guy? Didn't she see through that phony gallant routine?* The photo almost revolted him. *How could she ever . . .*

"So is this his backup drive?" said Michelle. She stood next to the desk that supported the three monitors. She pointed to a platinum-colored portable hard drive attached to the right-most computer.

Danny looked up. "Yeah. Yeah, I guess," he said without expression. He crossed the room and grabbed it.

"Then let's get our file and get the hell out of here. This place is giving me the willies," complained Charles.

"Unless . . . ," Michelle said.

"What?"

"Unless *that's* it." She pointed to a second drive, attached to the middle computer. It, too, was a platinum-colored, plastic-cased portable.

"Oh, my God. There's probably a third one, too," Danny mumbled, his mind still on the photo. He sneaked a glance at Michelle, who caught him in the act and gave him a funny look.

They found the third drive in Gam's familiar dingy blue nylon gym bag, which had been deposited beside the desk. Danny unzipped it, slipped his hand inside. There it was, cool and smooth to the touch, with rounded corners and a thick rubber-coated SCSI cable: a third identical hard drive.

He pulled it out of the bag. "Great," he said, trying to keep his mind on his work. "I thought we could just grab the thing and split. I didn't know were going to sit here playing a shell game.''

He stepped behind the faux-maple desk and connected the drive to one of the computers. ''Let's figure out which one is his backup drive and get the hell out of here,'' he said. ''Charles, can you do that first one?''

He flipped on the left-most computer. The drive spun to life with a faint whine, its LED activity lamp flickering.

When all three computers were on and displaying the contents of their respective hard drives, Danny checked each one. He knew it immediately when he saw it on the screen: one of the drives was called Hussein Backup.

Yup, that's it. Only Gam would name his drive Hussein . . . just one lovable guy toasting another.

He was just about to shut the system down when something unusual caught his eye. There was only a single folder icon on the screen: the System folder. Except for this stripped-down essential, the drive was empty.

''Oh, *no!*'' said Danny.

Michelle stared, too. ''Where's all his stuff?''

Charles flopped into Gam's desk chair. ''You didn't think Gam would make it easy, did you? He obviously erased the whole disk once the project was over.''

She looked at him, scowling. ''You've *got* to be kidding. What are we going to do!?''

Briefly—very briefly—Danny wondered when the applications to business school were due.

''Let me see . . . let's think a minute . . . ,'' he said. The files were all gone—but the System folder was still there. That meant Gam hadn't actually *erased* the disk, writing computerized zeros across its entire surface. Instead, Gam must have chucked all the other files and folders by dragging their icons to the on-screen Trash Can.

Which meant—

''We're not dead yet.''

He reached to the inside front pocket of his windbreaker and extracted his ''disk wallet,'' a padded nylon case that held and protected ten disks. He opened it, scanned the labels, grabbed an orange disk, and shoved it into the disk drive.

''What are you doing?'' Michelle said. She came over and perched on one of his knees so she could see the screen.

"He didn't reformat this disk. He just trashed all the files."

"So?"

"Aha," sang out Charles, suddenly getting it.

Danny explained as he worked. "See, the surface of a disk is like a bunch of post office boxes. When the Macintosh wants a particular file, it actually looks for its box number—in other words, by its position on the surface of the hard drive, right?

"OK. So when you throw a file into the Trash Can, the computer doesn't actually disturb the data at all. Instead, it just clears its directory—it forgets where everything is, like someone ripped off all the box numbers in that post office."

Michelle was listening intently. "OK."

"But the data is still there, as long as you don't copy anything *new* onto the disk. If you do that, the new information overwrites the old information, and that's that. Otherwise, if you use a file-recovery program like NeatUndelete, you can resurrect the files!"

"Well, great! So that's what's on this orange disk?"

"Right," he said. Its window opened on the screen: Neat-Undelete, it said. He used the mouse to point to it, and double-clicked the icon. The program ran.

From the main menu, he selected the Show File Fragments command, then sat back to wait.

In tiny type, wave after wave of file names rolled up the screen:

FILENAME	DATE	OK?
Arnie memo	12/9/93	Y
Beechcraft preflight	10/29/93	N
Infracorp handhelds	11/993	Y
Checking	12/31/93	Y
Lars revised contract	4/23/90	Y
MV status report/Lars	12/10/93	Y
MV source code FINAL	12/30/93	Y
Letter to Monica	7/31/90	Y

Danny whistled under his breath. "Look at this, you guys— his whole *life* is on this disk!" This was far juicier than the

LifeSaver files Danny had read; where those were just hints, clues, and one-sided records of correspondence, this was the hard-core stuff: the actual information. He hoped he wouldn't find any more disturbing relics of Gam's past romantic life.

"Just so the map thing is there," Michelle said. "Let's get it and get out of here. This place is giving me the creeps."

Danny clucked. "Let this be a lesson to you—don't leave anything on your computer you don't want other people to read after you die."

The list of deleted files rolled on.

Letter to Morton	7/31/92	Y
FAA Application	1/22/89	N
LightningWrite	1/22/89	Y
Artell. Email pswords	11/9/92	Y

"Oh, nice!" Danny said, pointing to the screen. "E-mail passwords. The guy's probably been reading our E-mail for months."

Charles groaned. "This just keeps getting better and better, don't it?"

Serial pinouts	2/2/92	N
InfoServe log	6/17/92	Y
InfoServe log2	3/13/92	Y
Steak recipe	4/22/89	Y

Danny looked at his watch. It was 6:15. Still the list rolled on.

Source code backup	4/2/92	Y
USA Onine log	9/14/92	Y
Huntington pswords	4/4/93	Y
Savings acct.	12/15/93	Y
MY prototype	12/29/93	Y
MY code map	12/30/93	Y

"*There*," Charles yelped, pointing. "Check out that one called 'code map.' That's gotta be it."

Michelle grabbed Danny's face and kissed him hard. "Nice going."

Danny's emotions were distinctly mixed.

"Lovely," Charles droned, looking around the room. "Now may we get our butts out of this place?"

Danny clicked the name of the file he needed to recover.

"Now recovering the file: 'MV Code map,'" it said on the screen.

In ten seconds, the job was done. Danny quit the recovery program and returned to the main desktop. There was the map file's icon, calmly sitting in the directory window as though it had never been erased. Danny felt a surge of pride. *You can call me Tex*, he drawled in his own head, tipping his invisible nine-gallon hat. *Data sleuth, private eye, lady-killer.*

His hand was halfway to the mouse to shut the computer down when they heard halting, shuffling footsteps behind them.

"You stay right there, youse. You stay right there. I'll carve ya. I will."

Danny turned slowly. There before him was a flabby, stooped woman wielding an electric cordless carving knife, which she held before her like a ray gun. She looked far older than her fifty-five years; her stringy hair, gray and unkempt, dangled listlessly across her forehead and cheeks. She clutched the front of her filthy white terry bathrobe, clamping it shut around her potbelly. She took one more step in toward them, switching the knife on and off once for effect. The twin blades whirred noisily to life, their interlocking teeth scissoring back and forth at 200 rpm.

"I'll carve ya. Don't you move."

Michelle turned as gently as she could to face her.

"Becca."

Becca looked shocked to hear her name.

"Becca, I'm Michelle Andersen. I'm Gam's friend. Don't you remember me?"

Becca squinted for a moment, and then her expression indicated she would not be swindled.

"I'm callin' th' cops. You don't move or I'll cut ya."

Becca glanced at the phone on Gam's desk. It was a foot from Danny's left hand. Charles tried to catch Danny's eye.

Michelle tried again. "Becca. We're not here to steal anything. We've been calling and ringing the doorbell, but you haven't answered. I let myself in, see?" She held up the key. "Gam showed me where the key was before he—before the accident.''

The woman took a step toward them. It was then that Danny noticed the smell; stale, sweaty, unwashed.

''What do you people want from me? What from an old woman?'' she said finally, starting to look panicked.

Michelle poured on the soothing voice. ''Not a thing, Becca. We're not here to hurt you. We need something from Gam's computer, that's all. We just need this box right here.'' She patted the hard drive.

Becca was on the offensive again. ''You're not taking *nothin'*. You get up now, you walk out. Right now. Or I'll carve ya! I'll do it!''

Once more, she gave the rattling electric knife a burst of juice, swiping it like a scimitar through the air. Danny was astonished: *this* was Gam's *mother*? Gam, with his stratospheric IQ? Gam, cynical, calculating, brilliant, was raised by this pathetic vision?

He gave the small of Michelle's back a little nudge. ''Pack up the drive,'' he whispered. ''I'll deal with her.''

She slipped into the chair behind him. Danny kept what he hoped was a friendly, nonthreatening expression on his face. Charles was made of stone.

''Mrs. Lampert. My name is Danny. I'm Gam's friend, too. He and I worked together.'' He started to move slowly away from the desk, creating more distance from the others; already Becca was having to split her focus between Michelle, Charles, and Danny.

Good girl, Michelle. Wait until I've got her complete attention.

''He's dead!'' Becca shrieked suddenly.

For a moment, Danny thought she was about to bawl, but the storm passed as quickly as it had come.

He took another breath. ''Mrs. Lampert. We're Gam's *friends*. Gam used to tell us about you. He told us how much he loved you. Didn't he, Charles?''

Charles nodded primly, still rooted to the spot.

She was listening now. One flap of her robe slipped away from her bony fingers, falling to reveal her naked, wrinkled body beneath. But Danny didn't dare shift his gaze from her eyes, as he continued his slow arc away from the desk and toward the doorway.

All right, let's go, Michelle. Pack that sucker up.

"Gam worked right next to me. Every day. He created something great, did you know that? He did something really remarkable on the computer. He's going to be famous."

Becca's nervous glances toward Michelle and Charles were coming less and less frequently as Danny kept moving. Now Michelle was almost directly behind her, and Danny peripherally saw her quietly going to work at the computer. *Screw the finesse, Michelle! Just rip the damn drive out and let's get away from this place.*

"Now, Mrs. Lampert. Just let us take this piece of equipment with us. You need to help us finish Gam's work."

"You people leave here," Becca finally said, her grip on the carver tightening. "Right away. Go now."

Michelle, for God's sake? I'm dyin' here, babe.

"Yes, Mrs. Lampert. In just a very short moment, we will leave here. And we'll just take this one computer box with us to—"

"*No!*" There went the knife again. "Don't you take nothing."

"All right, listen, Mrs. Lampert. We'll buy it from you. It's not doing you any good sitting on his desk, is it? We'll buy it from you. Five hundred dollars, right now. We'll write you a check right now. All right?"

Blissfully, Danny noted that money appeared to be a sensitive point with Becca. She suddenly lost interest in all other proceedings.

"You are going to pay? Five hundred?"

Danny nodded. *You* do *have your checkbook, don't you, Michelle?*

Michelle was standing. "Yes, Becca, we'll pay you right now."

Becca watched eagerly as Michelle took her checks out of her purse and scrawled one out in a hurry. Danny kept his eye on the gym bag. *Thank God you've got your purse...*

At last it was done. Becca held the little yellow check in her hand, reading it over and over again. "Thank you, Becca," chimed Michelle, nimbly stepping through the gap between the carving knife and the desk, to be with Danny. "You've done a great thing. You're a good person, and you've helped us very much."

"Yes...thank you," added Charles. The three of them sidled toward the doorway. Something deep in Becca's brain was trying to process the situation; a look of helpless confusion took over her face as she looked from the check to the two young people edging away from her.

"Uh..." was all she said.

"Thank you, Mrs. Lampert."

As they entered the hallway, Danny, Charles, and Michelle turned carefully away from the dazed woman in Gam's bedroom, still moving slowly. When they reached the stairway, they bolted. But even as they reached the back door, they heard nothing from the upstairs. They ran through the kitchen and burst into the backyard.

The tension broke—the drive was in their hands. Danny whooped, grabbed Michelle and kissed her happily. Her eyes were closed, her arms around him; Charles stood to the side, and finally gave Danny a self-conscious slap on the back. Suddenly, with the prospect of making things turn out right, Danny felt liberated, freer of Gam's shadow than he'd ever felt before.

They had the map. They could stop the virus.

"Be careful with that bag," Danny told Charles unnecessarily. "That drive's our one and only ticket out of this mess."

They trotted down the hill toward the cars, aware that the troubled woman upstairs might be staring at them through the window.

"All right, my heroes," she said, beaming. "You've got your Holy Grail. Now get back to Santa Clara and slay some serious dragon."

"We shall, O Princess," he responded.

Charles held the canvas handles of the gym bag in both hands. The weight of the drive made it sway like a pendulum.

"I'm off to Cupertino," she said, gesturing to her car with her thumb. "How late will you be at the office?"

Charles shot Danny a look. "Till about, uh...1998?"

"Then I'll see you when I get done," she said. "Keep a light on for me."

Danny watched her go. Even in the midst of this crisis, there was a bounce to her step.

It was going to be hard to leave this job, he decided.

As Michelle's Honda pulled away with a friendly beep, Danny fished his keys out of his pocket and stepped up to the car. He slipped the key into the lock, but for some reason it only slid in halfway.

He withdrew it and looked at it closely; he turned it upside-down and tried it again. No luck. He wiggled it, withdrew it, checked to see if it was straight, tried again. Something was jammed inside the lock.

"Here. Let the master try it," offered Charles.

Danny handed over the key. "I think there's something stuck in there. Wanna try the other side?"

A dark red Sentra slowed to a stop just behind Danny's Rabbit.

"Yes, even here in the moneyed hills of Woodside," chanted Charles in a life-styles-of-the-rich voice, "Good Samaritans take time out to aid motorists in trouble."

The man who got out of the Sentra was a tall, muscled fellow, wearing sunglasses and a thick brown mustache. He pushed the door shut and approached the two programmers. From the way he glared at them as he walked, Danny didn't think the guy was a Good Samaritan.

"Good evening, boys."

Danny looked at him. *Who is this guy?*

The big guy stopped just in front of them. "You boys from Artelligence?"

Danny looked at Charles, whose expression suggested he'd rather be at home asleep.

"Uh...can I help you?" said Danny cautiously.

"Gentlemen, I'll take what's in the bag, and then you can go on your way." He sniffed once, held out his hand for the gym bag that swung from Charles's fist, and glanced back up the hill.

Danny's mind did not compute. "I beg your *pardon*?"

"I said give me the bag." He took a step closer.

"I'm sorry, we can't do that. Charles, open the door." Charles wasn't thrilled about crossing the mustache guy.

As it turned out, he wouldn't have to. The big guy pulled open his blazer just enough for Danny and Charles to see the holster strapped across his torso. It contained what looked like a police pistol.

"Let's not make this any uglier than it has to be, boys. I want the bag. I'll even give it right back. And then we can forget this ever happened. But I want it *right now*."

One meaty hand was on Charles's wrist, and his hot massive body pressed him hard against the side of the car. Charles winced more with surprise than pain.

"Give it, buddy," the guy muttered, his other hand closing on the gym bag just below the handles, as though he were strangling a chicken. "Let me do my job, and you go on your way."

Danny was trying to think, trying to plan. *Gang up on him? Oh, right—this guy would squish us like cherry tomatoes. Run for it? Where? Back to Becca's? He'd shoot us in the knees...*

"Look, you don't need to force it, all right? Let go of him."

The burly guy relaxed his grip and stepped back. "All right, you're right. I don't need to get violent."

Danny relaxed—slightly.

"I just need *this*!—" the guy said, and he ripped the bag violently from Charles's hands, the cloth handles making rope burns across his palms.

"*Hey!*" Danny cried, but it was too late. The big man whirled the bag once around his head for momentum, then brought it down through the air to the pavement, smashing it with all his might. There was a sickening crack as the plastic case shattered inside.

And then again. And again. Danny jumped forward, grunting, and grabbed the guy's massive arm, clutching it to stop its motion, but with incredible force, the former policeman shoved him to the pavement like a dog. Danny tried to get up again, watching in horror; it looked like the man was beating a rug, or a slave. With each impact, the sound of jingling and clinking increased from inside the bag.

After the longest fifteen seconds Danny had ever endured, the muscular man shoved the battered nylon bag back to Charles, who took it with a shaking hand. Danny could see a few tiny rips in the fabric, and a gray plastic fragment fell through one and onto the pavement.

"You see? That's all, boys. No problem. No hard feelings, boys." The guy put on a mournful expression for Danny. "Oh, I *am* sorry about your door lock. I think a piece of metal may be stuck in there."

Danny watched the man stride off to the Sentra.

"What ... the hell ... was that?" asked Charles, his hands shaking. With conscious effort, Danny collected himself enough to unzip the bag that dangled from Charles's hands; the drive was pulverized. He knew that even if the motor and case had been shattered, the data could still be retrieved from the spinning platters themselves; but even those shiny coppery disks were hopelessly cracked.

For a moment, Danny considered leaping into his car and following the Sentra, to discover who had sent this unpleasant fellow—and then he decided not to bother.

He had a pretty good idea already.

chapter 15

THE NEW YORK POST

DEADLINE:

ELECTRONIC 'TIME BOMB' TICKS AWAY

Iranian Terrorist Group Claims Responsibility

Santa Clara, CA—A deadly "time-bomb" virus program has infected computer networks across the continent. Programmed to begin destroying computer data at midnight Sunday, the sinister virus has users, analysts, and Wall Street alike expressing grave concern for the safety of the victims' computer data.

At 1:30 this morning (EST), in a telephone call to the *Post*, the Shi'ite terrorist organization ANA claimed to have authored the deadly pro-

gram. The spokesperson declared that "We are
doing God's will," and that the group would
continue to pursue its terrorist tactics until "the
Western dog lies dead."

(Continued on page A4)

January 22, 1994—8 P.M.   LeMongelo Wiggins's first words
that Friday night were unpublishable. And they didn't stop—a
torrent of vulgarity that continued until the ringing phone was
actually under his fingertips.

"What the hell you want?"

"Good evening, Mr. . . ." There was a fluster of paper from
the other end. "Mr. Wiggins. My name is Martin. I'm calling
from the telemarketing firm Ascard and Philmore, and we're—"

"You sonofabitch, don't you call me wakin' me up to sell me
some kinda crap!" He tried to slam the phone down, but he was
still in bed, on his back, and the crazy angle his wrist had to take
messed up his aim. As he groggily tried to find the cradle, he
could hear the little voice coming from the earpiece.

"No, wait! Mr. Wiggins! Mr. Wiggins! We're not selling anything, Mr. . . ."

He sighed angrily. "All right then, what you want?" he
snapped, the receiver once again at his face. These people had no
idea what it was like to be a graveyard-shift worker; for Le-
Mongelo, eight P.M. was the middle of the night.

"Mr. Wiggins, we realize it's Friday evening, but we were told
this is an emergency message. May we read it to you?"

What the *hell* was this? "Let's hear it."

"This message comes from the Artelligence Software Corporation in Santa Clara. 'Dear Artelligence customer, We are delighted that you have recently purchased our Master Voice
speech-recognition sys——' "

"Look, man, I'm sleeping, right? You wanna tell me the deal
and lemme go back to bed?"

" ' . . . of our Master Voice speech-recognition system. While
we're sure that you'll be pleased with the system, we are calling
to tell you about a very dangerous condition that may exist in
your copy of the software.' "

LeMongelo was listening now.

" 'Through circumstances beyond our control, this software was infected by a computer virus when it was under development. We believe that your copy of the program may also be infected. Please listen very carefully and take the following steps. If you do not follow these steps explicitly, you risk severe data loss. If you do take the following precaution, however, we are confident your computer and your information are safe from harm. Are you ready for the instructions?' "

"Yeah, yeah, let's hear it."

" 'The virus in question is a so-called time-bomb virus. That is, it will do nothing destructive to your system until a specific time and date. That date is January thirtieth. Therefore, to protect your data, we advise you to set your Macintosh clock back one year, so that the Control Panel says 1993 instead of 1994. As soon as possible, we will ship you a new copy of the Master Voice software that is free from viral infection.

" 'Mr. Wiggins, are these instructions clear, or would you like instructions on how to set your computer's clock?' "

"Where the hell this virus come from?" asked LeMongelo.

"I'm sorry, sir, I have no information other than what I've read you. Would you like to hear the message again?"

"No, man, forget it. I'll do that. I'll set my clock back. *When I get the hell up, all right?*" Once again, his wrist was at the wrong angle to perform a proper phone slam.

The last sounds he heard from the little earpiece as he finally connected with the cradle were, "Thank you for listening, and we hope you enjoy many hours of happy computing with products from Art——"

"Look, Clark, I don't *know* what's causing the slowdown. All I can say is we're working on it. I have Accounts working on a backup carrier for you, but in the meantime you're just going to have to bear with us, OK?"

Silverstein knew they were in big trouble. The mainframes in Southbury, Connecticut, had been missing cycles—processor cycles that were only a few milliseconds long, but critical to the error-correcting routines built into its communication with COMSAT. And maintaining error-free signal traffic to the satellite was at the top of the COMSAT priority list; as semiannual bursts of sunspot activity always proved, a little static on the line could cause hellish problems for the communications satellite. And that could mean trouble for the TV, government, telephone, scientific, space, weather, university, military, and air-traffic systems that rented time from COMSAT, Inc., to bounce their signals off the cylindrical black orbiting machine.

For the moment, the trick was to keep the subscribers happy.

"Clark. Listen. I'm going to have to get back to you. I assure you we're onto the problem, and I'm sorry it's messing up your transmissions, and all I can say is it's messing up everybody else, too. Sorry. I'll call you. Bye."

Silverstein hung up and rubbed his eyes. He beeped down to Engineering.

"Max, it's Roger. Any progress?"

There was something wrong with the UNIX-system mainframes that operated the satellite. Something was making the processor miss a computing cycle once every sixteen seconds, and nobody could figure out what it was. The result, however, was becoming a problem. For the cable-TV broadcasters who leased time on the satellite, the missed cycles meant missed error-correction routines, and therefore thousands of viewers phoning in with complaints about picture quality. For mobile phone networks, the missed cycles meant that thousands of newly dialed calls failed to go through. For marine navigational equipment, it meant unreliable readings. For overseas telephone traffic, it meant a slowdown in response time.

"No progress here, Roger," said Max in Engineering. "We got some big trouble, I'm afraid. Whatever it is, there's more of it now."

What?

" 'Fraid I'm not with you, Max."

"Well . . . " Roger could hear Max sigh on the other end of the line. "The mainframe is skipping *four* cycles a second now. Whatever it is, it's replicating itself. Some kind of bug in the OS somewhere. It's gonna take a while to find it."

Roger swore out loud. His phone console was lighting up with phone calls from companies all over the planet who leased time on the satellite.

"All right, Max. Just get the goddamn thing fixed, all right? This is really messing things up."

He hung up. He wasn't even thinking about the phones, or the TV picture, or the news wires, all of whose operations were suffering through the COMSAT malfunction.

He was worrying about the shuttle launch.

Lars felt better than he had in years. The fog that had seemed to obscure his road to a bright, brilliant future had lifted suddenly after a decade. He beamed, savoring like fine wine the scene Nick had just described; oh, what he would have given to see Stroman's boys stand there while the hard drive got smashed to mulch. And oh, what he'd give to see Stroman's face when the news got back. For all practical purposes, Bob Stroman was history. For the first time in a decade, Lars knew at last that the world was his.

"Thank you, my friend," he said confidently, pumping Nick's thick, callused hand. "You did good work tonight."

"No problem," said Nick.

Lars turned and returned to his office, relishing the victory. It was a peculiar feeling, actually. He didn't sense any positive emotion, nothing uplifting like joy or victory; come to think of it, he wasn't sure if he had ever had those feelings. No, what he felt now was the death of a negative feeling, as though a curse had finally been removed. It was a vindication—an acquittal, really. So many times they'd told him his tactics would come back to haunt him. So many naysayers, so many doubters.

And they were all wrong. There was no evidence left in the world, no remaining bread crumbs left to follow. Huntington was home free.

And the software is the phoenix, really: Stroman slaves for a couple years, a business life cycle, and dies just in time to hand the completed project to me *on a platter. I rescue it from the ashes. I bring it to market. Too beautiful.*

He entered his office and closed the door, perversely happy that it was a Saturday, so he didn't have to dilute his massive feelings of relief by dealing with any employees on the way in.

Vincent celebrated his seventy-eighth birthday by opening a bottle of Martinelli's sparkling cider and sending out for steamed clams from that Italian place he loved. He walked over to the La-Z-Boy to sit down to wait for his meal and put on the TV; though the arthritis made walking difficult, he often thanked God that he could still walk at all.

Vincent paid $375 a month for his two-bedroom apartment in Queens, where he had lived since arriving in the forties. Only thing he didn't go for was these young crazy kids that seemed to be taking over the city. They had no sense of class, of style, of behavior, with their long hair and their loud music.

He had just reached for the remote when it began again: a door slamming in the apartment next door. Because of the design of the building, Vincent's living room was just through the thin wall from the next unit's bedroom, so he sometimes wound up learning a lot more about these crazy young people than he wanted to.

Male Voice:	Allie?
Female:	I'm home!
Male:	I need to talk to you. Come 'ere a minute.
Female:	Just a second, lemme get my coat off! (*Closer now*) What's the trouble?
Male:	Look at this.
Female:	What?
Male:	Don't you see this? Look. Right here. At the edge.
Female:	A little white spot. So?
Male:	Do you know what that is?

Vincent set the remote control down. This might get good, and he didn't want the TV sound from his own apartment to disturb the scene in progress; any discussion of sex lives beat ESPN any day.

Female:	So you've got a white spot up there. Who cares?
Male:	I was watching the news today…
Female:	Spare me, Michael.
Male:	…and they were talking about some kind of virus.
Female:	And you think that white thing up there is a virus.
Male:	I don't think you've been careful.

Vincent's eyebrows went up. He adjusted the chair so his ear would be parallel to the wall.

Female:	Michael, give me a break. You could have brought that virus home, too.
Male:	Oh, please. I do not go shoving my floppy into just anyone's slot.

Vincent's mouthful of Martinelli's exploded from his lips.

Female: I don't, either, Michael. I am *very* careful. Nobody at work has come near me for weeks. OK, well, Larry did; he wanted a closer look at this figure I've been working on.

Male: Oh, just great. You let him...

Female: And Bob, or Rob, or something, downstairs in the computer lab. Anyway, he said I was making a funny noise when I powered up, and said he needed to get inside there to poke around. But other than them, I've been practicing very safe—

Male: Jesus, Allie! You barely know these guys! You don't know who they've been sharing with, where they've been, who they dial up at night...

Vincent's doorbell rang...must be the clams. It took a moment to stand up, with his stiff joints and all, but he knew it would be worth it: the clams were his favorite. He hobbled toward the door, clucking his tongue at what today's youth had become.

"Well, Bob, for whatever it's worth...," Arnie said to Stroman, patting the side of his Macintosh, "your boys and I have just engineered the world's most effective virus. Too bad there's no market for 'em, huh?"

It wasn't really a joke—not when their emotions were at this low an ebb. It was actually the last remnants of pride in the team's work: in a nonstop, life-and-death programming marathon, they had produced a slick, simple, wildly effective shell of a program in less than a day.

A shell, because all it could do was furiously and systematically plunge into every disk, every file, every network cable it encountered. The team had sardonically dubbed their new virus Macrophage; Skinner, whose brother was an oncologist, said a macrophage was a cell in the human body that attacked invading cells.

Arnie had pointed out that Macrophage would set virus-protection programs beeping whenever it struck—but so, of course, had the original virus. Then, too, Macrophage wasn't intended for computer users regularly plugged into the national stream of Macintosh lore. Those power users—the kind savvy enough to use virus-protection programs to begin with—had, by this time, already heard about the Houston virus and how to protect themselves.

No, Macrophage was for everyone else: people who worked on computers purchased for them by their companies; people who were just learning to use their computers; people who had contracted the Houston virus by trying out some goody a friend had brought over on a floppy. The hope for Macrophage, of course, was that it would steal as swiftly and silently through the computing community as had its adversary—and that thousands of people might be cured before they even knew they were infected.

"It's lovely," Stroman responded.

It was, indeed, an elegant demonstration. Skinner and Rod had put the half-finished Macrophage through its paces. After successfully infecting a computer, the prototype Macrophage indicated its success by inverting, black for white, the *rest* of the computer screen. . .all except pixel (0,0), in honor of the Houston virus.

Stroman looked around: the entire R and D lab was filled with black computer screens that had white lettering, as though he were looking at a negative of a Macintosh factory. "By the time we're finished with Macrophage, it won't invert the screen like that," Rod explained. "This is just for now, to let us know it's working right."

Stroman smiled at the programmers, knowing that if he spoke, he would only defuse their morale. Realistically, they only had forty-eight hours left to finish, debug, and start distributing the Macrophage anti-virus nationwide; Stroman tried not to focus on the impossibility of the task.

He turned and was about to leave the lab when Danny and Charles burst in, stressed to the breaking point. Charles carried the shreds of a dusty, ragged nylon bag of some kind, which he threw disgustedly on the center table as he came in.

"Stroman," Danny panted. He had run, lungs bursting, from the parking lot and through the length of the building. "It's over . . . it's all over. They had a guy there. Big guy."

He panted for a moment, hands on his knees. "He was waiting for us when we got out of the house. He took the drive and wrecked it. He—"

Caught in a fit of coughing, Danny pointed at the bag on the table. Stroman picked it up and unzipped it slowly, a look of distrust and fear on his face.

The other programmers were frozen. They watched Stroman reach inside the opening. They saw his hand moving inside the bag; and they saw it reemerge holding a pie-shaped metallic wedge. It was a hard-drive platter shard.

Without a word, Stroman threw it on the table and stormed from the room. This was going too far—this was violence! This was vicious, premeditated, punishable! He strode toward his office, his mind racing. He'd sue. He'd fight. He'd. . .

He fairly leaped into his office, slamming the door behind him and collapsing in his chair. He covered his face, not knowing how to react, what to do. Everything was unraveling much too quickly; the breath was knocked out of him. He'd had no chance to counterstrike.

Shaking violently, he clutched the receiver, but kept his right index finger on the hang-up button. In his heart, he knew that he'd have to make this phone call sooner or later.

It had been a long time since he dialed this number, of course. So long that he no longer had it memorized. In fact, the number wasn't even in his Mac-based electronic Rolodex; he had to dig out his old real Rolodex to find it. *My God . . . it's been ten years.*

As he waited for an answer, his breathing began to slow. He thought at first that nobody would be there on a Saturday afternoon. But even by the fourth ring, he knew that—if his hunch was right—Lars would have to be at the office today.

Today, of all days.

"Huntington," said a woman who sounded as though she'd been smoking for thirty years.

"Yes. It's Robert Stroman. I'm calling for Lars Huntington." He glanced at his calendar. "I believe he's . . . ah . . . expecting this call."

"One moment."

There was no Muzak on the line today.

There was a click, and then the hollow plastic sound of somebody putting on the speaker phone.

"Well, *hel*lo, Bobby." It was Lars.

Stroman closed his eyes with the discomfort and the memories.

"You miserable *bastard.*"

"Why, *Bob*by! Is this the way we greet an old friend?" Huntington's voice oozed with condescension.

"Look, Lars. I'm sure you can imagine that I'm in no mood for small talk. We know what you've done, we know who did it, and I can imagine very easily why you did it."

"Now, *Bob*by. Why on earth would you call me up so full of piss and vinegar? We have a lot of catching up to do, you know ...'How's the company, Lars?' 'Fine, Bobby...' 'I'm sorry I've dedicated my career to destroying you, Lars.' 'That's all right, Bobby...' *That* kind of thing."

"Cut the crap, Lars. I'm gonna throw your ass in jail."

Lars chuckled. "*Are* you? What a sweet notion. Do you have a reason in mind, Bobby, or are you just feeling grumpy?"

"We're on to you, buddy. I believe they call it industrial sabotage."

"You haven't a shred of proof of wrongdoing, my dear friend. I'm afraid our country's criminal system doesn't work quite the way you think it does. You don't just show up at the police station, pointing fingers and saying, 'That big bully!' Let me help you along with this fine legal point: you have to have evidence. But oh, too bad, there's no evidence left to find, is there? What a shame about that hard drive! Such a noble, feeble attempt on your part, once again, to try to stand in my way. I guess I should refund the quarter you spent on this phone call, old friend."

If Stroman could have seen himself, he would have noticed that he was nervously, sharply, unconsciously jutting out his jaw every now and then, a tic he hadn't had since junior high school.

"Lars. I'm not in the mood to play around. You hired Gam to plant a virus in our code. We know this, Lars. But we shipped early, do you understand? We shipped the virus out on a hundred thousand disks. It's all over the goddamn place. The whole country is riddled with this thing."

For the first time, Huntington had no fast answer.

"Look, it's not about this stupid rivalry, all right? At this point, I'm willing to forget our personal differences. At this moment, I need you to help us kill the virus."

There was still silence on the other end.

"OK. Congratulations—you smashed the hard drive we were trying to get. Good for your guy. All I want to know is whether

or not you've got a copy of the virus code map we need to write
an anti-virus program. We still have time to avert some of the
catastrophe."

Lars cleared his throat grandly.

"Ah, Bobby. What an imagination! To think that I'm going to
come to the aid of the man who's done nothing but try to crush
me for ten years—and now he wants *help*! Now he wants *to-
getherness*! I don't think so, Bobby ol' buddy. It's *your* company's reputation the media is about to begin questioning. It is *your*
company's quality control that's about to be doubted by the computer users of this country. And you know what? It's *your
problem*."

Stroman drew a long, slow breath. "Think this through, Lars.
I'm offering you a chance, right now, to do something positive
To help people. If you close your door to us now, I swear you'll
live to regret it."

Lars only laughed. "Hoo, boy . . . I think you need to take a
couple of playwriting courses, pal. My character's got no moti
vation. Why would I *possibly* want to help *you*? I'm in good
shape, and you've got nothing on me. And your story's not be
lievable! How could you—a man whose company is about to dro
off the map—threaten *me*?" Lars was really laughing now, gidd
with his safety and his victory. "Makes a nice fantasy, Bobby
but nobody will buy it."

Stroman struggled for a comeback, but drew a blank.

"Well. Thanks for the call, Bobby. Nice of you to fill me i
awfully sorry to hear that your business is about to flop. *Do* sa
hello to Margo for me."

Lars hung up.

chapter 16

January 22, 1994 As a rule, Joni checked every file for viruses
when it was uploaded by an InfoServe member. As the system
operator—or SysOp—of the Macintosh Business Forum, she took
pride in adding, "This file has been checked for viruses by Antidote 3.0" to the description of any program she made available
to the membership. Since she started hearing about the Houston
virus business, she was especially careful to do so.

Antidote was a terrific program. It was advertised to be able to
detect and eradicate "any virus known to man or machine," and
she believed it; in the thousands of files she had posted in the last
five years, she could remember about ten being infected by known
viruses, and Antidote had nailed them all.

It didn't occur to Joni that Antidote was useless at identifying
unknown viruses.

She had the windows open tonight—one of the luxuries of
living in Savannah—and was working through her nightly ritual.
Answer questions posted in her forum by members during the

day. Download the new files members had sent to her. Check them for viruses, make sure they work, edit the descriptions; and if she indeed thought they'd be valuable to the computing community at large, post them in the library section of her forum so that InfoServe members could download them. Finally, credit the members who sent the files with a refund of the connection charges they spent doing it. That was to encourage people to participate, to contribute files, to keep the library constantly stocked with new and interesting software.

There were eight new files she had decided to post tonight. One of them was sent in by Rory Gershon, a regular uploader. She smiled when she thought of him; a nice, articulate man, an ad executive in Texas somewhere. Of course, she didn't know how to picture this guy any more than she could picture any of her best on-line friends; the electronic community just didn't work that way. On a modem network like InfoServe, you meet people. You get to know them. You have fights; you fall in love. But you never do see what these people look like, never hear their voices, never know a thing about their demographics.

With some embarrassment, Joni occasionally recalled the time she, a forty-year-old divorcee, had been getting to know a brilliant, mature, witty systems analyst she met on-line. His screen name was Lancelot. They'd send E-mail to each other every day, run into each other in the public electronic discussions, and eventually have private one-on-one conversations in secluded parts of the network. He'd make her laugh. He was a truly sensitive fellow. She really became attached to him.

Finally, one night, their on-line chatting had become somewhat philosophical—even a little romantic. Joni began to ask Lancelot to describe himself. *Funny thing*, she thought at the time. *The topic comes up only now, when we already know each other as few other souls do.* Suddenly looks and demographics were only a topic of conversation, nothing more: neither of them would draw any conclusions, make any judgments. *Isn't that how real society should be?*

He told her he'd been deaf from birth. He said he was an Orthodox Jew. He told her he was calling from Washington State, about as far away from her as she could get.

She smiled in surprise. That's nice, she typed.

Then he told her he was fourteen.

Since then, Joni had been a little more careful about falling in love with people typing on distant keyboards.

Rory Gershon was a good guy, too. He liked to send files to the forum, little programs he'd written himself. "Shareware," it was called; people were free to download this kind of program from InfoServe to try out at home. If they found such software useful, the honor system bound them to send some token amount—maybe twenty dollars— to the author. Rory once told her that he only made about $250 a year from the shareware he wrote; that for every fifty people who downloaded one of his programs, only one or two mailed him money.

But he still loves doing it, Joni thought as she ran his new little program through the Antidote virus-checker. It beeped, a little smiling-man icon appeared, and Antidote told her, "No known viruses found."

She was just about to run Rory's program, called Dbasement, when the phone rang. It was her mother . . . a delightful woman under most circumstances, but occasionally a runaway chatterbox. Like tonight.

Joni sighed and decided that the conversation would be one-way enough that she could continue to work on the forum while she chatted. *Aw, screw it,* Joni thought, *I'll try out Rory's thing later. Meantime, let me get these files posted.*

Absently, she posted all eight of the new files into the InfoServe Macintosh Business library. She had run all of them through Antidote. All were clean.

Had she actually *run* Rory's Dbasement program, however, she would have simultaneously run the virus embedded within it. It would have attempted to infect every program on her hard drive, and that invasion process would have triggered Antidote's secondary alarm—a watchdog feature that notified the user any time *anything* tried to modify programs on a hard disk. Antidote would have beeped once for each attempt the virus made. She would have realized that a new virus was along for the ride in Rory's program, and she never would have posted it on-line.

But as her mother filled her in with news about her garden, Joni posted the infected file on the nation's largest electronic bulletin board—one that was electronically visited each day by 90,000 people.

Bernard Meng had been Walter Reed's chief cardiologist for six years, and he'd never seen anything like this. The spikes in President Jurenko's EKG had been growing farther apart all morning—not wildly, but only slightly over the hours. It was an indication of hypokalemia—low blood potassium levels.

Hypokalemia shouldn't be surprising, Meng knew. Post-op patients were regularly given diuretics after the surgery, to help minimize the body's massive fluid shifts. And the nasal gastric tubes that compensated for the G.I. tract's shutdown during surgery also drained fluids away. With all of that fluid removal, losing a little potassium was to be expected.

But this particular patient was on Digoxin, given to prevent the heart from going into a frenzy of rapid, futile beating in the physical trauma of surgery. Digoxin and low potassium made for a dangerous combination, making the threat of irregular heartbeat—or even cardiac standstill—many times more severe.

And so Meng had administered potassium hourly since the cycle began, just after midnight. There was nothing unusual about that.

But what *was* unusual—in fact, frightening—was that the patient's blood-potassium levels were *dropping*, despite the injections. Where was the potassium going?

Meng turned to the computer terminal next to the bed. One of the two ever-present bodyguards was in his way. "Excuse me, I've got to see the monitor here," he said.

He called up the patient's most recent lab results. The system was splendid, Meng had always thought; every computer in the entire medical complex, stretching over a dozen city blocks, was linked to all the others. Standing right next to the patient's bed, Meng could instantly access the results of the tests taken only an hour before—even though the lab was in the basement of another wing of the building.

The screen indicated that Jurenko's potassium level was now 1.8. It made no sense; normal was between 3.5 and 5, and the patient's had been 4.1 for two days. Then, just around dinnertime it had plummeted to 3. Since then, Meng had ordered 10 milliequivalents of potassium per hour; after three or four doses, he was sure the level would return to normal. But the hypokalemia had only worsened.

He grabbed the phone and dialed the chief thoracic resident. "Debbie, give me Dr. Ankner please."

Ankner came on the line.

"Jay, it's Bernard. Listen, I wonder if you could give me a opinion. Our special cardiac patient here is having a little problem with his potassium levels. I want to know what you think." The surgeon promised to be on the floor in a moment. Meng hung up. The bodyguards looked jumpy.

He stared at the screen for a moment, wondering what was going on. He couldn't ever remember a body simply refusing to respond to potassium injections.

His thoughts were interrupted by an outburst from across the hall. "Judy!" yelled the nurse on duty. The supervising nurse materialized and ran across the hall.

Meng peeked out to see the situation. It was Mrs. Jelkenson. A Type II diabetic, he remembered. She was in for an angioplasty that Ankner had performed: a balloon was inflated inside one of her cardiac arteries to widen the corroded opening.

But now her muscles were locked in seizure, and her pupils were wildly dilated. The two nurses were frantically attempting to pull her out of it. Judy's fingers flew frantically at the computer terminal next to Mrs. Jelkenson's bed.

Insulin seizure, Meng thought. *Damn. Somebody wasn't watching her blood sugars.*

Ankner appeared at Meng's side. "Bernard, what's up?"

Meng showed him the president's chart, and showed him the bizarre results of his last few lab tests.

"I don't know, Bernard. Doesn't make much sense, does it?"

He sniffed once, the way he always did when he had a thought. "Funny about potassium, though. We've got a patient in the ICU with the opposite problem."

"What problem?"

"Guy's blood potassium is going through the roof. I don't know where it's coming from; we haven't given him a thing. Been going up all day."

"What the hell is going on around here, Jay?" Meng pointed to Mrs. Jelkenson. "Look at that—insulin seizure. Her blood-sugar levels must be in the hundreds. Why didn't Stokes check the damn lab tests?"

Within five minutes, the resident was called in. "What is it?" asked Stokes.

Meng demanded to know why Stokes hadn't administered any insulin to Mrs. Jelkenson that day.

"Why didn't I?" said Stokes. "Why *would* I? The lab tests were showing that her blood sugars were normal! Why the hell would I give insulin?"

Impatiently, Meng strode to the computer terminal. "Give me her patient ID," he snapped.

Stokes gave it to him. Meng stared at the monitor.

"My God, you're right, Stokes. Jay, look at this."

It was true. The most recent lab results, only thirty minutes old, showed Mrs. Jelkenson's blood sugar count to be normal.

"Wait a minute," said Meng. He held his hands up for silence and thought hard. He asked Jay to tell him about the hyperkalemic patient, whose potassium count kept rising. "Since around dinnertime," Ankner told him.

"Oh, Jesus," said Meng. "Tell everybody to stop administering anything." He looked grimly at the other two, who looked surprised and confused.

"I've got a terrible feeling about the lab." He pounded out of the room. "Get a cardiogram going!" he shouted over his shoulder.

As he would discover within minutes, nothing had gone wrong with the lab. The lab results were perfectly accurate.

What was wrong was the relational database, CTU-Base, into which the lab technicians entered the results of each test. It had staggering analytical powers, blinding speed at calculations, and the ability to handle huge numbers of requests for data—from all over the hospital complex—simultaneously.

The individual data files for the cardiothoracic unit lay grouped in a single electronic folder on the 1.6-gigabyte optical storage subsystem that hummed in Information Services a quarter-mile away. The CTU-Base program was extremely intelligent, and had been programmed to function even under less-than-optimum conditions; for example, the doctors in the CTU could access its data even in the event of a power brownout or a voltage surge.

Thus, when several of the individual patient files were erased from the optical drive by Clive Witmark's prematurely awakened Houston virus, the database did what it could to make sense of the remaining data. It cleverly omitted the missing files as it read data from the disk surface, loading in their places the next files available. In short, in the attempt to avoid any disruption of its normal functioning, the program did succeed in associating each patient's name and patient ID with a set of lab data.

But, like a child who has misbuttoned the buttons of her sweater, CTU-base associated each patient's ID with the *wrong* set of lab data—in fact, with the data of the patient with the next higher ID number.

Ankner, still on the ward floor, stared at the ever-widening rhythms on the printout from the cardiogram. He ran the strip through his hands in disbelief.

"Stokes! Get the hell over here! Nurse!"

The blips on the EKG monitor representing the rhythms of the atria and ventricles had almost merged into a sine wave. Something was horribly wrong with the patient's heartbeat. Stokes stood by, ready for action.

"Nurse! Call the code!"

Judy raced to the paging station. Within seconds, the PA popped to life: *"Code blue, code blue on the floor."* A team of four residents scrambled into action and burst into the room, dragging a cart loaded with cardiac crisis equipment.

"Get Meng! Look at the goddamn EKG!"

Even as Ankner spoke, the sine wave deteriorated into a shallow, jagged, jittery line. "Jesus," he shouted at the code team. "Ventricular fibrillation. We'll have cardiac arrest in a *minute*."

One of the code team rammed a tube down the president's throat; the bodyguards stepped forward, uncertain.

"Get the hell out of the way," Ankner glowered at them. Stunned with his ferocity, they stepped back.

Ankner seized the strip of cardiogram printout, now making sinuous curls on the floor.

"Dammit. No change. Defibrillators! Let's shock this mother back into rhythm. Give him two hundred joules."

One of the team held the two cereal bowl–shaped defibrillators as another ripped open the patient's gown, exposing his dark tan chest. "Clear!" the first resident shouted, and released a powerful jolt of electricity into the president's chest. Ankner waited for the EKG signal to recover from the shock; when it did, there was still nothing but a tiny jagged horizontal line.

"Give him three hundred joules!"

Another massive jolt; still no response.

"Oh, God," Ankner said to a nurse. "Get the State Department. This is bad. Stokes, get these guys out of here." He indicated the two hulking bodyguards, who were increasingly in the way.

Suddenly Meng arrived, out of breath.

"Give him calcium," he blurted.

Ankner stared. "What the hell . . .? Meng, that would only make him more hypokalemic. He hasn't got a drop of potassium in his whole body! Why the hell would you give him—"

"Shut up, Jay. Ten mils of calcium, *now*!" he shouted at one of the code team. He turned to Ankner. "He's not hypokalemic. He's *hyper*kalemic—he's got more potassium in him than a banana farm! We've been pumping him full of it! No wonder his heart rate went off the map. *The goddamn lab computers are screwed.*"

Ankner swore.

They tried the defibrillators again, this time applying a blast of 360 joules—"Clear!"—to no avail. Ankner injected a massive dose of epinephrine, then of bretyllium. The nurses prepared the operating room.

"God*dammit*!" shouted Ankner. "Get the chief resident down here!"

But within two minutes, it was over. The erratic spikes on the EKG monitor gave way suddenly to a flat line, static and still on the phosphor of the display—cardiac standstill.

The patient was dead.

Ankner fled from the room, unable to handle the situation. He ducked into an empty patient room and stood, forearm and head against the wall, panting, shaking with anger—and fear. Fear that his career was over. Fear that there was something he had overlooked; that in the inevitable investigations that would follow in the months to come, the guilt would be laid at his feet.

In Reston, Virginia, the phone rang. Secretary of State Masso reached out to pick up the phone.

"Yes?" he said. Sitting in his library in a leather-covered recliner, his feet resting on an ottoman, he listened silently.

He let the phone fall to its cradle less than one minute later. He was deathly pale, his breathing shallow, mouth dry. He swallowed with difficulty, letting the horrible news sink in.

How had it happened? The best cardiac-care hospital in the country; the top surgeons in the hemisphere . . . They'd assured him that the operation was, as heart surgery went, routine. That Jurenko had been recovering with excellent speed.

Masso was devastated. His gut churned; somewhere in his soul, he knew that this event would change his life. Without success in the Soviet negotiations, his career in Washington was over—and without Jurenko, there could be no such success.

Helplessly, as rational thought succumbed to deep-seated, suddenly unleashed fears, Masso made a shaky call to his analyst. At this worst possible of moments, Masso was greeted by an answering machine.

Crumpling, Masso buried his face in his hands. His jaw clenched in the effort to keep from sobbing.

The call slip was marked URGENT; even so, Stroman could barely bring himself to look at it.

What was the point? No code map, no Macrophage. No Macrophage, and the Houston virus would explode wildly, unchecked, taking millions of computers down with it—and, with them, businesses, lives, national safety.

And what was the point of returning a business call, when Stroman knew he no longer had a business?

But he saw who the call was from. He picked up the phone and dialed.

"Hirota."

"Mr. Hirota. It's Robert Stroman."

There was a pause. "Mr. Stroman, I am sorry to disturb you on a Sunday. But the chairman of Mika was watching the news yesterday. He was watching your CNN, which he enjoys very much. During a broadcast this morning, he heard a very unpleasant report. We would like you to tell us there is no truth to it."

"Mr. Hirota. Well. There may well be a problem, yes, but we think . . ."

Think what, Stroman? Think you'll find a time machine to take you back ten years? Think you'll glue a thousand hard-disk platter fragments back together again? Think a miracle is going to walk into Artelligence in the next hour?

"You think what, Mr. Stroman?"

Stroman cleared his throat. "Mr. Hirota, I'm very sorry. It appears that the report you may have heard is true. The Master Voice software has somehow fallen victim to a virus. And it appears that we've . . ." He swallowed. "We've shipped a hundred thousand copies."

Mr. Hirota was perfectly still on the other end of the line. A few moments passed.

When Hirota finally spoke, it was with his characteristic British-accented tone of controlled calm and courtesy.

"Mr. Stroman, Mika representatives will arrive at your offices on Tuesday at nine A.M. We trust you will deliver a certified bank check for the full amount of our investment in your company."

In his misery, Stroman said nothing.

"If you are unable to produce the full one-point-two million, Mr. Stroman, we trust you will arrange the transfer of all employee-held stock to our representatives at that time. Including your own, Mr. Stroman. These were, of course, conditions of our agreement."

Tears of loss welled in Stroman's eyes. *Cowboys don't cry,* he thought, viciously wiping them away.

"I understand," he croaked. He let the receiver fall back to its cradle.

After five minutes of listening to the roar in his ears, Stroman vowed not to let his self-destructive instincts take over. *People,* he thought. He desperately needed to be with other people right now.

He stood shakily, walking down each of the desolate, frightening corridors to the R and D lab, where he knew the programmers would be. He entered without a word.

They barely glanced as he entered. The blazing activity of the previous hours was over; Macrophage was as ready as it could be without the code map. There was literally nothing to do.

No one else spoke. No one stirred. Stroman slumped disconsolately into a chair in the corner, feeling his life ebb away.

"So I don't understand one thing, OK?" said Skinner at last. "OK, so this guy from Huntington came and got you, right, came and got the drive from you. OK, but what I want to know is how did he know how to intercept you, y'know?"

Danny hadn't thought of it. "I don't really know. He was just sitting there waiting for us out in front of the house. The only thing I can think of is that maybe they can read our E-mail. They do have our passwords, you know. There was a list of Artelligence E-mail passwords on Gam's disk."

"It's my fault," said Stroman softly, staring straight ahead.

They looked at him.

"I sent Ellie an E-mail where I mentioned that we were going over there to get the file. I'll bet they read our note and just went there to wait. Huntington's guy just stood there and waited for Danny to come to *him.*"

There was a bitter, despondent moment. Even Charles, half a Ho-Ho in one hand, honored Stroman's pain by sitting still.

"Mika is coming to claim the property on Tuesday," Stroman added. "I'm...I'm so sorry."

Danny and the others were horrified.

Not with a bang, but with a whimper, thought Stroman. *What's that from?*

In the ensuing silence, the sound of brisk footsteps could be clearly heard all the way down the corridor. The sound approached the R and D lab; Michelle flounced in, purse in one hand, car keys in the other. She looked ludicrously cheerful.

"Hey, guys, howzit—" She stopped, noticing the gloom. "Hey. What'd I miss? Someone lose the lottery?"

Nobody reacted. It was worse than she thought.

Danny finally summoned the energy. "Michelle, we're in a little trouble. We uh..." He glanced at Stroman, who probably didn't need any further reminders. "We lost the hard drive."

"You *lost* it!? Danny, after all that?! Oh, my God! But you had it when I left for Cupertino! How could you?..."

But Danny was staring coldly at her, trying to speak with his eyes, to protect Stroman's brittle feelings, to signal to her the gravity of the situation. She was altogether too cheerful.

"Huntington sent a guy to meet us. He jumped us right after you left."

Michelle had heard a story or two about Stroman's less-than-wonderful ex-partner. "Uh-oh."

In his depression, Danny resented her good mood.

"He grabbed the drive and smashed it to a million pieces."

"And the map file, let's not forget," added Skinner irritably, feeling only *slightly* furious that his excellent work on the counter-virus had been wasted after all. "We were ready to roll, OK? The rest of the Macrophage is done."

There was a distinct click from the minute hand of the wall clock as it made its jump to 10:19.

Michelle snapped her fingers. Hers eyes slammed shut at a sudden thought. "Oh...the map file!"

Danny looked at her. "What about it, Michelle?"

"Oh, gosh, I forgot to tell you. Course, I just got here..." She stopped to re-rubber-band her ponytail, gathering it behind her head. "My God, you wouldn't believe the setup at this PR firm! It's like an airplane hangar full of library carrels or some-thing—''

"What *about* the map file, Michelle?" Charles was less patient.

She looked at him. "My, aren't we crabby!"

She came farther into the room and sat on the corner of the table. "Well," she began, enjoying it. "*You* know how boys are." She unsnapped her purse. "Always messy, always losing things..."

Danny knew Michelle well enough to recognize when she was slipping into blond-ditz mode for maximum effect. He tried to catch Stroman's eye, but Stroman was nearly insensate. Something was going on.

"...and you know how Danny's always yelling at us to make backups of everything..."

She was rummaging in her purse.

"...so after we recovered the file at Gam's house, and Danny was arguing with Gam's mom, I thought..."

Maddeningly, she started pulling items out of her purse. A brush. A wallet. A lumpy zipper case.

"...yeah, I thought it would be a good idea to make a copy of the map file. I thought: *Be a good girl and make a backup, Michelle.* I put it onto a floppy disk. Here ya go."

She withdrew an orange square from her purse—the orange floppy disk from Danny's disk wallet—and tossed it to him.

Danny caught it in a state of shock.

Michelle studied their faces, each frozen in a look of catatonic ecstasy.

"What? What's the problem? That's what you wanted, isn't it? Isn't that what you needed?"

She turned to go. "Jeez, and here I thought I was being helpful."

They mobbed her, screaming and babbling, cheering and hoot-ing, and lifted her off the ground. Stroman gradually lifted his head from the table, blinking and unbelieving. Michelle was tou-sled, kissed, tickled, squeezed, and hailed.

They set her down at last, grinning foolishly.

"So...am I one of the guys now?" she teased them.

Danny ran over and, unself-consciously, mauled her with kisses. "Michelle, you are *brilliant*," he said over and over again into her ear. "What a masterpiece you are."

"Careful," she scolded him. "I don't like to get emotionally involved with my co-workers."

He grinned at her, feeling glorious. He kissed the floppy disk once, slipped it into the nearest disk drive, and started to work.

chapter 17

January 23, 1994   "This is going to take freakin' forever,"
moaned Charles.

"I don't mind," offered Rod almost cheerfully. For the thousandth time the programmers racked their brains to imagine what
Gam might have used as a password to encrypt his code map.

"Read that thing again, Danny."

For the fourth time, Danny showed them the E-mail he'd found
on USA Online that morning.

■□■■■■■■■■■■■■ **URGENT! READ ME!** ■■■■■■■■■■■■ ⬛

DATE POSTED: 1/22/94
SENT BY: Miss Brooks
MAILED TO: Danny the C
SUBJECT: Huntington etc.

Hello Danny. You and I have chatted a few times here on USA
Online. I have something very important to tell you. I'm an
employee at Huntington Systems, and I just learned that you will
be going to Woodside to try to get Gam Lampert's software code
map.

I must warn you of two things. First: a representative of this
company has been sent to intercept you. BE CAREFUL.

Second, you will not be able to read the code map anyway,
because it is password-protected. Fortunately, I was able to find a
folder of old E-mails here at Huntington, and (at some risk, I
might add) I managed to find a reference to the password. It's in a
memo from Gam, and it says: "The password is the same as last
time (my mom's name etc.)." I hope this helps you.

I hope you succeed in stopping the virus. One day you and I will
talk; I'm sure there will be much to say. Until then, it's best if you
don't know who I am. Contact me only via USA Online.

--Miss Brooks

[Forward...]   [**Reply...**]

"Danny!" Michelle had scolded him the first time he'd read
t. "Who is this *woman*?"

"Just some lady on USA Online. I barely know her. She's up
n Livermore."

"Livermore!?" said Michelle. "Danny, that's where Hunt-
gton Systems is! You mean you didn't know this chick worked
or Huntington?"

"She's not a chick, Michelle. She's like fifty."

"I thought you barely knew her?"

"Look," Charles had interjected, "the point is, we've got the goddamn password! Let's get going!"

But they'd tried every possible variation, based on the message in the E-mail message "my mom's name, etc.": first name, last name, name and age, name and address. They'd tried Becca, becca, BECCA, variants of *Re*becca, Mrs. Lampert, B. Lampert, and every possible permutation thereof. Every time, the computer beeped and denied access to the hard-won code map file.

"Michelle, are you *positive* that's how she spells her name?"

Michelle threw up her hands. "*Yes!* How hard can it be? It's B-E-C-C-A. Becca. There's no other spelling."

Danny regarded her politely, then turned to Rod. "Try B-E-C-K-A." Rod looked at him quizzically, but entered the name. The computer beeped.

"Nope."

"I'm telling you, it's B-E-C-C-A. I don't even think it's short for something," Michelle said. "Even Gam called her Becca, and not Mom or anything."

Skinner turned to Michelle. "So, like, did she have another name? Say she had a middle name or something, y'know?"

"Well, maybe," sighed Michelle, "but if she does, I don't know it."

It was getting late—and it was getting *too* late.

"The thing that gets me is, Gam just wouldn't *do* something so easy," Danny murmured, racking his brains. "You're not ever supposed to make up a password that's in English."

"What do you mean?" asked Michelle.

"Too easy to guess." He sighed. "I just can't believe Gam would use something as guessable as his mother's *name*."

"Well he didn't, OK?" replied Skinner, " 'Cause his mother' name doesn't work."

Danny noticed that Skinner had started wearing his earring again.

Charles collapsed into a chair. "First he dies with his hard drive. Then we find out he erased his backup disk. Then the file we need is password-encoded. We overcome all that, we even have some fink at Huntington *telling* us the password, for God sake, and we *still* can't open the damn thing!? Why does Gam have to make everything so goddamn *tricky*?"

Michelle shook her head, mystified.

Danny kept thinking about one phrase: *mother's name, etc.* "What do you guys think the 'etc.' means?"

"Beats the hell outta me," muttered Charles.

"Means that's not all there is to it, right?" asked Rod, seated at the keyboard. "Maybe it's backward?" He typed ACCEB. Nothing happened.

"Maybe it's code," suggested Skinner. "That'd be totally righteous, y'know? Like the code where each letter of the alphabet is a number? Try that, Rod, OK? Try two for the letter B, and five for E, and stuff."

Rod entered 25331. Nothing.

Come on, Danny. You know Gam by now. Everything's gotta be tricky, and hidden, and convoluted. Everything's gotta be inscrutable to everybody else. Everything's gotta show off his programming genius and leave us out of it.

What would he do?

Suddenly Danny yelped. "Hey! I bet it *is* code!"

Charles looked at him through smoky lenses. "What kind of code?"

"What kind of code?! What are you, kidding? *Program* code! The code we've been living and breathing for the last three months! Code the *computer* understands!"

Danny pushed Skinner out of the way and stood behind Rod. "Look, you bozos. Here we're typing in a bunch of numbers in *human* notation. But Gam would never do that! He'd enter it in *hex*!"

"Huh?" said Michelle.

"Hex. Hexadecimal notation," said Charles. Skinner unhooked his ubiquitous calculator from his belt and stood in readiness.

"See, look," Danny explained. "There are twenty-six different letters in the alphabet; how many different numerals are there?"

She looked blank. "Um . . . you mean ten?"

"Right! The numbers you can use are zero, one, two, three, and on up to nine, right?"

She nodded, understanding somewhat.

"OK. But we humans use those ten numbers 'cause we were born with ten fingers. We count in *base ten*. But a computer, because it's a binary machine, counts in *base two*. It's like it has *sixteen* fingers."

Michelle shot him a look.

"Well, OK, in a manner of speaking. We can count up to nine without leaving the 'ones' place, right? Well, the computer can count up to *fifteen* without leaving the ones place. So when we're programming, and we need to express a number like, say, *ten* to the computer, we use a letter. Letter A comes after nine. It's called hexadecimal notation. The computer counts like this: zero, one, two, three, four, five, six, seven, eight, nine, A, B, C, D, E, F!''

"A, B, C...?" Michelle repeated lamely.

Danny nodded. "Right. To the computer, A is ten, B is eleven, C is twelve..."

He grabbed an empty pizza box and commandeered a mechanical pencil from Skinner's shirt pocket. "Ready for this?"

On the back of the cardboard box he wrote:

B	E	C	C	A
=11	=14	=12	=12	=10

"OK, now this is like a five-digit number. In *our* system, the number four-five-six is really a hundred times four, *plus* ten times five, *plus* six, right?"

"Sure." It was fine with Michelle, as long as they knew what they were talking about.

"So in hex, you don't multiply the digits by powers of ten. You multiply by powers of sixteen—sixteen, two fifty-six, four thousand ninety-six...like this:"

B	E	C	C	A
=11	=14	=12	=12	=10
×65536	×4096	×256	×16	×1

720896 +	57344 +	3072 +	192 +	10

"OK, Skinner, add 'em up."

Skinner held up the calculator: "So, in hexadecimal, B-E-C-C-A is...seven-eight-one-five-one-four!"

Danny leaned close and watched as Rod typed in 781514. The computer beeped three times, and Gam's code map file dutifully sprang to the screen.

"*Yes!!!*" hooted Charles.

"We're in!" shouted Michelle happily. She kissed Danny on the cheek.

Danny pounded Rod's back and yelped. Rod just sat back, grinning with delirious relief. Skinner danced on tiptoe, arms in the air, like a football player after scoring a touchdown. For a perilous moment, Danny actually thought Skinner might spike his calculator.

"And the crowd goes wild!" yelled Charles.

"OK, we got it, y'know!? There it is, OK? OK?" burbled Skinner.

Rod was happy, but he was looking at Danny quizzically. "Danny? Why is your Miss Brooks friend helping us?"

"I don't even know." Danny shook his head. "But I know that when this is all over, I'm going to find out, and I'm going to send her one incredible bouquet."

"Hmph!" said Michelle. But Danny couldn't mistake the twinkle in her eye.

The code map on the screen was meticulously typed, annotated, formatted. Each fragment of viral code was set off by dual rows of asterisks.

"Guess he wanted to make it easy to clean out the virus when he had to," said Danny. "Thank God."

Michelle still didn't quite get it. "Hey, Danny," she asked him quietly while the others regrouped in front of their computers. "What if Gam's mom's name had different letters? What if it was, like, Suzy or something?"

Danny stopped what he was doing and looked puzzled. "You're right. You couldn't spell that one in hex." He pulled up his chair and got ready for business.

"Gam got lucky, I guess," he said.

Clive discovered that doing good felt even better than doing well. He'd been milking his contacts all weekend, telling everyone in sight about the Houston virus. The message went out on every electronic bulletin-board system he could think of; he made a speech at his user group (and another speech at the user group in Dallas); with his wife's help—and using his clean, newly initialized hard drive— he started putting together a flyer/newsletter on the virus issue. Twice already people from city papers had called. They got his name from user-group members, who told the reporters that Clive was the expert on this thing—and, indeed, he probably was.

It was exciting, really. Yes, he'd suffered a tremendous loss when his data was eaten. But something new and big and important was growing out of it. After numerous phone calls to the people at Artelligence, he knew they'd have only a matter of days to get their anti-virus program out in the world. Clive planned to be ready.

January 24, 1994   "It's a virus, Roger."

Roger Silverstein leaned over Max's shoulder to look at the tiny writing on the dark green monitor. It was the only response he could think of, under the circumstance.

"A virus."

"Yup. It's a mean one, too. Judging from the rate of missed processor cycles per second, I'd say we've got close to a hundred copies of it bouncin' around in there."

Roger looked in panic around the COMSAT communications floor, as though he'd be rescued by some white-clad team of programmers at any moment.

"Well, Jesus, Max, I can't afford downtime right now. Can't we live with it till after the shuttle launch at least?"

Max shrugged. "Well, right now it's just gumming up the works a little. It's throwing off some things that are timing specific. Mainly data-correction signals. But missing a hundred cycles a second ain't peanuts. And it's only gonna get worse; far as I can tell, it's not done reproducing itself."

"What about the backup system?" Silverstein correctly predicted the answer.

"It's infected, too. The virus must've come from the InterNet, 'cause it got into both of our redundant systems."

Silverstein wiped his face. "Well. Can you get rid of it?"

Max gave him the thumbs-up. "All I gotta do is replace the UNIX shell with a fresh copy," he said. "Only thing is, I'm going to need some time with the mainframes isolated. We'll hafta replace every affected module, and then I'll hafta have the guys redo our passwords and access levels."

"How much time, Max? Jesus. We've got a shuttle launch in two days!"

NASA's primary communications systems were handled by

bigger satellite fish than COMSAT, Silverstein knew. Nonetheless, NASA leased time on COMSAT as an off-site backup system. No backup comm in place, no launch. *And no business—now or next time*, he added to himself grimly.

Max scrunched up his face. "Aw, I don't know. If I called in all our guys, we could probably have it cleaned out by then."

"Max, I don't need it cleaned out *by* then. I need it cleaned out *before* then. Are you telling me it's going to take you *two days* of downtime to fix this?!"

"I don't know what to tell you, Rog. I don't know how the damn thing got in here, for one thing; must be pretty sophisticated. That's only going to make it harder to rip out." He wiped his sleeve across his mouth. "Yeah, I think you'd better count on a coupla days. Sorry, boss."

Roger hurried out of the communications floor and back to his office. He pounded the keys of his terminal and sent the printer buzzing into action. When the first pin-fed sheet emerged, he ripped off the printout.

"Current Accounts twenty-four-Jan-ninety-four," he read aloud. He looked down the list of current COMSAT time-sharing clients on the first page.

page 1 of 15

Transcoastal Comm Corp	United Press International
National Weather Service	British Broadcasting Corporation
CNN	Hugo Shipping Lines
MetroBank USA	Stanford Univ/Linear Research
NASA/Kennedy Space Center	Transtar Mobile Comm
ATT	Deutschefon
Western Union Inc.	CBS
Norcom Cable Systems	US State Dept/Classified

Telefax Data Services	United States Navy/
	Norfolk
NBC	Nasdaq Inc.
Metrolink Data Systems	Associated Press

Silverstein's heart sank.

COMSAT Corporation had contingency plans; it was time to put them into effect. Unfortunately, it inevitably meant downtime for the clients while alternative arrangements were made, losing revenue for the company, and breaking trust.

He picked up the phone. "Mark, call Mr. Steinbrink for me." He sighed. "We're going to have to shut the bird down for a little while."

"Oh, *gawd*, not another pizza!" hollered Charles, slap happy and world weary.

Danny had to admit that he was longing for some good New York Chinese food. Or a waffle at the very least.

It was 11:35 P.M., almost exactly five days before the Houston virus would awaken. The Macrophage anti-virus virus was complete. They had, in essence, constructed a little spaceship with a titanium hull: fast, indestructible, potent, with a little hollow inside to carry its passenger—a virus-eating virus.

At Danny's suggestion, they had designed more than simply a beneficial virus. Like the Houston virus itself, Macrophage would be borne into the world embedded in a normal Macintosh program. Technically, Macrophage was a Trojan Horse virus just as Gam's was; people would think they were getting a useful program, but the virus would be an added bonus hidden inside.

When the carrier program, which they dubbed Cocoon, was launched, it did two things. First, it would look around the current computer and eradicate any Houston-virus code it found there. Second, Cocoon would release the Macrophage virus itself. This virus was instructed to run rampantly through the computer and any connected to it, on a seek-and-destroy mission for Gam's brainchild.

The Cocoon program's opening screen instructed the user to turn off any virus-checking software, since the Macrophage virus would, by nature, have to modify every program on the hard disk (by removing the Houston virus code). It also informed the user

that turning off virus-checkers also gave the Macrophage anti-
virus a golden opportunity to infect everything in sight. *This has
got to be the* weirdest, Danny thought at the time. *We're actually
telling people that we're letting a virus loose in their system!*

By nine A.M., they were ready to test the Cocoon program—
and the Macrophage virus nestled inside. As they had done several days before, the programmers isolated a single infected Macintosh. Danny placed a floppy disk, containing the Cocoon
program, into the disk drive.

"Go for it, Danny," said Stroman. "You're Mr. Virus around
here."

Danny wasn't sure he cared for the epithet, but he launched
the program. The splash screen appeared, describing the program's function.

Welcome to the Cocoon anti-virus system, developed
by Artelligence Software Corp.

This program eliminates the so-called Houston virus
from your hard drive and any other computers on the
network. It works by releasing a BENEFICIAL virus into
your system, which immediately eradicates any copies
of the Houston virus. The beneficial virus will not harm
your computer in any way.

For more information on the Houston virus or this
program, call the Artelligence virus hotline at 800-338-
8800. To proceed with the virus removal, click Proceed.

(Cancel)   [Proceed]

Danny clicked Proceed. A small window appeared, saying,
"Now removing viruses from your system."

The hard drive's LED access light flickered wildly. Danny
grinned at Charles as they waited. Something was happening to
the files on that hard drive.

Rod looked at the screen and spoke dreamily. "We're undoing
all Gam's hard work."

And then there was a beep.

"Infection removed," said a little message on the screen. There
was a small, weary cheer.

Danny quit the program and began to examine the various programs on the disk. He compared their sizes with the notes Rod had taken, and each was two kilobytes smaller than it had been when they started—sure signs that a chunk of viral code had been removed from them. He checked the Master Voice program. Where before the test it had been 770 K, it was now only 758.

"Man alive," said Danny. "I'd almost forgotten how much fun computers can be." He pulled up a chair and flopped into it.

"Let me have that copy," said Arnie. Danny handed him a floppy disk containing the final version of Cocoon. "Pass out the cigars, kids; I'm sending this little guy out into the world." He switched on the modem, ready to begin uploading the anti-virus virus to every network, service, and BBS he could think of.

It took nearly an hour for the team to return to earth; an hour of exultation made slightly surreal by intense sleep deprivation.

Michelle was overjoyed to hear the news: that Macrophage was being released into the nation's bloodstream.

"Anyone watch the eleven-o'clock news last night?" she asked.

"What station?" asked Danny.

"All of them," she said. "CNN. All the networks. They all ran stories about the virus. I guess NBC's newsroom itself got infected—the network's network, get it?—so they ran the story at six; and by eleven, everyone else followed suit."

Arnie looked up, concerned. "But did they publicize Macrophage? Do people know that they can cure the virus before it wakes up?"

Michelle nodded. "They made a big point of it. As a matter of fact, they flashed our 800 number." She looked at her watch. "It's not even nine yet, and already we've had about a million calls. I called in some more temps."

Stroman nodded. "Good thinking."

"Know what? Maybe this is weird to say right now, but this might not turn out to be such a terrible thing for us after all. We're being painted as a concerned, socially responsible company that's been victimized."

Stroman looked at Michelle for a long, warm moment.

"Michelle," he said finally. "You, young lady, have done an incredible job on this thing. You have shown yourself to be amazing at spin control, publicity, people handling, and crisis management. And backing up data, I might add. If you ever go into politics—or *any* other field—God help your opponents."

She was stunned but delighted. "Bob! Bob, I can't tell you how much that means to me."

A permed blond head poked into the room. "Oh, *here* everybody is," she said. It was Tina, holding a clipboard. "Hey, we're a little swamped answering questions about the virus, you guys. Everybody saw the news last night. Do you think you guys could come and help answer questions?"

"Sure, Tina, we'll be right in," responded Arnie, grinning at the boys.

"Like, I don't know. A lot of people want to know if this thing can migrate to UNIX systems. Two people called and said they think it *has* gotten into their UNIX systems."

Danny felt a chill run down his arms. Charles looked up with alarm.

"That's not good," muttered Danny.

Michelle sensed the tension. "UNIX. That's the big computers? The phone system and all that?"

"That's the one," replied Charles. "And the military, and air traffic, and navigation, and just about every other computer that counts in this country."

"Or any country," added Stroman. His face was ashen. "Danny, I thought we decided this thing couldn't live under UNIX?"

No, wait a second. . . . Danny's brow was furrowed. "It *can't.* I don't know how this could have happened. It's got to be a mistake!" *What could I have missed?*

"Unless somebody jury-rigged Master Voice to run under UNIX," Charles offered.

Danny leaped to his feet. "Do you have phone numbers, Tina? Maybe I should give them a call back."

She handed him the clipboard. "Right there, Danny-man." She circled a pair of phone numbers on the top sheet.

Looks like the friggin' moon, thought Colonel Oskins.

Sitting in the comfort of a briefing room, he fiddled with the contrast on one of the bank of nine-inch monitors in front of him. *God, you'd never know Nevada could be so bleak. White Plains Missile Range, Nevada . . . nosir, no casinos to be found in this particular zone. Only gambling we're doing is tossing around some million-dollar chunks of hardware.*

This was a special day for Oskins, with the feeling of a day off from school. Four men from the Pentagon were on hand for the demonstration, a woman from the GAO, and the whole development group from Infidel were there.

Oskins looked at the monitor again and swatted Private Larsen on the back. "Looks like the friggin' moon, doesn't it, Larsen?" He laughed heartily.

Larsen, not quite twenty, shot back the kind of smile reserved for one's superiors when they're clearly missing a cog or two. An air force audiovisual technician, he had been responsible for setting up Oskins's monitoring station. From the comfort of a swivel chair in Hamilton, California, Oskins could sit back and watch the proceedings in the Nevada desert. He could speak to Duke, the swarthy project director on the site, over the radio as though he were in the next room.

There hadn't been much to see. As was customary in test programs, the ratio of sitting around to actual testing time was about a billion to one. Today hadn't been any exception; Oskins and his staff had spent nearly twenty-four hours sitting with Private Larsen and watching the bank of smallish TV screens show hour after hour of empty desert.

All right, not completely empty. In one monitor, he'd been watching some antlike figures milling around on a dune, with a large mobile something-or-other centered prominently in the frame. It was, of course, an Infidel missile on its launcher; the cab of a four-axle semi was visible in the corner of one monitor. One of the ants, Oskins knew, was Lt. Terry Gibbs, whom he'd handpicked to be on the first crew. She'd been training to voice-navigate the Infidels for two weeks in China Lake using computer simulators.

Today was her big day.

"Hey, Larsen, can't you at least get us the game on one-a these goddamn TV sets?" He laughed again. . .a big, hearty, colonel's laugh.

One hundred eighty miles away, Gibbs plucked at her undershirt collar; the desert heat was making the inside of the truck an oven. She glanced at the equipment, hoping the heat wouldn't affect it.

Today she hadn't even been told what her target was—only the boundaries of the desert patch she was to use as a battlefield. She and Infidel.

''And don't you be fallin' asleep at the microphone, either, Gibbs,'' Oskins had told her by radio. ''You lose control of that baby, the good people of Vegas are going to be in for a helluva surprise.''

Colonel Duke's voice in her headset told her that things seemed ready. The choppers and field personnel had finally confirmed that the test zone was completely cleared of anything living, and the artillery boys had approved the launch. Gibbs adjusted her microphone.

She sensed, but couldn't see, the row of air force brass at the consoles arrayed outside the truck. ''Colonel Duke, I'm ready to proceed at your order.''

''Affirmative, Lieutenant. We're ready to roll as soon as Video gives us the word.''

You better believe it, Gibbs thought. *Half the point of this little demo is to shoot some pretty footage to show the gang at the General Accounting Offices. They like to know where their money's going, I guess.*

Her thoughts would have been far less idle if she had known that the modified Macintosh Quadra computers next to her teemed with a virus that was eliminating data files even as Duke began to speak.

''All right, ladies and gentlemen. The cameras are rolling. Let's begin the test, please.''

She switched on the microphone.

''Stand clear of projectile,'' someone shouted.

''Clear!'' was the response.

The phone rang on the command console. Duke grabbed the receiver.

''Duke here.''

It was Oskins.

''Duke—good luck, man. Maiden flight time. Bombs away.''

Yeah right, thought Duke. *It's your ass on the line on this project—you'd better wish for good luck.* He hung up and threw a glance at the four Pentagon guys, overdressed for the desert heat.

''All right,'' he said finally. ''Let's roll.''

The boy with his finger on the trigger—something that looked more like a circuit breaker—snapped the lever downward. In a dramatic hiss of steam and smoke, the missile pushed off from its mobile launcher, like an overgrown model rocket. The smell

of sulfur and smoke wafted over the observers as the missile
shrank to a speck in the sky.

Inside the truck, Gibbs was riveted by the dark green displays
in front of her, waiting for the moment. On the right side, she
watched the altitude numbers climb: 00000, 00500, 01100...

Colonel Duke shifted his gaze to the truck. "OK, Gibbs. Start
talking."

He could hear what she was saying to the missile.

"Bow cameras on." Her Trinitron monitor flickered to life,
and suddenly she saw what the missile was seeing: deep blue sky.

"Down thirty," she said. The view changed with snap pre-
cision, and she could now see the rim of mountains poking up
at the bottom of the screen. She could faintly hear a muted
cheer from outside the truck as the onlookers saw the missile
respond.

On the hard drive of the computer beside her, another file
disappeared.

"Down ten," she said, hoping for a better scan for her target.

The view didn't change perceptibly, so she tried it again.
"Down ten degrees."

Still nothing; the missile proceeded on its horizontal course.

"Right ten." She frowned. "Right *thirty*." There was still no
change in the picture's angle or orientation.

She tried another tack. "Turn zero degrees north. Fly level.
Zero. Turn *zero*. Fly level, bow cameras on."

Nothing.

"It's not responding," she said shrilly.

"Jesus," Duke muttered. He shouted at the tech boys. "The
computer isn't responding! What the hell's the matter with it?"

He watched as they scrambled to bring the backup computer
on-line. Yet the diagnostics were still looking good, which puzzled them. As Gibbs spoke, they watched the needles dance in a
row of illuminated VU meters—the microphone was working.
They checked a row of LEDs on what looked like a recording-
studio mixing console, blinking in sync with her voice, telling
them that the commands were reaching the computer. And on a
computer screen, the once-per-second appearance of a row of
++++++ symbols told them that the computer was in good
communication with the missile.

Gibbs was getting frantic, but she tried to speak coolly to the
computer. "Down fifty. Left forty. Cameras off. Cameras on."

She felt as though she were talking to an idiot.

"I don't know, Colonel," said one of the techies. "All the links are working. The computer's talking. The unit's listening. The chip is fine. The unit's just not responding."

Duke glanced nervously at the GAO lady, who was scowling.

"What will happen if we can't control the thing?" he asked the techie.

The young man shrugged. "Nothing, really. Unless a breeze gets it, it'll just keep on its launch trajectory until it runs out of fuel, and then fall back down. In about four hours. Remember, it's got no flying smarts of its own; it relies on us to pilot it."

Oh, God, Duke thought. They'd been too ambitious! How could they have left a manual override out of the design spec? The situation was rapidly getting nightmarish.

"Shut off those goddamn cameras. *Now*," he barked at the video crews. The cameramen shut down, some swinging their cameras off their shoulders.

The woman from the GAO pushed forward. "What is it, Colonel? Where's the missile?"

"It's under control," he lied. "Stay behind the tape, please."

He bent over to whisper into the microphone for Lieutenant Gibbs's headset. "This isn't working," he said. "The missile isn't responding to you. I want you to keep trying for thirty more seconds, and then kill it."

"You sure?" she said.

"Yeah. Abort the goddamn thing."

She went back to it. "Fly level. Fly level. Cameras on. Cameras off. Ten right. Ten right. Fifteen down." Gibbs continued running through the Infidel vocabulary set, trying for some response; none came.

They would learn later that, in fact, none of these commands were any longer in the Infidel vocabulary; the virus had deleted the files that contained them. The ground computer was incapable of sending anything but error messages to the navigation computers on board the projectile, no matter what Lieutenant Gibbs said into the microphone.

With an icy shudder, Duke stared at the truck; heads would roll for this—if his own didn't roll first. Nobody botched his pet weapons-systems projects, not while a bunch of penny-pinching vultures from D.C. were watching.

He looked over at them, standing like worried sheep in three-piece suits. *Well, put up your umbrellas, you overgrown CPAs. You're about to witness a million-dollar hardware hailstorm.*

Gibbs asked Duke for confirmation one more time. Suddenly feeling very tired, he gave it. With a vague feeling of fear, Gibbs leaned to the microphone. "Abort," she said.

And then she said, "Abort. Abort. Abort. Abort."

But the yellow-white dot in the sky continued to recede; it flew just off fifty degrees from the horizontal, rocketing higher and higher into the stratosphere.

"She's still hot," said a techie. It was still transmitting its location and status, thousands of times per second, to the ground computers, and they, for their part, corresponded equally fast with the onboard navigation systems—but they had nothing to say.

Duke ripped off his sunglasses and smashed his eyes up to his binoculars. It was too late; he'd already lost it. He scanned the sky from horizon to azimuth, and couldn't see anything more than the rapidly dissipating exhaust plume. He swore bitterly.

"*Do something!*" he screamed at the startled techies, who stared at him as though he were deranged.

"Nothin' to be done, Colonel. Everythin's workin' on our end."

Duke turned savagely away and sought solace in the shade of the truck that dominated the scene.

It didn't take four hours for the missile to return to earth. Unaided by any navigation commands whatsoever, its launch trajectory slowly deteriorated until it flew, for a time, parallel to the ground. Finally, forty minutes after launch, gravity made the projectile's nose slowly begin to arc downward again.

Fifty-seven minutes after launch, the Infidel struck the earth in a township called Brush, Utah, just short of 350 miles away from White Plains Missile Range. Not until nightfall did news of the catastrophe reach Colonel Oskins and his staff: that the missile had struck the parking lot of a public campgrounds. Shrapnel sent eight picnickers to the hospital; two, sitting too close to escape the Infidel's blast, perished immediately.

It would be thirty-four months before another Infidel 10 entered the testing stage.

"Mac Storehouse, may I help you?"

"Yeah. I wonder if you can tell me if there's anything that

would let me run Mac software in a UNIX environment.''

"A UNIX environment?"

"Yeah."

"One moment."

Danny couldn't think of any other way the virus could have crossed the chasm between computer types. It certainly couldn't have done that on its own; it must have had some help. *This is what they call a shot in the dark.*

"This is Dave, how can I help you?"

"Yeah. Dave. Do you sell any product that adapts Mac software to run under UNIX?"

"UNIX? Oh, sure. We have CrossOver, from Quitex Systems; that's four ninety-five. And there's a new one coming out from TransAxle called Auntie Emulator. That'll be three ninety-five. We won't have it till next month."

Oh, my God... Danny gripped the phone more tightly.

"And how exactly does this stuff work?"

"Well, basically, it's a shell that puts a Mac screen up on your UNIX terminal. From there, it's just like you're using a Mac. It slows the performance down, and everything, 'cause in the background it's filtering every call to the Mac's 68000 chip, and interpreting it into something the mainframe can understand."

Jesus, we're in trouble, Danny thought. *It's a real interpreter.*

"OK, thanks a lot."

"Will you be ordering anything from us today, sir?"

How the hell can we catch it now? We'd have to convert Macrophage into a UNIX format somehow....

"Sir? Would you like to order that?"

"Oh—sorry. No, I—"

How can we convert it? There's no time!

"No, thanks. But listen, I appreciate your—"

Wait a minute! We're going to need this thing, too! We'll send Macrophage through the same rabbit's hole into the mainframe world....

"Yes," Danny interrupted himself. "Yeah. We need that Mac interpreter you just mentioned. And we need it fast. Where's your closest store to Santa Clara?"

The COMSAT technical team pulled out every stop to make a smooth transition. In anticipation of a satellite shutdown, they farmed out packets of leased time to INTELSAT and two other rivals in a six-hour convulsion of phone calls and modem transmissions.

A lucky few clients—those whose use of the satellite was confined to infrequent bursts—were barely inconvenienced by the temporary switch. Most, however, were forced to gear down to the most basic service, and some frills had to be sacrificed. MetroBank's primary data services experienced no slowdown whatsoever, so that large-scale transactions and hour-by-hour balance information was unaffected; a few secondary services, such as credit reports and remote automated teller machine transactions, suffered severe slowdowns.

The story that would later make the greatest impact, however, was the incident at the Chicago Stock Exchange that Monday morning. The stream of updated stock prices, beamed in from New York, was interrupted at increasingly frequent intervals, until the Chicago mainframe balked. Designed to be highly sensitive to anomalies in the incoming stream of price data, the mainframe's security routines kicked in and shut the stock market down. As the big illuminated ticker stream on the wall blinked to darkness, the floor full of traders went into an uncomprehending frenzy.

chapter 18

ARTELLIGENCE SOFTWARE CORP. ● VOICE-MESSAGING SYSTEM

Thank you for calling Artelligence Software. If you are calling with a technical question about an Artelligence software product, press 1. If you would like information about any Artelligence software product, press 2. For upgrade and registration information, press 3. For information concerning the Cocoon anti-virus program, press 4. For all other questions, press 5.

You have pressed 4. One moment please.

January 25, 1994   "COMSAT's down, that's why," explained Peggy.

"Oh, God. So where are the calls going? AT and T?"

MCI's vice president of marketing needed this like he needed a hole in the head. The East Coast circuits were completely flooded; millions of calls weren't going through, and the company was losing serious business to the competition.

Peggy flipped through her printouts, looking for the information she needed. "Yeah. Most people don't know how to hook into anyone else. They're using AT and T."

"How long before they restore service?"

"They say within the day," Peggy said. "We're working on

a temporary rerouting to the Albany substation, but in the meantime the lines are completely overloaded. The ground lines weren't designed to handle this volume of calls.''

"Nice," spat the vice president. "OK, thanks. I'll get Albany on the line and see if we can't get some of the pressure taken off. Thanks, Peggy."

Peggy nodded and left his office.

The vice president picked up the phone and dialed the Albany office. After dialing, he leaned back in his reclining office chair and held the receiver to his ear.

"I'm sorry. All circuits are busy now. Please try your call again later."

The American computing community had never been invaded by anything so fast or so rabid. The Cocoon program, weighing in at only nine kilobytes, was easy to post on electronic bulletin boards and dial-up networks everywhere—and, taking less than a minute to transfer over the phone wires, was equally easy for members to download to their own disks.

Among the first to download the program were computer stores. The owners of many of these dealerships were quick to capitalize on the situation, offering to distribute Cocoon at no charge to anyone who brought a blank floppy in to the store. Once the customer was in the store, of course, a salesman would introduce the store's special, two-day-only sale on anti-virus software like Antidote.

Consultants chucked Cocoon disks in their pockets and immediately made the rounds of their clients, in hopes of (a) preventing the Houston virus from awakening and (b) running up additional billing hours. Macintosh User Groups sold Cocoon disks for three or five dollars. *PowerMac* magazine, inundated with phone calls from readers seeking advice, worked a hasty deal with Federal Express: for a complete cost of ten dollars, a user who phoned in for the Cocoon program by midnight would have it delivered by noon the next day. Mail-order houses formulated similar deals, sometimes offering overnight shipping for as little as three dollars.

By far the most computer users, of course, got copies of Cocoon from InfoServe and USA Online. By dinnertime Monday the download count on InfoServe was over 225,000, and nearly 75,000 from USA Online.

On the InterNet, a specialized copy of the program made its rapid rounds. Danny and Arnie had run the program on a UNIX system by using the CrossOver Mac interpreter program. Like beef going through a grinder, the program emerged on the other side as a true UNIX application. They posted it—with the title VIRUSKILLER.URGENT—onto the InterNet, where no university, corporation, or government office could miss it.

There was a feeling of banding together, of community. College computer-science departments sent every computer user an E-mail, documenting the viral threat and how to solve it. At Williams College, in fact, there was so little time for elaborate planning that the Cocoon program was distributed at the health center, just like the free condoms that were normally handed out there. At M.I.T., by the end of the day Monday, "I Get a Boost In/Killing Off Houston" T-shirts were already for sale in the student center . . . along with Cocoon disks, naturally. The Berkeley Mac User Group, the largest user group in the country, went to the considerable expense of duplicating a Cocoon disk for every one of its members nationwide and sending it Express Mail.

Experienced computer users looked out for their novice friends; it made both feel good. And each time somebody launched the Cocoon program, the Macrophage beneficial virus was released. Thousands of hard disks were cleaned up before their owners were even aware they'd had an infection.

Once it was released, Macrophage worked like a charm. It multiplied in an explosion of clones, burrowing its way into millions of files, eating Houston viruses as it went. It leaped instantly across the cables that connected networked computers. It lodged on floppies and removable storage cartridges, spreading to otherwise inaccessible computers and purging them of the dangerous virus—and then cloning itself some more.

Jeremy Jason, for example, downloaded the Cocoon program from InfoServe after reading about it on the InfoServe's welcoming screen. He ran it on his hard disk; but the program reported that he had not, in fact, been infected by the Houston virus. Though Jeremy wasn't aware of it, the act of running the program had released Macrophage into his system. The next time he took a floppy disk to his job as an informational graphics artist at the Portland *Oregonian*, Macrophage succeeded in infecting the newspaper's entire network. By the end of the day, the offices were completely free of Houston virus infections, though not a soul knew that any of this had transpired.

In other situations, a combination of deliberate and accidental circumstances helped to spread the beneficial virus. At Credit-Cheque, a credit bureau based in Kentucky, the systems analyst deliberately let Macrophage loose as a preventive measure. One of the computers affected belonged to Colette Van Valkenberg, a vice president, who regularly transported her hard drive each night for use with her home computer. As a result, the Macrophage virus succeeded in eradicating the Houston infections both at work and at home, where Colette's secondary hard drive—as well as her backups—had been infected.

What the programmers of Macrophage had only fleetingly considered was the role of chance in the distribution of the original virus. In the time it had taken Gam's original virus to spread, there had been thousands of accidents, one-time visits, and fluke contacts between humans and computers. Some people had loaned floppy disks, swapped pirated software, tried out dial-up networks. Others visited clients, transported hard disks, sent disks to be mass-copied.... The result was an unimaginably complex infection path that infinite years of thought and planning could never completely duplicate.

Jenny hefted her sleeping two-year-old into her left arm and fumbled with her wallet. With some difficulty, she extracted her ATM card and pushed it into the cash machine.

The guy at the other machine, a short Hispanic man, looked over at her sympathetically while he waited for the machine to complete a transaction. "How old is he?" he asked.

Jenny answered with a city dweller's no-eye-contact disengagement. "He's two," she smiled. She looked at the cash machine's display.

Please enter your PIN code and press Enter.

Press Clear if you make a mistake.

She typed in her number.

"Oh, *man*," burst out the short guy. He pounded the meta casing of the cash machine with his fist. "Sonofa*bitch*."

He turned to her apologetically. "Stupid thing ate my card."
He picked up the Customer Service phone and waited for an
operator to come on the line.

Jenny looked back at her machine.

Not a valid PIN code. Please try again.

Again she typed in her number. The machine balked again,
and asked her to enter the code a third time. This time she
punched each number firmly and slowly. The machine beeped
once with each button-press. There was no *way* she'd messed it
up this time.

But the ATM beeped, and now there was some mechanical
activity in the card slot. She saw the edge of her card slither into
the machine. There was a clank.

Your card is being confiscated.

**Please contact a Customer Service
representative. Thank you for using
MetroBank™.**

"Aww, *come* on," she moaned.

She turned to the guy on the phone. He shrugged. "Nobody
there."

"It ate *my* card, too," she griped.

During the thirty-two hours of COMSAT downtime, the Con-
fiscate loop of the ATM's software erroneously ran seventeen
hundred times, in all regions of the country. MetroBank had that
many apologies to make when the problem finally came to light.

Sheila hadn't smoked for three years, but somehow snapping
the plastic off a new box of Benson and Hedges had the cere-
monial kick of opening a bottle of champagne. She sat, quietly,
and lit one up. A blank word-processing document was up on the
screen.

She turned and looked out the window to her garden. Somewhere along the time line of his life, she knew, Lars had derailed.
What afternoon was it? On what day of what year did he take
one step too far? When did his edition of the American dream
become a nightmare?

She tapped the cigarette on the mouth of her empty coffee mug.

The question of when Lars's corruption began wasn't an idle question, of course. She was going to have to find a starting point for this book. This candid, dangerous book . . . for which Sheila doubted there would be retaliation. It would be much too difficult for Lars to reach her from his jail cell.

And the book was the answer; she knew this now. In strait-jacketed frustration, she had watched Lars triumph over his rivals—at the expense of millions of innocent victims. And he had even destroyed the only possible incriminating evidence—the hard drive that Nick had disposed of so effectively. Rankert and Chad were out of the picture, cowed into permanent submission by Lars's threats.

And that meant there was only one messenger to tell the story. There was only one person who could set the record straight. *I alone escaped to tell thee . . .*

She sighed and set the cigarette down. Sunlight filtered through its rising curls of smoke from the garden windows. Sheila pressed the tab key a few times, peered through her half-moon glasses, and began to type.

SYSTEM FAILURE:

The Rise and Corruption of Lars Huntington

January 26, 1994 "Roger, Delta three-five-five, you are number three in line for takeoff," he said into the mike. Kevin rubbed his eyes, then turned to yell over his shoulder. "Yo, Peter! Any answers from Admin yet?"

"Kev, they're doing what they can. They've left messages for Carla and Joe-Joe. Ricky's on his way now. Nothing else they can do. I've told New York to start using Dallas."

Dammit, Kevin thought. *I don't like this a bit.*

He had little time to reflect, however; a United liner from Denver was entering Houston tower control. As the plane approached the five-mile radius of William J. Hobby International Airport, Approach Control handed United 262 over to him.

"Thank you, Approach. I have him."

The mainframes were acting as though they were waterlogged. Even a moment ago; just as Delta 939 was touching down, the radar still showed it at 0100 feet and a quarter mile from the strip. It made Kevin nervous; it was like driving on half-inflated tires.

The United flight radioed in. "Hobby Tower, United two-six-two is with you at five thousand with Information Hotel. Over." The scattered clouds were hanging low today.

Five thousand? We see you at six thousand! Kevin hit the mike button. "United two-six-two, descend and maintain twenty-five hundred. Report the outer marker."

"Roger Hobby Tower. Descending to twenty-five."

What the hell is wrong with the radar? He couldn't wait until the tech guys arrived.

"United two-six-two, turn right, heading oh-six-zero—I'm sorry. I'm very sorry. Turn right heading oh-*four*-zero to intercept localizer for runway thirty-right."

The pilot showed no reaction. "United two-six-two," he acknowledged.

Kevin muttered under his breath. His concern over the computers was beginning to affect his performance. "Look, honey," Jody always told him, "if you can't take the stress, work in Administration." Right about now, it was sounding like an attractive proposition.

There was indeed something wrong with the computers in the Hobby Tower air-traffic computers. The Houston virus lay semi-dormant inside the UNIX mainframes, having made its way over the InterNet. Once on board, it proceeded on its programmed path, reproducing every time it discovered an uninfected program.

But by 11 A.M., there were hundreds of copies of the tiny piece of code. Each polled the central processor once every sixteen seconds— "Is it January 30 yet?" Forced to take on the additional load of responding to those tiny requests, the machine took some of its attention away from the task it was designed for: monitoring and displaying air-traffic data. The result: the screen display was almost three seconds out of date.

The radio crackled. "Hobby Tower, United two-six-two. I have a possible intercept at eleven o'clock—"

The veteran liner pilot was typically contained, but Kevin knew near-miss situation when he heard one. He blinked tightly and stared at the scope.... Where was two-six-two again?

The radar screen, like all tower screens, identified blips only by two numbers: the plane's altitude and its transponder frequency code. The United flight's transponder code was 4401... there. Its blip had looked fine a moment ago, two miles out from runway 30-R, altitude 2,450. Another blip, ID'd on the screen by its altitude, 2,400, and a transponder code Kevin didn't recognize, hadn't looked dangerous a moment ago.

"I hear you, two-six-two. You should...ah, you..." He took his finger off the mike button, panicked.

"Who the hell is code twenty-nine-ninety-five?" he shouted to the departure controller. He grabbed for the "cigar box," the traveling container that contained the transponder codes and corresponding flight numbers on slips of paper. The radio speaker popped again:

"Hobby, Mayday. Aircraft at quarter mile, intercept imminent! I'm going hard right."

"That's mine, Kevin," shouted the departure controller at another console. "I had to send him out on thirty-right. Get your guy the hell out of there!"

Kevin grabbed the mike. "Ah... Yes, two-six-two. Go hard right, as per your..."

He stopped. Whatever happened was already over.

He waited tensely for another radio transmission.

"Two-six-two. We're clear now, situation normal. Approaching runway thirty-right as directed." There was a pause.

"Yo, Hobby. What the hell is going on up there?"

Kevin didn't know how to respond. "Thanks for your quick thinking, two-six-two. Approach thirty-right at twenty-one hundred."

He ripped off his headset and threw it down. "Get Paulson on the phone," he said to Peter angrily. "We're closing the airport."

This was what it must feel like in the eye of a hurricane, Danny thought. It was 11:55 P.M. on January 29. In a matter of minutes a tiny string of programming was about to become activated in untold millions of machines. In a matter of minutes, their future would become instantly sealed. Somewhere, out there beyond these very familiar walls, any computers untouched by the Macrophage virus would be touched by the Houston one. There was nothing to do now but wait.

The team lay draped on the furniture in the Customer Service room, almost nonfunctional with exhaustion. Wiring and duct tape were everywhere, making the room look like some high schooler's giant science project—a result of the temporary phone lines they'd had hooked up to handle the ocean of phone calls since the Houston virus story made the headlines. Shane, in Shipping, had made hourly runs to Federal Express with packages of the anti-virus, which Artelligence provided at no charge to any caller.

And now, minutes before Gam's clever little virus awoke, the phones were still for a moment.

Danny looked over at Charles. "So."

Charles lifted his head a half inch off the table. "So?"

Danny shrugged. "So you think we killed it in time?"

"Not in time for those army guys, y'know?" interjected Skinner.

It wasn't a topic dear to Bob Stroman's heart. He looked haggard.

The clock said 12:01 A.M. "Happy January thirtieth," said Charles woefully. The phone rang; they looked at it wearily.

Arnie picked it up. "Artelligence Software." He yawned. "OK, here's the story." The others had heard it too many times.

"There's no way to know if you've been infected. But let me take your name and address, and I'll send you the anti-virus. In the meantime, don't use your computer at all. OK?"

As Arnie went through the routine, Stroman stood and stretched. The hurricane of damage was taking place nationwide, but they wouldn't know how severe it was until another day; it was time to rest.

"OK, look, gentlemen," he said. "The worst is over. I mean the worst of the phone calls. Why don't you go home and get a shower? And a little sleep? At this point, there's not one more thing we can do. If our anti-virus did its job, then a lot of people are safe. If not..." He shrugged.

"Anyway. Let's call it a night."

"Let's call it a night*mare*," countered Michelle.

"Yeah." Stroman looked at her. "Well, whatever it was, our part of it is over."

chapter 19

Even two weeks after the crisis, the Houston virus was already being called the most widespread virus in the history of computers. Thousands of people and corporations lost at least some data; a few lost all of it. To them, it was little consolation that 8? percent of the infected computers nationwide were successfull rescued by the Macrophage counter-virus. The episode was bot a setback and a triumph for the computing industry.

Worse, there could be no accounting of the personal costs c

the episode: companies that foundered, security that was shaken, even lives lost. Secretary of State Henry Masso would have placed his experience at the top of the list: following Ukrainian president Jurenko's death—"in American hands," the Belorussian secretary asserted—the peace talks devolved rapidly into posturing and hostility. Despite the administration's protests that the president's death was unavoidable, the Ukraine declared that the incident was, medically speaking, highly suspect, and refused to participate in additional talks until an investigation was conducted and a culprit was found. Azerbaijan accused the United States of incompetence or worse; Russia found the U.S. inability to reconvene the different factions after Jurenko's death to be a sign of diplomatic weakness. Masso knew that he would be long out of office before another attempt could be made at reaching a lasting balance of power in the region.

Even some people who didn't receive Macrophage in time survived the damage—those who regularly made backup copies of their data. In most cases, of course, the backup files were infected just as badly as the primary files. But the Houston virus's behavior was extremely well publicized in the days following January 20. People were told, over and over again, the process for safely reinstalling their backup data: first, erase the existing data on the hard drive, because the damaging Houston virus cannot be deactivated once it's been awakened; second, set the computer's clock back to a pre-deadline time and date; finally, run the Cocoon program to destroy the sleeping virus.

In the aftermath, there were flurries of editorials, nightly-news segments about the rise of computer crime, even a made-for-TV movie about the episode, starring Telly Savalas as Lars Huntington. Sales of Master Voice took a drastic, albeit temporary dip; sales of virus-protection software—promoted heavily by their makers, who knew a golden opportunity when they saw one—skyrocketed. For many months, a good number of America's computer users were much more careful about their computing practices.

For Artelligence, too, there would be nearly endless repercussions. There were both civil and criminal suits to be brought against Lars Huntington. Securing evidence was no problem: Artelligence lawyers were armed with the LifeSaver typing files Danny had recovered from Gam's hard drive, as well as the testimony of ex-employees like Sheila Brooks. Lars Huntington discovered rapidly that he had chosen the wrong state in which to commit computer sabotage; few states had "computer contaminant" laws as explicit and harsh as California's.

Of course, Stroman had some legal problems of his own—a gaggle of lawsuits. A metallurgical-engineering outfit in Connecticut lost the entire contents of a removable-disk hard drive that contained the specs for an alloy they'd been developing for six months. A design firm in Minneapolis lost all of their clients' artwork; when they'd installed their backup copies, those, too, were promptly eaten. Stroman's lawyers told him he might well be liable for extensive damages.

But for two days after the release of Macrophage into the nation's bloodstream, Danny missed all the news. He slept.

It was one of those rare valley nights: there had been enough high pressure from the ocean to shove the murky layer of smog off to the east. Lying on their backs in the grass, the programmers were treated to a vast, twinkling, Disneyesque array of stars in the night sky. It was just chilly enough to require a sweater; with food in their bellies and the pressure off, they lay next to the pond of the Japanese garden with every muscle relaxed.

Danny thought about the way machines and people were connected. Each person's computer might have connections to only a handful of others—maybe by the phone wires, maybe through the exchange of disks; not many people could see the big picture. But multiply those few connections times the millions of machines and people, and the result was a staggering, overlapping, continual, unpredictable network all over the world. Every machine was eventually connected to every other. Information was meant to be shared; it was the right system. The more connections, the more useful the computers became . . . and the more vulnerable the world was to attack.

And the world was spinning faster and faster toward an even more universal computer standard. The very walls of incompatibility that used to contain a computer virus to a certain type of computer were crumbling every day. Danny had just read about the release of a new joint-venture Apple/IBM machine, a computer that would run software developed for either kind of system; in the past, it had been inconceivable to think that software (including viruses) written for one computer would run on another. UNIX system administrators had been secure in the knowledge that UNIX viruses were rare and easily spotted; they had always assumed that they were immune to attack from the far more common personal-computer viruses. But now emulators like CrossOver were even making it possible to run personal-computer software on big UNIX mainframe systems.

The walls were coming down. The world was on its way to becoming a single, glorious network, where every computer could speak to every other, and any program written for one could run on another. Glorious. . . and vulnerable.

But at the moment, Danny decided he had more pressing concerns—like what he was going to do with his life. He took a deep, slow breath: he was going to miss these guys.

"I can't believe we're outta here tomorrow," he said.

Their services as Reinforcements were no longer needed; the contracts had expired. "It's been so hectic, I haven't had a chance to make any plans at all."

He could just make out Orion off to the north.

"What're you gonna do now, Charles?"

From his vantage point, staring straight into the atmosphere, Danny couldn't see Charles; but he could tell that Charles was thinking.

"Well, I thought maybe I'd write a self-help book. *The Company You Keep: How to Keep the Japanese From Buying You,*" he said.

Rod's voice was dreamy. "What Japanese?"

Danny smiled. "Maybe you weren't aware of it, Rod, but a certain Mika Corporation came within about an inch of gobbling us up. Just be glad we nixed the virus as well as we did, or it would've been all over."

"Wowww," murmured Rod.

"Either that," said Charles, reconsidering, "or I'll go on a self-destructive streak, locking myself into my apartment with a stack of rented movies and the entire Keebler product line."

"I just want to keep programming, y'know?" said Skinner from flat on his back. "I gotta earn the money, you know? So I can treat my girlfriend right."

Danny lifted his head off the grass. "Skinner! You never told us you had a girlfriend!"

"Well, not really, OK, not yet. Not really a girlfriend. But I was in the Quik Mart today, y'know? And there was this girl there? And she was trying to figure out how many sub sandwiches she'd need for this party she was having and everything? And so I had my calculator with me and stuff. So I helped her figure it out, y'know?'' There was a mountain of happiness in his voice. "So OK, so she invited me to the party. She wants me to be there and everything. She was really, really nice. To'lly righteous.''

"Hey, Skinner, that's great!''

"I'm going to New York City,'' announced Rod.

Danny never would have imagined how much he'd grow to like Rod; for weeks after meeting him, Danny had dismissed Rod as a dunce. No, the guy wasn't quick as lightning, but there was something elemental and trusting about him.

"Listen,'' Danny said warmly. "Do you know what you're getting yourself into? I mean, I just moved *out* of New York City.''

"I know, but there isn't anything else out here for me to do, after this,'' he said. A moment passed.

"And I want to ride the subway,'' he added with great conviction.

"Maybe I can give you some pointers, then. I know a great Chinese-food restaurant,'' said Danny. At least it had always *smelled* good from his apartment directly upstairs.

"Will you guys write?'' It was Charles. Danny thought for a moment he was his usual dry, sarcastic self, but Charles was serious.

They murmured their assent, but they knew the future was too uncertain to predict.

"I hope we do,'' said Danny. He sighed. "If I can't find something out here, something more long-term. . .'' He could scarcely believe the words were coming out of his mouth. ". . . I'm probably going to apply to business school.''

Charles gasped in horror. "Danny! Let's not fly off the *handle* here . . . surely we can find you a job at Burger King—a car wash—*something* more creative than that!''

Danny chuckled. He listened to the swish of traffic on the highway for a moment.

There was a rustling of footsteps on the path to the garden. Danny tilted his head and saw a flowered peasant skirt making its way toward his field of view.

"My God! Look at you guys, lying here like a bunch of lawn ornaments!'' exclaimed Michelle.

She flounced to the grass and sat cross-legged near Danny, regarding them.

"Hey, come on, is *this* the high-energy, hardworking team I've come to know and love?" she said.

"Please, Michelle," intoned Charles. "Your voice threatens to disturb our state of perfectly focused inertia."

She made a "Hmmph!" sound, and said, "Well, then I won't risk further disturbing your inertial state by telling you the good news."

Danny grabbed her playfully and pulled her to the grass beside him. She nestled against him happily.

"You can tell *me*, Michelle," he said in a stage whisper. "You won't disturb *my* inertia."

She whispered something into his ear. He sat bolt upright.

"You're *kidding*!"

"Danny, Danny!" chided Charles, now roused reluctantly from his relaxed position. "*Must* you violate the stillness of the evening with your exclamations? Have you no self-control? What possible news could merit this nerve-grating noise pollution?"

Danny grinned. "Stroman's offering us jobs!"

"Yeeeee-*HAWWWW*!" belted Charles at the top of his lungs.

"Really!? You're kidding!" said Skinner, suddenly on his feet and dancing in his jittery fashion.

Rod was wide-eyed.

"It'll be nice for you guys to move up to full-time programmers' salary, won't it?" She shrugged. "All except Danny."

"What!?"

She clasped her hands around him, pulling him close. "Your pay scale's going to be a little bit different."

She paused for dramatic effect. "Bob wants you to become his R and D director for Macintosh software," she said. "And he's hoping you'll also consider being product manager for your first two programs."

Danny squinted at her. "First *two* programs? Master Voice and what else?"

"What's happening to your memory, young man? That antivirus program you wrote. Stroman wants to market it under the Artelligence label. Not only that, but he figures you're a minor celeb after your work in killing the virus. So he thinks he'll sell extra copies if he puts your name on the box."

He leaped to his feet, whooped, and lifted her off the ground in a spinning bear hug. Charles, Rod, and Skinner hooted for him.

Dear Dad: You can stop worrying that I'm Squandering my Gifts...

Danny set Michelle down lightly on the grass. They both sat and, after a moment, stretched out to look at the stars. She smelled sweet beside him.

"Listen, Media Goddess," he said softly after a moment. "This place is going to be on autopilot for a while. What do they have to do: just sell zillions of programs and hang out with a lot of lawyers, right?"

She was listening.

"So whaddya say we take a week to go someplace where they've never even heard of computers?"

She cocked an eyebrow. "Oh yeah?"

"I hear Mendocino is gorgeous...we could drive through San Francisco and take Highway One along the ocean. Might be just the antidote for all we've been through."

Michelle was smiling the sweet, irrepressible smile Danny loved so much.

"Really?" she said. "No viruses? No networks? No computers?"

"None of the above," confirmed Danny.

From the darkness a few feet away, Charles's bulky, prone silhouette interrupted them. "Don't do it, Michelle! He's a wolf, I'm telling you. He just wants to get you alone so he can seduce you and steal your heart away."

She feigned astonishment. "Danny! Is that *true*?"

"I'm afraid so."

She kissed him—warm, soft, through a smile.

"Oh good," she murmured. "When do we start?"

"Varley is the best writer in America.
This book proves it." —Tom Clancy

STEEL
BEACH

John Varley

"One of the best science fiction novels of the year...
Nebula and Hugo award-winner Varley makes a
triumphant return!"—*Publishers Weekly*

"Varley's first novel in almost a decade...skillful
science fiction epic...beautifully told."—*Omni*

Fleeing earth after an alien invasion, the human beings
stand on the threshold of evolution, like a fish cast on
artificial shores. Their new home is Luna, a moon colony
blessed with creature comforts, prolonged lifespans,
digital memories, and instant sex-changes. But the
people of Luna are bored, restless, suicidal— and so is
the computer that monitors their existence...

An Ace paperback

Coming in August